The Use of Heavy Water

by

D'Arcy Arden

The Valence Chronicles, Book 2

The Use of Heavy Water

Cover Art by *Jennifer Greeff*

The Wild Rose Press, Inc.
PO Box 708
Adams Basin, NY 14410-0708
Visit us at www.thewildrosepress.com

Publishing History
First Edition, 2022
Trade Paperback ISBN 978-1-5092-4450-8
Digital ISBN 978-1-5092-4451-5

The Valence Chronicles, Book 2
Published in the United States of America

Desmodian turned sharply back to Brog. His hand, which had been holding the card, opened and closed as if confused about its sudden emptiness. "What? You're keeping it?"

One of Brog's hands held the card, and another gripped Desmodian. That still left two arms free to cross over his chest in a challenging posture. "Maybe. No reason not to."

Desmodian gaped. "No reason...after what that man did to you. There's every reason to avoid him."

The pair stared each other down, Brog with one set of eyes and Desmodian with his whole body.

Pet's foot slipped over wet rock, and he nearly tumbled off the island. He had seen these emotions on his trio before, but rarely directed at each other. On the rare occasion they fought, it usually ended as quickly as it started. He hoped this time would be the same.

Xavis approached the argument with both wings outstretched. "Hey, guys, calm down. This isn't worth fighting over."

Brog let go of Desmodian, practically throwing his hand away. "If he thinks he can make decisions for me, then we got somethin' to fight over."

Desmodian's hammer planted in the sand again, hard enough to sink several inches. "It shouldn't even be a decision. It should be common sense. Yaivin Vels is the reason you ended up arrested and in Unit 22 in the first place. You shouldn't want anything to do with him."

Dedication

Dedicated to all the past fans of the first book, and all the future fans of this one.

Chapter One

After

It was cold.

An understatement, but Pet could think of no better description. Fanciful words like glacial or frigid had no place here. There was nothing artistic about bitter wind sucking the air out of his lungs, or the numbness creeping along his extremities.

It was simply cold.

Pet lay on his back, looking up at the morning sky. His breath created its own clouds against the pale backdrop. Ice-melt soaked into his coat, but he didn't have the energy to get up. Sheer walls of ice rose all around, trapping him at the bottom of a deep pit. Catching his breath provided a good excuse to delay the difficult climb to freedom that awaited him.

Voices sounded in the distance, too far away to hear in detail, but too close for comfort. He closed his eyes and waited for them to pass, trying to ignore the cold shiver taking root in his chest. Snow had shifted down into the pit, partially covering him. Hopefully, it would be enough to hide him if anyone wandered by.

The sky turned from washed-out morning gray to a cheery pastel blue. It would've been a pleasant day if not for the sub-zero temperatures.

Shouldn't he be more worried? He was alone in the

arctic, kept alive only by a poorly fitted coat and a thermal suit not designed for such extreme cold.

Thin glowing lines ran through the fabric of the thermal suit, changing color like a temperature gauge. Currently, the lines glowed neon red. The thermal suit worked as hard as it could to keep him warm, yet the cold still penetrated.

Finally, after an uncomfortable amount of time, the distant voices disappeared. Pet strained his ears for even the smallest sound and heard only hollow wind.

Getting up hurt. His joints creaked, and his muscles threatened to snap if he moved too quickly. On his knees Pet crawled hand over hand up the side of the pit.

At the top of the wall, he peered carefully over the edge. He was surrounded by a flat monochrome of ice and snow.

The only disruption to the colorless white landscape came from two unnatural additions.

The first was a grounded airship. An oblong bubble, with a solid metal bottom, and a clear dome on the top half. It had brought him there, and it now sat at an awkward angle, landing gear obviously not built for arctic terrain.

The second blight on the landscape was a dark jagged shape sticking out of the ice. It seemed small, but a shadow under the ice hinted at its true size. A few minutes ago, the structure could have been mistaken for a natural sheaf of rock. Now, a hole blown into its side revealed an inner metal skeleton.

Don't think about that structure. Don't think about how that hole got there.

Shaking away his apprehension and the fatigue that still clung to his limbs, Pet climbed out of the pit. He needed to focus on getting back to the airship.

More distance lay between his hiding place and the airship than he thought. The extreme size, coupled with the white surroundings, created an illusion that the airship was just over the next snowdrift. Yet what originally seemed like a short distance turned out to be over half a mile.

A strong gust of wind knocked him to his knees. The coat flapped around him, a twisting mass of silver fur too large for his frame. Frozen air snuck up his back and traced fingers along his spine. If it weren't for the thermal bodysuit he wore under the coat, he would've already succumbed to frostbite.

Another fit of shivers wracked his body. The coat's deep hood shielded his face, and he pulled it tighter. The last time he tried to move while the wind raged, he'd been sent tumbling over the ice. His scraped cheek bore the proof.

Eventually, the wind stopped.

He took a breath, and the cold stabbed his lungs from the inside. He could've composed a song to the beat of his chattering teeth.

Keep moving. He had to find his trio.

Dozens of footprints covered the area around the airship, stamping snow flat and cutting a path to the other structure sticking out of the ice.

Pet approached from the back of the airship, keeping glued to the metal hull as he inched toward the front.

His trio had been on the airship, but nothing stirred now. At least nothing he could see from the outside.

What would he do if they weren't there?

He reached the open hatch at the front and slipped

inside.

Even shut down, the ship was still warmer than the outside elements.

Pet breathed a sigh of relief and lowered his hood.

The hatch led into an open common room within the bottom half of the airship. It held plenty of luxurious furniture and even a bar. Everything except people.

Pet bypassed the common area to search the private rooms at the back of the ship. That was the last place he'd seen his trio.

Empty as well.

Growing more panicked, he sprinted up the stairs to the upper half of the airship.

A clear dome covered the many lounging areas divided by partial walls.

He ran the length of the ship, searching every corner and behind every door.

Empty.

Empty.

Empty.

He found only silence.

The airship was completely deserted.

Standing at the open hatch, he stared out over the barren landscape. He couldn't be alone. His trio had to be somewhere.

Frustrated tears welled up in his eyes. With a sharp gesture he brushed them away before they fell and pulled his hood back into place.

The airship's uneven landing created a gap between the hatch ramp and the ground.

It was only a small jump, but his feet slid out from under him. Snow cushioned the sound of his fall, but not the impact. Unforgiving ice rattled his teeth against each other.

He lay dazed in the snow. At least nothing was broken. His tongue throbbed where he'd bitten it, but he couldn't taste blood, so it was probably fine.

Sitting up, he remained kneeling as he found his senses again.

Useless décor. He couldn't even manage a two-foot drop without ending up on his face. He'd been designed to look pretty and decorate the homes of rich aliens. Over a year since he left that life behind, trying to become an independent person, and he still felt like useless decoration.

The tears he'd worked so hard to keep at bay came again.

No sobbing or wailing could be heard, just a hitch in his breath as the tears dripped down. They froze to his skin before they reached his chin.

A soft, barely audible noise caught his attention. If he'd been crying any louder, he wouldn't have noticed. He didn't immediately look up but turned an ear toward the sound of snow crushing under body weight. Someone was moving around outside the airship, and it wasn't any of his trio's footsteps.

This was a stranger, and they were coming closer.

Chapter Two

Before

The red button or the blue?

A drop of nervous sweat ran down Pet's temple. Normally, he stayed in his antigravity bubble whenever the *Vanguard* did anything difficult, like landing on a new planet, but they decided to try something different. Instead of floating in his bubble, Pet sat on Brog's lap.

The large four-armed Ocan held onto him, acting as his safety belt as Pet helped land the ship.

"Helped" was a generous word. Desmodian and Xavis did the bulk of the work. Pet had been relegated to controlling the landing gear, which was mostly automated.

Outside the control room's observation windows, their intended destination grew closer.

Syzygy was a mostly frozen planet. Ice covered the entire globe, except for a strip around the equator where the climate stayed pleasantly Mediterranean all year round. Little dots of land strung through the ocean, each island chain forming a separate country.

In his own chair on the other side of the room, Desmodian pulled up a lesser-used screen. Icy light from the planet reflected off the Dhen'in's green scales and indigo hair. "We're about to enter the planet's atmosphere. I'm starting the ship's decontamination process. Most planets that allow ships to land have a barrier to protect their natural atmosphere. If we're carrying any unacceptable bacteria, the barrier won't let us through."

Pet's trio rarely voiced their actions when working together. Desmodian's explanation was entirely for Pet's benefit. He noted the graph on Desmodian's screen, tracking the decontamination process before turning back to his own decision.

The red button or the blue?

Nothing happened when their ship entered the atmosphere, except for a slight increase in turbulence from air pressure. As they approached the planet, their ship aimed for an island on the very end of a string of five.

Aptly named Starthrone, it stood like a wedge pointing at the sky. One side tapered gradually. A large switchback road led from beach to peak, with low-lying buildings tracing its path. The other side of the wedge dropped in a sheer cliff. Holes pockmarked its rocky surface, too evenly spaced to be natural.

Pet noticed all these details, then promptly ignored them.

Since his trio built the *Vanguard* themselves, they hadn't adhered to standard labeling systems. He struggled to read under normal situations. The symbols and abbreviations along the controls made even less sense than written words usually did.

The landing pad was coming up fast. Red button or blue? The arms around him tightened, offering silent support, but Brog didn't say a word.

Blue button.

With a tap of Pet's finger, the screen turned to the

correct display. He deflated with relief, absently stroking one of Brog's arms as he activated the landing gear.

The *Vanguard* touched down with a satisfying lurch in momentum.

"Good job, Pet." Desmodian's tail reached across the space to brush his leg.

Xavis finished shutting down the ship, turning off screens one at a time. "You'll be flying the ship on your own soon." His chair's special design accommodated the large feathered wings on his back, and every button on the ship's controls was strong enough to withstand his sharp talons.

The very last screen to go dark was the Relativator, a ship-wide system associated with the artificial gravity.

Pet had accidentally activated it once and earned such an extreme reaction from his trio he vowed to never go near it again. He leaned away from the controls and raised his hands in the air. "You can do the flying. I'm happy to help from a back-seat position."

Brog's arms squeezed Pet again. "Speakin' 'a that. If you're goin' to be helpin' out, we should get you a chair. Not that I mind bein' your seat belt."

Pet barely heard this remark, too eager for their new destination. He practically bounced on Brog's lap in his excitement, and only the four arms around his waist kept him from tumbling to the floor.

After the adventures with the DPS agents and the *Trailblazer*, it had taken the Oculi government three months to pay the trio. With the money finally in the bank, they decided to make good on their idea for a vacation.

For the last several weeks, Pet had pestered them to

tell him where they were going, but they remained frustratingly silent.

Finally disembarking from the ship, Pet's first look at the planet Syzygy showed only the landing pad.

It was a self-contained area, open to the sky, but with grand walls on all sides. Huge, ship-sized stalls lay in rows along each wall. Half the stalls remained vacant while the other half held ships of various types. Even fully spread out, the *Vanguard* barely took up a third of its stall. Compared to the larger ships, still sporting their factory-new shine, the *Vanguard* looked like it had landed there by accident.

Pet followed his trio to a large doorway out of the landing pad. Gravity on the planet felt slightly lighter than on their ship, giving Pet an extra bounce in his step. Artificial gravity maintained a universal standard, but natural gravity came in a variety of strengths, a fact he forgot until he set foot on ground.

As the four of them crossed below the arch, a pale-blue light scanned them. It had no physical sensation, but Pet saw the vague image of his own veins under his skin. "Is this supposed to happen?" He held up his hand, pushed his sleeve out of the way, and wiggled his fingers. Veins shifted with his movement.

Desmodian gripped Pet's hand and ran a thumb over the pulse in his wrist. "It's standard when entering a new planet. They need to make sure we're not contaminated with anything dangerous." Instead of veins, the light showed each optical lens in the Dhen'in's scales, creating a spotted pattern against the green.

The light ended, and Pet took his hand back. He couldn't see the veins anymore but felt unnaturally aware of their existence. "We never do this when we go to the Penumbra Belt."

Feathers brushed Pet's skin as Xavis pushed past. "That's because we mostly visit asteroids or ships with artificial atmospheres." On the path beyond the scanner, he turned back to face them and held his arms aloft, framing the distant island between his talons. "This planet has its own natural atmosphere. Harder to maintain than an artificial one, but it comes with a lot more variety. So what do you think?"

Pet stepped through the archway. "This is where we're staying?"

Xavis's feathers wilted. "What? You don't like it?"

"No, it's just...not what I expected."

Desmodian gave him a smirk as he also stepped from under the scanner. "That's the point. Vacation is about doing something different."

Outside the landing pad, Pet was greeted by the sound of water slapping against metal.

The landing pad sat on a manufactured structure, anchored to the ocean floor on thick posts. This support did not extend to the bridge leading to the island, however, which rocked with each of their steps.

How much water lay below their feet?

When they were halfway across the bridge, the first signs of life appeared.

Pet looked between the people moving on the island in the distance and the landing pad they just left. "It looks busy."

Brog crossed one set of arms. "Islands around here are basically all resorts. Real popular with people who can afford it."

Pet glanced again from the lack of activity on one

end of the bridge to the whirl of activity on the other. "Why are there so few ships? Half the spaces in the landing pad were empty."

The second pair of Brog's arms also crossed, and he shrugged both sets of shoulders. "Most people that come here don't live on their ships. Just get dropped off and picked up. Even those ships in there weren't meant for livin'. Just for showin' off and takin' up space."

Ah, that said a lot. Pet kept the thought to himself, but he read between Brog's lines. This was not a place for ship-dwellers. No doubt that was exactly the reason his trio had picked it.

A building waited for them on the other side of the floating bridge. Right at the edge of the beach, the low structure bore a ceiling but no walls.

A single clerk waited behind an ornate desk at the center of the room.

When Xavis told Pet about the Rurarine, a race of sentient slug-like beings only two feet long, he had pictured something resembling Earth land slugs. The individual sitting behind the desk looked more like a sea slug.

A variety of bright colors patterned their body, predominantly green with red spots. Two frilled antennae stuck up from the top of their head, and a neon fringe framed their pale underbelly. The Rurarine sat upright in a motorized wheelchair, so they didn't stand when Pet and his trio approached, but their antennae perked up.

"Hello." They had no mouth, yet words emanated clearly from a speaker in their chair. "Can I help you?"

They supplied no name, so Pet dubbed them Clerk.

Desmodian stepped up, leaning the handle of his

hammer against the desk. "We're checking in."

Clerk's frilled antennae rubbed against each other like someone nervously washing their hands. "I'm sorry. Starthrone Island is a private resort. Reservations are required."

At Pet's back Brog scoffed but otherwise remained silent.

Neither Desmodian nor Clerk had visible eyes, making for a very awkward staring contest. "We know. We made our reservation a month ago. Desmodian of Gonthorn."

The title didn't fit Desmodian's voice. He spoke as if bending his words into an uncomfortable shape.

Xavis leaned in to whisper so only Pet could hear. "They never would've taken the reservation with the *Vanguard's* name. Des may be banished from his homeworld, but we're not above name-dropping for our own advantage."

Another way of saying ship-dwellers didn't belong there. His trio was in a mood for mischief. Pet almost felt bad for the unsuspecting staff.

Clerk had no limbs other than antennae, but their mechanized chair took the burden. Arms extended from the sides of the chair, poking at a holographic screen hidden just out of sight.

Pet leaned around the desk for a better look.

The chair seemed simple at first, but a series of wires and panels lay flush to the Rurarine's back. A dim glow along the seam where metal met flesh indicated some sort of connection.

Talons skritched against the polished desk as Xavis leaned with him. "It's a cerebral connection. They think something, and the chair does it. Never seen one before.

Wonder if I can convince them to let me take a closer look?"

"Do you mind?" Clerk's frilled antennae bent in their direction as if glaring at them. The chair's arms even stuck out to the sides like someone propping their hands on their hips.

Pet backed away, dragging Xavis along when the Scaacax didn't immediately follow.

They planted themselves at Brog's side.

The Ocan's arms stayed crossed, but his mouth had a telling upward curve. "You two gettin' us in trouble already?"

The crest of hair running over Xavis's head raised higher, and his feathers fluffed. "They should be used to curiosity, running around with that kind of tech."

The mechanical arms of Clerk's chair continued searching through files, but their antennae kept flicking in the trio's direction. They read over the information on their screen. Then they read it again. And again.

Checking reservations should have been a simple task. Why was it taking so long?

"Gentlemen."

Pet instinctively stepped behind Brog when an unexpected voice called across the otherwise empty room. A blush heated his cheeks for his foolish action, but he couldn't step back into the open without drawing more attention.

The new Rurarine would have resembled Clerk, except for their darker coloring and more intricately designed chair. They stopped right in front of the desk, forcing Desmodian to step back or risk catching his foot under a wheel.

The Dhen'in's tail thrashed, and he gripped his

hammer a little tighter.

If the new Rurarine noticed Desmodian's annoyance, they gave no indication. "I'm the on-duty manager. What seems to be the trouble?"

A brief crackle of green energy danced between Desmodian's fingertips, too quickly for anyone to notice unless they were looking for it.

Since finding out about his trio's Phazer abilities, Pet was always looking for it.

"Come on." Xavis nudged Pet and Brog away from the desk toward a circle of soft chairs. "Desmodian'll have an easier time without us looming."

So they waited.

The chair creaked when Brog sat down. All six of his limbs sprawled in different directions when he slouched in the seat, almost low enough to count as lying down. "Damn slugs."

Xavis chose to perch on the short table accompanying the chairs whose fabric didn't look like it would stand a chance against sharp talons. "We should probably avoid that word. Apparently Rurarine consider 'slug' to be a slur. It's not gonna win us any friends."

Pet sat as well but kept an eye on Desmodian. The conversation with Clerk and the manager wasn't going well, judging by the Dhen'in's increasing gesticulations.

It would be a shame if they couldn't stay. Pet hadn't seen much of the island yet, but it seemed like a lovely place.

The sky was a particularly royal shade of blue, sand along the beach sparkled bright white, and there was a heady perfume in the air that mixed well with the salt of the ocean.

Such a difference from their usual pit stops like the Gravity Well.

He forced himself to stop watching the conversation. Desmodian's back didn't tell him anything useful. Instead, he plucked at the hem of his long sleeves. Without knowing where they were going, he'd spent an hour picking an outfit that would work for nearly any circumstance. A pair of navy shorts clung to his legs and showed off their long lines. He forwent jewelry and instead chose an artfully asymmetrical top in a neutral blue. On the right, its hem rose all the way to his chest, while on the left, it circled around behind his knees. The semi-translucent fabric billowed with the slightest gust of air.

Desmodian needed to hurry up. If their conversation lasted much longer, Pet would end up completely unraveling the delicate material.

Fifteen minutes later, Desmodian was still arguing with the manager.

In that time the sun traveled farther across the sky than Pet expected. "The sun is already setting."

Brog looked over his shoulder at the skyline where the first hints of red appeared. "Oh, yeah, days here are shorter than the intergalactic standard."

This pulled Pet's interest away from the sky and back to his trio, or at least the two members currently available. "Wait, the length of a day can be different?"

Xavis had resorted to preening his wings for entertainment as they waited but stopped and let the feathers fall back into place, giving Pet his attention instead. "A day is just how long it takes a planet to spin. Different planets spin at different speeds, so their days are all different. You lived on a planet before joining the *Vanguard*. Didn't you notice the difference?"

Pet thought back to his time as Mister Stiril's décor. A day back on the Vunqril's homeworld hadn't felt any different than a day on the *Vanguard*, but he never specifically counted the hours until he learned the standard time measurements used on ships.

Now that he thought about it, he had no idea how many days Vunqril considered a week, or how many weeks to their month. He shrugged. "When I lived as proper décor, every day was the same. Time didn't matter back then. I was told what to do and when to do it. So long as I obeyed, I never needed to keep track of anything. Guess I assumed time was always measured the same way."

One of Xavis's loose feathers drifted to the floor.

Purple sparks danced along its veins until Brog picked up the feather and crushed it in one fist. Orange consumed the purple, then both lights died. "Yeah, it gets weird goin' from planet to planet, but you get used to it. Now, looks like Des finally made some progress."

Waving one arm to get their attention, Desmodian called to them from across the room. "It seems they've had a mix-up in their system. There's no room ready for us."

The manager bowed from their chair. "Terribly sorry. I'll be sure to address the problem. As I was just explaining to your companion, I can contact one of the other islands in the area and see if they have any availabilities."

Two of Brog's arms gave a lazy wave. "Don't worry 'bout it. We'll wait."

The manager's antennae drooped. "Excuse me?"

Pet pretended to cough so he could hide a smile behind his hand.

The lounge chair shifted ominously as Brog peered over at the manager. "Can't take that long for a room to be prepared. We don't mind waitin' right here 'til then."

"Sounds like a plan to me." Xavis stood from the table to lean against the back of Brog's chair, adding his weight to the already strained furniture.

Pet held his breath and waited for it to collapse.

They would have succeeded if Desmodian joined. Instead, he seated himself in another chair beside them. "This does seem like a good place to spend time. It'll give us a chance to meet the other guests. I think I see an Iknox ship approaching."

The manager hurried to place himself between them and the front entrance where a ship could be seen touching down on the landing pad. "We can't let guests just sit around, of course. Until we can prepare a room, you'll have to stay out of the resort's private areas, but we have several wonderful restaurants that are always open. I'm sure that will be a much more comfortable place for you to wait."

With a tap of his war hammer against the floor, Desmodian bounced back to his feet. "Sounds even better."

At the manager's prompting, Clerk handed each of the trio a visitor's pass. The cheap-looking things were obviously not meant for regular guests but would get them inside.

"We can check your luggage while you wait."

It was a simple offer. Why did Pet's trio look so affronted?

When Clerk turned his direction, Pet sighed over his own foolishness. By definition, décor fell into the category of luggage.

Brog laid an outer hand on Pet's shoulder while crossing his inner pair of arms. "He stays with us."

Whatever mechanism allowed Clerk to speak also allowed them to stutter. "B-but…"

Desmodian interrupted them. "He stays."

Clerk conceded and backed farther behind their desk. They still didn't give Pet a visitor badge but didn't stop his inclusion either.

As they left the reception hall and entered the communal area of the resort, Xavis snuck up to Pet's side and slipped an arm around his waist. "On the bright side, you do get in for free."

Pet shrugged but leaned into the embrace. "It's what I expected."

More than a year with his trio had left him spoiled. It was easy to forget other people still viewed him as an object.

However, the depressing reminder couldn't kill his enthusiasm for their new surroundings. What looked like plants from a distance turned out to be coral. It had grown up onto the land, as if stepping out of the water in a bid to claim the sky.

The slope of the island loomed over them like the height of a mountain, providing shade from the sun so that even when he looked toward the peak, Pet never had to shield his eyes.

Their temporary passes only allowed them access to the island's outer ring of shops and restaurants. With no guide, and not knowing one place from another, they chose to wait at the restaurant closest to the beach.

Like most buildings on the island, the restaurant was a flat one-story structure made of white sandstone. Only one wall stood at the back, with support columns holding up the glass ceiling, providing plenty of light and a fresh ocean breeze.

At a place like the Gravity Well, it was typical for people to notice when the trio and Pet arrived. They had an impressive reputation among other ship-dwellers. However, on a planet, the attention that turned toward them held less admiration and more bewilderment.

The restaurant had exactly thirty-six tables in a neat grid of six-by-six. Dozens of different species filled those tables, but although they existed in the same space, they didn't mingle together. Each table hosted one species, and only one species.

Pet didn't recognize most of them. The few species he could name weren't ones he interacted with often. A group of Vunqril off to the side caught his attention. This was exactly the kind of place his previous Owner would have enjoyed.

Memories of Mister Stiril were best left forgotten. They inspired a complicated mix of emotions, and he wanted to enjoy the start of their vacation, even if it was off to a rocky start.

With Brog leading the way, they claimed a table front and center, with a good view of the water. No one said anything as their group passed, but the number of stares pointedly not looking their direction weighed on the back of Pet's neck.

At the table they ran into a new problem. The style of chairs suited Pet and Desmodian, but the tall backs would impede Xavis's wings, and they didn't look sturdy enough to hold Brog.

Desmodian pulled out a chair for Pet to sit while directing Xavis toward the counter at the back of the restaurant. "Those don't look bolted down."

A row of stools stood along the counter. Most were empty, so no one could complain as Xavis stole one and carried it back to their table. "These won't work for Brog."

Brog waved away his concern. "I got it."

He turned to face the main room of the restaurant but hesitated after barely taking a step.

Tension grew along Pet's brow like a needle threading his skin as he scowled. Brog never hesitated once he decided something. After so much time spent studying the idiosyncrasies of his trio, Pet recognized when something was wrong.

This was a vacation. Nothing should be wrong.

The indecision only lasted a moment. Then Brog drew back his shoulders, stood as tall as possible, and marched to a group of guests in the far corner.

How had Pet failed to notice other Ocans in the room?

Three months ago, when the *Vanguard* was attacked by poachers in the Iota Cloud, they had encountered an Ocan even larger than Brog. Pet had assumed this was a fluke.

He was wrong. The smallest Ocan sitting in the corner would stand several feet taller than Brog. The largest of them, the matriarch of the group, was nearly double Brog's size.

Desmodian latched onto Pet's wrist, making him jump. "Don't bring it up."

The green-scaled hand gripped Pet a little too tightly for comfort. He looked between it and

Desmodian's masked face. That mask pointed toward neither Brog nor the group of Ocans, but Pet knew Desmodian watched them anyway.

"What? But, I…"

The hand squeezed harder. "I know what you're thinking, and you're right. He may seem large to us, but Brog is actually small for his species. Don't bring it up."

Xavis nodded along with Desmodian's explanation. "Never turns out well."

Pet agreed to stay silent and pulled his hand back into his lap.

Desmodian let him go, but a brittle tension hovered around their group.

Off in the corner Brog stopped before the table with the other Ocans, both sets of arms crossed. "You usin' that?" He gestured toward the empty seat at the table but never took his eyes off the matriarch.

No one except the smallest member of the group even looked at him. "Our family unit doesn't need any new members right now."

Pet could hear Brog's snort even from across the suspiciously quiet restaurant.

"Not lookin' to join you. Just want the chair."

The smallest member of the group nodded in a jerky movement, as if they had diverted a different gesture at the last moment. The rest of the group continued to give no response, like Brog wasn't there at all.

Brog grabbed the empty chair, easily lifting it despite its size, and carried it away. The display of strength turned a few of the other Ocans' heads, but they still said nothing.

When Brog returned, no one at their table spoke either. Brog made more noise than necessary as he set the chair down, and the screech of metal legs scraping over the floor emphasized the unnatural silence.

The awkward moment didn't last long as they were almost immediately interrupted by a bubbly voice. "Hi. Welcome to *Spring and Neap*. My name's Bug. What can I get for you?"

Another Rurarine had rolled up to their table while they were distracted, riding the most complicated chair Pet had seen.

Instead of wheels, it had treads like a tank. Along with the typical cerebral connection and mechanical arms, there was a complex series of machinery with no obvious purpose. At the center of it all sat a bright-pink Rurarine, with orange highlights and a yellow underbelly.

No one in their group had even glanced at the menu displayed on the table, but Bug showed no signs of impatience. Granted, it was much harder to read emotions on a face so different from his own, but Pet had been able to recognize such things with Clerk earlier.

Because of its large array of clients, the restaurant boasted an extensive list of food. Bug took a moment to point out which section of the menu each of the trio would probably prefer.

Mealtimes were always the most awkward part of Pet's day. Desmodian and Xavis both ordered something he recognized by name, but the words meant nothing without a memory of taste to accompany.

It didn't surprise him when Brog ordered three separate dishes for himself, but this was apparently odd enough to disrupt their waiter's professionalism.

"Um, sir, our meals are all proportioned based on species. We wouldn't make you order more just to meet a biological need."

Brog still looked tense after his interaction with the other Ocans, so luckily it was Desmodian who answered. "It'll be fine. Just bring him what he ordered."

The waiter's frilled antennae twitched, but their mechanical arms entered the information into a tablet. "All right. And what about you?" Their antennae pointed at Pet.

His shoulders curled toward each other as he hunched in his seat. "Ah, no, I can't...I'm décor. I can't eat regular food. Only nutriment." He worried at the hem of his sleeve again. The fabric creased under his repeated abuse.

Bug's chair rolled back in a brief jerk, yet the treads remained silent against the floor. "I'm so sorry. I should've realized. Well, that won't do. This is Starthrone's most popular restaurant. We're known for serving any guest who comes through our door. I can't offer you anything now, but I promise the next time you come, we'll have something for you."

The waiter bowed from their chair, just a small curving of their body so their head dipped downward, then rolled away toward the kitchen.

Pet's neutral expression crumpled. He hid his face in his hands, drawing his trio's attention.

Xavis's wing circled around his shoulders. "Sorry they don't have anything for you. We'll make sure to get your nutriment off the ship when we collect the rest of our luggage."

There was no point hiding his reaction when it was already so obvious. Pet lowered his hands and let them see the smile on his face. "It's not that. The waiter called me a guest."

He hadn't wanted them to see how such a simple word affected him. It gave away how much the previous dismissal hurt. Yet none of his trio showed any surprise. He should've known there was no point hiding anything from them.

They always knew.

While they waited for their food, they spent the time reviewing Pet's newest lesson. After the incident with the poachers, it was decided that Pet needed to know the signals and gestures his trio used to communicate without words. The system was surprisingly complicated. So far they'd barely covered the basics.

Desmodian ran his thumb over the largest knuckle of his first finger. "What's this one mean?"

Pet had seen it before, at least once, yet couldn't remember the meaning. He didn't want to disappoint his trio, so he stared hard as Desmodian repeated the gesture again.

They mostly focused on teaching him emergency orders. "Get down." "Stay there." "Run." However, those gestures moved across the body to indicate direction. This one remained stationary, so it must refer to an object.

Pet copied the gesture. The feel of his own hand making the motion finally triggered a memory.

It wasn't an object. It was a person.

Pet pointed toward Brog.

Desmodian smiled and rapped a knuckle against

the tabletop. "Yep. That's the sign for Brog. Xavis and I have our own as well." He demonstrated his sign by tucking his thumb inside his fist.

Pet copied it as well before turning to Xavis and asking for his symbol.

Xavis flicked every finger on one hand open, then curled them back together. "They're all simple things that can be done singlehandedly. We'll have to make one for you as well."

By the time Pet mastered the trio's identifiers, Bug returned with their food.

Pet kept himself occupied by practicing the other signals he knew as dishes were handed around. Being the only one at the table not eating was always awkward, but nothing could be done about it. His diet wasn't a choice. Décor were incapable of eating anything except nutriment, and his trio shouldn't feel bad about something they couldn't change.

Brog's three full meals took up most of the table space.

Bug still seemed skeptical when they handed the plates over, offering to bring takeaway containers for leftovers.

The offer earned a laugh from Brog. "Don't bother. There won't be anythin' left."

Bug rocked back on their wheels. "If you're sure."

"We are. Oh, by the way, you got a pronoun you prefer?"

Bug seemed stunned by the question. Their antennae perked up, and their pink coloring grew brighter, as if blushing.

At the obvious signs of their waiter's discomfort, Desmodian added a quick explanation. "We know

Rurarine are technically intersex, but we've met members from such species before that preferred one pronoun over another."

"Well…" Bug hesitated again and rolled a little closer until their treads bumped the table. "It's not really common around here, but…I've always preferred *she*. I'm not sure why, but being referred to as female just feels right."

Xavis waved one of his utensils like a salute. "If *she* feels right, then *she* it is." He then tossed the utensil aside and tore into his food with bare talons.

To their credit, Bug didn't even twitch at Xavis's antics.

To *her* credit.

Pet repeated the proper pronoun in his head several times to make sure the change stuck. She had been considerate of him. He needed to return the favor.

As usual, once they got over the awkwardness of Pet not eating, the rest of the meal passed with shared comradery.

An hour later, sunset was in full bloom across the sky when the manager from earlier found them at the restaurant. Their room was ready.

As they left, Bug waved them out. Genuine enthusiasm brightened her voice as she told them to come back soon.

The tip they left for her nearly equaled the cost of the meal.

After their luggage was collected off the *Vanguard*, the manager led them to an automated trolley which picked up passengers from the edge of the beach. "This is the best way to get anywhere on the island."

It looked like a fishbowl. A row of seats circled the

center of the glass sphere, facing outward for the best view.

As soon as they boarded, the trolley started moving along its track, following the long switchback road that led through the city to the top of the island. No one else joined their group, leaving the trolley mostly empty.

This might have been on purpose to keep them away from the other guests, but Pet enjoyed the extra space. It allowed him to move freely, taking in the sights as he bounced from one side of the glass sphere to the other.

Like the restaurant, most buildings only stood a single story tall. While they had ceilings, the walls remained open. Natural coral climbed right up the buildings and collected into living forests on the roofs.

Dozens of different species mingled between the various shops, restaurants, and clubs, but it was not so busy that people looked crowded.

Another trolley passed by.

The glass spheres allowed Pet a close view of its passengers. Someone from a crystalline species he didn't recognize carried a similar-looking child in their arms. As they passed, the child locked eyes with Pet. They shared a moment of connection, each acknowledging the other's existence.

The child waved.

Pet waved back.

Then they were gone in opposite directions down the tracks, and the moment ended.

The trolley looked like it was supposed to stop at regular pickup spots along the road, but theirs never even slowed down. At this steady pace, it still took them fifteen minutes to reach the top of the island.

Here they found the island's namesake. An elegant building, multiple stories tall, perched right on the highest tip. It looked like a throne, haloed by the open sky with not even the horizon in sight. Wind echoed between the open walls, whistling an invitation for people to enter.

Pet was so busy looking up he nearly missed what was right in front of him. When he did notice, he stopped abruptly, and Xavis bumped into his back.

On either side of the entrance to the throne building stood a pair of décor.

Pet hadn't seen other décor since leaving his previous Owner. They were as blank and perfect as he remembered.

The male and female were styled differently than Mister Stiril preferred. Their heads were shaved, and they wore glittering outfits of gold and pearls. Yet with such perfectly symmetrical features, so finely sculpted, they could've stood completely naked and been just as beautiful.

Pet felt bland in comparison. The gauzy material of his own outfit was nice, but it didn't draw attention like they did.

A memory of his pre-décor interview came to mind, and the starving husk he had once been. He'd needed a lot of work to look like he did now. Had the pair needed just as much work? Or did the secret of their beauty stem from natural perfection?

These were some of the most expensive décor on the market. Even his previous Owner would've struggled to afford them.

Pet hid his wrinkled sleeves behind his back just as Xavis touched his shoulder.

"All right?"

"Fine." Pet forced himself to keep walking, sparing one more glance at the pair by the door.

Perfect décor, they never looked at him.

He had no reason to be jealous, but what else could he call the acidic feeling bubbling in his stomach? Once past the entrance, he didn't dare look back. He didn't want to know if his trio lingered over the pair, and what expression they wore if they did.

Inside the throne building, dozens of elevators lined the structure's only wall. As they approached, several doors opened to deliver groups of people into the room.

Pet distracted himself by listing off the species he recognized.

Khaso.

Q'od.

Something a bit rodent-like that was either called Endret or Erndet.

The strangers barely looked at Pet, but they quickly noticed his trio.

Despite the presence of so many different species, ship-dwellers still stood out. It was in the way they carried themselves, the way they dressed, and even the way they walked.

People whose feet never left the earth walked with a certain confidence, safe in their knowledge that the ground under them would never change. The same wasn't true for ship-dwellers. Living on a constantly moving ship meant each step came with a level of distrust.

Even planetside, his trio walked as if ready to change direction any moment.

Did he walk that way too?

Probably not. A year and three months spent living on the *Vanguard* meant he had gotten better at ship life, but he still tripped far more than his trio did.

The departing strangers gave his trio a wide berth, though the sight of a manager eased tensions to some degree. At least no one spoke out against them.

On silent wheels, the manager brought them to the side of the room, away from the main elevators. "There were no regular rooms available, so we upgraded you to one of our waterfall suites, free of charge. You'll need these cards for the private elevator."

Mechanical arms handed out three engraved gold cards to the trio, once again skipping Pet. Then the manager hit a button on the wall that revealed a smaller, hidden elevator. Pet and the trio were ushered inside, but the manger didn't join them. "This elevator will take you directly to your room. Your luggage should already be waiting for you. We hope you have a wonderful stay here on Starthrone."

The doors started closing.

Desmodian leaned against the back wall, hammer in front of him, positioned so he would be the last thing the manager saw. "I'm sure we'll find some way to enjoy ourselves."

Then the doors closed.

The private elevator might have been smaller than the others, but it still dwarfed all of them. A whole family of Ocans could have fit inside comfortably. Yet it felt as if Brog filled the space with a single deep sigh.

"Ugh. I kinda wish they'd go back to openly hatin' us. That fake cheer was gettin' on my nerves."

The elevator gave a slight lurch as it began its

descent, almost unnoticeable compared to the *Vanguard*'s wild maneuvers.

Pet didn't even bother reaching for the railing on the wall.

Desmodian wrapped a steadying arm around his shoulder anyway. "I'd rather watch them bite their tongue. Now let's see what kind of *upgrade* we've got."

The way he said it made Pet wary of what they would find, but when the elevator doors opened, he was surprised in the best way.

They stepped into a room that looked like a cave set right into the side of the island. Glowing coral along the walls gave the dark space a soothing ambiance.

The suite was the size of a small villa. Different alcoves carved into the rock were connected by a meandering cavern, like a cave system. Each open-concept room came outfitted with blocky furniture that could be easily rearranged while also strong enough to support Brog.

A kitchen claimed the heart of the suite, filled with appliances set right into the rock. Bedrooms and bathrooms lay scattered around like an afterthought.

Pet and his trio could've each taken a bedroom for themselves and still left more than half unused.

At the farthest reach of the suite, they found the master bedroom.

Bigger than all the other bedrooms, one wall of the master connected to the outside. Instead of open air, like the architecture throughout the city, a curtain of water covered this missing wall.

During their descent to the planet, Pet had noticed a dual pair of waterfalls stemming from the top of the island.

Their suite, it turned out, was situated at the base of one of these waterfalls, right behind where the water hit the ground. A channel carved into the floor created a stream which snaked through the entire suite. Stone bridges provided access across the stream, and flowers floating on the water added accents of pink, teal, and purple.

"I thought so." Desmodian strode over to the waterfall and touched a button hidden among the rocks.

The water parted down the middle and drew aside like fabric, revealing an empty stretch of beach beyond.

"Our own elevator. Our own beach. This may be an upgrade, but it's also a way to keep us separate from the other guests."

"I'm not complaining." Xavis's voice didn't echo as much as expected when he called across the suite. He dismantled one of the other beds and dragged the mattress into the master bedroom. "Would've cost more than what the Oculi government paid us to afford this room. I mean, we could, but I'd rather not spend the money if they're gonna upgrade us for free."

Desmodian disappeared into one of the other bedrooms where he could be heard pulling the bed apart. "One of the advantages to being unwanted, I suppose." He brought the bedding over and added it to Xavis's pile.

It was standard practice whenever they visited somewhere new. Even places familiar with them, like the Gravity Well, never had beds big enough for all of them at once. That comfort could be found only on the *Vanguard*, so they made their own arrangements.

Usually Brog would help, but Pet didn't see the Ocan anywhere. "Where'd Brog go?" It was a large space, but Brog was hard to miss.

Xavis and Desmodian looked up from their work, Xavis by raising his head, and Desmodian by angling his body in Pet's direction.

Suspicion grew in Pet's belly when the pair smiled in unison. He narrowed his eyes, prepared to demand an explanation, when water exploded from the stream behind him. Just as arms wrapped around his waist and pulled him backward, he noticed Brog's clothes discarded on the floor.

He plummeted into the surprisingly deep stream before he could even shout. Cool water folded around him, and four arms kept him pinned beneath the surface. His back touched the bottom of the stream just as a mouth claimed his in a kiss. They resurfaced before Pet's lungs could protest.

Taking a deep breath, he clung to Brog's shoulders and pushed wet hair off his forehead. "Was that necessary?"

Brog's laughter sent ripples across the water. "You wouldn't be askin' if you saw the look on your face."

Over the sound of his own racing pulse, Pet heard Xavis and Desmodian laughing. He splashed water at them, but it fell short. "Jerks. All of you."

His arm slipped from Brog's wet shoulders. The stream was shallow enough for him to stand, but the water came up to his chin. He flailed without support. Wet cloth tangled around him, and his head dipped under the surface.

Four arms lifted him back up. "Whoa, hey, Pet. Calm down. You're fine."

The water he'd swallowed nearly went to his lungs instead of his stomach, and he coughed. "Sorry.

Panicked. Can't swim."

Some parts of the stream were larger than others. The two of them had drifted away from the edge, so Brog brought him over to an island at the center of the stream. "What do you mean, you can't swim?"

Pet's wet clothes clung to him as he shrugged. "When would I have learned?" Rather than meet Brog's eyes, he peeled himself out of his top. The billowing fabric had betrayed him, and he wanted it off. It made an unappealing splat against the rock when he tossed it onto the bank.

His waterlogged shoes soon followed.

The clothing could stay there for all Pet cared, but Xavis spread it out to dry.

"We'll have to fix that. Water's not my favorite thing either, but it's still good to know how to swim."

The bed had finally been arranged, and Desmodian threw himself across the pillows. "A goal for later. Until then, we'll have to keep hold of Pet."

Brog's concern turned into a leering smile. "Gladly."

Even though Pet sat on the smooth stone with his legs dangling in the water, Brog was still tall enough to lean over him.

He wrapped arms around Brog's neck and pulled the Ocan down until they were chest to chest. "They gave us this suite to separate us from the other guests. Think we can earn a few noise complaints anyway?"

Brog braced one set of hands on the island. The other set pulled Pet's legs around his waist. "Up to you. You're the loud one."

Pet lay back against the stone as his shorts were removed, leaving him completely bare. He raised his hands over his head and arched his spine, putting his body on full display as he ground their hips together. "Only when you make me scream."

Brog's sharp teeth nipped down Pet's neck without breaking skin, and the Ocan's already hard cock rubbed against his ass.

They weren't wasting any time.

Out of the corner of his eye, Pet glanced toward the rest of his trio.

Xavis perched at the edge of the stream, legs slowly kicking through the water as he watched.

Desmodian was less obvious with his voyeurism. He leaned back in the bed and removed his shirt, uncovering even more scales for a better view.

With such an attentive audience, they needed to put on a show.

Pet locked his legs around Brog's wide hips and pulled them closer, almost shoving the Ocan's shaft inside himself.

Brog's growl vibrated his pulse point. "Eager little thing. Fine. I won't be gentle."

At some point while Pet wasn't paying attention, Xavis tossed Brog a bottle retrieved from their luggage. Pet only learned this when Brog slipped a finger slick with oil inside of him.

The Ocan made good on his promise. A second finger quickly joined the first, and together they shoved roughly in and out of Pet. It hadn't been long since Pet and his trio last had sex, so the rough preparation didn't hurt. The slight burn as his body adjusted quicker than normal felt like a promise for what was to come.

Pet couldn't wait, and begged Brog to hurry up.

They never made it to a third finger. The two

fingers disappeared, leaving Pet empty just long enough for Brog to grab onto his hips and shove inside properly. The ribbed shaft forced its way into Pet's barely prepared hole, driving the air from his lungs.

Brog pressed as far inside as possible, then immediately pulled out.

There was no chance for Pet to catch his breath as Brog started thrusting in earnest.

He squirmed as he struggled to adjust while getting fucked. It felt good, but he was overwhelmed by the sudden stimulation. His fingers slipped over smooth stone. Each thrust sent him sliding up the rock, only to be pulled back into the next one.

The sound of skin against skin and slapping water was drowned out by Pet's cries echoing off the cave walls.

Brog's breathing increased, but he still looked far too composed as he hovered over Pet. "Regrettin' it now? Want me to slow down?"

"No." Pet shook his head against the slick texture of the rock. "No. More. Please, more."

Brog's pleasure rumbled deep in his chest. "Good Pet."

They kissed as Brog kept up his pace, eagerly fucking as hard and fast as Pet's body would allow. Pleasure tightened deep in Pet's stomach. He moaned into the kiss, trying to get as close to Brog as possible.

Off to the side, Xavis groaned. "Aw, Brog, let him scream. I wanna hear him."

With a flurry of feathers, Xavis flew over to the island and landed by Pet's head. Talons carefully coaxed Pet to end the kiss.

He arched back against the flat stone, and Xavis

pinned his wrists.

Brog sped up, hitching Pet's hips higher to slam into his pleasure spot with each thrust.

Restrained from two sides at once, Pet couldn't even squirm as he pushed closer and closer to his release. He made up for it with his voice. His cries of ecstasy bounced around the suite, echoing off rock and water alike.

Just as he approached the peak of his pleasure, Brog beat him to it. The Ocan's whole body shuddered through his orgasm.

In contrast to Pet's wailing, Brog was quiet when he came. His features pulled tight, and his mouth fell open, but his eyes never closed.

The heat that spilled inside Pet wasn't enough to satisfy him. After finishing, Brog pulled out and left Pet empty. He tried to sit up, but Xavis still trapped his wrists. Instead of chasing what he wanted, he had to rely on words.

"Please." He wiggled his hips and rubbed his legs together, drawing attention to his unsatisfied state. "Don't go yet. I'm not done."

Still kneeling by his head, Xavis leaned in to nuzzle his heated cheeks. "Such a lovely little slut. How can we say no when you beg so pretty?"

Xavis let go of his wrists, and Pet took advantage of the freedom. He couldn't see what he was doing since it was above his head, forcing him to feel along Xavis's legs until he found the closure to the Scaacax's pants.

Belts never lasted long against Xavis's talons, so he just used a knotted piece of rope.

Pet's hands shook with a combination of

excitement and need. No matter how hard he tried, he couldn't get the rope undone. He let out a high-pitched whine when his fingers slipped off the knot a third time.

Brog's laughter tickled his thigh, making him twitch.

While he'd struggled with Xavis's belt, the Ocan had ducked down in the water until only his head remained above the surface. "Better give 'im what he wants, Xavis. Or you're gonna lose those pants."

"He can have them. Here, Pet, let me help." Xavis's talons made quick work of the rope.

Pet waited only long enough for Xavis to shed his pants before grabbing him again. With the Scaacax kneeling above his head, it wasn't the best angle, but he refused to wait any longer and swallowed down as much of Xavis's cock as he could. The familiar sweet taste bloomed on his tongue. He moaned as the natural aphrodisiac hit his system, making his own arousal throb.

"Fuck. I swear he gets better every time." Xavis pushed more of his cock into Pet's mouth and down his throat. The position meant he was practically sitting on Pet's face.

He hesitated, but Pet squeezed his hips in encouragement to keep going.

Xavis started thrusting, and Pet swallowed him eagerly.

More hands ran over Pet stomach and legs as Brog nipped a trail up his thigh. The closer Brog drew to his arousal, the more Pet moaned, begging without words for the attention he craved. Yet, just when it seemed Brog was about to give him some relief, the Ocan retreated to repeat the process on the other thigh.

Pet screamed in frustration, and the vibration made Xavis's hips stutter.

"Ah, Brog, whatever you're doing, keep doing it."

That was the exact opposite of what Pet wanted. He kicked his legs, but they remained pinned in the water against Brog's shoulders. Frustration made Pet sob and suck harder at Xavis, chasing the only pleasure he could get.

Xavis's wings flapped, sending up a spray of water. "F-fuck. Pet. So good. Brog, give him whatever he wants. He deserves it."

"You don't want to tease him more?" Brog's breath ghosted over Pet's painfully hard cock.

Even such brief stimulation made Pet shudder.

Xavis thrust down into his mouth as far as he could go. "I want to feel how hard he'll scream when he comes."

Brog descended on Pet, flat lips enveloping his arousal and sucking him hard.

The threat of sharp teeth near such a sensitive area never occurred to Pet. He was too busy weeping in relief as that hot mouth sent sparks of pleasure coursing up his spine.

They fell into a rhythm, with Brog between his legs and Xavis kneeling over his head. Pet's cries turned to quiet whimpers against Xavis's flesh. Everything felt so good. Yet, every time he thought he was about to tumble over the edge of pleasure, the peak moved further away. He was left chasing an end he could never quite reach.

It was an agonizingly long process as he slowly caught up to his own orgasm. All the while Brog's mouth and tongue never stopped. Above him, Xavis grew tense.

The Scaacax desperately fought off his own end, waiting for Pet to join him.

They came at almost the same time.

The pleasure in Pet's stomach finally turned that extra notch tighter, which was all he needed to tip over the edge. His back arched as he came down Brog's throat, screaming through pleasure so intense his vision whited out despite his eyes being closed.

Xavis came as well, but Pet couldn't swallow much. Most of Xavis's pleasure slipped past his lips and was washed away in the stream.

Still gasping for breath, he disentangled from the pair and sat up. Blood rushed back to his head. Now that their shared pleasure had faded, the awkward angle he'd been lying on the rock caught up with him. Hands grabbed him when he swayed, but the dizzy moment passed, and he brushed them off.

Someone was missing.

Desmodian hadn't moved from the bed. He lounged among the pillows, seemingly content to watch their show, but the bulge in his pants belied his excitement.

Pet waved for Desmodian to join them.

With a smile and a shake of his head, Desmodian curled a finger and beckoned Pet to the bed instead.

It did sound like a good idea. Residual pleasure still coursed through Pet's veins, but when it faded, he would regret the unyielding nature of stone.

He needed Brog's help across the stream. From there it was only a few steps to the bed. Yet his legs felt as stable as sand, and he collapsed gracelessly onto the mattress.

With his face on fire, he buried deeper into the pillows and groaned. "That was sexy."

Was that right? He was still getting the hang of sarcasm.

Desmodian stroked his hair.

Pet didn't need to look up to know it was him. He could tell from the cool texture of the Dhen'in's scales.

The hand moved from his hair to his cheeks, soothing their flush and making Pet look up.

"Cute can be its own kind of sexy." The mask fused to Desmodian's face meant he didn't have much expression, but the soft upward curve of his mouth spoke volumes.

The two of them leaned in at the same time, trading a gentle kiss that lacked their usual heat. It didn't stay chaste for long.

Desmodian's tongue pushed its way into Pet's mouth, filling him just as Xavis's cock had moments ago. The Dhen'in fell backward, bringing Pet with him to lie on his chest.

Pet yelped in surprise and drew back from the kiss. "When did you remove your pants?"

Desmodian's smile turned sharp. "Don't you want it?" He thrust his hips up, rubbing his exposed arousal against Pet's ass.

Unlike Brog or Xavis, Desmodian had a dual pair of cocks that extended from a single root. Both stood hard and pushed at Pet's hole, eager to be inside.

Bracing himself against Desmodian's chest, Pet sat up and speared himself on both at once. "Yes. I do."

The uneven stretch of the dual cocks never failed to get him going, even after he had just come minutes before. They moved independently and hit all his best spots at once as he impaled himself as far as he could.

He wasn't going to last. His previous orgasm took so long to reach it left him overstimulated, and he sprinted toward his end.

Desmodian didn't seem to mind. Judging from how hard he was, watching them had left him equally on edge. He gripped Pet's hips, bouncing him on his lap and forcing him to go faster.

Pet threw back his head, moaning toward the ceiling as Desmodian drove him to orgasm like a strict taskmaster.

The Dhen'in's mouth latched onto Pet's exposed throat, sucking hard right over the hammering pulse.

Pet tangled his hands in Desmodian's indigo hair. He came, gripping hard enough to pull a few strands free.

Desmodian didn't give any indication that he noticed. He was too busy shuddering through his own orgasm.

They trembled together, both needing time to come down from their high.

When Pet breathed normally again, he collapsed against Desmodian's chest.

The Dhen'in lay back among the pillows, cradling Pet to him. Even after such exertion, his scales remained cool and soothing.

Pet was halfway asleep when he felt the mattress dip as Brog and Xavis joined them. They would undoubtedly have another round later, but for now he let unconsciousness take him.

Chapter Three

After

"Bug?"

When Pet looked up to see who approached, the last person he expected was the Rurarine waiter. He'd never heard a mechanized chair on snow, so hadn't recognized the sound.

She rolled slowly over the ice. Her treads found traction on the difficult terrain, but she didn't seem to be taking any chances.

"Pet? There you are. I was worried when I didn't see you."

Pet jumped to his feet, nearly tripping again. "Bug. How did... What're you doing here?"

They reached each other, and Pet would have hugged her—chair and all—if his arms were long enough. Her chair only reached his waist but was as wide as it was tall.

Bug wore nothing to protect her from the elements, yet she showed no signs of cold. "I saw them snatch you on the beach, so I followed. The airships are locked down at night, so I wasn't expecting it to take off. Luckily, I managed to stay hidden until it landed."

Pet glanced again at their surroundings. Bug's bright colors clashed with the bleak white. He scrubbed frozen tears off his face, hoping she hadn't seen him cry. "Sorry. Now you're stuck out here too."

"Pet." Her voice was too soft for someone abandoned in the arctic. "Are you apologizing for getting kidnapped? Because if you are, stop it."

He laughed. The broken sound echoed off jagged ice. "Sorry—I mean, not sorry, but...you shouldn't be here."

The wind shifted, and the airship groaned on its unstable landing gear.

Pet and Bug regarded it with suspicion.

"Neither of us should be here." Bug's antennae twisted around each other as the treads on her chair reversed. "Specifically, right here, next to this airship. It's a luxury ship. It's not meant for this kind of terrain."

Pet nodded and backed away from the airship one careful step at a time. "Agreed." As much as he wished he could run, he was forced to walk at a sedate pace for fear of falling over again.

Bug's chair had a much easier time on the ice. She rolled away quickly but doubled back when she noticed he couldn't keep up. "Hop on. It'll be easier." Her mechanical arms pointed him to the back of her chair. It wasn't built to carry passengers, but the boxy design had enough space for him to cling on the back panel.

The airship groaned again, accompanied by the crunch of shifting snow.

Pet found a grip on the chair and let Bug carry him away. A burst of warmth surrounded him. "Your chair is heated?"

"Yep." They charged forward over the snow, but Bug's antennae arched backward toward him. "Rurarine evolved in deep waters. Our species is pretty resilient to low temperatures, but even we have our limit. Besides, I like being comfortable."

He pressed as close to the chair as he could without falling off and resisted the urge to purr as he soaked up the heat. "I think I'm a little bit in love."

Although Bug's laughter was mechanical, there was nothing fake about it. "Sorry, Pet. You're not my type."

"Who said anything about you? I was talking about your chair."

"Oh, I see. You only want me for my accessories."

Thanks to Bug's chair, they escaped the shadow of the airship and headed for the uneven peak sticking out of the ice. They rolled to a stop near the hole blown into the structure's side.

Cracks spread along the outer surface, but the hole itself was surprisingly small. Only about ten feet across, it punched right through the side of the structure.

Pet stepped off the chair and approached the hole, placing a hand on the ragged edge of the opening. "Whoa. That's more than I expected."

The walls were so thick the hole resembled a tunnel.

Pet couldn't see the other side.

Bug bumped against him, facing into the dark opening. "This is an old lab that was shut down years ago. They're all over the planet. The global economy dropped, and it was more cost-effective to leave them than tear them down. There's still hope we'll be able to return to them someday. So they were locked up tight to keep them safe. They're impenetrable."

Darkness filled the hole, giving no hints about what waited beyond.

Pet couldn't decide if that was a good or bad thing. "Not so impenetrable, it seems."

"Yeah…" Bug trailed off and maneuvered her chair to face Pet directly. "Pet. I saw the explosion. The force it would take to break into this place… Honestly, I'm not sure how we're still alive. But you don't look surprised."

There was no actual question, but he knew what she wanted to know.

Wind caught the edge of the hole and swirled down into the darkness with a lonely wail. It tugged his hair and clothes, gently pulling him toward whatever lay inside. "I need to find my trio. They were taken. If they're not on the airship, they must be in there somewhere. That's why we're here. Because they're…"

He hesitated. His trio's greatest secret wasn't his to tell. However, he needed help, and Bug would be a more useful ally with all the information.

"My trio are Phazers."

This didn't earn the reaction he expected. Bug just looked at him with antennae twitching.

"I haven't heard that term before, but it sounds important. What is it?"

Oh, this was going to be even harder. Pet barely understood his trio's Phazer abilities himself. Explaining it to someone else would be a challenge. He tried his best, but even to his own ears it sounded like a work of fiction.

"Oh, wow."

Maybe Pet's explanation was better than he thought because Bug sounded suitably impressed.

"People can control atomic bonds? I didn't know that was a thing. So they came here to manage that explosion?"

Pet flinched as memories of his captivity on the airship surfaced. "Not willingly. They were forced to help break into this place."

If Bug had eyebrows, she would probably be scowling. The way her antennae angled toward each other imitated a furrowed expression. "How does someone with that kind of power get captured? An ability like that could overcome anything."

Shifting on his feet, Pet tugged at the sleeve of his oversized coat. Revealing his trio's abilities was one thing, but their weaknesses? That seemed too personal. Yet he couldn't see any way around telling her.

"Being a Phazer comes with some major problems as well. They're weakened by anything that creates its own field, like magnets and electricity. I saw them. They were being kept in these electrified cages. Don't know what the common term for it is, but I think humans call it a Faraday cage. Trapped like that, they were helpless."

If for some reason his mind was ever erased again, that was one memory he would give up gladly.

Something echoed from inside the blasted opening. It wasn't an organic sound but rather a clang of metal against metal.

Pet and Bug both backed away into a snowdrift.

Bug's heated chair melted any snow it touched. Water trickled to the ground where it refroze, forming a slick puddle under her treads. "So what's the plan? Rescue your trio?"

Pet's shrug was far more nonchalant than he felt. "That's all I can think of. Unless you know how to fly that airship so we can get out of here and find help."

Without a neck, Bug couldn't nod or shake her head. Instead, the treads of her chair rocked side to side as if she were shuffling her feet. She slipped on the puddle of her own making and lurched backward. "Even if I did, those things need a whole crew. We wouldn't be able to fly it ourselves…so we find your trio. They'll be easy to spot, at least."

"I hope so."

They continued to stare into the opening, waiting for something to happen.

Time ticked by undisturbed. Even the sound they'd heard earlier faded.

Sharing a look, they crept forward side by side until they stood at the very edge dividing ice and shadow.

"We'll only get colder waiting around." Bug sounded a little too cheerful to be genuine. She had to be as scared as Pet felt, but she hadn't run away.

That was more than Pet could say for most people. He placed a tentative foot inside the hole.

Broken metal offered better traction than ice.

"With my luck, there'll be guards standing just on the other side of the wall."

Bug didn't disagree, but she did follow him.

Together the two of them disappeared into the dark maw to face whatever waited within.

Chapter Four

Before

The sound of raining water greeted Pet when he awoke. He fell asleep surrounded by three bodies, but now only one remained. Xavis lay pressed against his back, feathers tickling his legs, but Brog and Desmodian were nowhere to be seen.

Pet sat up, still bleary-eyed. Nights on Syzygy were short, and they hadn't stopped at one round. Although he was able to nap in between, he hadn't truly fallen asleep until the small hours of the morning. Judging by the angle of the light coming through the carved windows, it was still morning, but he wouldn't be able to go back to sleep without locating the rest of his trio. Not knowing where they were left him feeling naked. Clothes wouldn't help, so he didn't bother putting any on as he climbed from the bed.

It was a short search.

Desmodian stood off to the side of the room, leaning against the opening to the private beach. Half the waterfall had been pushed aside, leaving him just enough space to stare out into the morning.

As Pet approached, Desmodian took the effort to *look* over his shoulder in Pet's direction and raised a finger to his lips in a bid for silence. Then he nodded toward the beach.

Pet leaned around Desmodian to see a reflection of color. Sky and ocean mirrored each other, a gradient of bright teal to soft purple that met in the middle. The usually white sand looked dusky pink under the sunrise.

Brog floated on the water a little way off the beach, completely relaxed as he watched the clouds.

Desmodian pulled Pet around to stand in front of him for a better view, wrapping one arm around his shoulders so he leaned back against the Dhen'in's chest. In his other hand Desmodian held a mug, half filled with a bitter-smelling drink. They watched Brog enjoy the ocean, Desmodian taking occasional sips of his drink as the sky lightened.

The mug was empty before he spoke. "I never think about it until moments like this. Ocans are an aquatic species. Brog won't admit missing anything from his homeworld, but…"

He trailed off, letting the implication of his statement speak for itself.

Pet tipped his head back until he could see Desmodian's masked face, noting the pinched edges of his mouth. "It makes me realize something too. Oceans like this are only found on planets. This is my first time on a planet since leaving my previous Owner."

He turned around so they stood face to face, allowing Desmodian to see all of him. The full-body vision affected more than what the other male could see. It also dictated what he looked for. From Desmodian's perspective, body language meant more than facial expression.

For this reason, Pet kept his posture relaxed. "It's been a year and three months. In all that time you've only accepted jobs involving other ships or asteroid colonies. Inhabited planets must have a lot more opportunities, but you've avoided them. Why? Because of me?"

Desmodian raised the mug to his lips, only to realize it was empty and set it aside. "Not necessarily because of you, and we weren't specifically avoiding planets. We were avoiding landowners who would kick up a fuss when they found out a trio of ship-dwellers got our hands on one of their precious décor. It would happen eventually, but we wanted to put it off as long as possible. Now that we've been investigated by Décor Preservation Services and gotten through it, there's no reason to avoid attention."

Instinct told Pet to lower his eyes when he apologized. It was an aspect of décor mentality he couldn't shake. "I'm sorry. You lost business because of me."

Desmodian tipped Pet's head back up and stroked a thumb over his bottom lip. "It'll be fine. If we play it right, this can be good for business. Supply and demand. A decrease in the supply of our services will increase the demand."

Pet shook his head, though not enough to dislodge Desmodian's hand. While he had heard the terms *supply* and *demand* before, he wasn't sure how it worked. He was still perfecting the ability to read. Lessons in economics remained far in his future.

Splashing from the direction of the beach caught his attention.

Brog waved at them from the water. "What you two standin' around for? Pet, come here. Want to show you somethin'."

The feeling of sand under his bare feet was not

what Pet expected. The white grains resembled powder more than sand, loose where it was wet, yet packed hard in dry areas. He picked up a handful. Hints of his skin could be seen through the nearly translucent grains.

Brog met him at the edge of the water, standing naked in the surf with waves dancing around his ankles. "You need to learn to swim."

"Oh no." Pet waved his hands and backed away. "That's all right. I'm fine."

He didn't make it far before Brog grabbed his wrist. "Come on. It's a good skill to know. We won't go far."

A shiver traced from Pet's feet up to his head, leaving behind a trail of goose bumps. The cold ocean water wasn't as pleasant as the stream in their suite. Here the water constantly moved, and the sand squished under each step he took.

They waded out until the water was up to Pet's waist.

Brog let go of his wrist to pick him up bridal style, so he was half in and half out of the water. "Start with floatin'. Lie back in the water and just relax."

Pet let his hand rest on the surface, feeling the constant shifting. "That sounds terrible. What if I sink?"

Brog held him close and lowered them both a little more. "You won't. There's a higher percentage 'a heavy water on this planet, so it's extra buoyant."

Droplets cascaded from his fingers when Pet removed his hand from the surface. "What's heavy water?"

"It's, um…" Brog cast his gaze from wave to wave, as if the ocean would answer for him.

As expected, it provided nothing more than the lapping of the tides.

Brog sighed but tried his best to answer. "Well, see, water is made from oxygen and hydrogen. In heavy water, the hydrogen atom has an extra neutron. This makes the water denser, so it supports more weight."

Pet wasn't convinced. The interaction of neutrons and atoms sounded very scientific, but he couldn't see these things. How could he trust something he couldn't see?

When he looked up into Brog's eyes, the answer was simple.

He trusted Brog. That was enough.

With a deep breath Pet forced himself to lean back, though he couldn't relax.

In the end Brog laid him in the water while keeping two hands on his back for support.

Pet let his ears dip below the surface. The world immediately went silent except for the sound of his own heartbeat.

It was horrible.

He hadn't minded the stream in their room, where he was too distracted by his trio to notice the water. This was different. The last time he'd experienced such a stifling of his senses, he'd been lying in a sensory deprivation chamber.

Brog's hand left his back so only the water remained.

Pet panicked. Fueled by instinct, he curled into a protective ball, trying to keep the silence out of his brain. He sank below the surface. Opening his mouth to shout in surprise, he choked around the taste of salt.

Four hands pulled him from the water into strong

arms. "Whoa. Calm down. It's all right."

Pet coughed and sputtered, desperate to get the horrible taste out of his mouth. "No. I don't like it."

Brog lowered him until his feet dangled in the water again. "It takes a little practice."

He tucked his feet up against his body and clung tighter to Brog. "I don't like it."

His desperation must have been evident in his voice. Brog's orange eyes widened, and he pulled Pet out of the water without further argument. "Okay. Think that's enough for now."

He carried Pet from the ocean and didn't set him down until they were inside the suite.

Compared to the shifting sand, Pet preferred the feel of smooth stone under his feet and eagerly wiggled his toes.

At some point Xavis had joined Desmodian watching from just beyond the waterfall. The Scaacax looked rumpled, still half asleep, but Desmodian was more alert than a few minutes ago.

"Everything all right?"

Pet shook his head. "I don't like it." He was too busy scowling at the ocean to pay much attention to the look that passed between his trio.

Xavis's feathers flattened, and his wings drew back. "Any particular reason?"

Should Pet tell them about the memory of the deprivation chamber? He didn't want them to worry, or worse, think there was something wrong with him.

He chose an equally true but safer answer. "It's cold, and it tastes bad. Why does it taste like that? The stream in our suite doesn't taste bad."

Xavis led him back inside, with Brog and

Desmodian not far behind. One wing draped over Pet's shoulders. "The waterfall and stream are artificial, so they use fresh water. The ocean is natural saltwater. It can be a bit jarring, but don't worry about that. There's a whole island of entertainment waiting for us."

Unlike on the *Vanguard*, the suite had enough bathrooms for each of them to get ready simultaneously.

Still, Pet didn't waste time. He jumped into a shower just long enough to rinse away the salt, then dried off and checked for bruises from the previous night. He never minded them, but décor with obvious marks on their skin would attract suspicion.

Desmodian claimed it was fine to draw attention since they'd already dealt with DPS, but there was no reason to invite unwanted questions.

Speaking of questions, another very important one waited for him. His trio were still getting ready, so he stood alone in their bedroom when he pulled out his luggage.

What should he wear?

It might seem like an inane thing to worry about, but for décor, it was an important choice. An outfit could dictate the entire day. Although his trio didn't treat him like typical décor, some habits never left.

The décor draped in gold and pearls from yesterday came to mind. He didn't want to imitate them, but gold and pearls were a smart choice. They wouldn't tarnish as easily in the briny ocean air.

Plus, if he rivaled the pair from yesterday, it would be a double win.

The outfit he chose was one he'd planned on saving for later in the vacation. However, after their lukewarm reception to the island, he needed to make a statement. The entire outfit was made from two ribbons of pale cloth. One wrapped between his legs and around his waist, the loose ends hanging in front and back. A belt of gold vines held it up. The metal leaves didn't meet in the front, and a hidden hinge in the back allowed the belt to be easily placed on and off. Most of his legs remained on display, with a few loops of white pearls on his thighs.

The second cloth wrapped around his back and crossed over his chest. It tied behind his neck, and the loose ends hung past his waist. They would flutter every time the wind blew. More pearl strands draped down his stomach and over his shoulders. Lastly, he donned a headpiece that matched the belt. Gold vines circled his head, not quite touching on his forehead, with pearls dripping from the leaves.

"Haven't seen that one in a while."

Pet spun to find Brog watching him from the other side of the room, still completely undressed. He raised his arms and twirled to show off the lightness of the fabric. "It seemed appropriately...beachy."

An orange glow built in Brog's eyes as he approached. He took Pet into his arms and tugged the bow holding the outfit together. "Easy to remove too."

Pet waited until Brog almost had the bow undone before swatting the Ocan away. "Not now. We're about to leave."

Brog tried again. "Nothin' that can't wait."

Their game was interrupted when Desmodian entered the room. "Are you trying to make us late? Again?"

Brog shrugged but let Pet go. "Late for what?

Nowhere we gotta be."

Xavis leaned out of his bathroom just enough to make eye contact with Brog. "I'm hungry. And we still gotta find a restaurant. No delays."

"Fine." Brog grumbled and gave Pet another once-over. "I'll 'ave that off you later."

It didn't take the trio nearly as long to get dressed as it took Pet. Their clothes were mostly variations of the same style. Meant to hold up against the rigors of travel, but not very fashionable. Only slight differences existed between the three.

Everything Desmodian owned had intentional holes, while everything Xavis owned had unintentional holes. All of Brog's clothes had been fitted with holsters for weapons, though security hadn't let him bring any off their ship. The empty holsters made him look half naked.

His trio's simplistic fashion sense meant that only ten minutes passed before they stepped off the elevator at the top of the island.

The communal lobby was more crowded than when they arrived. Elevator doors constantly opened and closed as guests ventured from their rooms for the day.

It was busy enough that most people ignored their little group of four.

A bottleneck formed at the pickup spot for the trolleys. The glass domes could carry several dozen at once, but even this was not enough to keep up with morning traffic.

Desmodian stayed to the front of their group, holding his hammer at a casual angle that kept people at a distance. Being crowded was never fun, especially for a species like Dhen'in, with long tails in danger of being stepped on.

When they finally boarded the trolley, Brog kept an arm around Pet so he wouldn't get separated. "Private beach. Private waterfall. Private elevator. What that suite really needs is private transport." Despite sitting next to Pet, he didn't bother to lower his voice. It was no louder than usual, but in the domed space every word echoed.

"What? You have a waterfall suite?"

On the other side of the trolley, one of the Ocans Brog spoke with the day before stood from their seat while the rest remained seated. The towering matriarch maintained her poise, casting a silent vigil over the exchange as one of the smaller members spoke for the entire family unit.

Brog released Pet to cross both sets of arms. "Yeah. So what?"

The other Ocans were a brighter blue than Brog and lacked the pale tones along his face and torso. Yet their skin showed more mottling. The entire group bore similar characteristics, so Pet assumed it was a regional trait. They must come from a different area of Brog's homeworld.

The smaller member of the family flushed, their face turning dark until it almost matched Brog's color. "How does someone like you afford one of the best rooms here?"

The trolley started moving, and the confrontational Ocan tripped.

Their matriarch caught them before they hit the floor. "Mel, sit down. There's no need to make a scene."

The smaller Ocan obeyed, but this didn't keep them from talking. "Matriarch, he's…" Two of their arms flailed in Brog's direction. "Someone like him shouldn't be here."

Pet rolled his eyes. This old argument again. Landowners would never miss an opportunity to discriminate against ship-dwellers.

He expected Brog to laugh and say something dismissive, maybe even a little condescending. That was his trio's usual reaction.

Instead Brog grew tense, and a growl formed in the back of his throat. "I ain't hurtin' anyone bein' here."

The smaller Ocan started to speak, but the matriarch raised a hand to silence them. She spoke, with a voice oddly soft for her size. "Perhaps. But you're not any use here either. The *Impotent* already have so little to offer our species. If you choose to make yourself useless, that's your responsibility to bear. It has nothing to do with us."

Brog fell silent. The growl died in his throat, and his face went slack.

This was apparently enough for the other Ocans. They immediately resumed ignoring him as if he never existed in the first place.

The handle of Desmodian's hammer struck out across Brog's lap.

Pet followed the line of the weapon to see orange sparks forming around Brog's fists as they squeezed dents into the arms of the chair.

The hammer briefly flashed green, and Brog's orange glow faded.

Yet it never left his eyes.

Leaning around Brog, Pet caught Xavis's gaze. The

Scaacax's purple eyes also glowed brighter than usual.

In the smallest motion possible, Xavis shook his head, imploring Pet to remain silent.

An awkward tension hung over them for the rest of the journey.

The other Ocans got off at a stop somewhere in the middle of the city, but it made little difference. Even with them gone, Brog remained so tense he seemed to have petrified.

They stayed on the trolley all the way to the last stop at the very bottom of the island. Then they had no choice but to disembark.

Brog didn't move when everyone else got up. It looked like he had no intention of ever moving again.

Xavis laid a hand on his shoulders, but Brog shrugged him off. The gesture spurred him into motion, but he still didn't speak as they stepped onto the street.

They wound up near the beach. Heading for the first place they spotted led them to the same restaurant as yesterday.

"Back again already?"

The familiar voice was a welcome surprise as Bug rolled up to their table. She looked more apprehensive than the day before and gave them extra space.

Pet could feel the metaphorical cloud that had descended over their group. It was no wonder other people picked up on it as well.

Brog's tension turned into listlessness as he sat hunched at the table.

Both Desmodian and Xavis were too busy throwing the Ocan concerned looks to notice their waiter's presence.

So Pet took over. "How could we stay away? This

place has the best view on the island."

Bug's antennae perked up and focused his direction. Even her chair seemed to sit a little taller. "We do. And it was hard-won. A lot of other restaurants wanted this spot."

"It must be fun getting to work right on the beach every day." He looked out over the sand and water. Honestly, he wasn't sure if it would be enjoyable. His experience with the beach had ranged from neutral to unpleasant, but he was probably the exception instead of the rule.

Whether true or not, it felt like the right thing to say, and the conversation seemed to set Bug at ease. He nodded toward his trio. "Forgive them. We're tired this morning."

Bug's mechanical arm hit a button on the side of the table, bringing up a projection of their menu just like yesterday. "Food will help with that. What can I get you?"

Desmodian and Xavis didn't notice the question, too busy whispering to Brog.

In response, Brog relaxed in slow increments.

Pet shouldn't interrupt them.

The hardest part of ordering for his trio turned out to be reading the menu. He often cooked for all of them, so he knew what each liked, but the text on the menu was small and written with an extra flourish. Shame burned his face when he had to ask Bug about some of the words. Each time she answered him easily as if needing help reading something so simple was a normal experience.

Maybe it was normal. The menu was written in the common language. Anyone who regularly dealt with species other than their own learned it as a second language, sometimes even a first language. However, this might not apply to everyone who came to the island. Some of the more sheltered guests might also struggle to read the menu. He hoped so. It would mean he wasn't as stupid as he felt, stumbling over words he should know.

Eventually, he managed to order for each of his trio. In a last-minute decision, he avoided traditional Ocan food. Brog didn't need a reminder of their encounter with the other Ocans literally served to him on a platter.

By the time Bug wheeled away, Brog seemed mostly back to himself. His orange eyes were dim, and Desmodian and Xavis sat a little closer, but it was a marked improvement from a few minutes ago.

Brog caught Pet's eye and rubbed at the fin on the back of his own head. "Sorry 'bout that, Pet. I don't...uh, really get along with other Ocans."

That was all the explanation he gave.

Why didn't they want to include Pet in the conversation?

He shouldn't feel hurt about being excluded. His trio had a right to privacy, even from him. It was their choice, but he wished they trusted him with something so obviously important.

What did they think would happen? He already knew about their criminal pasts. Surely, it couldn't be worse than that.

He shrugged but turned to stare at the table where the menu had disappeared to show a looped underwater scene. "I don't get along with other décor either."

This prompted a small smile from Brog, but he still

kept his secrets behind closed lips.

It wasn't long before Bug returned with their order.

Desmodian preferred to eat light in the morning, so Pet had only ordered him a salad of mixed fruits. For Xavis, he ordered a dish he didn't recognize but had heard the Scaacax mention before. It turned out to be thin strips of meat wrapped in an herbed flatbread.

Brog got a sample platter, usually meant for groups to share, that included a little bit of everything.

Pet's selections were well received, and he preened over being able to do at least this much for his trio. He might not know all their secrets, but he did know them in other ways.

Maybe it was the little ways that really mattered. What use would their secrets be to him?

To Pet's surprise, a bowl was placed in front of him as well. "What?"

He stirred with a spoon, inspecting the gray mush. It was nutriment.

When he looked at Bug in confusion, the arms of her chair twitched as if shrugging. "We have décor on the island, so I figured there must be supplies for them. This is supposed to taste like coconut. I don't know what that is, but I'm told it's a human food."

Something warm bloomed behind Pet's breastbone, adding a hitch to his breath. "I don't know what that is either. Thank you. You didn't have to."

"I said I would have something for you next time you came, and I've never gone back on my word. Now, wave me down if you need anything else."

Her gesture was not only appreciated, but also well-timed. In the chaos of his morning swim, then getting ready for the day, he had forgotten to eat. The nutriment they brought with them were his only supplies. He'd resigned himself to hunger since he didn't want to demand they go all the way back to their room after the drama that occurred on the trolley.

Oh, that gave him an idea. He stopped Bug as she turned to leave. "Hey, um, what activities on this island do Ocans usually enjoy most?" A quick glance at Brog showed the cracks that lingered around his strained smile.

Bug stopped to consider for a moment, her antennae furling in on themselves. "Deep-sea diving is usually popular with our Ocan guests."

Pet deflated. Of course, it was the ocean again. He clenched his fists under the table. If it would cheer Brog up, then he would endure being submerged again.

She gave him directions to the dock where they could find the boats to take them. The next one departed in an hour and a half, so they had plenty of time to finish eating.

He thanked her again before she left to attend other tables.

By then, the bowl sitting in front of him had caught the notice of his trio.

Xavis poked at the nutriment, grimacing over its unappealing texture. "At least there are some decent people on this island." His talons clicked against the glass bowl.

Had they heard Pet's conversation with Bug? Hopefully not. It would be more fun to surprise them, so he said nothing about his plans and focused on his meal.

Coconut, it turned out, tasted milky but with something extra he couldn't place. Even good-quality nutriment never made for an exciting meal, so he didn't loiter over it. He brought the spoon to his lips until the bowl was empty, then pushed it aside to talk with his trio while they finished their own food.

Conversation mostly returned to normal.

Brog even sounded like himself again, banging fists on the table for emphasis when he got excited about something and gesturing with his utensils as he spoke.

They could almost pretend like their encounter that morning never happened.

Yet the shadows in Brog's orange eyes never fully disappeared.

After the meal, Pet excitedly dragged them off to the docks, following Bug's directions.

The docks divided down the middle. One side held a line of airships, reserved for activities such as windsurfing and parasailing. The large dome structures had a clear rounded top like a soap bubble. On the opposite side sat another line of ships meant for the water. The two rows would've looked identical, except for the way one rested on landing gear and the other bobbed among the waves.

The boat intended for deep-sea diving was clearly labeled.

Pet didn't even struggle to read the sign.

Desmodian tapped his hammer against the walkway planks as he looked up at the ship. "You sure, Pet? You didn't seem to like the ocean this morning."

Pet's fists clenched again, and he hid them behind his back. "I'm sure."

Four hands gripped his shoulders and turned him around to face Brog. "This is to cheer me up, isn't it?

You don't 'ave to, Pet. I'm fine."

Pet stepped closer to wrap his arms as far around Brog as they would reach. "I want to. I'm sorry I couldn't enjoy the ocean with you this morning, so I thought this way might work better. Give me more control."

It was a lie. The thought of getting back in the ocean had no more appeal now than it did earlier. He'd never lied directly to his trio before. The words tasted sour.

Would they notice the lie?

No, they didn't. Or maybe they did but chose not to bring it up. Either way they agreed to his plan, and less than an hour later, he was sailing out to an isolated part of the ocean.

Pet and his trio claimed a group of lounge chairs near the back of the boat and watched Starthrone Island disappear. They weren't alone. Dozens of other guests came along for the ride, but the boat was so big that Pet barely noticed. The glass dome enclosing the top half allowed guests to enjoy the sight of the open horizon without being bombarded by the salty spray.

More Rurarine ran the boat. Instead of mechanized wheelchairs, a series of tracks had been built into the boat to carry them from place to place. Half an hour into their journey, a crewmember approached on one of these dolly chairs, offering to fetch them drinks.

Pet was about to assure the crewmember they were fine, but Desmodian beat him to it with a surprising request.

"We don't need anything, but we were wondering if there's a way for people who don't swim to still go diving?"

Pet expected laughter or maybe dismissal. How could a person go diving without swimming? That was the whole point.

However, the crewmember didn't even seem surprised by the question.

"Of course. We have diving bells that can take people to the ocean floor. They're free for anyone to use. When we reach the diving area, you can find the diving bells on the bottom level of the boat."

Desmodian thanked the crewmember before they left, then turned to Pet with a smile. "That should make things more comfortable."

"But..." Pet twisted his hands around themselves, unable to look any of his trio in the eye. This was harder to avoid with Desmodian, as looking at any part of him was the same as meeting his eye, so Pet kept his gaze pointed out over the water. "What's a diving bell? How can I use something I've never even heard of before?"

Talons brushed his skin as Xavis leaned against his side. "Don't worry. These diving bells should be made so anyone can use them. But if you're still uncomfortable, I'll drive."

Pet looked at Xavis with surprise. "You're coming with me?"

Xavis opened his wings, showing off their span before folding flat again. "I'm not really made for water."

A few hours later, Pet got his first look at a diving bell.

The ship came to a stop on a patch of water that looked no different than anywhere else. However, an announcement declared this to be their designated diving spot.

Brog and Desmodian departed for the area of the boat that catered to swimmers while Pet and Xavis sought out the diving bells.

They weren't the only ones, either. At least a third of the guests joined them in the lower level. Apparently, swimming was a common concern across species.

The room at the bottom of the boat looked like the inside of an organ piano. Tubes of all sizes lined the walls, some only a few feet wide while the largest rivaled the width of the trolleys on land. At the base of each pipe sat a diving bell.

Despite its name, the diving bell shared no qualities with a bell. Like all other modes of transportation on the island, it resembled a glass sphere.

Guests were guided toward the various-sized diving bells and given a brief rundown of the controls.

Xavis led Pet to a sphere that was plenty big enough for the two of them. The Scaacax rarely said so out loud, but his wingspan made him wary of tight spaces.

Even on the *Vanguard* rooms were as open as possible, so Pet wasn't surprised he chose a sphere larger than they needed. He looked but couldn't find any way inside. "Why's it called a diving bell if it's not bell-shaped?"

Another guest approaching the diving bell next to them bumped into Xavis.

What was that species called? Orei? Orik? It was something with a round sound at the beginning. A plump stomach and extremely short limbs forced them to waddle side to side as they walked.

What passed for their face resided at the center of their body and had features just familiar enough for Pet to recognize.

Based on their expression, their mumbled apology was clearly half-hearted.

Or it was until Xavis turned to look at them. As soon as they met Xavis's eyes they blanched and apologized again, this time with more sincerity. Then they shuffled off and chose a different diving bell farther away.

It was a strange reaction.

People were often intimidated by the sight of Pet's trio, but he always assumed it came from their reputation.

They were well-known out in the Penumbra Belt and beyond. However, that reputation didn't extend to civilized space. No one on the island knew who they were, yet the intimidation remained.

Was he missing something?

Xavis scowled but shrugged off the interaction and easily reclaimed the thread of their conversation. "Diving bells were actually bell-shaped when first invented, and the name stuck."

"Uh-huh." Pet nodded, but he wasn't really listening, still hung up on the stranger's reaction to the mere sight of Xavis.

One of the Rurarine crewmembers approached in their dolly chair. A long arm traveled along the ceiling, stopping just in front of them, with the Rurarine cradled at the end.

The image of a worm dangling on the end of a fishing line popped into Pet's head. He struggled to swallow his laughter and bit his bottom lip to keep quiet.

Luckily, the crewmember didn't seem to notice as their antennae stayed angled toward Xavis. "Is it just you?"

The common language spoken across the galaxy had a simple grammar structure. This made it easy for so many different species to learn, but also meant the "you" in the crewmember's question could've been singular or plural. There was no way to know whether they included Pet or not.

Xavis placed an arm over Pet's shoulders. "Yeah. Just us. We'll take this one for a ride."

If they were alone, Pet would've made a joke about what else he could ride. He kept it to himself, but imagining the crewmember's reaction to décor making innuendo almost broke him. An undignified snort escaped his nose, which he quickly hid behind a pretend cough.

Xavis squeezed his shoulders.

Pet's reaction hadn't gone unnoticed.

The crewmember offered to help them get started. They pushed a few buttons on the tube holding the diving bell, and a hole opened in the side of the sphere, like acid dissolving glass.

After Xavis and Pet stepped inside, it then closed the same way.

Inside, a flat floor divided the sphere in half.

Pet stepped carefully, unable to trust the floor under his feet. Walking on the perfectly clear surface was a lot like his first time on a spaceship. If he could adapt to that environment, this shouldn't be too hard to get used to, right?

Then he looked down.

Oh, the tube holding the diving bell extended all the way to the bottom of the boat. He and Xavis appeared to be floating in midair over a long dark drop with the barest hint of water below. This wouldn't be as easy as he hoped.

He was so busy staring into the abyss, it took Xavis calling his name several times to get his attention.

"Pet. We need to hold on for the launch."

A waist-high pedestal stood at the very center of the diving bell. It looked like it should be supporting something, but the top was empty except for several handles around the edge.

He and Xavis both grabbed the handles and waited.

Crewmembers gave them a countdown, then with a soft click of disengaging locks, the diving bell dropped down the tube. It was a smooth fall, but incredibly fast, and came to an abrupt halt when they hit the water.

Without the handles, Pet would have fallen over. He managed to stay on his feet but instinctively closed his eyes against the impact.

When he opened them again, the diving bell had already sunk below the ship. Open blue water surrounded them on all sides.

Pet looked to Xavis for instructions. "What now?"

"Now we go wherever we want. Watch."

Xavis placed a hand on top of the center pedestal. The surface bubbled, and another sphere emerged to float a few inches above. It looked solid as marble but swirled like sunlight reflecting off the bottom of a pool. With a careful touch Xavis rolled the sphere forward, and the diving bell moved the same direction.

"See? Simple." When Xavis let go, the diving bell came to a stop. "Give it a try."

Pet took hold of the control sphere with both hands. Its smooth cool texture created an illusion that it was wet, yet his skin remained dry. The sphere rolled without friction, and his first attempt to move the diving bell sent them lurching forward

He pulled his hands away. "Maybe you should do it. I'll probably crash us."

With a gentle hand on the small of Pet's back, Xavis guided him closer to the controls. "Don't worry. We can't crash. Look."

The hand not on Pet's back swiped over the top of the control sphere, sending it spinning. Around them the diving bell spun in a drastic whirl, but the floor remained level.

When Xavis grabbed the control sphere again, the diving bell stopped, no worse for wear. "These things are pretty much idiot-proof. Speaking of…heads up."

He pointed over Pet's shoulder where another even bigger diving bell approached. Several people stood inside, busy laughing at whatever one of them was saying, and not paying attention to the controls. Just before they collided, the control sphere beeped and both diving bells stopped in place. The other group looked up in surprise, then gave a sheepish wave when they realized what happened.

Pet waved back, but the other diving bell sped off so quickly they probably didn't see him.

After that, Pet grasped the controls with more confidence.

They gradually descended into the depths of the ocean, leaving behind the ambient noise of the world.

So much water pressing all around them created an unnatural silence. It almost reminded him of the deprivation chamber, but the diving bell offered just enough buffer to keep Pet from panicking like he had before.

They eventually sank too far to see the surface.

Pet had always known about oceans in theory, but he spent his days traversing the stars. Surely the limited depths of an ocean would feel small compared to the infinity of space.

Oh, how wrong he had been.

Space was large and empty. In many ways this made it more freeing because a person could travel any direction they wanted. The ocean, in contrast, was a vast weight. Anything that stopped swimming for even a moment would be dragged down.

Even the power of the sun failed against the ocean. It wasn't long before they descended beyond sunlight's reach. The water grew dark, making it feel even heavier. Flecks of detritus floated in the water, reflecting the diving bell's running lights.

With a little imagination Pet could pretend they flew through the night sky, instead of sinking to the lowest depths of the planet.

Something new flashed in the distance, long and indistinct. The dark water disguised its outline and turned it into a looming shadow.

Xavis's arm wrapped tighter around him. "It's all right. Just keep going."

"What is that?"

"I forget the name, but it won't hurt us."

The shadow ventured close enough to reveal a creature with a broad triangular head and a scoop-shaped mouth. Behind the head extended a serpentine body so long it seemed to go on indefinitely. Instead of scales, it had hundreds of segmented sections like an insect, each as iridescent as black ice. Along the belly where most insects had legs, this creature carried thin membranes trailing through the water like curtains closing on the end of a play.

Pet's hands trembled over the control sphere as he fought the instinct to run from the creature following alongside them. "You sure that thing is safe? It's big enough to swallow us."

Taking Pet's shaking hands off the controls, Xavis led him to the side of the diving bell. "Look closer. See the shape of its mouth and how it has no teeth? It's a filter feeder. It eats by filtering bits of matter out of the water. We're too large for it to see us as prey. We're safe as long as we don't startle it."

Xavis left Pet to observe the creature and returned to the control sphere so they could keep moving.

At one point the creature seemed to look at them, but otherwise paid the diving bell no attention. It swam parallel with them for a time, occasionally opening its mouth so wide Pet could see down its throat. The entire broad head was hollow, with a few slits at the back for the filtered water to escape.

After a few minutes of calm existence, the creature floated off into the dark, disappearing as quietly as it had arrived. Then they were alone again.

Had it gotten brighter?

The creature had provided such a distraction that Pet failed to notice the approaching ocean floor.

A carpet of glowing coral waited for them. Natural bioluminescence radiated off the coral, lighting up the water even brighter than sunlight. It looked like the same type that grew on the island, but much larger. By the time the diving bell reached the ocean floor, the coral carpet turned out to be a forest.

Xavis navigated them between the structures, drifting as close as he dared without running into anything.

Meanwhile Pet walked the circumference of the diving bell, marveling at the myriad of colors and twisting shapes. "It doesn't even look like plants. It looks like art."

He stopped to get a closer look at a coral structure growing in complex geometric patterns as if intentionally designed that way.

Noticing his interest, Xavis circled the structure. "Actually, coral isn't a plant. It's an animal."

Pet caught Xavis's eye in the faint reflection on the diving bell's curved walls. "That just makes it weirder."

"But also more beautiful. Makes you think about what it really means to be alive if something like this is considered a living being."

They moved on to a tall thin piece of coral shaped like a lace fan. It pulsed between pink and orange, starting at the base and traveling out to the edges. The diving bell could fit through the gaps in its structure, and they spent several minutes weaving between the natural latticework.

Even after they left, Pet kept an eye on the changing colors. "I wonder if it would still be classified as a living thing if it wasn't so pretty?"

Before Xavis could reply, a tapping sound caught their attention.

A figure floating outside the diving bell knocked on the wall. It looked humanoid in shape, with two arms, two legs, and a head on top. However, a dark suit covered their entire body and a complicated contraption on their head made them impossible to identify.

The only thing not covered by the suit was a long tail swaying through the water.

Oh, Pet knew that tail. "Des." He ran to the side of the diving bell nearest the Dhen'in. Desmodian wouldn't be able to hear him through the wall, so he gave an overexaggerted wave.

Desmodian waved back, then pointed to something out in the coral.

It disappeared before Pet could see what it was. He shook his head. The blank surface of Desmodian's diving helmet made communication difficult, and Pet couldn't tell if his confusion translated across the barrier.

Pushing off from the wall, Desmodian swam in the direction he'd been pointing, gesturing for them to follow.

The Dhen'in didn't have his hammer.

Seeing Desmodian swim with both hands free caused something cold to settle in Pet's stomach. The Dhen'in looked too vulnerable for his comfort, and he hoped the weapon had been stored somewhere safe.

They stopped near a patch of flat coral with clusters of smaller coral growing on top. Until then, the only sign of life had been the creature they encountered earlier. However, a number of fish and other sea creatures made their home among the safety of the smaller coral forest.

Desmodian tapped on the diving bell and pointed again.

Off in the distance, Brog swam among the coral. He looked even more powerful than normal compared to the delicate sea life. Thick corded muscle moved with a fluidity it never displayed on land. Brog's whole body rippled like a wave to propel him forward as his four arms controlled direction. His short tail acted as a rudder, allowing him to make quick turns in the water.

He also wore no clothes, not even a diving helmet.

Pet had known from day one that Ocans were an aquatic species, but it never occurred to him what that really meant.

Brog was not meant for land or even for space. He was a creature of water.

Like the coral, Brog displayed his own bioluminescence. Little dots of pale-blue light glowed under his skin, traveling from the top of his head down over his torso and legs.

It was beautiful. Pet could've watched him for hours.

He waved at Brog. Fish and other small animals darted between them, blocking his view. It took a few minutes for Brog to notice him, but Pet didn't mind. After the drama from that morning, it was great to see the Ocan so relaxed.

If only he could look that way all the time.

The unwanted thought had barely formed before Pet shoved it away so hard he outwardly flinched. So what if Brog looked more at home in the ocean than he did on the *Vanguard*? It didn't matter if water made Brog happy without even trying while Pet had to work for such a result. None of it made any difference.

Pet had never been a very good liar, not even to himself, but this seemed like the perfect time to practice.

Eventually, Brog swam over to the diving bell.

A conversation passed between him and Desmodian through a series of gestures, only three of which Pet recognized. A fluttering hand motion that signaled physical distress, but that was immediately counteracted by an open palm which signaled a need to stay. This almost made sense but was complicated by the addition of two fingers splitting apart to represent a separation.

Whatever they communicated, Brog remained relaxed. Yet Pet worried when Desmodian gestured toward Xavis with even more rapid movements. The only gesture Pet understood was a twisting motion for opening something.

Desmodian broke away from Brog and swam under the diving bell at the same time Xavis returned to the controls.

The clear floor of the diving bell gave Pet an unobstructed view of Desmodian floating directly beneath their feet.

Xavis twisted both sides of the control sphere in opposite directions, like cracking an egg. A hole opened in the floor of the diving bell with the same acid-on-glass effect as when Pet and Xavis first entered.

The water remained outside the diving bell as Desmodian climbed through the opening. A brief whiff of brine followed him before the hole closed, cutting them off from the ocean again.

"Ugh. I need to get this off." Desmodian's muffled voice finally rang clear when he removed the helmet. It fell from his hands to the floor, and he pulled off the top half of the suit. "It was fun at first, but this thing cuts off almost all my senses. I kept running into things."

Brog knocked on the wall, visibly mocking and pointing at Desmodian. Then he swam a lap around the diving bell before returning to the same spot.

Pet tried to hold in his laughter while watching Brog show off but failed when Desmodian flipped the Ocan a rude gesture.

The diving bell had been spacious with only two, but three was a tight fit. Pet pressed against the wall while Desmodian sat on the floor to avoid Xavis's wings.

Brog made another gesture from outside the wall. A double tap to the center of his chest.

This signal Pet knew.

Are you okay?

Pet touched his own chest and flicked his hand down, as if brushing a crumb from his clothes, giving the signal for *I'm fine*.

Oops, he must have done something wrong because Brog immediately looked concerned.

From his spot on the floor Desmodian tapped Pet's leg. "Other way." He demonstrated on his own chest, brushing upward.

Pet cringed. He'd accidentally signaled *I'm not okay*.

When Pet made the correct gesture, Brog's concern disappeared. He drew closer to the diving bell until he pressed flush against the glass.

From this proximity Pet could see the gills on the side of Brog's neck. On land they remained closed and nearly invisible, but here they opened rhythmically as they drew in water.

Pet turned to Desmodian. "Is that safe for him?"

Desmodian tipped his head in a silent plea for

clarification, so Pet pointed to Brog's gills.

"He's breathing water. But this ocean has more heavy water than normal. Is that safe for him?"

"Oh." Desmodian nodded. "Don't worry. He's safe. Gills don't breathe water. They don't even breathe the oxygen fused with hydrogen to make water. He's actually breathing by separating out oxygen from the air that's mixed in with the water. So the heavy water will pass through his gills just fine."

Assured that Brog wasn't being harmed, Pet let his gaze trail down the Ocan's figure, admiring the unfamiliar features along with the familiar ones. Every taut muscle in Brog's body stood on display, and the bioluminescence highlighted his lines. If only they were visible on land. Pet would have loved to spend time exploring them.

Would those places feel different when lit up?

Would they taste different?

Halfway through his inspection, Pet found another surprise waiting for him. He had seen Brog undressed so many times that he hadn't thought twice about the Ocan swimming naked. Now he realized why Brog hadn't bothered with clothing.

Apparently, in deep water, certain more delicate parts of the Ocan's anatomy retracted inside the body.

Pet looked back up to meet Brog's eye, raising an eyebrow at him.

Brog shrugged.

It felt like a challenge. Maybe it was foolish to think that way about a species' biology, but Pet was in a mood to challenge nature.

Desmodian's hand settled over his own on the glass. "You okay, Pet?"

Whatever expression Pet wore while looking at Brog must have been strange, because Desmodian sounded concerned.

He looked at the Dhen'in sitting beside him. "I'm good." The hand retracted, but Pet caught it before it left. "Although, I could be better."

Desmodian smirked as Pet took control of his hand.

He pressed Desmodian's palm against his chest, then moved it downward, trailing over his stomach to settle between his legs.

"Really?" Desmodian sounded shocked, but he rubbed Pet to full arousal.

Pet moaned and pressed that hand closer. "Why not? Who's gonna see us?"

A pair of arms wrapped around his waist as Xavis draped against his back. "You're not getting started without me, are you?"

Pet fisted a hand in Xavis's hair and pulled his head forward enough to kiss him. "Of course not."

Xavis and Desmodian worked together to divest Pet of his clothes and reposition him to stand over the Dhen'in still sitting on the floor.

A long blue tongue licked up Pet's thigh.

Pet braced his hands on the glass as Xavis rutted against him. Somewhere along the way Xavis' shorts had disappeared, but instead of immediately entering Pet, he took time rubbing his cock along Pet's hole.

The Scaacax's natural lubricant spread over Pet's skin. He shivered as the aphrodisiac took effect. A fog of desire settled over his brain, and he burned with the need to be filled.

Desmodian's tongue moved to the other thigh, and Pet's legs trembled.

Xavis's arms around his waist kept him steady. "Look. I think he's getting jealous."

A talon tipped Pet's head up to see Brog floating just beyond the clear wall. If only Pet could reach out and touch him, but the barrier kept them separate.

The Ocan watched them with a scowl, clearly annoyed at being excluded. His gills pumped harder, and even his bioluminescence pulsed.

Pet leaned forward and pressed a kiss to the glass before mouthing the word "later."

Message received, Brog's scowl lessened but didn't disappear.

Pet laughed at the image the strong Ocan made— like a pouting child being denied a treat—but his laughter turned into a moan when Desmodian's tongue finally found its mark.

The Dhen'in's tongue wrapped completely around Pet's throbbing cock. It slid up and down, milking him until his arousal dripped with a mix of saliva and pre-cum. Pet would have collapsed from sheer pleasure if not for the number of hands holding him up.

"Please." He wasn't sure if he begged for more or for mercy.

It didn't matter. The decision was made for him.

Xavis's hands clung tighter to Pet's hips, pulling him into just the right angle. "Don't worry, Pet. We'll take care of you."

He thrust inside, and Pet screamed. At least, it was meant to be a scream. What actually came out was no more than a shuddering gasp.

Xavis's movements were languid at first, smoothly sliding in and out with minimal friction, all while Desmodian's tongue never stopped its work. They had

Pet pinned between two types of slick pleasure.

Wet sounds of flesh against flesh echoed in the silent diving bell, drowning out Pet's aborted moans. Light from the glowing coral seemed to dance in time to their sounds, reflecting off the glass and painting them in a rainbow of flickering colors.

With his tongue Desmodian drew Pet's erect cock into his mouth and started sucking with more force.

Pet's hips stuttered, not sure if he wanted to bury himself in that hot suction or pull away. This caused him to accidentally fuck himself harder onto Xavis. He was trapped. Drawing away from one only pushed him deeper into the other.

He couldn't last much longer. With his hands braced against the glass, his harsh panting fogged the clear surface. He beat uselessly against the wall to warn them he had reached his limit.

Xavis's breath raged hot in his ear. "Go ahead, Pet. I'm right behind you."

Pet moaned as the pleasure tightened to an excruciating level. He hovered on that edge for a lifetime condensed into one moment. Then he tumbled over. Xavis kept pounding into him, and Desmodian kept sucking as he came. The two of them pushed Pet's orgasm higher and higher, until he was crying from the intensity.

When it finally ended, he sagged in relief. His palms dragged against the glass with a harsh squeal as he tried to hold himself up. Xavis continued chasing his own release, pounding hard inside him, and Pet wanted him to stop and keep going at the same time. He was oversensitive from his orgasm. The pleasure turned painful, but it was a pain he loved.

"Help. I can't…"

He could barely hear his own voice, but his plea was answered anyway.

Desmodian released Pet's spent cock, licking his lips to capture every last drop of Pet's orgasm. He helped Pet remain standing as Xavis thrust harder.

Then suddenly Pet was left empty.

A splash of heat hit Pet's back, then with a gasp Xavis collapsed against him.

"Sorry, Pet. Didn't want to come inside. Hard to clean up."

Oh. Pet hadn't thought of that. They weren't in the comfort of the *Vanguard*, or even their own suite back on the island.

A different kind of warmth spread through Pet's chest. Even in the throes of passion, his trio thought about his comfort.

While Xavis disappeared somewhere out of sight, Desmodian guided Pet to sit on the floor.

Exhausted, he leaned against Desmodian's side. "What about you?"

Desmodian's tail curled around his leg. "I'm good."

Pet looked up just enough to see the evidence of Desmodian's claim. Apparently, while they'd been busy, Desmodian had taken himself in hand. When, exactly, the Dhen'in had come was unclear, but he'd obviously found his own satisfaction.

A popping sound, like an airtight lid opening, preceded the smell of the ocean. Water lapped at the edges of the entrance hole Xavis opened, like questing fingers trying to climb inside. With the help of his talons, he tore a strip from his own shorts. Dipping it into the water, he then used it to help Pet clean up.

While Pet settled his clothing back into place, Desmodian and Brog held a gestured conversation through the glass.

The two of them reached some sort of decision.

Brog swam to the top of the diving bell as Desmodian turned back to Pet and Xavis. "Brog's ready to go if you want to head back."

Pet took a moment to admire the landscape at the bottom of the ocean one last time. It was like another world down here, but he was ready to set his feet back on land.

They turned the diving bell around and headed back to the boat, Brog swimming alongside the whole way. When they reached the surface, they parted briefly to return the diving bell and for Desmodian to collect his hammer. Once they had everything settled, they met on the main deck. Not all the guests had returned yet, but there were plenty of lounge chairs to enjoy the sun while they waited.

Xavis and Desmodian draped themselves across the chairs, eager to soak up the heat.

Pet chose to remain under an umbrella to avoid burning.

Brog joined him. An affinity for deep water also translated to an avoidance of strong sunlight. There wasn't enough room for both of them under the single umbrella, so Pet sat on Brog's lap. They could've found a second one, but it was more fun to cuddle together while taunting Xavis and Desmodian from the safety of their shade.

Plus, as they waited, Brog's hands were free to wander.

Eventually, all the guests returned.

The boat started moving again, this time pointed back toward Starthrone Island.

Just as Pet settled in for the journey, Brog suddenly stood. "Come on." He pulled Pet out of the chair and away from the deck.

Xavis and Desmodian watched them leave. Neither said anything nor looked surprised.

The boat rocked under Pet's feet, so he slipped a hand into the crook of Brog's arm for support. "Where're we going?"

Brog led him to a lower level of the boat. Not as far down as the diving bells, but far enough that the only people they passed were crewmembers.

"While the boat's movin', people won't be wanderin' around as much." The Ocan searched for something, opening doors only to shake his head and close them again.

Should he ask what Brog was looking for? If he knew, maybe he could help.

Brog finally opened a door he was happy with and brought Pet inside. It turned out to be a bathroom. Like on the *Vanguard*, appliances tucked into the walls while not in use. The metal box smelled like overly sweet flowers, probably to hide the harsh odor of chemical disinfectant.

A large mirror covered one wall, and Pet stared into his own reflection. He combed a hand through his disheveled hair. "Why're we here? I don't look that bad, do I?"

Brog answered by spinning him around and pressing him against the cold mirror. Then the Ocan leaned in until his arms formed a cage around Pet. "You promised me later. It's later."

The round pupils of Brog's eyes dilated with desire.

Pet smiled and ran a hand up Brog's chest to hook behind his neck. "I meant later when we got back to the suite. Why? Did you have something else in mind?"

Brog grabbed both his wrists and pinned them by his head. "Teasin' me like that. Makin' me watch when I couldn't touch. You're lucky I waited this long, and you know it."

Teasing Brog was too much fun. Pet struggled to keep his smile sultry.

Despite the Ocan's strength, it took little effort for Pet to free his hands. He calmly brushed the wrinkles from his clothes. "I don't know what you're talking about. Now, we should probably get back to the others before they start to worry."

He turned away from Brog as if he meant to leave and braced in expectation. Yet he made it all the way to the door unhindered. Looking over his shoulder, he found Brog standing alone, gripping his own hands as if he didn't know what to do with them.

The room was meant for a wide variety of species, so despite Brog's size, he looked lost in the empty space.

That wasn't what Pet wanted.

Maintaining eye contact with Brog the whole time, he reached out and turned the lock on the door. The soft click echoed off smooth walls.

Finally, Brog's eyes widened in understanding, before his expression turned into a scowl. "Wicked minx. You're still teasin' me."

"Am I?" As hard as he tried, Pet couldn't make

those two words sound innocent. Too much promise throbbed between them.

This time Brog picked him up and braced him against the wall. Two hands held Pet's legs around Brog's waist, and another supported his back so only his shoulder blades touched the metal. This left one hand free for Brog to remove Pet's clothes.

Pet grabbed that hand when it tugged his clothing a little too forcefully. "Careful. Don't rip it. I don't have anything else to wear until we get back."

Brog growled in frustration but took care when undressing Pet so nothing was damaged.

The imbalance of being so exposed while Brog remained completely covered sent a thrill up Pet's spine. Brog's thick belt chafed his thighs, and he fisted his hands in the Ocan's vest.

Due to the structure of Brog's shoulders, the other male avoided sleeves and preferred clothing with an open front.

This gave Pet plenty of access to the grayish-blue skin and well-defined muscle.

Their foreheads touched as Brog planted a kiss on his lips. "You know, this room ain't soundproof. Anyone could walk by and hear us. You'll 'ave to be quiet, or we'll get reported. Don't want the crew interruptin' our fun."

Pet arched his back and gripped his legs tighter around Brog. "I'll try, but no promises."

With some jostling, Brog opened his pants enough to pull out his already aroused cock.

Pet couldn't see it but felt it rub against him.

Brog repositioned them so his cock lined up with Pet, ready to push inside. "Oh, fuck. You're still slick from Xavis. You just been walkin' around ready to get fucked any moment."

The wall grew warm from the heat of Pet's skin, and he relaxed against unyielding metal. "Been waiting for you."

"Ah, Pet." Brog curled down enough to press his face against Pet's neck. "Always know just what I need."

He thrust inside. Pet's earlier activity with Xavis and Desmodian meant they didn't have to wait before Brog started pounding into him.

The ribs along Brog's shaft tormented his rim as they slid past, and the knobbed head ground deep into his most pleasurable spots.

Pet bit his lip between his teeth to keep silent, but it didn't work.

The boat rocked under them as it navigated the ocean. Turbulence pitched Brog forward and pushed him even deeper.

Pet went silent like an overloaded computer and didn't come back online until Brog pulled out again, drawing another moan from him.

"Quiet, Pet," Brog reminded him.

The Ocan shoved in, just as hard even without the help of the rocking boat. With unfailing accuracy, he kept hitting that same perfect spot deep inside.

"I can't." Pet panted, and a line of spit dripped from the corner of his mouth. "I can't. I can't. I can't."

"Let me help."

One of Brog's hands clamped over the bottom half of Pet's face. It not only silenced him, but also pinned his head to the wall. Their position kept Pet from moving or participating. He could only stare into

Brog's eyes, hands fluttering over the wall as he was pounded mercilessly.

Brog maintained complete control, and the Ocan took advantage. He slowed down, letting Pet feel every inch of the flesh sliding in and out of him. When Pet clenched internal muscles to try and spur him on, he laughed.

"Oh, no, Pet. This is what happens when you tease. You take it as long as I say you take it. No faster. No slower."

Pet screamed in frustration behind Brog's hand. The pleasure coiling in his belly stalled, not quite enough to push him over the edge.

How long had they been at it?

A haze settled over Pet's mind, like sinking inside his own skin. He surrendered to whatever pace Brog decided. Sparks danced up his spine with each of Brog's thrusts, just enough to jolt him back to awareness before he sank back into a pleasure fog.

Brog growled against his neck. "Good Pet. Takin' me like this. Deserves a reward." He sped up, thrusting harder and faster until he tormented Pet's deepest spots at a constant pace.

Pet thrashed against Brog's hands. He couldn't even scream when he finally came. His fingers gripped like claws at the wall behind him as he was seized in ecstasy.

Brog followed him a moment later, and they rode out their orgasm in unison.

Even after they finished, they stayed locked together and slowly caught their breath.

Pet traced lines over Brog's skin, trying to remember the pattern of bioluminescent light he'd seen earlier. They needed to give Brog access to water more often. It suited him.

Pet's hips ached when Brog finally put him down. He tripped on the rocking floor, and Brog helped him stand until his feet remembered how to balance.

Luckily, they were in a bathroom, so it wasn't hard for Pet to clean up. He retrieved his clothing and shook wrinkles out of the long fabric strips. "I've spent more time picking this outfit up off the floor than I have actually wearing it."

Two hands reached around him to help wrap the cloth into place. "If you didn't look so good, it wouldn't be a problem." Brog placed a kiss right over Pet's pulse.

It tickled, and Pet flinched with a laugh as Brog tied off the fabric at the nape of his neck.

Once Pet was dressed, he turned around and stood on his toes to press a kiss to Brog's lips. "Thanks."

Brog's hands trailed down Pet's sides and over his hips. "I should be the one sayin' that."

They left the bathroom together, arm in arm. No angry crewmembers waited outside the door to scold them, so maybe their activities had gone unnoticed.

They returned to Desmodian and Xavis on the deck, the pair still lounging in the sun.

Xavis breathed deeply in his sleep, dead to the world.

Desmodian, however, turned over to angle himself in their direction. "You didn't get caught? I'm impressed."

Brog collapsed onto the lounge chair still positioned in the shade, making the poor piece of furniture groan. "Ah, the crew probably knew what we were doin'. Just not worth makin' a fuss."

Pet joined him on the lounge, laying on top of the Ocan and using his chest as a pillow. A warm breeze toyed with his hair as two of his trio's calm voices mixed with the sound of the ocean.

The combination lulled him to sleep, and he didn't wake up until the boat docked.

The sun had almost set by the time they disembarked and once again stood on dry land.

Coral walls separated the public beach near the docks into alcoves, giving it a more private feel despite being open to anyone walking by. The coral must've been cultivated to grow this way. No natural growth formed such straight lines.

One of the walls had crumbled long ago. A new wall grew in its place, but the remains of the old structure still poked through the sand.

Pet climbed on top of these remains.

It formed an island at the edge of the water, one side glistening with moisture while the other stood completely dry. Blue coral with orange highlights grew on the wet side, while green coral grew only on the dry side.

Pet explored the crevasses of the wet side. While it lacked the glow of its deep-water counterpart, a different type of beauty could be found in its swirling patterns.

Xavis called to him from the dry side of the island. "Careful up there. Those rocks can be sharp."

Pet peered over the edge of a round spiraling coral with a design at the center that resembled an eye. "I'm fine. The water's worn this part smooth."

Farther away, Desmodian and Brog walked the

edge between water and sand.

Pet waved at them from his island to get their attention. He meant to ask what the trio wanted to do with the rest of their evening, but he never got the chance.

"Brog?"

A voice Pet had never heard before spoke just out of sight. Judging by the faces his trio made, it was not a stranger who stood at his back.

Chapter Five

After

A thin layer of ice covered the walls of the room Pet and Bug found when they stepped through the hole into the lab. Based on its size, the room only acted as a type of doorstep. A ramp led down into the ice, presumably leading into the rest of the building.

Sunlight from the outside didn't reach into the shadows, and there weren't any other lights.

Pet and Bug were forced to navigate the ramp by feeling their way along the frozen wall.

Thin glowing lines on Pet's thermal suit cooled from red to orange to yellow the farther they descended, eventually settling on a very cheery shade of green.

All except for the hand he kept on the wall, which stayed red. Slick ice covering the smooth metal chilled his fingers, forcing the suit to heat that part of his body. "At least it's warmer down here."

Warm was a relative term.

Any other time, he would call the temperature brisk, but anything was warm compared to the literal arctic outside.

The ice coating the wall slowly disappeared, until the lines on Pet's glove turned green like the rest of the suit.

They had reached the main body of the lab.

Pipes and wires ran over every surface, dipping in and out of the walls and clustering in the corners.

Despite their small size, Bug's people had an affinity for open space. The ceiling was so far above Pet's head that even Brog would have fit comfortably. It rippled with an uneven texture, interrupted by skylights every few feet. Instead of sunlight, however, the skylights showed a layer of sheer ice. It tinted the light coming through the windows and created fractal patterns on the floor.

Pet stepped into a patch of pale-blue light and looked up at the ice. "For something that's supposed to be impenetrable, I wasn't expecting so many windows."

Bug remained at the edge where light met shadow, just under a structural arch. "Don't be fooled. Those windows are probably the strongest part of this building."

Looking down the hallway, Pet counted a dozen identical skylights until they grew too far away to see properly. The building seemed to stretch into infinity, and he was hit with a tunneling sense of vertigo. "This place looked big from the outside, but now that we're here, it's worse than I thought. How are we going to find anything?"

"We could follow the signs."

Pet looked around but didn't see any writing. Even if it was a language he didn't know, he should still be able to recognize intentional lettering. "What signs?"

Bug's mechanical arm pointed to the archway. When he still looked around and frowned, the mechanics of her chair gave a strange wiggle. "Oh, right. Humans have eyes."

He observed the arch again, this time looking

closer. Hundreds of small nozzles covered the entire thing from top to bottom. "So the sign is invisible?"

"No, it's… Remember Rurarine communicate through scent. We don't have eyes or mouths or ears. All we have are these." She wiggled her antennae to show them off. "This is like our nose. Our chairs can translate other senses for us, but our natural language is scent based. When someone passes under the archway, it lets off a combination of scents to relay information."

The entire lab smelled like ice and metal. The cold stung Pet's nose when he breathed deeper. "I don't smell anything."

Bug's antennae twisted in a complicated pattern. "It may be outside human senses. Come on. There's an information hub just ahead that could tell us more about this place."

Pet had to put his faith in Bug's mechanical hands. He couldn't read the signs—was *read* the right word for interpreting scent?—and the lab was an underground labyrinth. Only three or four doors resided in each hallway, but if the lab was as big as he suspected, even that was too many for him to search.

So he followed Bug through a nearby door into a circular room. A large skylight let in even more fractured blue light from above, illuminating a central platform.

It was unnaturally silent, even for an underground lab in the arctic.

The lack of any sound pressed on them, and Pet popped his ears just to make sure he hadn't gone deaf.

His boots slapped against the floor and kicked up small billows of dust.

They were alone for now, but that would change.

There had been plenty of people on the airship, and the dust on the floor showed a parade of footprints.

"There's nothing here."

Bug's chair created almost no sound as she rolled onto the central platform. "There is. It just needs to be activated. Labs like this were left intact because the experimental technology was too difficult or expensive to move. There should still be power running."

The hand on each arm of her chair transformed into a plug that attached to hidden ports in the floor. A series of rings rose around the platform, each lined with more nozzles like the archway in the hall.

Static screeched from Bug's chair. "This will take some time. We don't have authority to access the system. There's a screen on the wall over there that'll translate for you."

The translation screen turned out to be hidden inside another panel that took some searching to find. A series of numbers and symbols flashed on its surface, all equally meaningless to Pet. "Whatever you can get is more than I'd manage on my own."

Bug gave no outward sign of what she was doing; her antennae didn't even twitch, but the symbols on the screen shifted and changed.

Pet would have to be patient for the outcome.

While Bug concentrated on her task, he explored the rest of the room.

There were a lot more pipes and wires here than in the hallway. Due to the Rurarine need for open floor plans, almost everything had been built into the walls.

Almost.

A few pipes here and there extended off the walls, creating tripping hazards for the unwary.

Unfortunately, Pet was so busy looking around he wasn't watching his feet.

His thick fur boots muffled the sound of his shin hitting the pipe but couldn't cover his pained shout. The oversized boot slipped from his foot, causing him to fall. He grabbed onto another pipe for balance, but it shifted under his hand. One of the bolts attaching it to the wall came loose, and the pipe hung at a catty-cornered angle.

"Ugh. Why's it so hard to find human-sized clothing?" He retrieved his fallen boot but really didn't want to put it back on. The thermal suit covered his feet. It wouldn't protect him out on the ice, but in the shelter of the lab, it would be enough to get around.

A metallic click came from Bug's chair, followed by a previously hidden side panel popping open. "You could store them here. They should fit. Then you'll still have them if we need to go back outside."

Pet slipped between the rings of the scent-based computer to kneel beside her chair. The bulky coat and boots together would be a tight fit. He rolled up the boots first and shoved them as far back into the compartment as he could.

Meanwhile, Bug continued working on the computer.

"This is all I'm able to access."

The speaker on Bug's chair wasn't visibly noticeable but apparently rested right next to Pet's ear. He jumped and banged his head on the chair's open panel. "Ow. What?" He clutched the back of his head, feeling a goose egg forming there. It hurt but didn't bleed.

"Sorry." Bug's voice was much softer this time.

Not like whispering, but like someone turning down the volume on a recording.

When the pain lessened and Pet's eyes uncrossed, he looked over the screen. It showed a flat design, mostly made of straight lines and rectangles. Various symbols hovered in the open spaces.

Pet stared at it for a few moments and from several different angles. "Is that a blueprint of this place?"

"Sort of. It's not the whole facility. Just this immediate area. And it only shows maintenance. It's all I could open without authorization."

The heavy coat hung off Pet's shoulders as Bug's explanation stole most of his attention. "Can we do anything with this?"

"We can read it. Other than that, I have no idea."

A room at the far corner of the blueprint caught Pet's eye, specifically the jagged lightning bolt symbol drawn inside. "What's that?"

With the screen positioned on the other side of the room, Pet had to repeat himself several times, pointing as best he could with his arms tangled in the half-removed coat.

Finally, Bug found the right spot on the blueprint. "Oh. That's a power monitoring station. It doesn't control anything."

Fed up with the bulky fur, Pet extracted himself from the rest of the coat and spread it over the floor. "It may not control anything, but a monitor would show us what areas in the lab use the most power, right?"

He folded the coat with care, then rolled it tight. It kept sliding over the smooth floor, dragging a clean path through the dust.

Bug turned a tread on her chair so it rested on the

opposite end of the coat and kept it in place. "It should, assuming we can get access. Since it doesn't control anything, security might be less than on this computer. But how will that help?"

Pet kept a tight grip on the rolled-up coat and shoved it inside the compartment of Bug's chair, right next to his boots. "My trio are being kept in electrical cages. Those things would need a steady supply of power, and I didn't see any cables coming from the airship outside. That means they're drawing power directly from the lab."

He didn't need to continue the explanation.

Bug caught on to his idea before he finished the first sentence. "The monitoring station would show a power spike in those areas."

It took a few shoves, using all his body weight to compress the thick fur, but with effort he managed to store the coat and close the panel.

"Once we know where my trio are being kept, then we can figure out how to free them." Pet stood and brushed the dust from his knees.

Hopefully, he wouldn't need the coat or boots again until he, Bug, and his trio all left the lab together.

Dressed only in the thermal suit, he felt much lighter. They had the beginning of a plan, and he was free from the ill-fitting garment.

The blueprint might only show a section of the lab, but even that was more than Pet could remember on his own.

Luckily, the mechanics in Bug's chair attached directly to her nervous system, giving her an eidetic memory. Anything she experienced could be accessed again with the ease of opening a file.

They shut off the scent-based computer and followed Bug's mental map down the hall.

It was too quiet.

Pet didn't trust the silence, especially when he remembered his own kidnapping. He never heard the kidnappers coming.

Granted, he'd been at a party. The music and crowds provided plenty of distraction, but he was usually more aware of people invading his space. He wouldn't have been able to fight off his kidnappers, but he should've noticed them.

This made him nervous about the silence surrounding them now. He followed Bug's directions, but when they reached the first turn in the hall, he stopped her. "Wait. Let me check first."

Even without eyes, Bug still managed to give him a curious look as he pressed against the wall. Moving slowly, he revealed as little of himself as possible while peering around the corner. At the same time, he kept an ear open for any suspicious sounds.

Around the corner lay an identical hall to the one they just left, including skylights, tubes along the walls, and absolutely no one in sight.

Still frowning, he waved Bug forward so he could once again follow her. "Sorry." His voice echoed, and he flinched. "Maybe I'm just being paranoid."

One of Bug's antenna curved backward to face him while the other pointed ahead. "I'd be more worried if you weren't. If there's ever a time to be paranoid, this is it."

They reached another turn in the hallway, and Bug directed them to the right this time. Still, they found nothing and met no one.

Was he the crazy one? There'd been a whole team of people piloting the airship that brought them here. Right? Pet had been too busy keeping himself safe to really look around. Maybe there hadn't been as many kidnappers as he thought. It seemed like a small army at the time, but surely that many people couldn't disappear so quickly.

As he thought, Pet watched the floor passing beneath his feet. He and Bug both left tracks in the dust, but they weren't the first ones. Others had passed through recently. Pet tried to count them, but the dust was thin, and the footprints were from a species he didn't know well. He couldn't judge how much space one person would leave between each step, and the tracks all jumbled together.

Patches of light from the skylights added to the chaos. Stepping from light to shadow to light again left his eyes in a state of constant adjustment.

It gave him a headache.

Just as they were about to make the next turn, Pet grabbed Bug's chair. The mechanics pinched his finger, but he didn't notice the pain.

Something was wrong. The rectangular shape of the skylights gave each patch of light and shadow a hard straight edge. He'd been studying the floor so closely the pattern felt burned into the back of his eyes.

Just around the corner, almost out of sight, one shadow had an irregular edge.

There could've been a simple answer.

Maybe one of the skylights was broken, but it was the only inconsistency he'd seen since stepping into the lab.

Bug turned back to face him, only inches from the

corner. "What is it?"

Pet shushed her with a finger to his lips.

The gesture probably meant nothing to a Rurarine, but Bug got the message anyway. She fell silent and backed away slowly.

Pet didn't approach the corner like before. Instead, he kept his eyes on the irregular shadow, barely daring to blink as he waited to see what would happen.

A minute passed. Pet scolded himself for literally jumping at shadows.

Then the shadow moved.

"This is ridiculous." Someone spoke just around the corner.

Pet held his breath, every muscle tense with the effort it took to stay still.

A second voice answered the first. "Not our problem."

The first voice grew softer, as if farther away. "Doesn't it bother you? We came all this way, blew the front door wide open, and now we can't find the damn thing."

A grunt came from the second speaker, also farther away. "Still not our problem. First-in-line says we're here, so we're here."

"Jail is where we're going to end up. Can't even use the damn computers to look it up. Honestly. Why didn't we plan for this?"

"Don't think anyone expected the place to be so big. Rurarine are tiny. What do they need all this space for, anyway?"

The voices disappeared.

Pet could only assume they'd left, because he never heard any footsteps.

He held up a hand for Bug to stay back and approached the corner. The voices didn't return, and he risked a look.

Empty. The pair must've left down another hallway or ducked through one of the many closed doors.

Once she knew it was safe, Bug joined him in peering around the corner. "Sounds like they're having the same trouble we are. Can't access any of the systems without authorization."

"Yeah, but they at least know what they're looking for. We don't even know that much. This lab is big, but it's not infinite. They'll find what they want, eventually. Then they'll leave, and we'll be stranded here."

"Not if we find your trio first. Come on. The power-monitoring station is just around this next corner."

A subtle change overcame the hallways. The area near the front entrance had been moderately sized, with the ceiling about eight or nine feet high.

Looking up now, Pet judged the ceiling to be at least a dozen feet up. Even Brog wouldn't be able to reach it, though the larger Ocans they'd encountered earlier probably could.

Were they descending deeper below the ice? The floor felt flat, but a very shallow decline might not be noticed from one step to the next.

Slipping through a door no different from any other, Pet and Bug found themselves in a dark windowless space, taller than it was wide. Compared to the information hub with its large platform, the monitoring station looked like a broom closet.

Pet stood with his back pressed against the far wall as Bug accessed another scent-based computer.

The nozzle rings rose out of the floor in jerky movements, and one of them sat a little crooked.

"This should only take a moment. Either I'll be able to access what we need, or I won't."

An even smaller translation screen than the one before came to life. It only showed static at first, with a crack marring one corner. Then a series of numbers and symbols flickered too quickly for the naked eye to follow. Eventually, a blueprint appeared. Unlike the previous one, this blueprint showed more than the immediate area.

Pet stepped forward, pressing against Bug's chair for a better look at the screen. "Is that it?" The blueprint might be larger, but the smaller screen made it hard to decipher. It looked like a circuit board.

"This should be the layout of the entire lab. The black represents walls, and the red represents electrical lines. So, if I just…"

Her mechanical voice grew fuzzy and faded away, a clear sign she was concentrating. Some red lines on the blueprint grew dim while others pulsed like a living heartbeat.

Bug's voice returned like the pop of a balloon. "There. This shows the electrical lines currently in use. There's definitely…oh."

Pet clenched his fists at his sides. No one said, "Oh," like that to indicate anything good. "What's wrong?"

With her arms still plugged in to the computer, Bug couldn't move far, but she turned to face him as directly as possible. "Pet. You were right. Some spots are using a lot more power. There's no way to know the cause, but the records show it's a recent change."

"That's good, right? Those energy spikes are from maintaining the electrical cages. That means we can find where my trio are being kept."

Bug's antennae deflated. Her whole body expanded and contracted, like someone heaving a sigh, before she looked up at him again. "Probably. But Pet...there're only two."

Chapter Six

Before

Waves crashed against the beach, spraying salty water around Pet's coral island.

The hot press of unfamiliar eyes burned between Pet's shoulder blades. It was décor's job to be stared at, and he had borne the weight of so many different gazes over his remembered life. He knew a stranger stood at his back even before he heard their voice.

"Brog?"

Pet turned toward the speaker, not sure what he'd find.

He had seen Iknox before. His previous Owner sometimes hosted them as guests.

The faun-like species had delicate angled features that always looked a bit sad. Downward-pointing ears only increased the effect. They walked on two legs but had the sloping posture of a species that once walked on four legs and didn't stand up until late in their evolution. Instead, wide hips gave them stability the rest of their figure lacked.

The perky feathered tail didn't fit the rest of the species' aesthetic, like an afterthought.

Pet would've loved to learn about the Iknox's evolutionary history, but now probably wasn't the time to ask.

The individual on the beach wore primarily dark colors, contrasting with their pale-lavender skin. Black fabric hung from one shoulder like a toga.

It was a deceptively simple outfit. At first glance, the Iknox would seem no more than middle class. Yet the quality of the material and the delicate hand-stitching spoke of money.

Assuming this was a friend of his trio, Pet started to wave.

Xavis reached up and pinned his wrist at his side.

Neither Xavis nor Desmodian greeted the newcomer.

Desmodian even stepped in front of Pet's island, planting the end of his hammer in the sand.

Brog, however, greeted them easily. "Yaivin? What're you doin' here?"

At least Pet could now give the newcomer a pronoun. Technically Iknox had no binary gender. They chose a gender to fit in with other binary species. Yaivin was a masculine name among several Iknox cultures, so their family line must have chosen to identify as male.

The Iknox's response came just as easy as Brog's had. "On vacation. What else? Although, I'm surprised to see you here. This doesn't seem like your kind of place." As he spoke, he looked up at Brog through long lashes. The tilt of his head lent intimacy to the conversation despite the casual words.

"Yeah." Brog shrugged both sets of shoulders. "We decided to try a change 'a pace. You know, somethin' different."

Only then did Yaivin seem to notice the rest of them. He stared from Desmodian to Xavis, and surprisingly, also at Pet. "I see."

Before he could say more, a new voice interrupted. "Yaivin. What're you doing?"

Yaivin sighed, and the intimate tilt of his head turned submissive as he stepped back from Brog. "It's nothing, Father."

The owner of the new voice approached from the direction of the docks, walking briskly across the sand until he stood beside Yaivin.

Iknox's asexual reproduction meant all members of a family line looked identical. Yaivin and his father had the same skin tone, the same white speckles over their cheeks, and the exact same facial features. Even their outfits matched, with only a gold sash draped over the father's shoulder to mark a difference.

Yet it would be impossible to mistake one for the other. Yaivin's father stood as if his spine had been replaced with a titanium rod, making him loom over his son despite their identical height.

The father cast his son a look but quickly turned his attention to Brog. "You."

He spoke that simple pronoun with such weight it sounded like a name.

Brog gave a lopsided shrug that couldn't have been less sincere if he tried. "Tradius Vels. Wasn't expectin' to see you here."

The newly identified Tradius narrowed his eyes, but otherwise showed no reaction. "I could say the same." He turned sharply to his son. "Was meeting up with this...man your plan from the start? Coming here was your idea. Did you think I wouldn't notice?"

Yaivin took another step back, out of his father's direct line of sight. "Of course not. I just thought this planet could benefit from your ideas. That's all."

Pet shuddered in sympathy. He recognized Yaivin's posture. It was the same one Pet had taken for years as décor, trying to merge with the scenery.

Brog stepped forward, forcing Tradius's attention onto him. "Don't get angry at him. We're here for vacation, just like everyone else. Didn't know you'd be here."

Tradius looked away from his son to survey Desmodian and Xavis. "You've made some new friends since we last met." His eyes lingered on Pet. "And you have décor. Expensive taste for a ship-dweller. I bring mine when I travel as well. Familiar decoration always makes a place more comfortable."

Standing above the others on a coral island felt eerily similar to how Pet's previous Owner displayed him.

Should he get down? Moving might just draw more attention to himself.

He would wait and see how his trio handled the situation.

Both Desmodian and Xavis seemed hesitant to interfere. They hung a few steps behind Brog, obviously present, but outside the conversation.

Meanwhile, Brog squared his shoulders, making himself look even bigger. The effect was extreme compared to the Iknox's svelte figure.

Brog could've snapped Tradius in half with ease. Why bother posturing?

One of Brog's hands drifted toward his hip where he usually kept a couple of guns holstered. Armed weapons weren't allowed on the island, so he grasped empty air. To cover the aborted movement, he braced both sets of hands on his hips in a posture that took up even more space. "Yeah. Things 'ave been good lately."

In contrast to Brog's shifting, Tradius clasped his hands in front of himself as if glued there. Iknox hands had only two fingers with a thumb. Hard dark patches over their knuckles kept their hands stiff, a holdover from the cloven hooves of their primordial ancestors.

It was a motif that Tradius Vels seemed to take to heart. He stood so unbending it was a wonder he could tie his own shoes.

Although, if he was as rich as Pet suspected, he probably had servants to do such menial tasks for him.

The only part of Tradius that moved were his eyes. He never stopped looking around. "If you're able to afford a room here, then you've been doing very well indeed. It seems you've made quite a few changes since your time in Unit 22."

Brog clenched his fists. Such a small movement, but a clear sign that the Ocan considered violence to be a reasonable response.

"Brog." Desmodian's sharp voice cut the tense atmosphere. "We were going back to the room, right?"

Brog jolted and looked back at the rest of them. "Uh, yeah. One minute."

Tradius stepped back so he stood next to his son. "Your commander has the right idea. The day grows late. We should all retire. That includes you, Yaivin."

He nodded for his son to follow. The older Iknox walked with a stately posture, never once looking back, but shifting sands revealed a slight difference in his footsteps. His right footprint on the beach dragged a little more than the left.

An old injury maybe? Or perhaps something he was born with? He hid it well. Under any other conditions Pet never would've noticed the limp.

Although he disliked the man's attitude, he was impressed. Tradius Vels exuded the type of natural authority that Pet's previous Owner would have given anything to possess.

Yaivin trailed after his father with reluctant steps. As he passed, he flashed Brog a warm smile and slipped something from his pocket. While maintaining eye contact with Brog to make sure the Ocan noticed, he wedged the item into one of the coral structures lining the beach. Then he rushed to catch up with Tradius.

When both father and son were gone, Brog retrieved what Yaivin left behind. It was a room card, just like the one to their own suite. Setting sunlight glinted off the card as Brog turned it over to reveal the room number, turning the gold a bloody red.

The sound of the shifting tide at their backs kept silence at bay until Desmodian stepped up to Brog's side. "Some nerve. Acting like nothing happened." He plucked the card from Brog's hand. "Not even an apology."

Desmodian's usually soft footsteps kicked up a torrent of sand as he marched toward the ocean.

Brog followed him. "What're you doin'?"

"Getting rid of it. What else?" Desmodian cocked his arm back, ready to throw the card into the surf, but Brog grabbed his wrist.

"That's not your choice. It was given to me." He took the card back.

Desmodian turned sharply back to Brog. His hand,

which had been holding the card, opened and closed as if confused about its sudden emptiness. "What? You're keeping it?"

One of Brog's hands held the card, and another gripped Desmodian. That still left two arms free to cross over his chest in a challenging posture. "Maybe. No reason not to."

Desmodian gaped. "No reason...after what that man did to you? There's every reason to avoid him."

The pair stared each other down, Brog with one set of eyes and Desmodian with his whole body.

Pet's foot slipped over wet rock, and he nearly tumbled off the island. He had seen these emotions on his trio before, but rarely directed at each other. On the rare occasion they fought, it usually ended as quickly as it started. This time would be the same, right?

Xavis approached the argument with both wings outstretched. "Hey, guys, calm down. This isn't worth fighting over."

Brog let go of Desmodian, practically throwing his hand away. "If he thinks he can make decisions for me, then we got somethin' to fight over."

Desmodian's hammer planted in the wet sand, hard enough to sink several inches. "It shouldn't even be a decision. It should be common sense. Yaivin Vels is the reason you ended up in Unit 22 in the first place. You shouldn't want anything to do with him."

Brog shrugged but wouldn't look directly at Desmodian. "Tradius Vels had me arrested 'cause he didn't like me sleepin' with his son. Yaivin had nothin' to do wit' that. Not his fault his father's an ass."

"He was paying you for sex at the time."

"And I was the one being paid for sex, so what

does that make me?"

"Then it made you a victim. Now, it would make you an idiot." Desmodian looked like he had a lot more to say, but he took a deep breath and ran a hand through his hair. "I can't believe I have to argue this. No. Sleeping with that man already got you arrested once. You're not doing it again."

His words may have sounded calm, but they had the opposite effect on Brog. The spines on Brog's outer shoulders raised, and orange light sparked in his eyes. "You givin' me orders now, Commander?"

The title hit home. Desmodian flinched and stepped back, his foot landing in the water.

Xavis pushed into the space between them. "Brog, that's too far."

Desmodian cut Xavis off. "No. If he's got something to say, let him say it." The Dhen'in stood firm but didn't move any closer.

Pet crouched on top of his island, making himself small and unobtrusive. The air between his trio crackled with tension. They weren't yelling, but that only made it worse. They were seething. Too many emotions bounced between his trio for Pet to keep track.

Brog planted himself firmly in the sand. "You're always puttin' on a show, sayin' you're not our captain. But words mean shit if you're gonna order me around just 'cause I'm doin' somethin' you don't like. I'm not yours to command."

Desmodian's tail lashed, splashing water in either direction. "We're tied together. There's no changing that. If you follow your dick back into prison, Xavis and I will be hurt as well. I tolerate your fucking around, but I won't let you put us all in danger."

The light in Brog's eyes spread past their sockets and seeped into his skin. Sand beneath him began to melt, turning to a puddle of liquid glass. "Tolerate? You 'tolerate' me? Fuck. Seems the commander hasn't changed at all. Still as much a prude as ever. Shouldn't 'a got my hopes up."

A crackling sound interrupted the rhythm of the tide. The water around Desmodian's ankles turned to ice, rooting him to the spot.

"Your hopes? You were hoping I'd change?"

Desmodian's voice sounded more fragile than Pet had ever heard, like a cracked mirror. Its frame still held the pieces together, but one wrong move would shatter everything.

Even in his anger, Brog must have realized the effect of his words. He looked away from Desmodian, shoulders tense as he scoffed. "Just thought you were finally over your whole…" He vaguely waved one arm toward Desmodian. "…thing."

Desmodian's hammer tilted downward, knocking against the ice at his feet. "My whole thing?"

The pieces of his voice shattered like broken glass, cutting everything they touched.

"Des." Xavis approached the frozen water, reaching out for Desmodian, but it was too late.

Green light pulsed in Desmodian's hammer as he raised it to stand strong at his side once again. "You can do what you want, Brog. I won't stop you, but I want no part of it. Go make yourself useful somewhere else."

Xavis called Desmodian's name again, this time in warning.

With an unintelligible shout Brog pushed past Xavis and stomped right to the edge of the water.

Footprints of molten sand followed him.

Compared to his actions, when Brog finally spoke, his words were soft. "I may 'ave ended up in Unit 22 as a criminal, but you only joined 'cause you had to. It was the only way people would tolerate you."

Desmodian gripped his hammer in two hands, just like he did before swinging it at someone.

Bright feathers bisected the air between Brog and Desmodian. Xavis shoved at Brog's shoulders, forcing him out of reach of Desmodian's weapon. "Brog, that's enough. Walk away. I know seeing other Ocan reminded you of your family, but this isn't..."

Brog slapped his hands away. Orange light sparked as he rounded on Xavis. "Don't talk about family like you know anythin'. You've never even had one."

Xavis drew back, much more than needed to avoid Brog's flailing hands. His purple eyes flicked glances between Brog and Desmodian, tracing the space between them. "Fine. I won't talk. Figure it out yourselves."

Then he turned and walked away, disappearing around one of the coral walls.

Brog and Desmodian watched him go, then looked back at each other. They scoffed at the same time and stormed off in different directions.

The beach emptied in a matter of moments.

All except for Pet.

He remained alone on his island.

The last rays of sunshine cast long shadows over the beach.

His silhouette stood large and tall across the sand. How pathetic he was when his shadow showed more confidence than him. He just watched his trio completely fall apart and hadn't said a word to stop them.

Most of their conversation made no sense, consisting of half sentences and thoughts the three of them already knew. However, Pet still recognized the emotions. They were angry at each other and hurt at the same time.

Anger and hurt he could deal with. He knew how those felt.

Determined to erase the fissure that had formed between his trio, Pet climbed down from his island. Careful feet skirted patches of frozen water and molten sand. He had no idea how to fix the damage to the beach, so he left it for the island's maintenance staff to figure out.

Which way had his trio gone?

He'd been too distracted by the horror of the fight to pay attention when they stormed off. Xavis had gone to the left somewhere, but he needed to find either Desmodian or Brog. They were the heart of the fight.

He followed a path to the right that trailed along the far side of the beach. The few people he passed paid him no more than a cursory glance.

It was a large island, so Pet expected to spend several hours hunting for his trio. Instead, his search barely lasted a few minutes.

Farther down the beach stood a series of pavilions, also cultivated from living coral. A popular spot for guests to hang out during the day, but with the sunlight quickly disappearing, they now stood empty.

Brog sat on one of the tables with his back to the beach. His feet rested on top of the bench, and he slumped forward so both sets of elbows anchored against his knees. Broad lips twitched as he grumbled to himself.

Pet approached with an unnecessary amount of noise, stomping sand off his shoes to avoid startling the distracted Ocan. "Brog?"

Sad eyes peered at him over dual shoulders. "Hey, Pet."

Taking a deep breath and standing a little straighter, Pet stepped into the pavilion. "I don't know what just happened, but are you okay?"

Brog urged him closer until he stood between the Ocan's spread knees. His hands carded through Pet's hair in a soothing gesture, though it was unclear which of them he meant to comfort. "Don't worry 'bout it. Just an old fight we've had before."

The bench kept Pet from closing the distance between them, so he braced his hands on Brog's knees to lean closer. The edge of the bench pressed uncomfortably into his legs. "It's not fine. I've never seen you fight like that before."

Brog's deep sigh ruffled Pet's hair. "We 'ave. Just not while you've been here. Was hopin' we were done with that, but…" He ended the sentence with a shrug.

"Can I do anything?"

Brog smiled, but it didn't put Pet at ease like normal. What made the expression different this time?

"Yeah." One of Brog's arms wrapped around Pet's waist. "You can help me forget."

He pulled Pet closer and kissed him.

The edge of the bench dragged painfully across Pet's knees. He wouldn't have minded, but the kiss felt wrong. It was the same as always, yet something chafed like sand in his shoes. He tried to relax and grabbed onto Brog's shoulders, moving his lips in time with the kiss. No matter what he did, their mouths never lined up.

Like most things the Ocan did, Brog kissed aggressively.

Pet usually enjoyed surrendering to the attention, like the rush of sinking into a hot bath. This time, however, the bath was only lukewarm. Some comfort remained in the familiar connection, but it was half-hearted and stale.

He broke the kiss and pushed away, just enough to get a look at Brog.

The broad flat planes of the Ocan's expression pinched around the edges.

Pet ran a hand over his face, tracing the crease along Brog's brow. "You're still angry."

The crease deepened. Brog pulled Pet onto the table and laid him over the surface. "Course I'm still angry. Only been, like, an hour. But you can make me feel better."

Cloth slid against Pet's skin as Brog unwrapped his top. They were going to have sex right there on the table. Not the first time they got intimate in public. Sometimes when they used a back room at the Gravity Well, they left the door open just for the thrill of knowing other people could hear them.

That was fun, and Pet basked in the envious stares he got afterward. This should be the same. It was Brog. They'd gone through these motions a thousand times.

Brog's hand moved to the rest of Pet's clothing, but his touch felt like a harsh drag instead of a firm caress.

Pet grabbed his wrist. "But you're angry."

Brog knelt on the table, looking down at him. "It's fine. I'm not angry at you."

Before the Ocan could kiss him again, Pet braced both hands against Brog's chest. "Sex is about pleasure, not anger."

Brog hovered, neither coming closer nor backing away. "It can be. Sex is great at workin' through bad emotions."

Pet pushed against Brog. There was no way for him to move the Ocan on his own. Four arms caged him with the solidity of iron bars.

Warning alarms went off in Pet's mind, similar to the ones on the *Vanguard* that blared whenever they were about to crash into something. If only humans had controls like spaceships to tell him what was wrong. He felt uncomfortable, and he didn't know why.

In all the time he'd known the trio, he'd never once told them *no*. This was unfamiliar territory. But of course, Brog would accept his answer. His trio would never make him do something he didn't want.

Right?

Brog sat up and removed two of his arms from around Pet. "Why're you lookin' at me like that?"

"I'm...um..." Pet lay motionless, unable to speak. Different emotions warred within him. He wanted to make Brog happy. The Ocan clearly needed comfort that Pet could easily provide. Maybe he should just go along with it. Brog was the more experienced one. He understood sex better than Pet.

Yet that wasn't what Pet wanted. It would be easier if he could at least define what he did want. All he knew for certain was that this wasn't it.

Pet longed to explain these conflicting thoughts.

Brog always helped him understand when he didn't know something. He tried, but all he managed was a soundless gaping, like a landed fish swallowing air.

Frustrated tears gathered in his eyes. He needed to explain, but he had no words.

At the sight of his tears, Brog shoved away from the table so hard it slid over the floor with a horrid sound of cracking stone. "You're afraid 'a me?"

Pet gathered up the other half of his clothing. "No. I'm...I'm not afraid."

This seemed like a good thing to say, but it only made Brog more agitated.

"Well, you're definitely not happy."

"No, I..." Pet trailed off.

No was a strange word. Such a simple little sound could have so many meanings depending on why it was said. Pet wasn't afraid. He knew what fear felt like. So why was he saying *no*? Was it okay to dislike something without a reason?

He tried a new explanation. "I don't want to have sex like this, but I don't know what to say."

Two of Brog's arms waved wildly while the other two tucked close to his body. "You say *no*. It's simple. If you don't want something, you say *no*. You've said it to other people just fine."

Pet stood from the dislodged bench. "But this is different. It's you."

Orange eyes widened, and Pet saw in Brog the very emotion he'd previously denied.

Fear.

Brog backed up until he bumped into another table. "So...you sayin' you can't tell me *no*. Fuck. I just..." Like a bridge missing its supports, Brog collapsed onto the table behind him. His slouched posture looked even more despondent than before. "You should leave. Or don't. Fuck. Do whatever you want. I'm not tellin' you what to do."

Pet reached out to Brog, but the Ocan flinched, unable to look him in the eye.

He pulled back. There were only two things he could offer Brog, his actions and his words. Physical contact would not be appreciated, and he couldn't figure out what to say.

There was nothing he could give Brog right now.

"I'm sorry."

Those two measly words felt inadequate.

He left but didn't go far. As soon as he stepped off the pavilion and onto the sand, he second-guessed himself.

Was it right to leave Brog like this? It wasn't the Ocan's fault Pet failed to explain himself properly. Maybe he should try again.

A sliver of sunlight remained on the horizon, just kissing the tops of the sand dunes.

Pet hid in the shadow of the pavilion, leaning against a coral pillar as he debated with himself.

"I didn't get you in trouble with your friends, did I?"

Pet peeked around the pillar. That was not a voice he expected to hear again.

Yaivin approached Brog from the opposite side of the pavilion, footsteps silent over the smooth floor. The Iknox paused at the sight of the table shoved out of place but passed it to sit by Brog's side.

Brog slouched on the intact table, feet up on the bench. "You heard that, huh?"

With a delicate gesture Yaivin settled the folds of his toga over his legs. "No, Father and I had already left by then, but one of our servants heard and told me. If you don't mind me saying, that Dhen'in sounds jealous."

Brog glanced back toward the beach.

Pet ducked behind the pillar to avoid being seen. Because of this, he couldn't read Brog's expression or body language when the Ocan finally replied.

"Jealous? Des? Nah, don't think so. No offense, but you're not his type."

Pet didn't want to admit it, but the Iknox had a nice laugh. It danced on the breeze and bubbled like seafoam.

Yaivin's laugh lingered even once he stopped. "Oh, I'm sorry. I didn't mean he's jealous of you. He's jealous over you."

"What'd you mean?"

The scuff of boots shifting over stone echoed from the pavilion, indicating Brog had moved, but Pet couldn't guess what he was doing.

Softer sounds from Yaivin followed.

"I mean, that Dhen'in seems like the type that needs to be in control. He's jealous something is interfering with that control."

The words were harsh, but the tone was soft, and Pet couldn't help glancing back into the pavilion.

Yaivin and Brog sat together on the bench, much closer than before. One of the Iknox's hands rested on Brog's knee.

Brog didn't even seem to notice, or if he did, he didn't bother to push it away. "It's not like that. Des and I just don't agree on some things."

Yaivin let go of Brog's leg, and Pet breathed a sigh of relief. Should he leave? This seemed like a personal conversation, but he also hated leaving Brog alone with someone who was clearly interested in him.

Someone Brog had slept with before.

Pet gasped and slumped against the pillar, remembering only at the last second to stay out of sight. Yaivin wasn't just some passing interest Brog met at a bar. He was basically Brog's ex. This man knew Brog even before Xavis and Desmodian. Technically, Yaivin had been paying Brog at the time, but based on the way Yaivin looked at him, there were obviously more feelings involved than just a business transaction.

With the hand no longer on Brog's leg, Yaivin touched the center of his own chest. "I'm not saying that Dhen'in is anywhere near as bad as my father. At least he doesn't track your every movement. But I'm very familiar with what it's like to live with someone controlling, and I just wanted to let you know I understand."

Brog slouched until he was almost equal height with Yaivin. He scowled, then shook his head. "No, that's not... Wait, what do you mean Tradius tracks your movements?"

"Hm?" Yaivin looked startled. His downturned ears perked up, and even Pet had to admit it was a cute expression. "Oh, no, it's not just my father. Every Iknox gets tracked."

He pulled aside the collar of his toga. A bright-gold symbol rested on the center of his chest. It resembled a sun with a maze inside, and the metal looked fused directly to his lavender skin.

Brog reached out and traced an edge where metal

met flesh. "Always thought this was decorative."

Yaivin shook his head. "Iknox family lines are just that. A straight line. One person stands at the front, and everyone else follows in single-file order. Where you stand in that line dictates everything about your life. Since members of a family line are identical, we need a way to tell one from the other. So we're implanted with unique identifiers the moment we're born. Not every culture on my home planet does this, but where I come from, it's pretty common. The identifiers track our movement, so we have no secrets."

A delicate lavender hand gripped at his own chest, fingers digging into the edges of skin and metal as if he meant to tear it out. With a deep breath he relaxed and smoothed the toga back into place, hiding the symbol.

"My father stands at the head of our family line. As his heir, I'm the second-most-powerful person in our family, but honestly, I'd give it all up to be free of his control."

Brog fidgeted, his stare never leaving Yaivin's chest where the gold symbol lay hidden behind black cloth. "Can't you, I don't know, remove it?"

With a gentle touch, Yaivin tipped Brog's head up so their eyes met. "The identifiers are wired directly into our hearts. They can never be removed. But that's not your problem to solve. I must return to my room before Father notices I'm missing. Come back with me? I have a waterfall suite all to myself. Father prefers to stay in a throne suite at the top of the island, so we'll be alone."

Brog smiled.

Pet hid behind the pillar again. His heart pounded in his chest.

The last ray of sunlight disappeared, and stars took their turn to decorate the sky.

Pet closed his eyes, but he could still see the soft look on Brog's face.

What was this emotion? It was more than anger. This settled much deeper in his chest. Anger burned like fire, but this was cold and bitter, like being plunged into dark water with no way to breathe.

This was loathing. Not at Yaivin or Brog, but at himself.

He should've been the one to make Brog smile, not this intruder. Instead, he caused Brog more pain.

It took a few deep breaths for Pet's racing pulse to calm. He prayed Brog would turn down the invitation, but already knew what the answer would be even before he heard it spoken out loud.

"Sure. Got nothin' better to do."

Those few simple words broke Pet's heart. He could almost feel the pieces clinking against each other and pressed his hands over his chest to hold them inside.

Of course, Brog wanted to pursue something pleasant. After such a devastating argument, he deserved whatever made him happy. It was only temporary. Like every time he went off with someone else before, he'd enjoy himself, then come back.

Brog and Yaivin left together but didn't pass by Pet's hiding spot.

When Pet finally looked around the pillar, the benches were empty.

One table sat perfectly aligned, while the one Brog shoved out of place remained off to the side where it didn't belong.

Pet doubted it would be fixed anytime soon.

Chapter Seven

After

Pet shivered as if the ice outside had found him again.

Red lines intersected with black lines. Pet traced one across the screen, static jumping from the smooth surface to his finger. Most of the red lines were dull, but two spots stood out bright as new stars.

Only two spots.

Pet tucked his hand against his side. "It's fine. We only need to find one of them."

Bug regarded him with a heavy tilt to her antennae. "Pet, if there's only two, then—"

"I said, it's fine."

He didn't want to talk about it. More importantly, he didn't think he could talk about it. Just thinking about his kidnapping left him speechless.

The memory of screaming would haunt him. Putting it into words would be impossible.

Bug still looked like she wanted to argue, so Pet pointed to a spot on the blueprint. "This is us, right? Then this is the closest energy spike. We just need to find a way to get there and free whoever we find. Then we can all get out of here, and Tradius will pay for what he's done."

"Wait, Tradius?" Bug jerked and nearly ran over

his foot. "You mean Tradius Vels? The Iknox we talked about before? That's who's responsible for all this?"

Pet stumbled back to save his feet from the heavy treads. "He had help, but he's the one who captured us. I thought you knew. Didn't you see him on the airship?"

"I kept myself hidden in the lower level. I barely saw anyone."

"Oh, well, yeah. That's who's to blame. I don't know what he's looking for, but he came to this planet specifically to get his hands on something in this lab."

Bug's antennae didn't even twitch, but mechanics in her chair whirred a little faster. "Well, fuck."

Pet hid a laugh behind his hand. He'd never heard Bug curse. Something about the straightforward pitch of her mechanical voice made it even funnier. "Yeah. Fuck. So how are we getting to the closest electrical spike? We can't just keep wandering aimlessly through the halls. Someone's going to notice us."

They turned their attention to the blueprint. Knowing who was behind their current situation changed nothing. The plan remained the same. Free his trio and get the hell out of there.

Fifteen minutes later they had a plan. Not a very good one, but a plan, nonetheless.

A series of vents ran through the walls, bringing fresh air to the underground rooms. Following the vents from their current location to the nearest energy spike would be a circuitous route at best, but it was possible.

A green line appeared on the blueprint, mapping the path Pet would have to take. He stared at the opening to the vent near the ceiling. It would be a tight squeeze.

"Why am I the one crawling through the vents? Without the chair you're a lot smaller than me."

Bug turned from her work with the scent-based computer. "Pet, I can only communicate through scent. My chair translates everything else for me. Without it, I have no way of communicating with anyone who isn't Rurarine."

"All right, all right. I get it. I'm just not looking forward to this." The pipes along the wall provided adequate footholds for him to climb up.

Once he reached the top, Bug tossed him a small manual screwdriver that she carried for emergencies, so he could detach the grate covering the vent.

Bug lingered just below. "You've got the path memorized, right? Two lefts, a down, and a right. Then you'll have to get out and pick up a different vent. From there it's another down and a right."

Two lefts, a down, and a right.

Two lefts, a down, and a right.

He'd repeated that sequence dozens of times to himself, over and over to drill it into his brain. However, he appreciated hearing it one last time. Not because he needed the reminder, but because it showed how worried Bug was about him.

That meant she cared. He wasn't used to people other than his trio caring about him. Even his friends at the Gravity Well had known his trio first. He could never be sure if they actually liked him or were just friendly to stay on good terms with his trio.

With Bug, however, it was the other way around. She was his friend first and only cared about his trio because of him.

He saluted her with the screwdriver. "I'll be fine.

Wait here for me. Hopefully, I won't come back alone."

The inside of the vent pressed on him from all directions as he wiggled inside. There was just enough width for his shoulders. His stomach slid along smooth metal as he pulled himself forward. The limited space made his legs mostly useless. They flailed behind him, trying to take some of the burden off his arms.

At least he could see. He'd feared he would have to navigate the vent entirely by feel. However, every few dozen feet a grate let in ice-blue light from the main part of the lab. As he passed the first grate, he looked down into an unfamiliar room, vacant except for a series of glass tubes and jars. All empty now, but he could picture them bubbling with experimental chemicals under a scientist's careful observation.

For an uncertain amount of time, all Pet knew was the small world inside the vent. Smooth metal walls stood only a few inches shy of suffocating him. Occasional glimpses through the grates saved him from claustrophobia. After the room with the glass tubes, he passed a computer station, a supply closet, an office, and a strange cavernous room completely empty except for a seamless chrome pyramid at the center.

He reached the first intersection in the vent and turned left. As he crawled, he repeated the first half of his path over and over. "Two lefts. Then a down."

The vent didn't always travel in a straight line. Sometimes it angled up or down, and once it curved so drastically it felt like a corner.

Hopefully, that didn't count as his second left turn. On the blueprint, every turn he needed to take lay at a cross section, but maybe he was wrong. He still struggled to read written words. What were the odds he'd misunderstood a complicated blueprint?

He had no choice but to trust his memory. At the next intersection, he turned left again and kept his eyes open for a way down. He found it just a few feet later.

The good news—he was still going the right way.

The bad news—he had no idea what to do.

An opening in the floor of the vent led to a new tunnel heading straight down. The blueprint had showed the drop, but it never occurred to him there would be no safe way to climb down.

Why would there be? Vents were only meant to carry air, not people.

Pet pulled himself to the edge of the drop. Too dark to tell how far it went. If he fell, how long would it take to hit the bottom?

He couldn't breathe.

Rough gasps tore at his throat. Pushing away from the drop, he curled up on the floor of the vent as best he could. His knees pressed painfully into one wall, while his back pressed into the other. The unmoving metal didn't budge.

"It's fine." No matter how quietly he spoke, his own words yelled back at him. "It's fine. It's Fine. IT'S FINE. YOU'RE FINE."

He closed his eyes, trying to get his breathing under control, but that let his imagination run wild.

How far down did the drop go? It could be dozens of feet, or maybe even hundreds. Falling that distance would break his neck, and the vent would become his coffin. Or worse, what if the fall injured him but didn't kill him? He would lie at the bottom of that darkness, calling for help that never came until dehydration and starvation caught up with him.

Since landing in the arctic, he'd desperately pushed away his growing panic. Having Bug around helped. She gave him a distraction. But the fear remained, and once it took control, it paved the way for every other unpleasant emotion he'd been trying to ignore.

Pet's gasping turned into sobs. What if this was all in vain? He'd been clinging to the hope of finding his trio. What if they were already dead? Those electrical spikes on the map could be something else, and he was only chasing shadows.

The memory of screaming returned, stronger than ever. He'd only heard his trio cry out in pain like that once before when Xavis had been attacked by the DPS agents. It had been bad then, but this time it was so much worse.

Pressing his face into the dusty metal floor, Pet wept. He imagined the tears dripping down his cheeks filling the vent and drowning him. His fear of deep water would finally catch up with him in a flood of his own making.

The tears eventually stopped, as they always did. No matter the weight of his emotions, the human body only had so much water to spare. Finally able to breathe normally, he resorted to his usual self-soothing method. He started to hum. By now he knew many songs, but there was only one that always calmed him down. It was melancholy but hopeful. Even when he'd been proper décor, broken fragments of it bounced around in his head. Three months ago, he finally learned the whole thing, but only the tune. If there were lyrics, those remained lost.

It took several repetitions of the song before he felt normal again. He wiped the remaining moisture from his cheeks, surprised it was hot to the touch.

He needed to keep moving. Until proven otherwise, he would assume his trio still lived, but there was no telling how long that would last.

Wriggling on his stomach, he peered over the edge of the drop again. Just as dark as it had been moments ago, but it wasn't very wide. He crawled past the opening, then slid his legs backward into the empty space. From there, he worked the rest of his body inside the tunnel. His feet braced against one wall of the vent, and his back pressed against the other. Only the strength of his legs kept him from plummeting to his death.

Careful to always keep one foot braced against the wall, he inched down the vent. It was easier if he thought of it as simply crawling backward and ignored the drop below. If he couldn't see it, then it didn't exist.

With no grates in this part of the vent, the only light came from the small open square above. Pet kept his eye on that patch of light, letting his feet feel their way down. It grew smaller and smaller.

Just as he started to panic, his foot hit empty air. He slipped and dropped down the vent.

Luckily, the bottom lay only two feet away. His foot had found the next branch of the vent before the rest of him. He landed, sending a jolt up his spine that echoed off the surrounding metal.

Pet cursed and rubbed his abused tailbone. "I'm going to be one big bruise at the end of all this."

The pain faded quickly. He squirmed around to lie flat and crawl down the next branch of the vent. The grates returned, giving him light once again. Compared to the vertical decent, navigating this part of the vent was easy.

When he reached the next intersection, he turned right.

This part of the vent continued undisturbed for a while, with only the occasional glimpses into different rooms to break up the monotony. At one point he thought he heard voices, but when he looked into the room below, he saw no one.

The vent dead-ended.

Pet pressed against the grate blocking his path to see the space beyond. Larger than most of the rooms he'd passed, it held rows of tables like museum displays.

Using Bug's screwdriver, Pet detached the grate and pulled it inside the vent so it wouldn't fall and make noise. Getting out of the vent was a process, and he nearly tumbled over the edge headfirst. After some trial and error, he sat on the edge of the opening and grabbed onto pipes higher up the wall. Then he shimmied his legs free and climbed down to the floor.

The other air vent lay on the opposite side of the room. He wove his way between the tables, intent on getting to the vent as quickly as possible.

One of the displays caught his eye.

It would've looked no different than the rest of the technological clutter, but this display sat under an icy skylight. The fractal blue light shone on a miniature spaceship model.

Pet didn't know the name of this design, but he recognized some of the parts.

The *Vanguard* had been made from salvaged pieces of other ships. Four independent arms extended from the main spherical body, each arm constructed from a different design. The arm that housed their garden had been made from a ship just like the miniature model in front of Pet now.

In fact, as he looked around the room, he found more familiarity. Two rows down, a table held the same heat-resistant paneling that could be found on the *Vanguard's* outer hull. A half-finished structure in the far corner resembled Pet's antigravity bubble. A collection of disassembled engine parts sat just under the vent Pet needed, some of which he recognized from their own engine room.

Everything on display related to spaceship design. Spaceflight must've been the lab's primary focus.

What did Tradius want in a place like this?

Never mind that the Iknox was a landowner and didn't spend much time in space. Tradius came from the Vels family, which mainly focused on intergalactic politics. He should have no interest in spaceflight technology.

This was a question for when they were all safely out of the arctic, not standing in the middle of an abandoned lab. Tradius could take whatever he was looking for and choke on it.

Pet abandoned the model spaceship and headed for the wall on the other side of the room. Near the ceiling lay an opening to another vent. He climbed the pipes along the wall, unscrewed the grate, and slipped back into the claustrophobic space. From there he followed his memorized directions. Shimmying down another vertical shaft was not as panic inducing now that he knew what to expect. Turning right and following a straight line, he reached another dead end.

This was it. If he'd followed the directions

correctly, the source of the electrical spike lay in the room beyond.

Taking a deep steadying breath, he gazed through the slits in the grate.

Three Iknox stood in the moderately sized room. Their backs were toward Pet, but he could already tell none of them were Tradius or Yaivin. Instead, he was more concerned with the large cage at the center of the floor that sparked with electricity.

Caught inside its bars, like a domesticated bird, was Xavis.

Chapter Eight

Before

Pet's thin clothing billowed in the warm night breeze as he walked along the beach, listening to the crash of the tide.

Land-coral glowed in the dark, just like it did under water, while high above, three moons illuminated the sky.

For someone used to the darkness of space, the island looked too bright for nighttime.

He wandered aimlessly over wet sand, avoiding the boardwalk where people gathered. Where should he go now? Back to their suite?

Brog wouldn't be there. The Ocan was busy in the other waterfall suite with Yaivin.

However, Pet might run into Desmodian or Xavis. This should have brought him comfort, but he'd already messed up with Brog.

What if he made things worse with them as well?

He ended up at the front of the island. The sight of the distant landing pad brought a deep and unexpected feeling, like dropping a coin in a well and waiting for it to land. Except the splash of metal hitting water never came.

This was a new feeling. They came less often as Pet gained more experiences.

He headed for the landing pad, determined to find a name for the feeling so it would stop bothering him. Past the reception entrance and halfway down the floating bridge, it occurred to Pet that he had no way back. Décor were luggage. They didn't receive guest passes.

Would he be able to get back to the island on his own?

That problem could wait until tomorrow. With a shrug he turned his back to the island and kept walking.

On the other side of the scanners, the *Vanguard* sat right where they left her. At the sight of that familiar shape, the round body and the four arms spread over the floor, Pet finally found a name for the emotion plaguing him.

Homesickness.

Due to its name, he imagined homesickness to feel pestilent and moldering, like acid building in his gut. Instead, it felt like longing. He wasn't sick at all. He was just sad.

The bottom hatch of the *Vanguard* opened, and Pet froze.

Who was on their ship?

Brightly colored feathers answered his question as Xavis jumped to the floor. It seemed Pet wasn't the only one longing for something familiar.

Xavis closed the hatch behind him. Instead of leaving, he headed for the back of the landing pad.

Pet followed him. A hidden door on the back wall looked ridiculously small compared to the surrounding ships. Xavis's wings barely fit, and even Pet had to duck.

The landing pad was an artificial structure, but over

time, sand and coral collected around its edge, creating a natural beach.

Xavis sat in the sand, just out of the water's reach. He tucked his knees against his chest, and his wings wrapped tightly around his shoulders, making him look small and vulnerable.

Pet hesitated in the doorway. If Xavis wanted to be alone, he shouldn't intrude, but the way the Scaacax watched the night sky spoke of the same sadness clouding Pet's heart.

"I can feel you worrying from here." Xavis turned to look at Pet over his shoulder, purple eyes missing their usual glow. "If you want to join me, you can. I wouldn't mind the company."

As an emphasis to his invitation, he pulled one wing back, opening a space at his side for Pet to sit.

They were a perfect fit. Feathers rested lightly against Pet's shoulders as he leaned into Xavis's arm. Without either of them needing to think about it, their fingers laced together.

Pet kept his eyes on the contrast of human skin and Scaacax talons. "I think I messed up."

Those talons squeezed his hand, sharp tips careful not to press too hard.

The silent encouragement was easier to accept than words. Pet took a deep breath and explained his encounter with Brog back in the pavilion.

When he finished, Xavis didn't let the silence last long. "Just to be clear, you're not afraid of Brog, right?"

Pet's other hand joined the first, so his grip surrounded Xavis's talons. "No, that's not the problem. Ugh. My emotions are all over the place. I don't know how to explain them."

"Give it a shot. Silence definitely won't explain anything."

"It's… I've never done this before."

Xavis's feathers ruffled and pressed closer. "Been in a relationship?"

"Said *no*."

The wind blew, picking up sand around them.

Pet closed his eyes and turned his face into Xavis's shoulder. "I've never said *no* to any of you. Never even wanted to before. This is the first time, but it's harder to say *no* to you because I care about you and want you all to be happy. I want to be the one who makes you happy. Brog was angry, and I wasn't comfortable with that. I know he wasn't angry with me, but I don't want anger to be involved with sex at all. But that's what would've made Brog happy. My wants are conflicting with each other."

Xavis's breath brushed Pet's ear when he spoke, tickling his skin.

"That happens. Emotions are complicated things. They don't follow rules."

"They should. Then I would always know what to do. I'm not sure if I even should say *no*. Like, I've already agreed to the relationship. Is it right to turn around and say *no* when I've already said *yes*, or is that wrong?"

The wind kicked up, and sand stung when it hit his skin. Pet opened his eyes to see a purple tinge in the air. Above him Xavis's eyes regained their glow.

"Of course you can say *no*. Being in a relationship doesn't change that."

Oh, this was an emotion Pet recognized. Anger was

too distinct to forget.

He leaned back to stare into Xavis's eyes. "Don't say 'of course.' There's no 'of course' about anything. I don't know these things that people seem to think are natural."

Like a bonfire that burned too hot, his anger quickly turned to cold ash. He was left with a defeated slump to his shoulders and the bitter taste of melancholy. The truth of his own words hadn't occurred to him until he spoke them aloud.

"People grow up learning how to interact with one another. Maybe I knew all this once, but I don't remember anymore. I need people to tell me things in order to know them. No one has ever said, 'Pet, it's okay to reject people even after you're in a relationship with them.' I don't even know what I don't know, so there's no way to ask."

Xavis took a deep breath. The wind fell still, but his eyes retained an ember of their usual spark. He pulled Pet back to his side but didn't speak immediately. Tension remained in his shoulders and wings, indicating he wanted to say something.

Pet was intimately familiar with the struggle to find the right words, so he waited.

When Xavis finally spoke, he didn't look at Pet but stared at the night sky. "I grew up in an orphanage. Never had a family, and I wasn't close with the other kids. I don't know what a family is supposed to be like, or if we even count as one. I don't know if it's normal for families to fight, or how to handle it if they do. I just know I don't like it, and I wish I could make the problem go away."

Ah, it was time to address the heart of their

troubles. It had hovered around them like a cloud of diseased insects that Pet assumed was meant to be ignored. Talking about the problem directly was a refreshing change.

He pulled Xavis's wings closer around his shoulders and stroked the feathers. "What was that fight about? I didn't understand half the things they said."

Xavis looked away from the sky to stare down at the line where water met land. "I'm not sure how much I should tell you."

Pet started to protest, but Xavis cut him off.

"Not because you can't handle it, but because it's not mine to tell. The three of us...our lives are already so entangled it's easy to lose track of where one of us stops and another begins. We need to maintain the borders that make us separate people. I can't tell you what the others think or feel because it's not mine to tell. I have no right to reveal it."

The familiar concept left Pet nodding along. It was the same reason he hated sensory deprivation. Although the process was common for décor and didn't cause any pain, it felt like a violation when something took ownership of his thoughts. He never wanted to intrude on someone else in such a way.

"Although." Xavis spoke that one word as if rolling a new food over his tongue, trying to decide if he liked the taste. "I could give you some context. As a species, Ocans value size. Different cultures on their world focus on different kinds of size. Like strength, or the number of children they have, but there is a general idea that bigger is better. The predominant culture on their planet values height above everything else, and that's the one Brog comes from."

Pet made a face. He had no idea what the face looked like, or what emotion it meant to convey, but he felt his facial features distort. The image of Brog standing before the Ocan family, significantly shorter than even the smallest, played out behind his eyes.

Xavis gave a solemn nod. "Exactly. When a male Ocan reaches adulthood, they call it 'going into season.' The male is supposed to show off and catch the eye of a matriarch who then adds him to her family unit. Most are usually claimed within five years, but sometimes one will go unclaimed. When that happens, they are labeled 'Impotent' and put into worker colonies so they're still some 'use' to society."

Pet could practically hear the quotes Xavis added to certain words. Another memory came to mind of Desmodian telling Brog to "go make himself useful somewhere else." What seemed like a general dismissal had been a deliberate choice meant to hurt as much as possible.

Xavis ran a hand through Pet's hair, and Pet couldn't tell if it was an offer of comfort or a plea for forgiveness.

Maybe it was both.

The Scaacax sighed, though his hand never stopped. "Des is harder to explain. He's not a very sexual person."

Pet snorted. The crude sound was a perfect expression of his disbelief.

Xavis smiled at Pet's reaction. "It may sound ridiculous to you, but it's true. Pet, you don't realize how amazing you are. Desmodian is rarely interested in anyone physically."

This was one truth Pet couldn't accept yet also had

no doubt it was true. Xavis wouldn't lie to him. Like assembling a puzzle, he thought he knew what the final image would be but suddenly found a piece with a completely different pattern.

He traced symbols into the sand, nonsense at first, but it turned into music. Since he hadn't learned how to write music yet, he'd invented his own system. Using a mix of lines and dots, he drew the song that often played in his head, slowing it to match the rhythm of ocean waves.

Just below the dry top layer, the sand grew damp and clung to his skin.

"So Des is picky when it comes to sex, and I just happened to be the right person?"

Xavis's answer interrupted before he even finished speaking. "No. It's not that simple. You'll have to ask Des about why he finds you attractive, but I can say it has nothing to do with how you look. The few people he's been attracted to in the past looked nothing alike. It's more complicated than that."

Interesting information, but what did it have to do with their earlier fight?

A year ago, Pet would've waited for Xavis to get to the point. Now, he just asked.

Another heavy moment passed before Xavis answered. "That fight you saw today isn't the first time it's happened. Brog needs sex to be happy in a relationship. The three of us come from species that aren't very compatible physically. We could figure something out if we tried, but Des and I aren't interested in trying, so we can't give Brog what he needs. Des at least has the excuse of his sexuality being complicated. For me, it's simple, and it's stupid. I'm not attracted to people who are taller than me. I wish I could change it, but I can't."

Pet started to reassure Xavis that he was allowed to have a physical preference, but the Scaacax entered full rant mode.

He spoke at the sky, nearly yelling, and gestured with his arms as if demanding an answer from the stars. "I mean, how horrible is that? 'Sorry, Brog. You're not tall enough for your own people, but you're too tall for me.' And the worst thing is, I get what he's going through. As a kid, well, they called me a *late bloomer*, but the truth is I was severely underdeveloped. Even the younger kids at the orphanage were taller. For years it seemed like everyone looked down on me. It's why I'm not attracted to people taller than me now, because looking up at my partner makes me uncomfortable. The difference is, I grew out of it. Now I'm an average height for a Scaacax, but for Brog it's never going to change. I should be sympathetic, but I'm just making it worse."

He came to an abrupt halt and looked at Pet with wide eyes. Putting an end to his rant, Xavis nervously cleared his throat and scratched the crest of hair on his head. This made the hair stick out in all directions, just like his ruffled feathers.

He looked cute, but Pet kept that observation to himself.

"Anyway." Xavis cleared his throat again and struggled to meet Pet's eyes. "This has caused a lot of tension between us, especially Brog and Des. So we decided to add a fourth. We tried twice before you. Both were a disaster. Finding you seemed to solve the problem, but it was only set aside. It's still a problem, and I don't…"

His breathing shuddered, and he cut off.

Trembling feathers tickled Pet's skin. Xavis tried to hide it, clutching his own hands to stop their shaking, but in such close proximity, Pet saw everything. From the way Xavis's eyes darted around without focusing, to the way his throat bobbed when he swallowed several times in a row. Pet saw it all.

He took Xavis's hands in his own but kept his grip loose.

Xavis's words trembled almost as much as his hands. "I don't know how to fix it. I love them, but I can't be what they need. I don't even know what they need. Maybe if I was better at dealing with people, I would know what to do. Maybe I could've stopped it from getting this bad. But as I am, I'm just…useless."

The more he spoke the harder he shook. Small tornados of purple air twirled an intricate waltz across the beach.

Just holding Xavis wasn't enough. They needed more contact. Pet threw a leg over Xavis and sat on the Scaacax's lap with their faces nearly touching. Running hands up the sides of Xavis's head, he buried his fingers into the ridge of dark-red hair, scratching at the coarse roots. "You're not useless. You can't be. You do so many things for all of us. If you're useless, then there's no hope for me. I'm only good for one thing."

The tornados died, leaving behind little pyramids of sand.

Xavis grabbed Pet's wrists and stilled his hands. "You better not be implying what I think you're implying. Pet, you're more than just some pretty bed warmer."

Unable to free his hands, Pet bumped their foreheads together. "Hey, I'm not saying it as a bad thing. Not to brag, but I'm pretty good in bed, and I'm proud of that. It's a skill I didn't have before. I'm learning how to be useful in other ways, but it's a slow process, and I'm trying to be patient. Better to focus on what I can do. Which is this." He leaned forward and kissed Xavis.

The other male hesitated at first, but soon wrapped his arms around Pet.

They kissed, slow and unhurried. Pet might not be great with words, but this was a language he spoke fluently. Through the slide of lips and tongue, he conveyed all the warm feelings that lived within him for his trio. The press of his palm as he cradled the back of Xavis's head was a poem of gratitude. The moan building in his throat was a whole monologue of love and acceptance. When he pressed small kisses along Xavis's lower lip, each was its own promise of devotion.

Both of them were panting by the time they parted. Sitting in Xavis's lap, Pet felt the bulge of the Scaacax's arousal, and it brought a flush of pride. He had done that. His trio held so much power, yet he left them desperate with barely any effort.

Sharp talons held him carefully as Xavis flipped them over. Pet landed on his back in the sand with Xavis kneeling over him. Broad wings opened wide, blocking out the stars and the light of the triple moons.

Only the glowing fire of Xavis's eyes brightened the intimate space between them. "Little vixen. I swear, there's no sating you."

"Good. Otherwise I wouldn't be able to keep up

with you three."

Xavis wore little clothing so he undressed with ease, carelessly casting his shorts aside to land somewhere out of reach. Once naked, he immediately rolled back on top of Pet. Wings extended as if shielding Pet from the stars.

Pet took care of his own clothes and carefully folded the delicate material. His jewelry, however, he left on. A particular pleasure came from being completely bare except for the cool touch of precious gold and pearls.

He wrapped his legs around Xavis's waist. They kissed again, and Pet's cock throbbed when it brushed Xavis's stomach. He moaned and thrust his hips in a desperate search for more friction.

Yet one little detail kept it from feeling as good as usual.

Pet pulled out of the kiss. "Wait. Hold on. Maybe we should go back to the ship."

Purple eyes, dazed with pleasure, struggled to focus. "What... Why?"

"Well, sex on the beach sounds like a great idea, but this sand is getting everywhere." He gestured to the particles already clinging to his skin. Xavis had some on his arms and legs, but most of it gathered on Pet. The coarse grains chafed.

A groan built in the back of Xavis's throat until his whole body vibrated. He didn't let Pet up. Instead, he slammed one hand down on the beach. The area around them flashed purple, and the sand turned hard, as if air had been sucked out from between the particles.

"Oh."

It was a lackluster response, but what else could

Pet say? Even the sand clinging to him had disappeared to be vacuum sealed with the rest. Since Pet learned about his trio's Phazer abilities, they had been more cavalier with such displays, but it was the first time any of them used their power for something so frivolous.

"There." Xavis tore his talons from the sand. "Problem solved."

The Scaacax then kissed Pet hard enough to press him into the beach.

Maybe they should upgrade their bed. Vacuum-sealed sand was surprisingly comfortable, cradling him like a specialized mattress.

Pet trailed his hand down Xavis's side. He went slow, teasing, before finally gripping the other male's hard cock. Natural lubricant coated his skin.

Never breaking the kiss, he twisted his hand around to slip two fingers inside himself. The aphrodisiac made him especially sensitive, and he groaned against Xavis's mouth.

Xavis ended the kiss to bite Pet's neck. "So eager."

Pet moaned again and tipped his head back as far as it would go, exposing the full length of his throat. Quickly preparing himself, he removed his fingers and hooked both arms around Xavis, burying his hands in small feathers under the Scaacax's wings. "Please. I need to feel you."

Pleasurable bursts of pain from Xavis's bites moved up his neck to his jaw.

Xavis breathed heavily into his ear. "Don't worry, Pet. I won't make you wait." He lifted Pet's hips, so they no longer touched the sand, and shoved smoothly inside.

Lubricant eased the way. All Pet felt was the

satisfying stretch of being filled. He cried out and clung to the base of Xavis's wings.

As he started thrusting, Xavis rested his weight on his elbows.

Rough hands encircled Pet's head, and

talons tangled in his hair. After such an emotional day, it was cathartic to be surrounded so completely.

With each thrust, Xavis slid a little deeper until he sheathed himself to the root. Pulling almost all the way out, he slammed the full length of his cock inside and hit Pet's most pleasurable spots with deadly accuracy.

They both shouted as Pet arched his back and clenched tightly around the invading flesh.

"That's it." Xavis picked up the pace but kept hitting that same spot over and over, driving Pet wild. "Let the whole island hear you."

Despite the encouragement, Pet's cries sounded like kitten mewls. Every time Xavis pulled out, Pet sucked in a lungful of air, only for it to be immediately driven from him again. Tears built in his eyes as divine fire burned through his veins. His arms and legs trembled but stayed tightly locked around Xavis.

The Scaacax couldn't move more than a few inches away.

Not that he showed any desire to leave. Xavis kept his face buried against Pet's neck, breathing heavily as he pounded Pet into the sand.

It was relentless.

Pet came quickly. His climax lubricated the slide of their stomachs against each other and dripped onto the sand.

Xavis followed almost immediately, groaning and filling Pet with a rush of heat. Yet his cock remained hard. Before either of them finished their first orgasm, he started thrusting again.

"I'm not done with you yet."

The words vibrated against Pet's pulse point. "I hope you're never done with me."

It was an easier slide now, and an obscene squelch accompanied each time Xavis's arousal filled him.

With a contented sigh Pet relaxed against the beach as Xavis fucked him with unusual desperation. He was a mess, and he loved it.

Pet surfed on the high of his first orgasm as Xavis kept going, coming twice more. They held each other tight, and Xavis shouted his pleasure against Pet's skin each time.

After reaching his third peak, Xavis abandoned Pet's neck to rest their foreheads together. His thrusts slowed to a languid pace but never fully stopped.

"Come for me again, Pet. I want to see you."

In the shadow of those large wings, Pet could almost feel the purple sparks from Xavis's eyes landing on his cheeks.

Pet chased his building pleasure as Xavis slowly increased their pace. When they finally fell for the last time, they did so while staring into each other's eyes and breathing the other's name against their lips.

Even once they finished, they stayed wrapped tightly together. Xavis moved onto his back with Pet tucked against his side. His wings became their mattress over the sand.

A year ago, Pet would've been too scared of hurting Xavis to lie on top of his wings. They resembled the wings of a bird, and it was easy to assume they suffered the same fragility. Now he knew better. Scaacax wings did not share the hollow-boned delicacy of their avian look-alikes. It would take a lot more force than Pet's body weight to damage Xavis's wings.

They lay together under the night sky, caressing heated skin and sharing slow sweet kisses. A startling contrast to the intensity of their earlier embrace, it soothed the remaining ache in Pet's soul. "Four times? I must not be taking care of you properly if you're that pent-up."

The sheepish blush that bloomed over Xavis's face made Pet laugh, and he buried the sound against the other male's chest.

After a moment, Xavis laughed as well. "Sorry. Thought I had it out of my system, but I guess not."

Pet stroked Xavis's flushed cheek. "I'm not complaining. Just surprised."

Talons wrapped around his hand, and Xavis kissed Pet's palm. "When all three of us feel the same emotion at the same time, it can create a feedback loop. Enjoyable with pleasant emotions, but something like anger is dangerous. You saw the state of the beach after our fight?"

He waited long enough for Pet to nod.

"Our Phazer abilities are usually tied to our intent, but when all of us are angry enough to lash out, it can manifest in ways we don't want. I came back to the *Vanguard* to siphon off the energy that built up during the fight. Brog and Desmodian are lucky that way. Their means of control are easier to manage. Desmodian's hammer can take the excess energy, and Brog can convert it into physical strength so long as he's got a steady supply of food, but I need the ship. I thought I took care of it, but I was more agitated than I realized. Sorry. That's the reason you walked away from Brog, and I just used you the same way."

Xavis still held his hand, so Pet couldn't force the other to look at him, but he didn't have to. Even if those purple eyes remained fixed on the sky, he knew Xavis would hear him. "It's not the same. I'd gladly help any of you work off some energy. I said *no* to Brog because he was angry. You just wanted pleasure."

A bright fluttering above them caught his eye. Large creatures darted through sparse clouds. They looked like moths, with a wingspan large enough to block out dozens of stars, even from a great distance. Several swarmed together, each a slightly different shade of orangish-pink.

What was the name of that color? It stood out so bright against the night sky.

Xavis twitched at the sight of the creatures above them. "Oh, Aura moths." He spoke the name with wonder.

Pet looked at Xavis, then back at the giant moths. "Are they special?"

Xavis's talons toyed with Pet's hair. "They're a rare sight and a sign of good luck. Their full name is Roluna Auralux, but most people just call them Aura moths. The dust from their wings is the reason this ocean has more heavy water. See?"

Far above, farther than Pet could accurately guess, the Aura moths broke their huddle to dance figure eights around each other. A puff of orangish-pink dust burst between them each time their giant wings touched. The dust floated down to land on the water, forming a thin film over the surface.

With a sigh Xavis raised the wing Pet wasn't lying on and pointed it to the sky, letting the triple moonlight filter through his feathers. "Look at them. They fly with more grace than I ever could. Coming here was originally my idea. I wanted to see them when they gather during the yearly syzygy, when the three moons fall into alignment. This is the only inhabited planet where a syzygy happens every year. The planet is even named Syzygy because of it. See how close the moons are, almost overlapping? The syzygy will be soon. That should be fun. The sky will be full of Aura moths then."

The wind changed, and some of the dust from the moths reached the beach. Orangish-pink contrasted with white sand.

Oh, he remembered the name of that color. It was coral.

****

Pet and Xavis fell asleep on the beach. It was a comfortable night, but when they woke, they were encrusted with a layer of sand, salt, and even a little moth dust. Short days meant short nights, so only a few hours had passed since they fell asleep. The sun had barely risen so early in the morning, and they snuck back onto the *Vanguard* to clean up.

After a thorough shower, Pet tossed his outfit into the laundry so he could wear it again. The choice had worked well for him so far, and he saw no reason to change.

While he waited for the laundry to finish, he applied a layer of makeup to his neck. Xavis's attention the previous night left a series of love bites up and down his throat. His bruise ointment would take care of it in a couple of hours, but until then, he needed to avoid awkward questions.

This, unfortunately, didn't solve his worst problems. The first one reared its head as soon as they returned to the island.

"What'd you mean you're not coming?"

Xavis shrugged as he lingered on the bridge leading back to the landing pad. "It's best if I stay on the ship while things are still so tense. I'll make sure you can get onto the island, but then I'm going back to the *Vanguard*. At least for now."

Should Pet be upset about this? Xavis would be safer in the ship. Yet Pet wanted Xavis's help. He refused to leave Brog and Desmodian on their own but had no idea what to do for them.

Inches from stepping onto the island, Xavis fidgeted at the end of the bridge. A few loose feathers floated down to land in the water.

Pet recalled their conversation from the previous night. Xavis was afraid of igniting another angry feedback loop. Staying on the ship would allow him to siphon off any excess energy that might build up between the three of them.

The only thing worse than external conflict was internal conflict. Pet wanted two things at once, Xavis's support but also his comfort. It wasn't possible to have both.

He chose Xavis's comfort.

"All right. I can get back to our suite on my own."

The look of relief on Xavis's face gave him confidence in his choice but didn't drown out the sense of loneliness when Xavis returned to the *Vanguard*.

Pet had to go back to their suite. Brog was engaged elsewhere, but he might find Desmodian there. That was the first step to solving the conflict between his trio. Find them. The second step would be harder. Talk to them. He tried to plan what he would say to Desmodian if he found the Dhen'in but second-guessed every sentence he strung together.

By the time he reached the line for the trolley, he hadn't even decided how to start the conversation. The early hour kept the crowds small, and soon it was his turn to step onboard.

He turned away.

Without thinking about it, his feet led him to the same beachside restaurant they already visited twice. Just like the trolley, the restaurant had plenty of open seats, including the table where Pet and his trio sat before. He ignored the few other customers who were either too awake or half asleep and claimed a seat overlooking the water.

Pale morning sun skipped along the tops of ocean waves. One reflection caught him squarely in the eye, and he turned his back on the water to face the shade of the restaurant.

If he'd boarded the trolley, he would be halfway back to their suite by now.

"Alone this time?"

Pet jumped. He'd been so lost in self-flagellation that he failed to notice Bug roll up to the table. Considering the size of her motorized wheelchair, this was a considerable oversight. "Yeah. Just me."

Before he could say anything else—not that he knew what to say—she placed a bowl of nutriment in front of him.

"I'd take your order, but there's no point. This is the only nutriment option we have."

He shrugged and stirred the spoon around the bowl. "It's fine. Nutriment's not meant to be enjoyed."

Her job was done. A typical waiter would leave. Bug, however, lingered with her antennae twitching erratically. "Are you waiting for the rest of your group?"

The extra-large seat Brog had dragged over from another part of the restaurant still stood at the table, as did the backless stool for Xavis.

Pet tried not to look at them. "No...it's just me."

The tank-like treads of Bug's wheelchair whirred as she rolled closer. "You know, I'm almost done with my shift. If you're not doing anything, I could show you around the city. I doubt you've seen everything in just two days."

Pet dropped the spoon. It hit the side of the bowl with a loud clink, sending drops of nutriment splattering over the table. "What? Why?"

Bug didn't have shoulders, but the arms of her wheelchair shrugged for her. "Why should you come with me?"

"No, I mean, why are you asking? You don't need to pity me just because I'm décor. I won't fall apart if I'm left alone for a bit."

Her chair pulled out a rag and wiped up the spilled nutriment, but her attention stayed on Pet. Apparently the chair acted on instinct just as any biological limb could. "It's not pity. Promise. I need to pick up some things and thought you'd like to get a better look around. Starthrone Island has a lot to offer."

He took a moment to fish out the spoon, which had sunk beneath the surface of the nutriment. "Yeah. All right. Sounds good."

Was that the right response? He'd never been asked to just "hang out" before. When he spent time with his friends at the Gravity Well, invitations weren't needed. They were already at a club. This felt more official. He had no idea if he would like it, or what was expected of him, but it felt like the kind of thing a real person would do.

"Great. Give me half an hour, and I'll be done here."

Her enthusiasm over Pet's acceptance didn't feel earned. He still suspected she was pitying him but promised to wait.

The next half hour was spent slowly emptying his bowl and watching the sun rise over the beach. It was as beautiful as the day before, as if nothing on the planet ever changed. The boardwalk grew busier as morning progressed, and many people sought breakfast at the restaurant. It was a popular place, based on the number of customers coming through the door.

Bug returned just as people started eyeing his table with its three empty seats.

"All right. I've handed things over to the breakfast shift. Let's go."

They left the restaurant behind.

Pet followed her lead. He hadn't felt this awkward since the first morning-after with his trio when they invited him onto their ship. The *Vanguard* was his home, but back then he felt like an intruder.

That same feeling plagued him now.

If Bug noticed the awkward atmosphere, she didn't bring it up. Instead she filled the air between them with pleasant conversation. "So how did the diving go, yesterday?"

Oh, right, that had been her suggestion. So much happened since then, it felt like months had passed.

"It went fine. I can't swim, so Xavis and I took a diving bell, but Brog and Desmodian got to swim around. Brog didn't even need diving gear." He didn't mention what else they'd gotten up to at the bottom of the ocean. She didn't need to know about that.

Despite Rurarine being the native species of the planet, Bug was a minority among the crowds. Guests from other planets filled the boardwalk. Very few motorized wheelchairs could be seen among the sea of legs, tentacles, and other various appendages.

This didn't seem to bother Bug. She kept on rolling as crowds parted around her like a diverting stream. No one wanted to get run over by the intimidating treads of her chair.

"Remind me, which one of your friends is which? I see so many people every day I can never keep the names straight."

This was a topic of conversation Pet could handle. He fell into an easy explanation about his trio. Although he stuck to surface information such as species, general personality, and what they all did for a living, it felt good to talk about them. He had never needed to explain his trio before. Everyone he knew was someone he met through them.

As he and Bug boarded a trolley, Pet realized he'd dominated the conversation. Bug had barely said anything since he started talking.

He dropped into an open chair, hands clasped in his lap and eyes down to hide his embarrassed blush. "Sorry. I don't usually talk so much."

She stopped just in front of the seat next to him.

"Don't worry. It's good to hear you sound so happy after how sad you looked earlier. You obviously care about them." The trolley seat collapsed into the floor and Bug backed her chair into the space left behind.

With eyes still downcast, Pet watched clamps emerge from the floor to secure her chair in place. "Of course. My trio are everything. I wouldn't have a life without them."

The trolley started moving, taking them to an unknown destination.

Bug's chair barely shifted under the change in momentum. Her vocalizer, hidden somewhere among her chair's mechanics, made a strange humming noise. "Hmmm. That sounds a bit..."

Although the voice was artificial, the concern in her words came through loud and clear.

Pet met her sincerity with his own. "I know that sounds a bit obsessive, but you have to understand. I'm décor. I'm not supposed to have relationships at all. It's only because of them that I'm even able to talk to you like this. So, to me, they really are everything."

"As long as you're happy, that's all that matters."

Pet tugged at the fabric wrapped around his torso, almost untying the knot behind his neck holding the whole thing together. "I am. Life with them has been...it's beyond words. They're having an argument right now. It's new for me, and I'm not sure what to do. How do you handle it when people you care about are unhappy?"

Commotion on the other side of the trolley caught his attention. Two people of the same species spoke with raised voices and wild gestures. Other people around them leaned away or sought another seat.

Was it an argument or just the way this species naturally communicated?

The exchange only lasted a few moments. Eventually, the raised voices quieted, and the wild gestures calmed.

If only his trio's argument could be resolved so easily.

From the angle of Bug's antennae, she also watched the exchange but turned back to him once the excitement settled. "It depends on why they're unhappy. I don't know enough about your trio or what happened between them to judge."

He explained the fight as best he could, without revealing the trio's private information. It took a few tries for him to find the right words. By the end, he wasn't sure if he'd given her an explanation or a jumbled mess.

Some part of his explanation must have translated because she thought in silence for a moment. "This sounds like a very personal conflict for them. Your trio need to figure it out on their own, but you can support them. The best thing to do would probably be to just remind them that you care and listen to them when they talk."

Pet sighed. He feared that would be her answer.

However, Bug wasn't done. "That person you mentioned. Tradius Vels? I've heard of him. His visit has been big news on the island for a while."

"Really? I know he's an important politician, but I didn't think that would matter outside his own homeworld."

Bug's antennae moved up and down, imitating a nod. "Usually it wouldn't, but Tradius Vels is a primary supporter of the Traditional Evolution Party."

Pet looked to see if anyone could hear their conversation. Throwing around the name of someone with political power seemed like asking for trouble. He had enough trouble already. He didn't need more. "I spend most of my time flying through space. I don't know much about current political movements."

She followed his lead and lowered her voice, not enough to seem suspicious, but just enough to keep their conversation between them. "Me neither. But you overhear a lot when you work at a place like this. Waitstaff are invisible to most people. They forget we can hear them. The Traditional Evolution Party promotes separation between species and wants to increase travel restrictions between planets. There's been a big debate about it for a while."

More separation between species? What was wrong with species interacting with each other? That was how Pet lived every day.

The person on Pet's other side grew excited over something their companion said and accidentally elbowed him. They were an Apha, so their vine-like limbs lacked proper elbows, but Pet still leaned away from them and closer to Bug. "Why would Tradius come here? Just looking around, I can tell half this island is populated by immigrants from other planets, not to mention the guests. Traditional Evolution won't be popular here."

Bug also leaned to the side, giving Pet room to encroach on her space and avoid the gesticulations of the person next to him. "That's exactly why he's here. He doesn't need to worry about the governments that already agree with him. He needs to persuade the ones that don't. But you're right. It's not a popular idea on this island, or any island in this chain. Can't say what the other countries think, but ours is one of the most influential, so it makes sense to start here."

"Tradius Vels sounds insufferable, showing up in someone's home just to tell them that they're wrong. I guess that's why Yaivin was eager to hook up with Brog. It's the only way he can rebel against his father."

Pet scowled and crossed his arms. He forgot about the person on his other side and sat up, only to immediately duck again as another careless gesture nearly hit him in the face. "If Brog wants to sleep with other people, that's fine. We never promised to be exclusive. But he deserves more than being used like that."

He expected Bug to agree, but her mechanical arms merely shrugged, and her antennae tipped indecisively to the side. "I don't know. I mean, it's his choice. If he knows he's being used and is fine with it, then it's not your call."

Oh, that sounded like Brog and Desmodian's argument on the beach.

Pet deflated, practically slumping against the side of Bug's chair. He sounded just like Desmodian, trying to dictate what Brog could and couldn't do. But he only said it because he was worried about Brog, so surely that made it all right.

Except Desmodian had probably also said the things he did out of love.

They didn't stay on the trolley much longer. A few stops later, they disembarked right into the busiest part of the city.

Shops of all kinds lined the streets, with walls

completely open to show off their wares. The sun had fully risen by this point, turning the inside of the shops darker by comparison. Coral grew along the buildings, making them look like undersea caves, except without water.

People of all sizes, shapes, and species bustled from place to place, but no one seemed to be going anywhere.

"This way." The arm of Bug's chair waved him along as she rolled down the street. They occasionally stopped to look at a shop display but never lingered long.

Pet spent so much time out in empty space with only his trio for company it was easy to forget what a city felt like. Moving bodies and half-overheard conversations pulsed around him, like the many cells of a living body. The city felt alive.

They eventually stopped at a shop Pet would've overlooked if he were alone. It was larger on top, like a wedge hammered between the buildings on either side. Its front displayed several bizarre outfits on mannequins of various design, none of which resembled species Pet knew. However, it was the spiral staircase at the center that drew the most attention.

Bug headed straight for the staircase. "Don't bother with anything down here. The real prize is upstairs."

The treads on her chair angled and rolled right up the stairs.

Pet watched her until she reached the top, marveling at the machine's ingenuity.

Following her upstairs, he found racks upon racks of cloth. Every color and pattern imaginable hung together, a meticulously organized gradient that traveled all the way up the walls and even hung from the ceiling. A long, thin table formed a circle at the center of the room. Inside that circle stood the shop's only staff.

Bug headed straight for the table. "Pet, this is Ochaid. She owns this place and can make anything you need so long as it's made of cloth."

Ochaid was a Q'od. A member of the same species that tended the bar in the Gravity Well.

Her main body resembled a weather balloon, floating several feet off the ground due to the lighter-than-air gasses stored inside. A ring of eyes surrounded her entire body, and a triple layer of frills hung below like a skirt. From under the natural skirt extended many tentacle arms that curled to keep from dragging on the floor.

The bartender at the Gravity Well was tan and red, but Ochaid was an exploration of the color blue.

When she spoke, Ochaid's whole body expanded and contracted like bellows. "You brought someone with you this time, Bug? That's unusual. Thought you only knew customers."

Without feet, Bug fidgeted by rolling back and forth on her chair's treads. "Well, um…"

Pet stepped up to the counter. "I'm a guest here, but the rest of my group's busy right now, so Bug offered to show me around."

A dozen eyes scrutinized Pet from top to bottom.

"You're décor?"

He stood as tall as his human spine allowed.

"Yep."

If she had shoulders, Ochaid probably would've shrugged. Instead, her tentacles curled and uncurled repeatedly. "Well, have a look around. I've got a little bit of everything. There should be something you like."

Rather than correct her that he wasn't looking for anything, Pet took the opportunity to end their exchange on a positive note. He followed Bug to a wall filled with an array of cloth in various shades of red and pink.

Bug's arms absently sorted through the fabric. "Sorry about that. Ochaid is nice, but she's blunt."

"I'll take blunt over fake any day. What're you looking for?"

From the selection on the wall, Bug pulled out a bright-red cloth, though she barely seemed to be paying attention. "I usually get new ribbons to decorate my chair for the Dust Party, but I haven't picked anything out yet."

"Dust Party?"

Bug's antennae stood up straight. "You don't know? I assumed that's why you're here. It's why everyone's here this week. Even Tradius Vels is probably here because there are so many influential people visiting right now."

Pet let his fingers trail over the cloth, selecting by touch rather than color. He pulled out a soft, heavy fabric that turned out to be a dull-rose color. It was not a choice he would ever make for himself. He'd never been fond of pastels, but it gave his hands something to do. "I haven't heard of a Dust Party. What is it?"

More importantly, were his trio also unaware, or had they forgotten to tell him?

Which was worse?

His internal questions went unnoticed by Bug as she pulled out another brightly colored cloth. "Well, our planet has three moons. They move in different patterns, but one week of the year they line up."

"Oh, the syzygy. I know about that. It's why this planet is called Syzygy in the first place." At least his trio had told him this much.

Pet dropped the rose cloth and selected a darker scarlet this time. A more favorable color, but its coarse texture had him immediately moving on to something else.

Bug swapped out the cloth in her hands for a shade of red with subtle threads of purple woven throughout. "Starthrone Island is right in the middle of the syzygy's effect. Aura moths flock here for their mating season. There's so many that the dust from their wings covers the island like snow. We hold a big party in the dust."

Pet dropped the cloth and braced his hands on his hips. "And you need ribbons to wear during this party?"

Bug shifted on her wheels again. "Yes, but I'm not very good at picking out colors. Rurarine only have olfactory senses, and you can't smell color. I don't get why some colors work together and others don't. You're décor. You know what looks good. I was hoping you could help me pick out something that won't get me mocked this time."

The bulk of her chair distracted from how small Bug really was. Like most Rurarine, her whole body only measured two feet long. Curled up in her chair with antennae drooping to either side, her delicate stature had never been more obvious.

Pet pulled the cloth out of her hands and hung it back on the rack. "Well, we should avoid red. It tends to clash with pink."

He walked around her, noting her various colors.

Bug perked up and sat tall in her chair. Her body was primarily pink with a yellow underbelly, but the problem came from the contrasting cool tones in her metal chair. Finding something that complemented both would be difficult but not impossible.

With color-wheels turning in his mind, he led Bug to the other side of the room full of blue and green cloth.

An hour passed as Pet pulled various fabrics off the racks and draped them over Bug to compare the colors. They laughed over the more outlandish choices and fell into serious conversation whenever they found a potential option. For the first time, Pet took the role of teacher instead of student. Bug was an avid listener as he explained the basics of color theory, and he enjoyed being the knowledgeable one for once.

They finally decided on a dark-cyan fabric that fell perfectly between blue and green.

The color complemented Bug, but the best part was the satin texture. It flashed copper when it moved, tying into the metallic tones of her chair.

They brought their choice to Ochaid at the circular counter where she immediately began turning it into several long ribbons.

As a last-minute addition, Pet included pearl-white cloth for a few smaller ribbons to accent the main ones.

While she worked, half of Ochaid's eyes remained fixed on Pet.

"What about you?"

"What about me?" Pet couldn't decide between watching the chaotic tentacles cutting and sewing all at the same time, or the many eyes staring at him.

One of Ochaid's free tentacles gestured around the

room. She seemed to think this was enough explanation because she didn't say anything more.

When Pet realized what she meant, he stepped back from the counter. "Oh, no, I don't need anything."

Ochaid made her curling and uncurling shrug again. "Humans usually wear clothes. The Dust Party takes place on the beach. Do you have a swimsuit?"

Unlike Ochaid, Pet's shrug included shoulders. "I'm not even sure if we're going to the party. My trio are…having some trouble right now."

The movement of Bug's antennae and the shifting of her chair announced that she wanted to say something.

Pet waited for her to speak. It wasn't long.

"If they don't want to go, then they're missing out, but…you could go anyway."

Nothing changed. Silence didn't fall, and the planet didn't stop turning. Yet that's exactly what if felt like.

It also felt like being thrown into the sensory deprivation chamber again, but Pet didn't want to think about that. "You mean go to the party alone?"

"Or we could go together if you don't want to show up alone. But, yeah. There's nothing stopping you from going to the party even if those three don't."

Was it possible? Yes.

Would he do it? Maybe.

It took some back and forth, but eventually Pet and Bug agreed that he should try talking to his trio again. If they settled their argument, then everyone could go to the party together. If not, then Pet would still meet up with Bug on his own.

Either way, Pet would need a swimsuit. Even if he never entered the water, a party on the beach made getting wet inevitable. He chose some water-safe cloth in basic black but faltered when it came to the suit's design.

Turning to the most knowledgeable person in the room, Pet asked for Ochaid's suggestion.

"Easy." She activated a holographic screen that projected from the worktable. "I've made plenty of outfits for the resort's décor."

The holograph displayed a generic image of a human male. Then, with the touch of a few buttons, an outfit appeared on the model.

At first the model still seemed naked until Pet took a closer look.

"That's not a swimsuit. It barely counts as a piece of string."

Ochaid gestured at the small triangle of cloth over the model's crotch. "It covers all parts necessary for human male modesty."

Pet also gestured at the image, his hand accidentally going right through the holograph. "Modesty is not the word I'd use for that."

Bug circled the holographic image, getting a good look at the model's exposed ass, saved from true nudity only by a barely visible thong. "What's the problem? It's a beach party. Most people will be showing up in as little as possible. A lot of species don't wear clothes at all. You'll be one of the more-dressed people there."

"Well, yeah, but…" How could he explain clothes to someone who didn't wear them? It wasn't about comparing himself to other people. The last time someone other than his trio saw him so undressed was when DPS agents examined him. He didn't want to be reminded of those invasive touches during an event that was supposed to be fun.

Ochaid didn't wear clothes either but working with fabric apparently gave her insight to his problem. "How about this?"

She held up a swath from behind the worktable. The material couldn't be called fabric. It resembled woven netting made from thread-thin strands of black nebula diamonds.

When Pet worked up enough courage to touch the netting, it was even lighter than he expected. "I can't afford this."

Technically he couldn't afford anything. He didn't have his own money. Anything he bought would be charged to the room for his trio to pay. He already felt guilty for buying a basic swimsuit without their input. This would be too much.

When he tried to push the netting away, Ochaid pushed it back. "Not too expensive. It's fake."

Pet gave her a narrow look of suspicion. A difficult task when she had so many eyes to meet. "Then why were you keeping it behind the desk?"

Some of Ochaid's eyes stayed on him, but most of her attention moved to the holographic screen. "Sometimes stupid guests bring their kids but don't watch them. Can't keep the delicate merchandise out on the floor. Now, look at this."

The model on the screen still wore the thong swimsuit but with an additional cover-up made from the diamond netting. Minimal stitching held it closed at the model's solar plexus. Other than that, it hung open to show off the model's chest and the swimsuit beneath. Draping loops of slightly larger diamonds formed sleeves that ended at elbow length.

It didn't actually conceal anything but gave the illusion of wearing more clothes.

A number appeared below the model.

Surely it had to be a joke. Pet waited for the number to double, or even triple.

"That's the price?"

Ochaid held up the delicate netting again. "I'll make this outfit for that price."

After being offered such a bargain, Pet could do nothing but agree. Continuing to refuse would only insult the person trying to help him. "I guess I'll take it, then."

"Good." Ochaid nodded, and her whole body bobbed. "Over here, now. I need measurements." Without giving Pet time to change his mind, she ushered him to a corner of the shop and onto a short pedestal. "Stand here. Arms out—no, not like that— stand natural. Now don't move."

The pose, relaxed but with each part of his body on easy display, felt like being proper décor once again. However, he found he didn't mind Ochaid's attention in this situation.

Two of her arms pulled a measuring tape from seemingly nowhere, and even more arms proceed to run the tape over each of his limbs and around his body in multiple places. Nowhere went unmeasured, more than seemed necessary for a simple cover-up.

"Why are you doing this?" He stared into her nearest set of eyes, which were several times larger than his own. Each eye bore three pupils, so it was obvious when she met his gaze.

"Need measurements to make your outfit. Otherwise, it won't fit right."

"No, I mean, why are you helping me like this? Even if those diamonds are fake, a garment like this should still cost more than you're charging. I doubt it even covers the materials."

Her arms never stopped, but her eyes flickered in Bug's direction.

While she waited, Bug had wandered to the other side of the store, idly looking through the fabrics. Too far away to overhear them.

Still, Ochaid lowered her voice so it was more vibration than sound. "She comes in every year, excited for the Dust Party. Always alone. This is the first time she's shown up with a friend. I want this year to go better for her."

Pet crossed his arms, staring down the Q'od that had stopped measuring him. "Are you trying to bribe me to be friends with Bug?"

Ochaid's measuring tape resumed its movement. "If you have a good time, she's more likely to have a good time. Now, you wait while I make outfit for you. Will only take a minute. Not much to work with."

Pet stepped off the pedestal now that they no longer needed the ruse of measuring him to keep from being overheard. "I'll assume you're talking about the fabric and not me."

Ochaid neither confirmed nor denied his assumption, but he swore he felt her smirking at him even though she had no visible mouth.

True to her word, the outfit didn't take long to make, and a few minutes later, Bug and Pet left the store with their purchases safely boxed in decorative packaging. They boarded the trolley together, but Bug disembarked after only a few stops. Before parting ways, she gave Pet directions to her apartment so they could meet later.

Then Pet rode the trolley to the top of the island, surrounded by other guests but alone.

Two décor still stood at the entrance to the elevator lobby. The building sat at the peak of the island like its architectural crown, and they were the crown jewels.

Pet straightened his own clothing as he passed.

They might be worth more than him on the décor market, but at least he was free to go where he wished.

Or maybe not.

The private elevator to their suite needed a special key. Without it, he was stranded in the lobby.

Now what?

Chapter Nine

After

Cold air blew through the vent, reminding Pet of the ice somewhere above his head. How far below ground was he now? The lab seemed endless.

In the room beyond the vent, flame-colored feathers contrasted with dull metal. There was barely enough space in the cage for Xavis, and his wings pressed against his back to avoid touching the sides. Electricity snapped at him whenever he got too close.

Pet couldn't see Xavis very well from inside the vent, but he could tell the Scaacax's eyes lacked their usual fire. In fact, everything about him looked dull. Even his feathers had lost their healthy sheen.

Three Iknox stood in the room with the cage.

At first Pet thought he was looking at Tradius in triplicate. The Iknox clustered around the cage all looked identical. Except their posture was more slumped in the shoulders, and they spoke with a slightly different cadence.

These were members of Tradius's family. Iknox reproduced asexually, so parents and children always looked identical. Entire cities could share the same face.

Unlike Tradius, these people wore clothing of much lower quality. The cloth was rough and crudely stitched. A simple tie at the shoulder maintained the toga style. Each outfit would have been indistinguishable from the others if not for the different colors.

It was the clothing of a servant. These individuals stood far below both Tradius and Yaivin in the family line.

The three servants never noticed Pet as he unscrewed the grate, too busy trading complaints.

"How long do we have to watch this thing?" The most animated of the servants wore red and waved their arms as they spoke. Their lavender skin flushed to a dark eggplant color.

Pet had never seen an eggplant. Due to its name, he had once imagined eggplant to be a white color. His incredulous surprise when he found out it was actually a shade of purple had sent his trio into hysterics.

The second servant wore green. Standing closest to the cage, he leered between the bars. "You think its eyes are like that on purpose, or is it just an ugly side effect?"

The servant wearing red shuddered. "I don't know, but it's freaking me out."

Their conversation hit a lull just as Pet detached the grate.

Metal scraped against metal.

He froze and held the grate in mid-air with shaking hands. Had he given himself away?

Thankfully, the servants remained unaware, but familiar glowing eyes turned his direction.

Xavis's wings bristled when he saw Pet hanging halfway out the vent.

Quickly, Pet raised a finger to his lips in a plea for silence. He didn't know what the servants were talking about. Xavis's eyes might be a little strange, with their lack of pupil or iris, but they were a lovely purple. Pet once looked up a name for that color. They shifted constantly between violet, orchid, and amethyst. All much better names than eggplant.

Those eyes looked between Pet and the servants, Xavis's feathers bristling even more.

Conversation picked up again when the third servant, wearing yellow, finally chimed in. "Doesn't matter what it looks like. We just need to keep it here until First-in-line is done."

Pet carefully pulled the grate into the safety of the vent as the servant in red started shouting again.

"But why're we even still here? This should've taken, like, an hour at most."

The servant wearing green looked away from Xavis to whisper harshly under their breath. "Hush. If someone hears you questioning First-in-line, you'll get us all disowned."

The servant wearing red scoffed. "I'm not questioning anything, but it's obvious this wasn't the plan." The three fell into quiet discussion of what they thought had gone wrong while at the same time denying anything was wrong.

Pet would've loved to listen in on the strange contradictory conversation but was too worried about Xavis.

With attention off him, Xavis looked up at Pet and tapped his chest in a familiar signal. *Are you okay?*

Pet signaled back that he was fine. It was mostly accurate.

Xavis asked the same question with the addition of the hand signal for Desmodian.

The meaning was clear, but Pet couldn't answer, and signaled back that he didn't know. He hadn't seen the Dhen'in since their initial capture.

The drooping of Xavis's wings made Pet want to embrace him, especially when a few feathers drifted too close to the cage and electricity crackled along the bars.

Xavis jumped and pulled his wings tight.

The servants spared him a glance, but Xavis kept his eyes away from both them and Pet. Even after the three returned to their conversation, he waited an extra moment before looking back up.

Then flashed a single hand signal.

Brog.

Pet hesitated. How should he answer? Did Xavis want to know Brog's condition, or was it some sort of warning? Claiming that Brog was all right seemed dishonest, even if technically accurate. At least it was true when Pet saw him just before escaping the airship.

All he could do was shrug and turn their gestured conversation to a different question.

You. How?

He didn't know the signals needed for a more detailed question, so he supplemented with a game of charades and mimed breaking out of a cage.

Xavis made a frantic series of gestures.

Other than Brog and Desmodian's names, Pet didn't recognize anything. His trio had just started teaching him their system of nonverbal communication, and those lessons had focused on emergencies. Anything else went right over his head.

Xavis's hands slowed and fell to his side.

Pet shrugged again. The other members of his trio would've easily communicated with Xavis. He'd seen it many times. Whole conversations passed between them with a few taps of a finger and a pointed look.

However, Pet was the one hanging from the vent, so Pet was the one Xavis had to rely on.

The Scaacax looked again between Pet and the gossiping servants.

Pet could almost see the wheels turning in his head, even from a distance.

Xavis tried again, this time sticking to simple gestures. He started with the symbol for his own name, then repeated Pet's charade of breaking out of the cage. Then he made the gesture for Desmodian and Brog, followed by slashing a finger across his throat. That last one was not part of their system, but the meaning was obvious.

Xavis. Free. Brog and Desmodian. Dead.

Pet wanted to smack himself across the head. Why hadn't he thought of that? Freeing any of the trio alone risked Tradius killing the others.

Yet Xavis wasn't done. He looked Pet in the eye and gave one final gesture.

Follow.

What did that mean? Pet frantically shook his head and waved his hands as if pushing away an unwanted advance.

Xavis merely held up a finger, asking for Pet to wait. Then he called out to the servants. "A bunch of little gossipmongers, aren't you? No wonder your First-in-line can't get anything done."

The servants fell silent.

The one wearing red approached the cage while the other two hung back. "Caged birds should hold their tongue."

Xavis shrugged and stepped closer until he was eye to eye with the servant, just out of reach behind the electrified bars. "So should lowly servants. And based on the color of your cloth, you're about as low as they come."

The two fell into a staring contest.

Xavis's eyes briefly flashed with their usual spark.

The servant flinched. "Fuck this." He retrieved a long pole from the corner of the room.

Still inside the cage, Xavis stood tall and crossed his arms with a smirk. "Servants are supposed to be silent, yet you're all talk. What does that make you?"

The servant in red stormed back to the cage, pole in hand. The other servants tried to stop him, but he batted them away. "What would you know about it?"

Purple eyes narrowed and flashed again. "Yellow and green over there should outrank you, yet they defer to everything you say like they're used to taking your orders. That cloth you wear is also newer than theirs, yet you all look about the same age. You were recently demoted. What happened? Did your temper get the best of you? It doesn't take three people to watch one prisoner in a cage. This isn't guard duty. They're here to babysit you."

The servant in red broke free from the others and shoved the pole between the bars. It struck Xavis square in the chest with an electric spark.

Xavis collapsed, screaming and beating his wings as his body spasmed.

Pet gripped the edge of the vent so tightly he would have bent the metal if he was strong enough. Was this planned, or had something gone wrong?

The servants wearing green and yellow pulled their

companion away by the arms.

"What're you doing?"

"We were ordered to keep the captive safe. Not kill it."

Sighing heavily, the servant in red retracted the pole.

Xavis grabbed the end with one hand and yanked it back. The servant slammed face-first into the bars of the cage, and Xavis's laughter sounded like a hiss of leaking air.

The wounded servant remained on the floor, clutching his nose. He moaned and cursed through the thick black blood dripping between his fingers.

Xavis raised the end of the pole like a gentleman tipping the brim of their hat. "There. Now you can dye your cloth black and pretend you're at the front of the family line." He sounded weak, with an audible wheeze in his voice, but even that couldn't diminish his arrogance as he stared down at the servant on the floor.

The amazing moment left Pet awestruck, but it didn't last long.

The servant in green stepped over their companion and took hold of the pole still sticking between the bars. "Let's see what color we'll get out of you."

The pole struck Xavis again. He screamed and twitched on the floor, unable to escape. Large wings filled the cage, sparking electricity as they thrashed against the bars.

It only lasted a few moments, but to Pet it felt like years. Stuck in the confines of the vent, he could do nothing to stop Xavis's pain.

The pole was finally removed. On shaking limbs, Xavis curled into a tight ball, as far from the sides of the cage as possible.

The servant in green tossed the pole aside. "There. That'll shut you up."

At his feet, the servant in yellow helped their injured comrade to stand. "Come on. Let's get you cleaned up."

The pair left, with the one in red leaning against the one in yellow.

Only the servant in green remained but seemed content to lean against the far wall and ignore Xavis now that he had gotten the last word.

The pole lay forgotten on the floor.

Pet would've paid it no attention, but Xavis looked up just enough to catch his eye and pointed at the pole.

A single orange feather clung to the end.

Unnoticed by anyone but Xavis and Pet, the feather rose as if stirred by an unfelt wind. It floated up to the vent and balanced on the tip of its quill in front of Pet's face.

Purple energy danced along the edges of the feather.

Xavis stirred in his cage, flashing a signal to Pet without catching the servant's attention.

Follow.

The feather flipped a quick circle before coming to rest in midair again.

Pet looked at the feather, then at Xavis, then back at the feather. How could he just leave when Xavis was hurt? Unable to fight, or use his Phazer power, the other male would be completely helpless.

Xavis repeated the signal again with more force.

Follow.

Closing his eyes and swallowing his frustration,

Pet nodded.

That was all Xavis needed. As soon as Pet agreed, he lay on the floor of the cage and huddled in the protection of his wings.

There wasn't enough room in the vent to turn around, so Pet crawled backward. The feather followed him. When he reached an intersection, he flipped around in the right direction. Retracing the path he'd taken to get there, Pet turned to the left, but the feather slipped in front of his face. It sparked again, getting his attention, then floated to a different branch of the vent.

"Not yet. I have to go back for Bug first."

The feather hovered unmoving, but Pet refused to back down.

He was arguing with a feather. This had to be the strangest thing he'd ever done, and he couldn't even appreciate the hilarity of the situation.

The feather turned another circle, and the purple spark faded. It followed Pet through the vents without getting in his way again.

Climbing back up the vertical shaft he'd shimmied down proved to be a nearly insurmountable challenge. His feet struggled to find purchase on the smooth metal. More than once, he slipped and plummeted several feet before catching himself. His heart beat an irregular rhythm in his ears when he finally managed to pull himself out the top of the vent unharmed.

All the while, the feather hovered just over his shoulder.

Pet's path through the vents remained dangerous but unhindered, right up until he reached the display room full of spaceship technology.

It had been empty earlier, but now he was met with

the sound of unwanted voices.

"Is this what we're looking for?"

The voice had the same cadence as Tradius's but lacked the sharp edges, so probably another servant.

A second identical voice followed the first. "Something like that. Yeah. That's a model of what it's supposed to look like, but the technology was still being developed when the lab shut down."

Pet pressed close to the grate. As much as he wanted to know what they were talking about, he didn't dare get closer. It would be impossible to slip out of the vent into the room without being spotted. He needed to find another way back to Bug. The mystery of what Tradius was looking for would go unanswered.

For now.

He backed up and tried to remember the blueprint Bug showed him. They had plotted several routes through the vents, just in case, but there hadn't been time to memorize them all. Pet stopped and ran his finger through the dust inside the vent, drawing what he could remember of the blueprint.

If his memory was correct, there should be another way to connect with the path he needed if he backed up and turned left. From there he would need to travel the length of several rooms and turn right twice to circle back around.

For luck, Pet drew a circle in the dust and slammed his fist in the middle. It was something he had seen his trio do before, a ship-dweller gesture to ward off the ill will of the universe. Right now, Pet could use the universe's help.

Crawling backward through the vent made his skin tingle with a sense of vulnerability. If anything snuck up behind him, he wouldn't know until he literally rear-ended the danger.

Xavis's feather sent sparks bouncing off dull metal, lighting the gloomy confines of the vent.

Pet sighed and shook his head at the feather. "Don't mock me."

It was probably his imagination, but the feather stopped sparking and rested on his shoulder as if keeping lookout behind him.

Luckily the intersection wasn't too far away. He managed to make the turn and crawl forward again. Pet peered through each grate he passed, counting the rooms. He needed to turn after the third room, or he would end up in a completely different part of the vent system.

The first two rooms contained broken equipment, mangled beyond recognition and mostly free of dust, as if recently tossed aside.

In the third room, another cage stood alone. Electricity buzzed along its bars, just like the one holding Xavis, and the blue-white glow illuminated the slouched figure trapped inside.

Chapter Ten

Before

The sound of ocean waves couldn't reach Pet at the top of the island, but the smell still found him. Half an hour passed as he sat on the low wall overlooking the cliff edge. From this vantage, he could see the shadow of another island on the horizon, the fourth in this chain of five.

Out of all the people on those islands, were there any décor like him, halfway between object and person?

Probably not.

"Pet, what're you doing out here?"

While Pet had been lost in thought, watching sunlight tap-dancing on the waves, Desmodian entered the lobby unnoticed. He stood in the entryway rather than the elevators. It seemed no one had returned to their suite since the fight.

Desmodian approached with the hesitancy of someone not certain of their welcome, barely making a sound as the handle of his hammer tapped the floor with each step.

Pet closed the distance between them, rushing to Desmodian's side. "Where have you been?" He regretted the question the moment he spoke. It sounded like an accusation.

Desmodian transferred his hammer to the other hand so he could wrap an arm around Pet. "Walked around for a while. Found a bar that's open all night. Just needed some time to think. Why're you sitting out here?"

Just beyond Desmodian's shoulder Pet could see the décor posted at the entryway. He remembered standing in their position, eavesdropping on people's conversations, and wanting to roll his eyes at their drama. Hopefully, the pair were too far away to hear them.

With one hand he gave an unenthusiastic gesture toward the elevator. "I couldn't get into the room. The elevator needs a key."

Desmodian flicked his tail, mimicking an irritated cat. "Have you been out here all night?"

Pet pressed close to Desmodian's side, mindful of the frill along the underside of the Dhen'in's arm. The partial embrace gave Pet a sense of stability, and he pulled the room key from Desmodian's pocket. "No. I went to the *Vanguard*. Xavis was there."

The elevator dinged when Pet swiped the key over the sensor, and the doors opened.

When they reached the suite, elevator music was replaced by the much more soothing sound of running water.

Desmodian left Pet to search out a drink from the well-stocked kitchen.

Pet scowled. Alcohol didn't seem like an appropriate response. It wasn't going to fix anything. At least Desmodian wasn't drunk. He'd seen Desmodian drunk plenty of times, and it always made the Dhen'in more affectionate. This silent stoicism was an entirely sober reaction.

Setting aside his package from the clothing shop, Pet squared his shoulders and joined Desmodian in the kitchen. He chose a stool at the counter that fit human proportions and fortuitously set him right across from Desmodian. "You need to tell me what's going on."

With a heavy sigh Desmodian reached to refill his already-empty glass.

Pet grabbed the alcohol bottle and set it on the other side of the counter. "Des, please. I'm in the dark here. Xavis told me some things, but nothing about you and Brog. That's for you to tell me. So what's going on with you?"

Without a single word, Desmodian conveyed an entire journey of emotions through movement. He propped his elbows on the table, slouched to run his hands through his hair, then leaned back in the chair and looked up at the ceiling.

His tail sounded like a wirehair brush cleaning a dirty pan as it swept the floor, quickly at first but gradually slowing.

When it fell silent, he sat up straight. "I'm not a very sexual person. That probably sounds ridiculous to you. But, Pet, you don't realize how special you are."

The alcohol bottle took a dive off the table when Pet leaned back and forgot its place near his elbow.

He caught it before it hit the floor, but some of its contents splashed onto the stone. Not wanting to stop the conversation to clean up, he placed the bottle back onto the table and tucked his feet on the stool to keep them out of the puddle. "It doesn't make sense to me, but I don't know all your experiences. I'll listen to them if you want to tell me."

Though he didn't have eyes, from the angle of his body, it was obvious Desmodian watched the bottle. In the end, he chose to leave it alone and ran his hands through his hair again. "I grew up most of my life thinking I was incapable of sexual feelings. I never felt the same desires as my peers. My family comes from a culture obsessed with children and continuing the bloodline. They desperately wanted me to bed a woman. Any woman. Didn't even matter if we were married, although they did try to arrange a marriage for me. I was resigned to doing what I had to, but the more they pushed me to it…"

Desmodian slouched, eyeing the bottle in his own way again.

Pet finished the sentence for him. "The more they pushed you to it, the more it turned you off."

Short but sharp nails clicked against the tabletop as Desmodian restlessly tapped his fingers. "Exactly. It stayed that way until my parents hosted a party for my birthday. I had finally reached my majority, so it was a big event. Not that they needed an excuse to show off. I barely knew any of the guests, so I was shocked when one of them propositioned me.

"This person came from a very xenophobic culture, so having sex with an alien was the ultimate taboo for them. That was the appeal. It was the first time I'd ever felt turned on. We slept together that night. It wasn't even that great, but it helped me find my sexuality. I don't care what my partner looks like. I don't have a physical type. What interests me is when someone enjoys doing what they're not supposed to do. Does that make sense?"

Pet's gaze drifted to the nearest window. He stared

out at the beach, seeing neither sand nor water. A few more pieces of the puzzle that was his trio fell into place. "It does. If you're attracted to relationships that are taboo, then you'll never be attracted to Brog or Xavis. There's nothing forbidding them."

Desmodian raised his empty glass in an equally empty toast. "That's the crux of it. No matter how much I love them, I'll never feel anything sexual for them. It would already be difficult for us if we did try. To put it in the crudest terms, sex may not have to include penetration, but we do prefer it, and none of us can take that role."

It was midday. The beach outside the window shone bright and sunny.

However, Pet saw a different beach. His eyes filled with an image of white sand stained red by the setting sun as hurtful words struck their mark. "Based on Brog's reaction, I take it he wants a sexual relationship."

"He did, but he accepted that it wouldn't happen. Especially since Xavis wasn't interested either." Desmodian stopped speaking abruptly and shifted in his chair.

The weight of the Dhen'in's stare pressed against Pet like a hole drilling right through him. Knowing his trio as he did, he could guess Desmodian's concern. "Because you're both taller than him. He told me."

Desmodian's posture relaxed. "We decided to bring a fourth into the relationship. Finding someone small enough for Xavis but able to handle Brog was hard enough. Trying to find someone I'm also attracted to was nearly impossible. We got really lucky with you."

Before Pet could come up with a response, Desmodian leaned across the table and snatched the alcohol bottle. Instead of pouring another drink, he stood and stored it away in a cabinet. "This may be an old argument, but it's time to put it to rest."

"How're you going to do that?" At the last moment Pet remembered the puddle on the floor and hopped over it as he stood from the stool.

Desmodian offered him a hand. "First I have to find him. He wasn't on the ship, right?"

Pet flinched, accidentally pulling away from Desmodian. No, Brog hadn't been on the ship, but Pet knew where he'd spent the night.

Of course, Desmodian noticed his reaction.

"What is it?"

There was no use hiding the truth. Even if the Dhen'in weren't so perceptive, Pet sucked at lying. Taking a deep breath, he told Desmodian about his last interaction with Brog, ending with Brog going off with Yaivin.

Would Desmodian be upset? Pet was at the time. He still was, to be honest with himself.

It turned out, no, Desmodian wasn't upset. He laughed a little, in the not-really-happy way that irritated Pet. Then he headed out of the kitchen. "I'm not surprised, though it'll make things more challenging."

Pet followed him. Instead of going out the main door, they moved deeper into the suite. "I thought we were going to find Brog?"

"We are." Desmodian didn't stop when he reached the master bedroom and made a direct line for the curtain of water blocking access to the private beach.

Or as direct as possible when one had to circumnavigate the streams running through the floor to get anywhere in the suite.

The waterfall parted at a touch to the hidden switch. "If Brog is with Yaivin, that means he's in the other waterfall suite. Without a key, we can't even get past the elevator to bang on the door. We'll have to find another way to him."

Past the waterfall curtain and out onto the private beach, Pet's sandals sank into the sand. They were mostly decorative, with gold hardware and straps wrapping up to his knees. Yet, like most of his shoes, they had sturdy soles that helped keep his balance on the shifting terrain.

Natural coral walls divided the private beach from the public one, with a door that only opened from the inside.

In the public area, hundreds of feet had trampled the sun-bleached sand into a firm surface. At the hottest hour of the day, guests enjoying the beach gravitated toward the cool ocean water.

Pet and Desmodian stayed to the other side of the beach, closer to the cliff. Its sheer face shaded them from the sun. Pet craned his neck to look straight up at the peak cutting a dark wedge against the royal-blue sky.

Just barely visible at the top of the cliff sat the throne-like building. It gave the island its name and housed the lobby of elevators as well as a few private suites. Somewhere up there, a pair of décor stood quiet, making Starthrone a little more beautiful with their presence.

Rows upon rows of uniform holes decorated the

face of the cliff from top to bottom. At a distance they didn't look very big. Yet the ones closer to the ground revealed the holes to be balcony windows cut directly into the rock. Each one represented a room housing any number of guests.

Two sets of footprints trailed behind them in the sand, one slightly bigger than the other and separated by a line of circular imprints from Desmodian's hammer. While Pet's footprints left an even impression, Desmodian's pressed deeper in the ball of the foot than the heel, as if ready to spring forward any moment.

Desmodian was holding back, maintaining a pace Pet could easily match. Was Pet getting in the way? His trio kept saying they were lucky to find him, but how could that be true when he was keeping them from their reconciliation?

"Des?" The question left his mouth before he could second-guess himself. "Xavis mentioned that you tried including a fourth before. What happened?"

It might be rude, but he had to know. Twice before, someone stood in his place. Twice before, something had gone wrong. Was he already on the same doomed path?

The hammer passed between Desmodian's hands, so it no longer separated them. "The first time it was a spur-of-the-moment idea. I wasn't particularly attracted to them, but I liked them well enough, and they had chemistry with Brog and Xavis. It was fine with me, but they kept insisting that not wanting to have sex with them meant I didn't like them, so eventually they left.

"Then we decided to try and find someone I was attracted to. It took time, but we came across someone who'd run away from their landowner family to live as a ship-dweller. But Brog was too much for them physically, and they eventually grew tired of the ship-dweller life. After that we gave up on the idea for a while until we ran into you."

A cloud passed over the sun. The cliff's shadow turned a little darker around them.

It distracted Pet enough that he didn't immediately notice when Desmodian stopped walking, and he had to backtrack a few steps. "Des, what's wrong?"

A hand covered in green scales cupped Pet's cheek and tipped his face until he stared directly at Desmodian's mask.

"Most people assume décor aren't even capable of having sex." Desmodian's voice was quiet, contemplative, as he stroked a thumb along Pet's cheek. "I'll admit, I was one of those people. After we saw you that first night at dinner, Brog immediately looked up the biology of humans to see if sex with one was even possible. He was so excited when he found that it was. Back then I thought he was pursuing something impossible and got into an argument with him."

The wind changed direction, and the scent of the ocean surrounded them. Surprisingly, it wasn't as strong as on their private beach, smelling mostly of salt and missing the bitter brine.

Where was Desmodian going with this story? Pet couldn't see the end of the conversation, but he could fill the unspoken gaps. "Décor aren't supposed to have sex, so when you saw me with Brog and Xavis, that's when I became attractive to you."

A child screamed somewhere in the direction of the water. It would have sounded distressed, but it trailed off into laughter at the end.

So many strangers gathered to enjoy the beach at the same time, but Pet and Desmodian didn't even look at them.

Desmodian's hammer remained standing on its own when the Dhen'in let it go. He held Pet's face with both hands and pressed their foreheads together, bone against skin. "You're right. That first night, when I saw you doing the most rebellious thing décor could do, and enjoying it so enthusiastically, I wanted to take part. It wasn't even about the sex. I desperately wanted to help you break that taboo. For the first time it felt like Brog, Xavis, and I were completely aligned. As if you'd provided a bridge we'd been missing."

"Like you're the planets and I'm the space between you."

"Yes. Exactly." Desmodian sighed but didn't relax. "Hearing it out loud, I realize how much expectation that puts on you. It's selfish. You shouldn't have to solve our problems."

He tried to pull away, but Pet grabbed his hands and kept them in place. "It's not about *have to*. I don't *have to* do anything. I want to. Isn't that what it means to care about someone?"

A wave crashed, and a child screamed again.

Desmodian kissed him. It was brief, and when it ended, they remained close enough for their lips to brush. "For someone who doesn't know much, how do you know so much?"

At such proximity, Pet saw nothing but Desmodian's mask. Hopefully the Dhen'in's crossed senses would let him feel Pet's answering smirk. "I think it's called learning."

No one could have missed Desmodian's laugh. It

probably even caught the attention of people down by the water. "Okay, smartass. No need to brag."

Pet shoved him away, still smiling. "If I'm a smartass, it's because you taught me to be."

Desmodian barely flinched against Pet's shove, and even that was probably for show. "And we couldn't be prouder. Now, come on. Let's go find our wayward Ocan."

He turned to pick up his hammer but stopped. and looked back at Pet, with a strange twist to his mouth. It seemed as if the words he intended to say had tangled behind his teeth and he was chewing on the knot.

"This isn't..." It took a few false starts for Desmodian to find the right words, and when he did, they weren't as fluent as usual. "When I talk about our first night together...it's not... Sexual attraction may have been what started everything, but it takes more than sex to keep a relationship going. We wouldn't have lasted this long if our relationship with you was only about sex. Understand?"

Pet nodded. "I think I get what you're saying."

Maybe Pet was getting better at lying.

After his trio spent so much time explaining how he was the only one they were all sexually compatible with, what else could it be about? He wanted to ask, but Desmodian already looked uncomfortable as he struggled with words. Pet didn't want to make it harder for him.

"Good." Desmodian nodded, but it seemed to be more for himself than for Pet. "I just wanted to clear that up before we tackled a more unpleasant conversation."

"I'm sure it'll be fine."

Was that a lie as well? It was hard to tell. Pet hoped Desmodian and Brog would settle their argument but doubted it would be easy. Maybe it wouldn't count as a lie so long as everything turned out all right in the end.

It took longer than expected for them to reach the other side of the public beach. Guests with ground-floor balconies watched them with wary eyes as they passed, but no one stopped them. Still, an hour of the already short day was lost to the journey from one side to the other.

At least they were in the shade the whole time. During their walk, Pet realized why the public beach didn't smell as strongly as the private one. There was no seaweed. On the private beach, vegetation accumulated at the edge of the shore and decayed in the heat of the sun. With so many people running around the public beach, it had no chance to build up.

How strange, to think that paying more for something could make it worse.

By the time they reached the end of the public beach, all thoughts of seaweed left his mind. He was done with sand and sun and longed for a cooler environment. They reached another private coral wall with a single locked door.

Pet looked up at Desmodian. "Can you get it?"

Desmodian bent to inspect the door. "You mean pick the lock? If I was Xavis, probably. He's better with the tech stuff. However, I may have another solution."

He ran a hand over the door, tapping the smooth surface like a woodpecker searching for prey. Halfway down he stopped, right where a lock would be. His fingers tensed, and his hand rotated as if turning a handle that didn't exist. A thin circle traced the same spot on the door, burning right into the surface and glowing a shade of green only found at the center of a copper fire. When Desmodian pulled his hand back, he drew out a perfectly cylindrical piece of the door that had been punched all the way through.

With a flourish, Desmodian held up the cylinder, showing off the severed mechanism inside, and opened the door with a push. "It's not as subtle, but it works."

The removed lock was carelessly tossed away while Desmodian's other hand clutched tight to his hammer. The weapon flashed green, and Desmodian relaxed.

To Pet's relief, no alarms went off when they stepped through the door. It was only a hotel room, but he'd never broken in anywhere before.

Hopefully, it wouldn't become a regular occurrence.

This private beach looked just like their own. The sand remained undisturbed, except for a single track of footprints leading from the waterfall to the edge of the beach. Several sets stacked on top of each other, as if someone had traveled the same path multiple times.

The handle of Desmodian's hammer shot out and kept Pet in the shadow of the doorway. "We're not alone."

An Iknox stood at the edge of the ocean, bending to dip their hands in the water. They looked the same as Yaivin and Tradius, but instead of a black toga, they wore navy cloth. The color difference would have been hard to judge in a dimly lit room but stood out starkly in bright daylight.

Pet pushed Desmodian's hammer away. "It's just a servant."

Desmodian frowned. "How can you tell? Tradius or Yaivin could have changed clothes."

"Trust me. I've spent years watching people. Servitude and leadership sit differently on a person's shoulders. A servant and a master don't walk the same."

The navy-clad servant stood and held a vial of water up to the light. It had a complicated cap, with a wire sticking down into the water.

Pet leaned closer to Desmodian. "What's he doing with the ocean water?"

Desmodian frowned and whispered, barely loud enough for even Pet to hear. "Looks like he's testing for something. There's a dial on the cap showing some sort of measurement. Although I don't know what they'd be looking for."

"What about heavy water? You said there was a lot more in this ocean."

"Possible, but why? Heavy water can be found on a lot of planets. Why look for it here?"

For that Pet could only shrug. "What's heavy water even used for?"

"I don't know much off the top of my head." Desmodian thought for a moment.

During that time, the servant tucked the vial in their pocket and hurried back up the beach, following the trodden path in the sand to the waterfall.

"Xavis would know more. The only things I can think of are medical uses and observing magnetic fields. I'm not sure why the Vels family would be interested in either of these things, though, so it's probably something else."

A section of the waterfall parted, and the servant

disappeared inside just before the water closed again.

Desmodian waved Pet forward to follow the servant's path. They stepped carefully over wet rocks as they approached the spot at the base of the waterfall where the servant entered. The tips of Desmodian's fingers dipped into the water. Another flash of green, and the water froze into an icy archway, giving them dry passage to the room beyond.

Thankfully, it wasn't the master bedroom. Knowing Brog slept with someone else was bad enough. Seeing for himself would have been too much for Pet.

The waterfall opened to a sitting room. The servant was still there, standing with his back to the water curtain. He opened a large case holding a dozen identical vials of water and added the new one to the collection.

Using the servant's distraction to their advantage, Desmodian let the ice melt, hiding their entrance to the suite. He then slipped into one of the chairs, slouching and throwing a leg over the armrest as if he'd been there awhile.

Pet copied him, perching on the other arm of the chair.

Barely a moment later, the servant turned around and jumped at the sight of them. "What're you doing here?"

Desmodian didn't bother pretending to look at the servant, instead twirling his hammer on its end and letting it dig into the stone floor. "We're here to speak with Brog."

At the mention of Brog's name, the servant's eyes turned shifty, and he fidgeted on his feet. "You're mistaken, sir. There's no one with that name here." His voice was surprisingly steady, but he didn't look at Desmodian or Pet.

"Really?" Desmodian went through the motions of *looking* at Pet. "Maybe we were wrong. Though we should probably check, just to be sure."

Pet shrugged and nodded. "We did come all this way."

Patting Pet's thigh, Desmodian stood and headed for the doorway. "Just a quick look around should do."

"No." The Iknox moved between Desmodian and the rest of the suite. "You don't have to do that. Just stay right there, and I'll tell our Second-in-line that you're here. He can help you."

The servant's blue toga flapped behind him as he hurried out of the room.

A moment passed, and then another. Desmodian looked back at Pet with a grin. "Well, he didn't say we couldn't look around. Shall we?"

"It would be faster than waiting."

They left the sitting room together.

It looked the same as their own suite, but in reverse. The same bioluminescent lights illuminated the same stone walls and organic architecture. Even the streams cutting through the floor followed the same pattern, but in opposite directions.

Unlike their suite, however, furniture of an obviously different design cluttered the open layout. As he and Desmodian moved through a dining room, Pet trailed his finger over the back of an ornate chair. "Did Yaivin bring his own furniture on vacation?"

Pet never heard Desmodian's reply. He stopped abruptly, his hand dropping from the back of the chair to hang limply at his side.

Furniture and staff weren't the only things Yaivin brought. He'd also brought his own décor.

It was such an expected sight that Pet hadn't thought twice about the humans standing around the suite until he saw a familiar face.

"Three-One-Five-Five?"

He must be wrong. The décor who once stood beside him at his old Owner's estate couldn't be here. Yet the longer he looked the more familiar she became. The clothing was different—Mister Stiril would never have dressed them in so many overlapping layers—but her face was unmistakably the same.

"Three-One-Five-Five? What're you doing here?" He grabbed her shoulders, fighting off the urge to shake an answer out of her.

His recognition was not returned. Her eyes remained blank, looking through him rather than at him as she flinched away from his touch. "I am Four-One-Zero-Four."

Pet stumbled back and only Desmodian's hand on his shoulder kept him upright.

4104?

No, that was wrong. He distinctly remembered her number. When they both belonged to Mister Stiril, she had come immediately after him in line. He heard that number every day.

Desmodian led him from the dining room into an unused bedroom as Pet kept repeating the same question.

"Why is she here?" He felt the words coming out of his mouth but couldn't stop them. There was only one reason she would be standing here with a new number, unable to recognize him. She'd been resold, but why?

Desmodian's grip on him tightened. "Pet, we reported Stiril's arms-dealing. That can't have ended well for him."

"So he sold his décor?"

"Or they were seized when he was arrested. Either way, they're probably better off now. Stiril's actions were going to catch up with him eventually."

A deep breath calmed the last of Pet's shock. "You're right. I didn't want to be resold because I would lose my memories of you, but for most décor it's not the same. One item number is no different than another."

While this may be true, it felt like shallow consolation.

In the waterfall suite, only the bedrooms had walls on all sides and a door that closed. This made the bedrooms more soundproof than anywhere else. Yet, in the moment of silence after Pet's declaration, he caught the faint sound of voices from another room.

Desmodian dropped his hand from Pet's shoulder. "I know that voice." He wandered almost absently out the door.

Pet followed but stopped on the threshold when movement caught his attention.

A black pillar stood hidden in the shadowed corner of the room. It would've looked like a strange piece of furniture, or maybe a display of modern art, but it had moved. Like a stack of coins reshuffling themselves, it had been chaos one moment, then a smooth pillar the next.

One of Desmodian's books came to mind, full of

articles about organic species that looked artificial. Pet had been seeking information about Oculians, the species they rescued from poachers a few months ago. While flipping through the pages, he had passed an image of a simple black pillar with one word written beneath.

Schade.

That was it. The book provided no further information about the species other than a name and a single picture.

What was it doing here?

Could it have been hired by the Vels? If so, what for? Pet didn't know enough about the Schade species to guess.

Maybe he was wrong. Maybe there was a perfectly reasonable explanation for the Schade's presence. Yet Pet was well acquainted with the feeling of being watched. This living pillar watched him with intent.

The crash of something breaking in another room shook him from his stupor. Pet ran after Desmodian, and the sound of raised voices coming from the master bedroom chased all thoughts of the Schade from his mind.

Desmodian had already reached the door and stood outside looking more and more furious with every word the voices spoke.

"What are you doing here? I thought you were giving a presentation."

That was Yaivin's soft tone, barely audible through the door.

"You haven't left your suite since yesterday, immediately after running into…him. Did you really think I wouldn't notice?"

Tradius had the same voice as Yaivin, yet the sharp speech pattern made him sound like a completely different person.

Compared to the precise enunciation of the two Iknox, Brog's strong cadence was unmistakable. "Haven't broken any laws. Nothin' you can arrest me for this time."

Tradius's voice turned a few degrees colder. "I'm sure I could find something, although I doubt it would do much good. Your time in Unit 22 only seems to have aided you."

Surprisingly, it wasn't Brog that responded.

Instead, Yaivin pleaded for his father's silence. "Father, please, that's enough. Brog hasn't done anything wrong."

Desmodian's hand hovered over the handle to the door, indecision weighing on the corners of his mouth. Brog seemed to be handling himself against Tradius. Interference might make it worse.

Tradius laughed like he rehearsed it in a mirror. "I doubt he's as innocent of wrongdoing as he claims. I did my research on you and your friends, Brog. I wanted to know why you were no longer serving in Unit 22 like you should be. That commander of yours led you on a suicide mission. Got everyone but you three killed. After being MIA for months, you turn up and are awarded an honorable discharge. After that, a lot of interesting rumors started floating around. They say your ship flies as if the laws of physics don't apply to you, pulling off navigational feats that should be impossible. You've only remained free because no one has bothered to pay those rumors much attention, but eventually, I'll see you behind bars again."

The indecision on Desmodian's face melted, and he stormed through the door.

The master bedroom looked identical to the one back in their own suite, except for Brog and Yaivin standing on one side and Tradius standing on the other.

"Don't you dare threaten him." Desmodian stood in front of Brog, acting as a wall between him and Tradius.

So many different types of anger filled that single room. Anger had always seemed like a simple emotion. How could it come in so many shades of fury, shock, and hate? This wasn't one emotion masquerading as another, which Pet often struggled to understand. No, this was a glimpse into the true depths of an emotion. What had once seemed like a deep well was revealed to be a bottomless pit. Pet stood on the edge of something he couldn't fathom, steadily growing emptier and emptier. That bottomless pit also existed inside him somewhere, and he had nothing to fill it with.

Unable to think about it for long, Pet clung to the doorframe for support.

Brog stepped aside so he was no longer behind Desmodian, putting him closer to Yaivin. "Des? What're you doin' here?"

Desmodian stood perfectly still with arms slightly outstretched to expose as many of his scales as possible. It was the pose he took when he was focusing in multiple directions at once. "I was looking for you."

Stuttered sounds from Brog took several attempts to turn into words, and then even longer to turn into words that made sense. "What? Why? If you wanna talk, you could wait 'til I come back."

Before Desmodian could explain, Tradius

interrupted. "Ah, the commander. Or are you more of a jealous lover? Either way, you need to keep your man in line."

Brog bristled, literally. The spines along his shoulders raised, a defensive gesture as much as an aggressive one. If an opponent managed to hit him, they would hurt themselves in the process.

Unfortunately, Brog's aggression wasn't only focused on Tradius, but also against Desmodian.

The Dhen'in seemed to sense it as well. Although he kept his back to Brog, his posture tensed, and the spikes at the end of his tail opened like the teeth of a hunter's trap.

"Brog won't bother you, and you won't bother us. We'll all go our separate ways."

"Hey." Brog grabbed Desmodian's shoulder, forcing the Dhen'in to give him more than his back. "You can't just make that decision for me."

Desmodian tore his shoulder out of Brog's grip. "It's hardly a decision to leave the person threatening you alone. It's common sense, although you seem to be lacking it lately."

"Don't be surprised." Tradius shook his head like scolding a child. "Prostitutes have no self-preservation."

Brog shoved past Desmodian to grab Tradius by the collar of his toga. "Watch me snap your neck with one hand. Then talk about self-preservation."

The delicate cloth ripped.

Tradius's right leg gave out, and he stumbled into the wall, sliding to the floor. Gold glinted on his revealed skin. Just like Yaivin, he too bore an identifier fused into his chest, but unlike Yaivin, his took the shape of a diamond with inverted points.

Surprisingly steady hands clutched the split fabric together. "First prostitution, and now assault. That won't look good in front of a judge." He stood, favoring his right leg much more than usual.

Brog stepped forward as if to grab Tradius again. "You keep callin' me a prostitute. Startin' to think you're just mad you didn't hire me when you had the chance."

Desmodian jumped in front of Brog and pushed him away from Tradius. "Brog. That's not helping."

All four hands slapped away Desmodian's touch. "You're the one not helpin'."

From the safety of the doorway, Pet longed to cover his ears. It would be easier to block out the angry voices, but this was something that affected his trio. He couldn't just hide while people he cared about hurt each other even more.

Maybe, if he removed them from the emotions bouncing around that room, Brog and Desmodian could calm down and talk to each other.

The situation had devolved. Brog, Desmodian, and Tradius all argued at the same time, talking over each other and drowning out what the others said.

Out of everyone in the room, only Yaivin remained silent. In fact, he displayed no emotion at all. As soon as Desmodian showed up, he retreated to the corner of the room. His face remained blank and his posture slack. If not for his darting eyes, he would've looked like a life-sized doll.

It was the same response to conflict Pet had when he first joined the *Vanguard*. His trio hadn't argued often, but back then, even the smallest disagreement sent him into hiding.

Luckily, his trio noticed this reaction and refrained from disagreeing with each other in front of him. It had given him the time he needed to get comfortable in his new environment and build confidence in himself. Although he still hated hearing his trio argue, it no longer sent him into total shutdown.

Yaivin had evidently never been given such consideration.

They all needed to leave. Nothing good could come from staying here.

Bracing himself, Pet stepped into the room.

No one noticed him, too wrapped up in their argument to pay attention to anything else.

He resorted to pulling on Brog until the Ocan finally looked his direction.

The sight of Pet took Brog out of the fight. "Pet? What're you doin' here?"

Pet couldn't physically force Brog to move but kept pulling at his arm anyway. "Des and I came to talk to you. This isn't talking. We need to leave and talk properly."

Orange eyes flickered between Pet, Desmodian, Tradius, and Yaivin, unable to settle on one place. Then he nodded with a deep sigh. "Yeah. All right."

Without another glance at Pet or Desmodian, Brog headed for the waterfall. The Ocan disappeared through the natural curtain, sending a spray of water over the floor.

It took less effort for Pet to get Desmodian's attention.

Once he noticed Brog's absence, the Dhen'in immediately forgot Tradius and chased after the Ocan.

Pet followed them, but unlike Brog or Desmodian, he couldn't help looking back.

Still standing at the center of the room, Tradius watched them leave without a word. He stood with more weight on his left leg than his right, his face a stoic mask.

Iknox had black eyes. Not a wet glistening black like most black-eyed species, but rather a matte consistency, as if they had no light inside.

Those unsettling eyes turned Pet's way, giving him an appraising look that Pet was unfortunately used to. It was the kind of look he'd been subjected to every day under his previous Owner. Eyes that only saw him as an object and evaluated him for his price.

Based on Tradius's eyes, the older Iknox found him favorable, but not worth further consideration. They turned from him quickly, making him invisible once again.

Just over Tradius's shoulder, Yaivin still stood in the corner. The younger Iknox stared at the floor, hiding his own eyes.

Repressing a shudder, Pet darted through the waterfall to escape the room.

Both Desmodian and Brog passed through the waterfall without trouble, so the force that hit Pet's shoulders came as a surprise. It drove him into the ground, and he barely managed to pass through the falling water before he dropped to his knees.

Pet knelt on the stone, watching water drip from his hair as he caught his breath. "Good job, Pet. Very smooth exit."

Taking a moment to laugh at himself, Pet shook his soaked hair out of his eyes and stood. His wet clothes clung like they were trying to merge with his skin. The pale cloth turned transparent, putting his body on as much display as possible without being naked.

In a different scenario, the waterfall would be considered temperate, but against the warm air blowing off the beach, it felt cold by comparison.

Pet shivered and wrapped his arms around himself as he took off after Brog and Desmodian.

The pair had left the private beach by the time Pet caught them. They didn't stop once they were on the public beach and headed toward the cliff face.

Desmodian called after Brog, who led their little three-person caravan.

Brog looked back at them but continued stomping his way across the sand. "Not here."

They found a door in the side of the cliff that led to a series of normal elevators. Luckily, no one else was around to witness the strained atmosphere hanging over the three of them as they waited for an elevator, dripping water over the floor.

The silence lasted until they were alone, riding their way to the top of the island. Even the bland elevator music seemed quieter than normal. Pet stayed to the corner as Brog and Desmodian stood side by side, facing the same direction rather than each other.

Brog broke the silence first, speaking to Desmodian without looking at him. "Why'd you do that?"

Desmodian indulged the side-by-side conversation, his full-body vision allowing him to look at Brog from any angle. "I wanted to talk to you."

A twitch of Brog's double shoulders gave away his instinct to face Desmodian, which he stopped at the last moment. "I meant why'd you jump in like that? I can fight my own battles. Don't need you to save me."

The word "save" was said with such bitterness that even Pet flinched.

Desmodian's tail swayed, and his nails tapped a staccato rhythm against his hammer. "I wasn't going to stand aside while that bastard threatened you."

Brog twitched again as if he meant to face Desmodian but crossed both sets of arms instead. "I can defend myself. Didn't need your help."

The tapping of Desmodian's nails fell silent. "If that were true, you wouldn't have been there in the first place. Getting involved with Yaivin is dangerous. His father has already put you in jail before, yet you're determined to throw yourself into danger just to prove your own virility."

Finally, Brog gave in and turned to Desmodian. "So it's okay for you to make an enemy 'a him instead? Fuck, Des, you just can't let go 'a that martyr complex 'a yours."

Pet sighed and stared at his feet. A puddle formed on the floor around him.

This wasn't what they needed. More accusations wouldn't solve anything. Less than a minute into the conversation, and he'd already given up on them reaching a resolution this time.

Staring at the floor, he could still see Brog and Desmodian's feet. The two of them drifted closer.

"Martyr complex?" Desmodian's hammer thumped the floor, an extra punctuation to his question.

Brog responded with an imitation of Desmodian's voice. He even managed to capture the aristocratic accent that sometimes slipped into Desmodian's speech. "Isn't it great how selfless I am? I sacrificed everything for you. Be grateful and do as I say."

Pet rocked on his heels, torn between comforting the angry pair and staying in his corner. They weren't talking about Yaivin or Tradius anymore. This was something from their shared past. Just a few months ago, Pet had learned about Desmodian killing his own brother when the man threatened Brog and Xavis. Since then, it had never been mentioned again.

Until now.

Desmodian pulled away from Brog. His back hit the wall when he tripped over his own tail. "I didn't protect you and Xavis so I could control you."

Brog's footsteps echoed off the metal floor as he closed the space Desmodian put between them. "No, but you didn't give us a choice either. We could'a found another solution. But you just ran off and decided to sacrifice yourself on your own."

Very hesitantly, Pet looked up to see the expression on their faces.

What little distance remained between the two crackled with opposing colors. Orange light glowed in Brog's eyes as he scowled, and the corner of his mouth pulled into a partial snarl.

Green light danced over Desmodian's scales, but he looked more shocked than angry. "You and Xavis were only in danger because of me. I had to be the one to fix it. My brother would never have given up. The only way to protect you was to stop him. Permanently. There's nothing you could've done to change that."

The elevator slowed as it reached the top of the island.

With a deep breath, Brog stepped back, and the

orange light died. The doors opened, and he stepped out of the confined space but stopped on the threshold to look back at Desmodian. "You're right. I couldn't do anythin'. And I'm reminded 'a that every time I look at you."

Then he left, passing the décor at the lobby entrance and disappearing into the city.

Desmodian walked off the elevator as if in a daze. The end of his hammer dragged on the floor, making a horrid scraping noise.

Pet scurried off the elevator just before the doors closed. He stood behind Desmodian and raised a hand to the Dhen'in's arm but dropped it before making contact. There was no comfort he could offer, not physical or verbal, that would make things better.

They had tried to fix the conflict between Desmodian and Brog, but in the end it seemed they only made it worse.

Chapter Eleven

After

A chill that had nothing to do with arctic temperatures ran up Pet's spine. Ice-cold light shone through the skylight, illuminating the electrical cage at the center of the room, along with its prisoner. He almost called from inside the vent and clamped both hands over his mouth to hold the name behind his teeth.

Desmodian.

It had been less than a day since Pet last saw him. At least the Dhen'in was conscious now. He sat on the floor of the cage with one leg bent and his arm braced on the knee. The other leg stretched out in front of him, almost touching the bars. His barbed tail never stopped moving. It swept back and forth, using every last inch of available space within the cage.

From this angle, Pet got a good look at the cables running from Desmodian's cage. If only he could cut those cables. Then Desmodian would be free.

Yet that still left them with the same problem as before. Freeing one of the trio would get the others killed.

A door opened directly below Pet. He pressed closer to the grate until metal slats indented his cheek. No one entered, but a bulky lopsided shadow stretched across the floor.

Desmodian didn't look up, though his posture changed slightly. "You find it yet?"

A single shadow detached from the cluster, and Tradius Vels stepped into view. He approached Desmodian's cage with slow even steps. "The Relativator has to be here somewhere. My people are looking for it. They'll find it soon."

Pet gasped and sucked in dusty metallic air. He buried his face in his elbow to hide his coughing fit.

A Relativator? That's what they were here for?

The *Vanguard* had a Relativator, as did all spaceships. It was the one piece of technology on their ship Pet was never allowed to touch. His trio wouldn't even show him the controls.

Tradius stopped just in front of the cage. The gold sash hanging off his shoulder slipped out of place when he leaned forward to peer between the bars.

Desmodian looked up, pointing his mask in Tradius's direction.

"So you haven't found it yet. Is that why you're here? I know you're a man used to getting what he wants. This setback must be frustrating. Are you hoping some good old-fashioned gloating will make you feel better?"

Tradius seemed unsettled. He kept fidgeting, raising his arms as if to cross them, then changing his mind and clasping his hands in front of him. "With an attitude like that, I see why your family was eager to shuffle you off to the military. Normally, I'd say this is just business, but I'm going to enjoy grounding that ugly ship of yours."

The crackle of electricity should've drowned out Desmodian's nails tapping on the cage floor, but Pet had heard that clicking so many times it played in his brain anyway.

It was a sign of Desmodian's mind in overdrive, even when the rest of him remained unresponsive.

"I think you're suffering delusions of grandeur, Tradius. Even if you find this advanced Relativator, all you've got is a piece of tech slightly better than what's already out there. That's hardly going to ground the *Vanguard*."

Tradius raised a single finger in the air. "A piece of tech that is necessary for any spaceship to function. Once Traditional Evolution passes, those other companies producing Relativators will be shut down. I'll be the only one with the tech that ship-dwellers like you desperately need."

Desmodian shifted again so most of his body faced Tradius. "Why would your xenophobic politics affect the production of spaceflight technology?"

Instead of answering him, Tradius looked over his shoulder to address someone still standing in the doorway. "I thought you said he was smart?"

Barely audible footsteps preceded the second person as they entered Pet's view.

Yaivin placed himself just behind his father, gaze glued to the floor. A bag hung across his shoulder. Its bulk rested against his hip, shifting with every move, while his hands stayed locked around the strap. "He is. But I'm also told he doesn't care about politics."

Tradius looked at his son with a strange expression. Pet only saw it from the side, so maybe he misinterpreted, but Tradius looked to be waiting for something.

A moment passed without any reaction from

Yaivin, so Tradius turned back to Desmodian. "He's a ship-dweller. He should be concerned. Astronautic companies hire a lot of different species. When Traditional Evolution passes, it'll restrict their labor force. Then, while they struggle, I start production on a crucial piece of technology better than anything they can offer." Tradius stood proud. The frozen skylight glinted off his gold sash.

Despite the display, Desmodian scoffed. "That's what this is about? A monopoly on spaceflight technology. I didn't realize you were so petty."

Tradius stepped out from under the skylight, into the shadow of Desmodian's cage.

The electricity sparked only inches from the hem of his toga. "Traditional Evolution will bring order back to this chaotic galaxy, re-establish the boundaries set down by nature. Yet ship-dwellers are the ones who fight us the most. Controlling spaceflight technology means controlling ship-dwellers. Politics is all about control. You were a landowner once. You should know that. But then, you weren't a very good landowner, were you?"

He shifted a little closer to the cage.

Yaivin shouted for his father to look out, but it was too late.

Desmodian's hand shot between the bars and grabbed Tradius's sash. The Dhen'in screamed as he was electrocuted but didn't let go as he pulled Tradius into the side of the cage.

Tradius writhed, and Desmodian's own scream morphed into manic laughter.

Yaivin tried to pry his father out of Desmodian's grasp but couldn't touch the older Iknox without being electrocuted himself.

An orange light snapped between Desmodian and Tradius, forcing them apart.

Desmodian was propelled to the other side of his cage, and Tradius slumped to the floor.

Yaivin knelt at his father's side. "Are you all right?"

Tradius stood and glared at Desmodian, nearly stepping too close to the cage again. "Bastard. Get used to that cage, because you're never leaving it. Once we're done here, I'm selling you to the highest bidder."

Yaivin tried to pull Tradius away from the cage, but the older Iknox slapped his son away.

A new set of footsteps approached the room, strange and lopsided. Every other step was accompanied by a strike of metal against metal.

An Ocan entered the room. "That was reckless."

Pet recoiled, pushing away from the grate back into the depths of the vent. That person couldn't be Brog. The voice sounded the same, but everything else was wrong.

Xavis's feather wrapped over his eyes like a blindfold.

Pet tried to peel it away, but it clung tighter. Purple light zapped his skin like static. "Please. If it's him, I have to see."

The feather let go, though it did so slowly.

Pet crawled back to the grate.

An Ocan definitely stood below. Their skin was the same color as Brog's. Dark grayish blue glowed with orange light. Yet, if this really was Brog, he had withered in a matter of hours. Once-broad shoulders sagged, and thick muscle had disappeared, leaving skin hanging off his bones. Each rib stood out in stark relief, even through his shirt.

He looked like a man dying from years of starvation.

Brog carried Desmodian's hammer tucked under his arm like a crutch. Orange light invaded the hammer, crackling as it fought with the weapon's usual green.

Step by painful step, Brog made his way over to Yaivin and Tradius. "Told you not to underestimate him. Desmodian ain't someone you want to go pokin'. He'll take you down with him if he has to."

Tradius brushed dust from his toga, hands shaking until he clenched them tight and forced them to remain still. "I thought Phazers were contained by electricity."

Brog shrugged as best he could with the hammer braced under his arm. "Electricity contains our powers, not our bodies." Tradius tried to argue further, but Brog turned to Desmodian. "You look terrible."

Desmodian braced one hand on the floor of the cage to keep himself upright as he panted heavily. "Look in a mirror. You've overextended yourself."

"I'll be fine." Brog's words were calm, but he gripped the hammer in tight fists.

Desmodian sighed. His tail twitched faster. "No, you won't. My hammer isn't made for you. It'll only help so much. If you don't get something to eat soon, you'll burn up trying to contain that much backlash."

Brog turned so only his shoulder faced Desmodian. Orange light glowed brighter, but the green light within the hammer pushed back.

Yaivin stepped in front of Brog to block him from Desmodian's sight. It was a futile attempt, considering the size different between Iknox and Ocan. "Brog, go sit down. You've already done your part. We can find the Relativator without you. Then we'll leave."

"Yes. Get him out of here." Tradius gave a dismissive wave of his hand.

Brog shrugged again and stumbled. The hammer screeched as it slid over the floor. He struggled but, with Yaivin's help, remained standing. "All right. Just stay away from the cage and don't be stupid."

He turned to leave, but Desmodian called out from behind the bars. "Brog, please. This'll kill you. It'll kill all of us. No amount of money can be worth that."

For a moment Pet thought Brog had spotted him in the vent when the Ocan looked up toward the ceiling, but nothing happened. Those orange eyes had always brought Pet comfort before. Now he didn't know what to think as they glowed like fire inside hollow sockets.

Harsh lines etched across Brog's face. With a deep breath, he closed his eyes and looked back over his shoulders. "The money's just a bonus. I'm tired 'a puttin' up with you. This is my chance to make it on my own."

Then he left the room, limping along with the help of Desmodian's weapon.

Pet pressed against the grate. He needed to go after Brog. Demand an answer, an excuse, anything that would explain the male's actions.

Surely, there had to be an explanation.

He reached for the screwdriver tucked in his pocket, but before he could remove the grate, Xavis's feather covered his eyes again. No matter how Pet struggled, the feather would not be removed.

"Please. I need to go after him. I need to free Desmodian. I need to…I need to…"

The surge of adrenaline evaporated, and he lay on the floor of the vent. His limbs shook, and tears gathered, but this was not the heaving panic-filled crying from before. This was a silent version, too deeply rooted in sadness to make a sound.

Each droplet that escaped him absorbed into Xavis's feather.

"You're right." He spoke so quietly his vocal cords didn't even vibrate, yet his voice seemed to echo back at him. "I need to keep going. Chasing after Brog won't solve anything, and I can't free Desmodian like this. But I don't know what to do. Where should I go?"

The feather slipped from his eyes, pointing down the vent.

Pet wiped away the moisture still clinging to his eyelashes and nodded. Before he left, he checked on Desmodian one last time.

The Dhen'in looked hurt, but not in immediate danger. Tradius seemed to have forgotten about his prisoner as he engaged in a whispered conversation with his son. Their words were too soft to hear, but their body language spoke for them. Tradius gestured with his hands much more than normal while Yaivin clung to the bag on his shoulder.

With a final emphatic gesture, Tradius turned from his son and marched out of the room, forcing Yaivin to trail behind him.

Desmodian was left alone, imprisoned but at least safe for the moment.

Pet turned away and followed the vent in a different direction.

Xavis's feather led him on a circuitous path. His knees and elbows ached from crawling around on unforgiving metal. By the time he finally reached the end of the vent, ice-blue light had never looked so inviting. He grasped the edge of the open grate but stopped before pulling his head out.

Back in the monitoring room, Bug remained right where he'd left her. Rather than working with the scent-based computer, she sat unmoving on the platform. Her whole body drooped like a wilted flower stem at the end of summer.

Pet would have thought she was dead, if not for the occasional twitch of her antennae.

Maybe she was asleep?

"Bug?"

She jerked in her chair, causing it to almost roll off the platform.

"What? Pet?"

Remembering his lesson from before, he managed to climb out of the vent without falling. "I'm back. Are you okay?"

"Yeah, I'm fine. I'm just... Yesterday I woke up at home. My biggest concern was getting the night off so I could go to the Dust Party. Now I'm wondering if I'll make it back to work at all. I've been trying not to think about it, but..."

The soles of Pet's thermal suit cushioned his feet when they touched the floor. "I get it. We just need to keep moving, and we might have a plan."

Xavis's feather turned circles over Pet's head as he explained everything he'd seen. He skipped over both of his breakdowns in the vent and tried to include only relevant facts about the incidents with Xavis and Desmodian.

When he finished, he expected Bug to question the

efficacy of following a feather. However, at the end, she only had one question.

"Brog's working for Tradius Vels now?"

The feather flashed purple.

Pet cupped it in his hands, smoothing ruffled barbs and letting sparks crackle against his skin. It gave him an excuse to avoid looking at Bug.

"I don't want to talk about it."

Bug rolled closer.

"Pet, if he's helping Tradius, then he's a threat."

"I said I don't want to talk about it."

The feather squirmed as Pet gripped it too tight. He let go, and it perched on his shoulder like a weightless bird. If Bug was allowed to not think about unpleasant things, then he was allowed to not talk.

He didn't think he could talk about it if he tried, anyway.

Chapter Twelve

Before

Water trickled down a glass spiral, filling a bathtub big enough to hold Pet and all his trio. Yet Pet floated alone.

With the lights turned down low, reflections off the water danced patterns on the stone ceiling.

He watched them as he thought back over the last few hours.

After the fight in the elevator, Brog left, and Desmodian wandered off into the city. Although he let Pet back into their suite first.

Now Pet was alone, soaking away his worries.

He'd tried talking to each of his trio individually. He'd tried getting them to talk to each other. No matter which way he turned, he kept hitting the same roadblock.

The dripping silence of the bathroom weighed on him. Sometimes he found solace in silence as he organized his thoughts, but today he wanted noise.

He drove away the quiet by humming a familiar tune. The song had existed as bits and pieces in his head as long as he could remember. A few months ago, when he saw a recording of his interview to become décor, he finally heard the song in its entirety. There weren't any lyrics—maybe there never had been—but the tune was at least complete.

Pet drifted on his back, keeping his ears above the surface. He didn't need to be reminded of his experiences with sensory deprivation on top of everything else. The last note of the song hung in the air like steam from the bath. When it faded, he started the song again, repeating it until the bath turned cold.

"Fuck it."

He stood, and water slid down his body to land back in the tub. Droplets hit the surface like little bells, echoing against the stone walls and creating a liquid symphony.

Just because his trio were being unreasonable didn't mean he had to spend the evening sitting around moping. He would go to the Dust Party and enjoy himself without them.

The party wouldn't start until after sunset, so Pet took his time getting ready. He even styled his hair and added shimmer to his eyes, things he didn't usually bother with when his trio's attentions would just mess it up again.

A package sat on the table by his elbow, waiting for him. Inside, the black swimsuit and cover-up nestled among protective wrapping. Black nebula diamonds cast reflections on the wall in a prismatic pattern, reminding him of the stars he usually called home.

The swimsuit covered even less than Ochaid's picture promised. It sat as low on his hips as possible without falling off. Only a string's worth of fabric connected the sides, and even less in the back. Pet didn't need to look in the mirror; he could feel air against his skin. Despite its name, the cover-up didn't cover anything. The wide netting showed everything underneath.

He thought the outfit would make him self-conscious, but the moment it settled over his skin like mist, he felt like a work of art. There was no reason for him to be shy about showing off. He never had been before. The incident with the DPS agents and the poachers had affected him more than he realized.

It was time to take his confidence back, even if he had to do it by himself.

An hour remained before sunset, but he didn't want to sit around any longer. He left the suite, deciding not to worry about how he would get back inside. If necessary, he could always go back to the *Vanguard*.

On his way to catch a trolley, he barely paid attention to the décor by the elevators.

A large apartment block for permanent residents sat at the very center of the city. More crowded than the areas dedicated to tourists, and obviously not as lavish, it still looked clean and functional. Unlike the architecture at the edges of the island, which utilized natural coral structures growing on the land, the apartment block needed synthetic construction. Whoever designed it had tried to make the artificial structures match the natural ones, but it was like comparing plastic decorations in a fish tank to the actual ocean.

Pet knocked on the apartment he thought belonged to Bug, but a Rurarine he didn't recognize answered the door.

"What'd you want?"

Either the stranger didn't recognize décor, or they didn't care. Despite their rude attitude, it was refreshing to be treated like anyone else.

"I'm looking for Bug. Is she here?"

"Oh, that one." The strange Rurarine gave an impression of rolling eyes by curling their antennae in a rippling movement. "Should've known they were getting up to something when I heard noise coming from that apartment again."

Pet clasped his hands behind his back to hide their fidgeting. "We're just going to the Dust Party."

Pet's terse tone was impossible to miss, but the strange Rurarine continued their rant. "Why? That's for tourists. Not us. Don't know why that one keeps trying."

Taking a deep breath through his nose, Pet pushed away all the words he wanted to say and chose something polite instead. "Well, I am a tourist. So, if you could just point me to the right apartment, I'll be out of your way."

The simple design of the strange Rurarine's chair didn't allow much arm movement. It couldn't shrug or express emotion like Bug's chair. All it did was point. "Around that corner and three doors down. The one with the weird stuff on the front."

Pet smiled. "Thank you." The door closed in his face. "Asshole."

He shot the neighbor's door a rude gesture, then left.

At least their directions were helpful. A wreath made from spare cogs and wires decorated Bug's door. It clashed with the building's fake coral architecture, but it fit Bug's personality.

He knocked.

No answer.

Waiting a moment, he knocked again. Still nothing.

Was this the right door? He'd already been wrong once. Yet the door fit Bug's aesthetic so well. Some of the pieces in the wreath looked like they had come right off her chair.

Pet knocked a third time to the same result.

Now what? Should he leave and try to meet up with her at the party, or just forget the party altogether? Neither of these options seemed like the right answer.

On a whim he tried the handle, and to his surprise the door opened.

"Hello?" He stopped on the threshold. "Bug? You here? It's me."

The apartment had an open floor plan and almost nothing else. He supposed someone who got around in a mechanized wheelchair wouldn't need much furniture. Instead, rows of shelves lined the walls, stuffed full of mechanical parts and tools.

Bug's chair sat in pieces at the center of the room. Her pink-and-yellow body lay on the floor, disconnected and unmoving.

"Bug!" He charged the rest of the way into the room, panic flooding his mouth. The door bounced off the wall and closed again.

Just as he reached her, Bug's antennae twitched. He hovered over her, debating whether to pick her up or call for help. She didn't speak, but her body began to slide across the floor. "Slug" might be a slur for Rurarine, but the way she moved made it hard to avoid the comparison.

She also traveled at the same speed as a slug, so it took time for her to wriggle into a part of her chair that seemed to contain the neural connection.

Static crackled before refining into Bug's familiar

voice. "Sorry, Pet. Lost track of time."

He looked around at the scattered chair pieces. "What happened?"

The arms of the chair attached to the neural connector on Bug's back. They dragged against the floor, allowing her to crawl around like an insect. "Oh, nothing happened. I was decorating the chair and had an idea for an update, so I took it apart, and then I just…got lost."

Her explanation started out energetic but quickly lost momentum until her voice was barely audible.

Pet crossed his legs and sat on an open patch of floor, ignoring the cold surface against his bare skin. "Got lost?"

With a sigh Bug's antennae drooped as her mechanical arms sorted through the chair's many scattered parts. "It's hard to explain. One moment I'll be fine, and then it's like my mind turns into quicksand, and I can't think. Working on my chair can help, but sometimes…ugh, sometimes I just feel like such a slug."

She slumped on the floor, and even her mechanized arms went limp.

A proper friend would say something to make her feel better. Although he didn't know what that would be, he hoped Bug saw him as a friend, so he gave it a shot. "You know, living on a ship can be a lot of fun. We're always traveling around, visiting new places and seeing new things. But, sometimes, all that newness gets to be too much. Maybe it's because I'm décor and I've forgotten how to process things. It's not the same as what you're feeling, but I get how quickly you can go from okay to not okay."

Mechanical arms jerked, and Bug sat up enough for her antennae to point at him. "I don't feel overwhelmed, more like I'm sinking. Different, but similar. What helps you get over it?"

Pet plucked at the hem of his cover-up, watching light inside the diamonds glitter as it moved. "I don't know if 'getting over it' is ever really possible. There's plenty of isolated corners on our ship for me to sit quietly until I feel like I can function again. My trio are always patient and know not to bother me until I come out on my own. That's what I need. So what about you? What do you need, and what can I do?"

Bug picked up a few pieces off the floor and put them back together with the help of nearby tools. It looked to be part of the treads to her chair. "I need to keep moving. If I let myself stop for too long, it's harder to get going again. That's why I like my job. It's engaging enough to keep me distracted, but simple enough to handle even on my bad days."

She pointed at another piece just out of reach.

Pet handed it to her. "So you need a distraction. I can do that. Do you still want to go to the party, or would a different kind of distraction be better?"

With the treads reassembled, the chair almost looked recognizable again. Bug turned her attention to the intricate mechanics inside the chair.

One by one, small cogs and wires slotted into equally small spaces. Bug never hesitated as she fit the puzzle back together. "I want to go to the party. I look forward to it each year, and I'd hate to miss it. But I don't know how much fun I'll be. I don't want to ruin it for you."

Last to be reassembled was the panel where the

neural connector attached. With that done, the only thing missing from the chair was Bug herself.

Pet found the ribbons they bought earlier, unspooled over the floor and waiting for their chance to shine. "Don't worry about me. Just being around people who're enjoying themselves is enough for me to have fun. Now, let's get you decorated so we can go."

Once Bug crawled into her usual place in the chair, Pet helped tie the ribbons around the mechanics in a way that wouldn't hinder the chair's movement. Up close, the unique complexities of the chair were even more obvious. Especially after seeing the simplicity of her neighbor's chair, Pet just had to ask about it.

Bug twitched but held still as Pet kept wrapping the ribbon. "I studied engineering for a while. Have to put that knowledge to use somehow."

Pet reached the end of the ribbon and tied the whole thing off with a fancy bow right at the center of the chair's back panel. "Is that why you're a waiter? To pay for your education. I've heard it can be expensive."

"No. There's just no jobs for engineers. Being a waiter actually makes me more money than an engineering job would."

Finishing the bow, Pet stepped around to the front of the chair. "That doesn't seem right. Engineers build stuff. It's a really important job."

Bug spun a few circles to show off how the ribbons fluttered when she moved, and to check that they wouldn't get caught in anything.

"Engineering is important, but around here it's not profitable. Syzygy is relatively new to the intergalactic community. At first we tried to establish ourselves as traders in advanced technology, but no one took us seriously."

Pet glanced over the neural connection attaching Bug to her chair. Xavis had been impressed at the mere sight of their technology.

What did Xavis see that the rest of the galaxy didn't?

She stopped spinning and faced him. "Ignore the chair and just look at me. To most people we're nothing more than fancy slugs. Buyers refused to pay what our technology is worth, and our economy suffered. A few years ago, representatives of each country around our planet got together and decided to shut down the research labs we couldn't finance and focus on building our global economy back up. For this part of the planet, that means tourism. So there's more money in hospitality jobs than engineering."

Although Pet had never pursued a career, not that he could remember anyway, he understood what it was like being stuck in a role he didn't enjoy. It was the reason he'd traded typical décor life for the life of a ship-dweller. "I'm sorry. That must suck, but I'm sure it'll change eventually."

This was apparently the right thing to say because Bug's posture straightened, and her antennae pointed toward the ceiling. "Being a waiter isn't bad. I enjoy it for the most part, and my chair gives me an opportunity to invent new things. But thanks. Usually, people just say I should be happy to have a job. It feels ungrateful to complain when others are unemployed."

Thinking back to the neighbor Pet spoke with earlier, he could imagine exactly who had said such things. "That's stupid. You can appreciate something without liking every part of it."

"That's what I said, but they didn't listen."

Bug and Pet left the apartment together and caught a trolley. They were lucky to claim the last two available seats in the crowded space.

Would his trio be at the Dust Party? They could've had the same idea and gone on their own.

Halfway down the island, the last ray of sunlight disappeared. The stars emerged, but the true indigo of night never settled. Three moons aligned as one, completing their syzygy and glowing brighter than ever.

Coral-colored moths appeared in the sky. Just a few at first, but more and more gathered until thousands of Aura moths swarmed together.

When they reached the bottom of the island, Pet stepped off the trolley onto a fine layer of orangish-pink dust which fell from the moths' wings like snow.

"It's magical." The beach had been completely redecorated, becoming a mix of dance stage, market, bar, and buffet. Neon lights had been added to the natural bioluminescence of the coral, and moths darted in front of the moon, creating their own strobe-light.

Dust mixed with water and sand, diluting the smell of the ocean into something softer, like saltwater candy.

Pet still had no desire to swim, but under these conditions it didn't seem as intimidating. If not for the extra-loud rush of the tides, pulled by the force of the syzygy, he could almost forget the ocean existed.

Guests from many different species gathered on the beach. Some wore swimsuits, and many wore no clothes at all.

Pet's outfit wouldn't stand out for anything other than its beauty.

Bug, however, did stand out. There was a

surprising lack of Rurarine in attendance.

They spent some time wandering between the market stalls as they eased into the energy of the party. First to greet them were the stalls selling food. They passed one place serving some sort of grilled fruit that smelled like it would taste good.

What would it be like to eat? Watching people pull bits of the cooked fruit off skewers with their teeth, Pet found the process impossible to imagine.

Bug also had no use for food, as Rurarine ate by absorbing nutrients directly through their skin. They left the stalls behind and discovered one of the many dance floors set up along the beach.

Music with a heavy bass played from hidden speakers. The lyrics contained sounds no human vocal cords could make. While obviously not human in origin, music was a universal form of communication.

Pet didn't need to know what the lyrics said to feel the beat of the song. It made him twitch with a desire to move, like a puppet with tangled strings.

However, Bug pulled away when he suggested they join the dance floor. "Rurarine aren't meant for dancing."

Before she could retreat any farther, Pet stepped behind her chair. "No one is *meant* for dancing. That's not the point. It's about moving in a way that makes you feel good."

Her chair could have rolled right over him if she wanted. The fact that she let him push her toward the dance floor proved she wanted to join.

"But I'll just get in people's way." They crossed from sand onto the sturdy surface of the dance floor, and Bug brought them to a stop. "One time I tried dancing, and I ran over someone's foot. They were furious."

Pet crossed his arms and stared her down. She didn't have eyes, but thanks to Desmodian, Pet had plenty of practice with this type of staring contest. "If getting their foot stepped on makes them that upset, then they shouldn't be on a dance floor in the first place. But if you're worried about it, we can stay to the edge where there aren't as many people. I promise I won't mind if you run over my foot."

They started simple. Pet grabbed one of the arms of Bug's chair and convinced her to turn in circles. From there they advanced to drawing figure eights and other patterns. By the end of the second song, they had transitioned into something that could almost be called dancing.

For Bug this mostly consisted of wildly waving her mechanical arms while her real body wiggled back and forth in her seat, but at least she was laughing.

Pet matched her flailing while also throwing in an occasional move taught to him by Oi back at the Gravity Well. The two of them probably looked ridiculous. He felt people staring but ignored the attention. Pointing it out would only make Bug self-conscious.

They passed a few songs unbothered until Pet grew tired and begged for a break.

The bars held no appeal since neither of them could drink. Nor did Pet have any interest in the market shops. He still felt guilty about buying his current outfit and couldn't imagine spending more. Instead, he and Bug gravitated to the games at the other end of the beach.

They were meant for children. Simple challenges like hitting a target or solving a puzzle were surprisingly difficult to the point that Pet suspected they were rigged.

Very few players boasted any success. Yet none of this mattered. The children just had fun playing. Most of the games were surrounded by a swarm of children, but one booth off to the side remained empty. It held a type of dice game that was apparently not as popular as the others.

The game reminded Pet of the way his trio would sometimes divide unpleasant tasks by rolling a die. Except this game had multiple dice rolling at the same time. He and Bug played a few rounds, losing terribly each time, but a pattern began to emerge.

These dice were definitely rigged. The numbers differed each time, but they always alternated between landing on odd and even numbers.

Armed with this information, he and Bug started winning more regularly. Neither of them had any use for the toys and trinkets awarded as prizes, so gave them away to nearby children. This drew attention, and before they knew it, they had an eager audience.

Half an hour later children crowded the booth, eager to try the game themselves, so Pet and Bug left the games behind. This put them on an empty section of beach at the very edge of the party space.

Dust falling from the Aura moths had collected several inches deep and turned the sand into powdery dunes.

Pet turned his back to the beach and faced the party again. "Want to check out some of the stands on the other side? Or maybe find another dance floor?"

Bug, however, rolled out into the open. "I have a better idea. Hop on."

"On your chair?"

Her mechanical arms directed him to the chair's back panel. "Yeah. Just hold on there and put your feet there."

They started rolling down the beach and quickly gained speed until sand and dust sprayed behind them like a pair of granular wings.

When he didn't immediately fall off, Pet quickly overcame his fear and relaxed. They caught air as they hit a particularly tall sand dune. At the crest of their arch, Pet's stomach floated up behind his ribs, as if disconnected from his other organs.

It reminded him of bouncing around his antigravity bubble when the *Vanguard* made a drastic maneuver.

The mechanics of Bug's chair stuttered when they landed, but the chair was sturdy, and Bug only laughed as they kept going even faster than before.

Pet threw his head back and howled his excitement to the night sky.

A few Aura moths startled at his sudden outburst and sent an extra dusting over them.

After days of worry and stress, it felt good to let go. What a shame his trio couldn't enjoy it with him.

Where were they? Was Xavis still on the ship? Had Brog returned to Yaivin's suite? Did Desmodian have a plan for how to rectify things, or was he as lost as Pet?

These were questions for tomorrow. Tonight was only for fun and laughter.

They turned around when they reached one of the coral dividers. Their path zigzagged, hitting every dip and dune they could find.

When they returned to their starting point near the games, they found a group of excited children watching them.

"That was awesome."

"Can you do it again?"

"How did you not fall off?"

There was no way to tell which child said what. The group clamored for attention, some even climbing onto the chair.

Pet didn't have much experience with children. He never knew what to say to them and found their enthusiasm overwhelming.

Bug, however, obviously loved the attention.

He let the nearest child take his place. "You should give them a few rides, Bug."

A child overestimated their climbing ability and tumbled from the chair. Mechanical arms caught them before they hit the sand.

Bug set the child back on their feet without looking away from Pet. "You wouldn't mind? It might take a while."

"It's a party." Pet threw out his hands to frame the entire event happening around them. "It's about having fun. If you think it'll be fun, then do it."

With minimal arguing, the children decided to let the youngest and smallest of their group go first. The whole process barely took two minutes.

Adults could stand to learn from their children.

Pet stood at the edge of the open sand and watched Bug run children up and down the beach. Listening to Bug and the children laugh as they navigated the dunes was even more entertaining than the music pumping from the party at his back.

Bug gave each child one lap to the coral wall and back, then swapped them out for the next in line.

During one of these moments, as a new child struggled to find their bearings on the chair, Pet's attention wandered back to the chaos of the Dust Party.

The concentration of so much energy and life gave him an odd feeling of peace. So many people enjoyed themselves at the same time, completely unaffected by him. His troubles seemed small in comparison. No matter what happened in his personal life, the universe kept turning, and people kept living.

Something in the crowd caught Pet's eye. He was so used to being surrounded by aliens that casually seeing a human walking around caused his brain to short circuit. It was like looking at the moon and seeing a face among the craters.

Even stranger, he recognized that face.

What was 3155 doing here?

Yes, she was 4104 now, but he had known her for years as 3155. They once belonged to the same Owner, and he couldn't think of her by any other number. He also couldn't imagine her current Owner giving her the night off to attend a party.

3155 disappeared into the crowd.

Without thinking about it, Pet followed her. He skirted the edge of the game booths, trying to catch her without elbowing his way through a sea of children.

Just as he rounded the farthest booth, something grabbed his arm.

"What?" The sudden change in direction strained Pet's shoulder in its socket.

A Schade stood beside him on the beach.

The being had no eyes to meet or an expression to

read, just a smooth black pillar.

Pet's forearm stuck to the side as if magnetized. "What're you doing?"

The Schade didn't answer. A faint vibration traveled across its surface, but this didn't translate into an explanation.

Further demands for answers were cut off as the Schade started dragging Pet along. The living pillar glided over the beach without leaving any tracks.

Pet tried to pull away. "Hey, wait, let me go."

A shock ran up his arm. The sudden pain made him trip, but the Schade never hesitated, dragging Pet through the sand until he found his feet again. A numbness spread through his arm, along with a dangerous buzzing just under his skin.

Calling out for help resulted in a similar shock, stronger than before. This one left the entire side of his torso numb. It made no difference. His voice didn't carry over the pounding music, and even if someone did hear him, they wouldn't interfere. To an outside observer it would look like an owner taking control of their own décor.

He didn't dare resist a third time.

The Schade brought Pet to the docks where he and his trio had met the boat that took them deep-sea diving.

Pet stumbled when his bare feet hit the boardwalk. "What do you want with me?"

The Schade still remained silent.

They passed the boats and instead headed for the airships also resting at the dock. Used for activities like wind surfing and parachuting during the day, the airships should have been shut down at night just like the boats. Yet a dozen Iknox servants swarmed around one, hauling barrels of ocean water onboard.

The servants never looked up from their work as Pet was dragged onto the airship. Instead of heading for the clear upper half of the dome, the Schade brought him down to the enclosed lower half.

Pet's bare footsteps echoed with a slap of flesh against metal. If the Schade made any noise, Pet couldn't hear it over his pounding heart.

The airship was built to accommodate scores of guests in comfort. Various styles of plush furniture filled the enclosed half of the airship. An unmanned bar service stood on one end, illuminated by crystal structures on the ceiling. Porthole windows allowed a glimpse of the sky, filled with Aura moths and flickering moonlight.

The Schade pulled Pet to the other end of the airship, into a private lounge room kept separate from the common area.

His arm suddenly detached from the Schade, and he collapsed to the floor. Luckily, there was carpet to cushion his face, or he would've walked away with more than a sore nose.

"What's this?"

Pet recognized that voice. It brought an acidic mix of anger and fear welling up from his stomach. He knew who he would see even before he looked up.

Tradius Vels sat primly at the center of a U-shaped couch, dressed in his typical black toga with gold sash. One leg crossed over the other, a deviation from his usual perfect posture, as he waited for an answer.

He didn't look at Pet, still sprawled at his feet. Rather he stared expectantly at the door.

Trying not to draw Tradius's attention, Pet looked over his shoulder with as little movement as possible.

A line of living pillars stood together, forming a black wall that effectively blocked the only exit.

Pet remembered seeing the Schade hanging around in Yaivin's suite. At the time he'd wondered what it was doing there. Now he had his answer. They were guards.

The centermost Schade vibrated, and the disks that comprised its body rearranged.

Tradius sighed and rubbed at his temple. "Yaivin?"

Carefully, Pet raised his head more and took a better look around.

Yaivin stood in one corner, appearing almost as inanimate as décor. "You told the Schade to bring the ship-dwellers here. This décor lives on their ship so it's technically a ship-dweller."

Beside Yaivin, a few servants copied his submissive posture, wearing his face but different-colored clothes.

"Should've been more specific, Tradius."

Pet jumped at the sound of that voice, finally looking up all the way.

In the opposite corner from Yaivin and the servants stood three intimidating cages. Two remained empty, but the sight of the third one sent Pet into a panic.

"Des."

He scrambled off the floor and rushed to the cage. No one tried to stop him until he'd almost reached the bars.

Desmodian called out. "No, wait."

Pet stopped only inches from the cage. "Des?"

"Don't come near. It's electrified." To

demonstrate, the Dhen'in extended a finger toward the side of the cage. A sharp crack of electricity jumped between the bars and his scales.

Desmodian shook his hand. Green sparked for a moment but quickly died like a candle without air.

Pet winced in sympathy. "What happened?"

Tradius interrupted, ordering Yaivin over to their corner. "Get that décor away from there. I don't need DPS breathing down my neck if it damages itself."

Yaivin tried to shepherd Pet from the cage. "Please, come over here." A bag slung over his shoulder shifted and knocked into Pet.

It was an unusual addition to Yaivin's attire. The bulky thing looked unwieldy and bounced against his hip every time he moved. Whatever it contained was hard, with curved edges and smooth sides.

Pet and Yaivin ended up circling each other in an awkward dance. Unlike the Schade, Yaivin refused to lay a hand on décor, and Pet refused to leave Desmodian's side.

"Pet, it's okay." Desmodian raised his hand as if meaning to comfort Pet but caught himself before he touched the cage. "Just do what they say. It'll be fine."

His trio said the same thing when they were captured by poachers a few months ago. Everything had worked out then. Surely there would be a similar outcome this time.

Pet complied and joined the servants at the side of the room. He stood against the wall, imitating the obedient décor he used to be. The numbness caused by the Schade had faded, but he still felt its echo deep in his bones.

Desmodian remained in his cage while two empty

ones loomed with obvious intent.

Electricity was a weakness for Pet's trio. He still remembered the agonizing sound of Xavis's screams after being hit with a simple neural disruptor. How much damage could an electrified cage do? Desmodian's Phazer abilities obviously didn't work while inside the cage, or else he would've already broken free. Plus, his hammer was missing. The Dhen'in had no way to defend himself.

Tradius sighed again. "This is taking longer than I thought. You told the Schade where to find them, right?"

Yaivin dipped into a small bow while clinging to the strap of his bag. "I did. It shouldn't be long now."

The younger Iknox turned out to be right. A few moments later more Schade appeared, dragging along a whirlwind of feathers.

Xavis filled the doorway, wings raised out to either side as if preparing to take flight. "Des? What?" His burning eyes flashed when they landed on the Dhen'in in the cage but quickly transferred to Tradius. "You're going to regret this."

A snarl carved deep caverns on either side of Xavis's mouth, turning the familiar planes of his face into a hostile wasteland of peaks and shadows. He stepped toward Tradius, but a Schade slid into his path. Sharp talons sparked purple when they struck the side of the living pillar but barely left a mark on the smooth surface.

Xavis growled louder, then suddenly stopped. His feathers drooped, and his wings snapped close to his body.

What changed?

The solid purple of his eyes made it hard to figure out where Xavis was looking, but Pet had enough practice to follow his line of sight.

Tradius hadn't moved from the couch. He'd barely even twitched except to raise a small handheld device with a single button on top.

"You're rather uncouth for a Scaacax." Tradius ran a thumb over the button. "But at least you're smart enough to recognize this. One push of this button, and your friend gets electrocuted. And you don't do well with electricity, do you?"

"You'll die before you can twitch a finger." Xavis's declaration would have carried more weight if his wings weren't drawn in close to his back, making him look smaller.

Tradius nodded. The brief angle of his head signaled acknowledgment, but not agreement. "If we were alone, that would be true. That's why I brought them." With the hand holding the device, he gestured toward the Schade. One finger always remained on the button. "Even someone with your abilities couldn't fight through them before I pushed this button."

Xavis's feathers ruffled before falling flat again. He glared unblinkingly at Tradius. "What do you want?"

"I want you to do what you're told. Starting with getting in that cage."

The Schade drew closer, crowding Xavis when he didn't immediately comply.

Tradius raised the device with the button a little higher.

The standoff didn't last long.

Xavis slumped and nodded. "Fine. You win. For

now." He let the Schade herd him toward one of the empty cages.

Servants opened the waiting door.

In that moment all Pet could see was the hatch to the deprivation chamber he'd once been locked inside. The suffocating dark and silence had suppressed every thought and feeling until he was completely hollow. That cage would do the same to Xavis. It would suppress his Phazer abilities, something deeply inherent to him, and leave him helpless.

Pet gritted his teeth and leaned on the wall, resisting the need to pull Xavis away from that door. Desmodian said everything would be fine. He needed to believe that.

Yet even Desmodian seemed to doubt his own words. He tried reaching for Xavis, shocking his hand against the cage. "No, don't. I'll be fine. Just leave."

Xavis stopped at the edge of the open cage and gave Desmodian a sad look. "Come on, Des. You know that's not gonna happen."

One of the servants grabbed Xavis to force him into the cage.

Desmodian snarled, and his tail lashed. "Don't touch him."

Pet pressed his hands flat on the wall, desperately holding himself up. Should he try to intervene? There wasn't much he could do. He couldn't fight off the normal servants, let alone the Schade guards.

Tradius turned just enough to watch the scuffle happening by the cages. "You, Dhen'in, tell your friend to get in the cage, or you're the one that's going to regret it."

With one last glare at the smug Iknox, Xavis

stepped into the cage. The door closed behind him.

Pet's blunt nails pressed crescents into the paint decorating the wall. It wouldn't have been a surprise to find himself bleeding. Watching the glow of Xavis's eyes dim felt like someone slipped a knife between Pet's ribs.

Stomping footsteps shook the floor. Someone approached the room.

"You better have a good reason for this." The private lounge wasn't sized for an Ocan, and Brog had to duck to fit through the doorway as the Schade brought him inside. Yanking his arms out of their hold, he scanned the room with a grimace.

Orange eyes skipped past Pet like a stone over the surface of a lake.

Brog crossed both sets of arms and leaned against the doorframe. "Guess you do. So what now, Tradius?"

"Same thing I told your Scaacax friend. Get in the cage, or the Dhen'in won't be alive much longer." Tradius let his unyielding posture bend. He leaned forward and placed both hands on his knees. The button remained in his grip. "I was annoyed when I first saw you here, but then I realized I'd been given a gift. Your abilities will be great use to me. I even have to thank you. After your little argument, the Dhen'in was so distracted he was easy to capture."

Brog looked back at Desmodian and Xavis locked behind bars, and the one empty cage. An emotion Pet couldn't decipher flickered across his face. Lines pulled tight around his eyes like a grimace, and his lips thinned even more than normal.

Then it all dropped away to be replaced by something new. Pet recognized this expression but wished he didn't.

An arrogant sneer pulled at one side of Brog's mouth, and he shrugged his outer set of shoulders. "Nah. Not gettin' in that cramped thing."

Tradius raised the button again, holding it tighter. "You'll get in if you don't want your friend to experience a very painful death. Don't test me. I'll do it."

Still leaning against the doorframe, Brog shrugged both sets of shoulders this time. "Then do it. Haven't been gettin' on anyway."

Do it? Had Pet heard that right? He must be wrong. Brog would never sacrifice Desmodian like that.

Yet Brog kept going, confirming everything Pet wanted to deny.

"Bastard's always tellin' me what to do. Probably time to move on. If you've got a job for me, I'm in."

Narrowed eyes regarded Brog. Tradius's grip on the button relaxed just a little. "I don't believe you. Why would you willingly work for me? You hate me, and the feeling is mutual."

Straightening from the doorframe, Brog stepped into the room until he loomed over Tradius with every inch of his considerable height. His head nearly brushed the ceiling. "You're right, I hate you, but I also hate bein' ordered around. Attacked one 'a my own commanders when I was stuck in the Unit. So fuck 'em. I'm done. Don't gotta like you, so long as you pay me. And I know you can afford to pay me."

Xavis interrupted Tradius's silent contemplation. "Brog? What're you doing?" He raised his wings but quickly snapped them closed when a jolt of electricity jumped between cage and feathers.

The sharp popping sound caught Brog's attention, but he looked away without a word.

Tradius summoned his son. "You know the Ocan better than I. Is he telling the truth?"

Yaivin stood beside his father, head tipped forward in respect, but snuck an uncertain look at Brog out of the corner of his eye. "I don't...I don't know. He and the Dhen'in weren't getting along, but I didn't expect... I'm sorry. I just don't know."

Pet's stare refused to settle on one place. Brog's strange actions, Xavis's panicked demands, and Tradius's arrogance all competed for attention.

Yet, in the middle of it all, Desmodian remained calm, like the eye of a storm.

No, that wasn't right. Desmodian wasn't just calm. He was motionless. The Dhen'in stood limply in the cage as if he lacked the energy to raise his own arms, let alone speak.

During Pet's momentary distraction, Tradius ordered Yaivin to fetch something. By the time he looked back toward the Iknox pair, Yaivin returned with a hinged box.

He offered it to Brog. His back was to his father, so Tradius didn't see the hopeful expression on Yaivin's face.

Pet saw it, and he was sure Brog did as well.

Brog opened the box but didn't touch whatever it contained. "What's this?"

Tradius returned to his immaculate posture, but a slight tilt to his head indicated much deeper emotions at play. "It's simple. I don't trust you. You say you want to join me, but I'm going to need more than your word."

Hesitating for a moment, Brog reached into the box and picked up a device similar to the one Tradius held. "I'm a whore, not a murderer. I'm not killin' anyone."

"I'm not asking you to. That's not the kill-switch. It stays with me and only me. That one will deliver an electrical shock just low enough not to kill. Don't want to destroy something as valuable as a Phazer if I don't have to. Pain is also an effective means of control."

"And you want me to…" Brog trailed off, leaving an open question for Tradius to fill.

"You said you're done with them. If you really want to join me, prove it."

Brog looked at the device, then looked at Desmodian again.

Desmodian stood in the cage, arms wrapped around himself. Even when captured by poachers, he hadn't looked so cowed. "Brog."

At the sound of his name, Brog averted his eyes to stare at Yaivin instead, taking in every inch of the young Iknox's hopeful face. Then he sneered. "Sorry, Des. It's just not workin' out."

He pushed the button.

A small flash, a pop of electricity, and Desmodian's whole body seized.

Then he screamed.

That scream would haunt Pet for the rest of his life. He clamped his hands over his ears but could still hear it.

Desmodian's usually calm voice tore itself apart. He didn't even writhe around. The electricity kept him imprisoned within his own seizing muscles, unable to escape the pain.

Xavis shouted from the other cage, calling out to

Desmodian and cursing Brog, but he could barely be heard over Desmodian's ceaseless screaming.

Pet closed his eyes, pressed his hands harder over his ears, and prayed for it to stop.

It did, eventually, but not soon enough.

Pet looked up just in time to see Desmodian hit the metal floor with a thud.

Luckily, the Dhen'in landed in the middle of his cage, away from the electrified sides so they couldn't hurt him anymore. He didn't move.

For a moment Pet feared he was dead, but his chest rose and fell. The breaths were worryingly shallow, but at least Tradius had been telling the truth.

The shock hadn't been enough to kill him.

Overcome with relief, Pet collapsed to his knees.

Xavis pressed as close to the bars of his cage as he could. "Des! Des!"

Desmodian didn't respond, but his breathing grew steadier.

Xavis rounded on Brog. "You bastard. You just...you...fuck." His dull eyes shimmered with tears running down his cheeks.

Brog shrugged and tossed the button to Tradius. "That proof enough for you?"

Tradius caught the button with one hand and returned it to the box. He still didn't relinquish the kill-switch, but his grip was more relaxed than before. "Impressive. I'll admit I thought you were bluffing. Well then, Brog. Welcome aboard."

Brog smiled.

Pet shuddered.

Hurting each other should never make one of his trio smile like that.

Chapter Thirteen

After

Why had the Rurarine scientists built their lab in the middle of the frozen arctic? Was it for the cold temperature or the distance from civilization? These questions raced through Pet's head as he and Bug followed Xavis's feather through the halls.

He assumed Xavis had a plan to get them all out of there, but unfortunately had no way to ask. When Xavis's feather led them around turn after turn, he and Bug followed on blind faith.

They traveled slowly, listening around each corner before stepping into the open.

Whatever the feather's destination, it seemed to be deeper in the lab. The hallways grew steadily taller the more they traveled.

"What's a Relativator?"

The sudden sound of Bug's voice didn't startle Pet as much as her question. "You don't know?"

"I've never even been on a spaceship. That technology is completely foreign to me."

Pet stopped under one of the skylights that kept getting farther away. When he looked up, the layer of ice blocked his view of the sky. "Living on a spaceship is my everyday life. I forget it isn't normal for everyone. To put it simply, time is relative to gravity.

Since there's no gravity in space, time moves a lot slower. I don't know how it works, but a Relativator keeps time moving the same on a ship as it does on a planet."

Bug rolled into the patch of light with him, but the bulk of her chair didn't quite fit. "That sounds complicated."

With a last look at the sky he couldn't see, Pet focused back on the friend at his side. "Living on a planet is complicated too. Just a different kind of complicated."

Xavis's feather waited for them at the end of the hall.

When they caught up, it turned left.

Just after they rounded the corner, Bug stopped and looked back the way they came. "Wait a minute. This seems familiar."

She mumbled to herself, repeating the path they had taken so far. Her voice phased in and out like a transmitter skipping between frequencies. "Yes, I'm sure of it. We're following one of the lab's main electrical lines. I think I know where we're going. Come on."

They remained careful but picked up speed.

Pet didn't bother to ask about their destination. He would see for himself in a minute.

Xavis's feather brought them through a double-wide door. The room inside reminded Pet of the bottom of the ocean. With no skylights, the only light came from a large metal structure. It looked like a sea urchin, with a fat round body and twisting metal arms branching out to every wall. Artificial lights ran in long lines from the center of the machine out along the arms, just like bioluminescent coral.

Pet stared up at the glowing contraption, trying and failing to measure its immense size. "This looks important."

Bug rolled to a stop at his side. "It's one of the generators that powers the lab. Now, if we're doing what I think we're doing, you're going to need to climb up there." Her mechanical arm pointed to a spot on the side of the generator.

To someone trained as an electrical engineer, it probably made sense, but to Pet it just looked like a bunch of metal. "Where?"

Before Bug could answer, Xavis's feather flew into the air and hovered at a spot near where Bug pointed.

"Right there." Bug left his side to detach a section from the base of the generator. "Find a way up there. We'll have to work together, but I think your Xavis can help."

Pet left Bug to mess with the generator, trusting that she knew what she was doing. Instead, he puzzled over how to climb up such an intimidating structure. It would be a stretch to reach the lowest of the generator's arms. He grabbed onto the metal and kicked his legs in the air as he pulled himself up. It wasn't as thick as expected, and he nearly flipped over the other side. He hung upside down, the metal arm pressed into his stomach, catching his breath as he regained his balance.

In this way he managed to climb up to Xavis's feather. The entire time he kept repeating the same words over and over to himself. "Don't look down. Don't look down. Don't look down."

Navigating the vent had been hard, but at least there had been a solid surface beneath him. Climbing up the generator was just as difficult as the vent but without the safety of walls.

He reached Xavis's feather and planted himself on the base of an arm, wrapping his legs around the metal for stability. With the screwdriver Bug gave him earlier, he opened the outer panel. Inside he found a mess of wires reminiscent of living veins.

It was like suddenly being asked to perform open-heart surgery.

He called down to Bug. "I'm here. Now what?"

Bug's voice called up from below. "That's the signal coupler. You'll need to redirect it."

This was worse than open-heart surgery. At least in that scenario he would be able to find the heart.

Xavis's feather slipped between the wires and lit one up with a purple glow.

Pet pinched the wire between two fingers. "This one? But what do I do with it?"

The feather curled around the screwdriver in his other hand. A dial Pet hadn't known existed turned on the base of the handle.

The screwdriver head retracted, to be replaced with a hinged blade.

"Oh." Pet turned the tool over, examining the wire cutters he now held. "Didn't know it could do that. I assume this means I need to cut the wire?"

When the feather made no move to stop him, Pet accepted this as agreement and cut the wire.

Lights inside the machine flashed, but nothing exploded.

Pet took this as a good sign and waited for the next step. Together, he and Xavis's feather cut a few more wires, reattached others, and removed something that looked like a microchip to uncover several small switches underneath.

The switches, flipped in a specific order, made all the lights on the panel light up.

Xavis's feather then directed him to cut a wire deep inside the panel.

Pet wormed his fingers between other tightly packed wires and only knew he had the right one from the warmth of Xavis's light.

When he pressed down on the clippers, there was more resistance than a single wire should've created. Something was wrong.

The panel surged with electricity.

Pet jerked his hands away and shielded his face, nearly falling from the branch.

"What happened?"

Xavis's feather blocked some of the electricity and revealed the problem.

Pet hadn't just cut the necessary wire but the one next to it as well.

The whole generator went dark, taking all the light in the room with it.

"Fuck!" No longer able to see the floor, Pet's high perch felt even more precarious. He clung to the metal branch with all the strength in his limbs.

Bug's voice reached him in the dark. "Pet, you okay?"

He clung even harder. "I'm so sorry. I messed up."

One simple task. All he had to do was cut the right wire, and he couldn't even manage that. He'd been so proud of becoming more self-sufficient since meeting his trio, yet when they needed him, he was still just useless décor.

A familiar purple light emanated from inside the panel. Faint at first, it quickly grew brighter.

Pet released one hand from his death grip on the branch to part the top layer of wires and see what was happening.

Xavis's feather wrapped around the wire he accidentally cut. It curled tighter and tighter until, in a shower of purple sparks, it completely fused with the wire.

Pet's mistake was undone, and the generator came back to life, lighting the room.

But Xavis's feather was gone.

"Pet! What happened?" Bug rolled back and forth on the ground below, looking for him among the many arms coming off the generator.

Pet sat up, his whole body trembling. "I cut the wrong thing. Xavis fixed it, but now he's gone. I don't know what to do next."

"What have you done so far?"

He tried his best to describe every step he had taken under Xavis's instruction.

Bug fell silent. She paced in a circle, and her antennae curled toward her body as she thought. "Hmmm. I think you're almost done. If I've got this right, then all you need to do is reattach the ends of that wire you just cut. Can you manage if I walk you through it?"

Taking a deep breath, Pet picked up the ends of the correctly cut wire, trying to ignore the one next to it that had caused all the problems. "I think so."

"Great. Now, one side of that wire should be attached near a red light. Take that end and reattach it to the remaining half of the very first wire you cut."

Pet found the appropriate wire and twisted the two severed ends together so the copper filaments entangled. If he were Xavis, he would be able to reform the metal.

A proper technician would at least wrap the newly connected wires in electrical tape.

Unfortunately, he was neither of these things. So he twisted them as tight as human fingers could manage and hoped that would be enough.

When he finished, he called down the result to Bug.

Even out of sight, her response came immediately. "Good job. Now take the other end of that last wire and attach it to the open slot behind that piece you said looked like a microchip."

This was harder to locate. The *open slot* ended up being a needle-thin opening on the side of the chip. He had to double-check with Bug several times before he felt confident enough to try attaching the wire.

The entire panel went dark, except for a single flashing light right at the center.

Pet fumbled and dropped the wire cutters. They tumbled end over end, bouncing off the generator's arms and sending up a riotous clang of angry metal. Unable to do anything but watch, Pet stopped breathing when the tool landed inches away from Bug's treads.

Her mechanical arm picked up the tool without further ceremony and stored it away. "It's fine, Pet. The panel was supposed to turn off. Climb down while I finish up here."

Pet heaved a sigh, grateful to Bug for ignoring how close he'd come to almost impaling her. That would certainly have put a damper on their new friendship.

Climbing down the generator was harder than climbing up. He couldn't see where he was going, and his legs barely spanned the distance between branches. On each transfer he hung in open air, praying his feet would find metal.

He could have kissed the floor when he finally reached it.

"So what have we achieved?" His legs shook, and he collapsed onto the dusty floor as he waited for Bug to explain.

Bug finished whatever she was doing and resealed the outer panel. When she returned to his side, she carried a small device that looked even more patchwork than the *Vanguard*.

She held up the device with pride. "This is a remote for the generator. With this, we should be able to turn it off from anywhere in the lab."

It didn't look like an off switch. If anything, it looked like a cluster of dynamite. He trusted that it would do what she said but refused to touch it.

She tried to place the makeshift remote in her chair's storage compartment but found Pet's coat taking up the space.

Pet shifted the coat inside the compartment to make room for the remote. "Why don't we just turn the generator off now? Cut power to the whole lab."

Mechanical arms tried to help, but even Bug's artificial strength couldn't compress the faux fur any more. "There are two generators. Either is enough to keep the lab going, at least for a while. Cutting power to only one won't work, and if anyone discovers one of the generators has been tampered with, they might kill your trio."

There wasn't enough space in the compartment for both his coat and the remote.

Pet removed the coat yet was hesitant to leave it behind. Someone might find it, and he would need it if they ended up back out on the ice. "We need to turn off both generators at the same time. So you made a remote."

With the remote safely stored, Bug shut the compartment lid. "Exactly."

Pet stayed on the floor with the coat draped over his knees. "But Xavis's feather is gone."

Bug pulled him to his feet. "Each of the generators is located at the end of a main electrical line. I recognized the path we took to get here from the blueprint. If we follow the other main line, we'll find the other generator."

Pet shook dust from the coat. He might need it later, but they needed the remote now. Bringing the coat would only slow them down. "Even with Xavis's help I still messed up. I don't know if I can manage on my own."

Bug placed a hand on his arm. "We don't need to make another remote. Just turn it off. That'll be easier."

Nodding, Pet rolled the coat up and hid it behind some machinery at the far side of the room. If everything went as planned, it wouldn't be needed. They would free Xavis and Desmodian from their cages, then use the airship to get away.

The two of them stepped out into the hall, following Bug's mental map of the powerlines to the next generator.

He hoped their plan worked.

If it didn't, they had no alternative.

****

Finding the other generator turned out to be the easy part. Bug's directions led them to a set of double doors even more grandiose than the first. According to her, the previous generator had technically been the backup. This was the main one.

The room was double the size of any other room Pet had seen so far. However, the generator looked the same, with a round body and branching arms. Once again, there was no skylight, and being so far down in the lab meant the room was even darker than the bottom of the ocean had been. Lights ran along the main generator, trailing over the floor and walls to form a whirlpool pattern on the ceiling.

More machinery hid in the corners of the room. Thick electrical cables trailed from the generator to each machine. Some were small while some stood as big as the generator itself.

It was also warmer than anywhere else in the lab. The lines of Pet's thermal suit changed from green to blue as the suit switched to its lowest setting.

"So we just need to shut it off?"

Bug rolled to a stop in the middle of the room, surrounded by a dozen towering metal structures. The dust was thicker here, and her chair left long tracks over the floor. "Yep. It'll take me a few minutes, but I should be able to get it."

She opened a panel in the bottom of the generator. Her hands moved with confidence, never once hesitating, even in such a stressful situation.

An acidic emotion took root in Pet's stomach, the same one he'd felt when he'd seen other décor back on the island.

Envy.

If only he had such a useful skill. He looked pretty and was good in bed, but what else did he have to offer? When they got out of here—and they would get out of here—he vowed to learn as much as he could. He would find a skill, and he would become more than just a pretty piece of decoration.

Faint voices broke his self-reflection.

He put an ear against the door. "Bug. Someone's coming."

Her hands never faltered. "Hold on. I'm almost done."

The voices grew louder and too numerous to count.

When they sounded right outside the door, Pet abandoned his post and hurried to pull Bug from the generator. "No time. If we're spotted, it's over."

Her chair wouldn't budge. "Wait. Maybe I can…just…there."

Exposed wires flashed and went dark, but the rest of the generator continued working as normal.

Bug shoved the panel back into place, hiding the evidence of her tampering.

The two of them hid as far from the door as possible, behind a machine that looked like it belonged in an industrial kitchen.

Pet peered through a gap between two pipes.

Tradius stepped through the door with Yaivin right behind him.

The sight of the two Iknox didn't surprise Pet, but when Brog entered the room, he had to cover his mouth to stifle a gasp. The Ocan's condition had deteriorated even more since Pet last saw him. Cracks ran through his skin, glowing orange like molten lava fighting to burst free from a thin layer of earth.

Desmodian's hammer seemed to be the only thing keeping Brog upright.

More identical Iknox spilled into the room, differentiated only by the color of their clothes. They dragged the electrical cages containing Desmodian and Xavis with them. The bulky cages took a dozen people working together to move, and even more to manage the thick cables trailing behind.

Inside the cages, Desmodian and Xavis looked exhausted. Neither as bad as Brog, but their weariness was evident as they sat slumped behind bars.

Last into the room came a group of two dozen Schade. The living pillars formed a solid black wall in front of the door and planted themselves at equal intervals around the room.

Bug's antennae nudged Pet's cheek. "That's a lot of people."

Pet nodded. "I know. No way we're getting out of here without being caught."

Tradius stepped to the center of the room, walking right over Bug and Pet's footprints without noticing. "The Relativator is in here?"

Yaivin remained just a step behind his father, still clutching his bag in desperate hands. "Apparently, it's hardwired directly into the generator."

The father and son duo passed the generator without sparing it a glance. Instead, they came to a stop right in front of the machine hiding Pet and Bug.

Pet pressed deeper into the shadows but hit a wall. There was nowhere else to go.

Tradius scoffed. "This thing? It doesn't look so impressive."

Yaivin was barely visible over his father's shoulder. "The Relativator is inside. We'll need to remove the whole thing. Relativators are volatile if not contained properly."

A nod from the father sent the son shuffling back to the rest of their people with orders to prepare the Relativator for transport.

Pet sought Bug in the dark, keeping his voice to the softest whisper possible. "We need to turn the generator off now."

Bug's antennae twitched frantically, brushing against him. "It's almost done. There wasn't time to shut it down from the inside, so I deactivated the dampeners."

Pet waited for further explanation, but none came. "Sorry, I don't know what that means. Will that turn it off?"

"Instead of turning it off, we'll overload it. The fuses will trip and shut it down." One of her arms moved into the light, just enough to reveal a single finger. "See that panel on the wall over there where one of the generator's arms is attached? That's the regulator. Turn that dial to max, and it'll shut the whole thing down."

Pet found where she was pointing, and his momentary hope deflated. "You mean the dial on the other side of the room?"

"Yep."

He sighed. Of course, it had to be in the hardest place to reach.

"All right. You stay here with the remote for the secondary generator. I'll go for the dial. Be ready to hit the remote as soon as this generator shuts off."

Her hand retracted from the light. "Do you think you can sneak past that many people?"

He heard her moving around but couldn't see what she was doing. "Probably not." Her movements stopped, and he felt her getting ready to argue. "But I have a plan. Part of a plan. I have an idea, at least. Just stay out of sight and be ready."

Before she could talk him out of his probably stupid idea, he slipped from their hiding place.

Keeping his back to the wall and using the shadows as cover, he inched around the edge of the room.

It worked at first. The Iknox were so focused on the Relativator they never noticed him passing through the dark only inches away.

Halfway to his goal, he bumped into an unexpected wall. The metal felt strange, slightly pliant with microscopic grooves running from top to bottom. He strained his eyes against the darkness to see what stood in his way.

It wasn't a wall at all. It was a pillar.

"Fuck."

He tried to pull his hand away, but it was too late. His palm stuck fast to the surface.

The Schade dragged him into the light.

"No. Let go."

It was useless, but instinct made Pet keep struggling.

All movement ground to a halt as people noticed him. By the time the Schade brought him under the center point of the whirlpool lights, the room had grown deathly silent. Even the hum of the various machines seemed to have stopped.

He still fought to pull his hand free, so when the

Schade suddenly released its hold, he fell to the floor. A cloud of dust billowed up around him. He coughed and waved a hand to clear the air.

When the dust settled, he found himself kneeling at the feet of Tradius Vels.

Chapter Fourteen

Before

Liquid sloshed in the myriad of glass bottles surrounding Pet. The airship was moving, with no indication of where it was headed.

Pet sat huddled on the floor behind the bar service.

Once Brog had proven himself to Tradius, they promptly forgot about everything else. Brog was given a seat in the lounge and even offered a drink. The Ocan draped an arm over the back of the couch around Yaivin and fell into whispered conversation with the younger Iknox while Xavis and Desmodian were wheeled away in cages. Desmodian was still unconscious, but Brog didn't spare them a glance.

No one, not even the servants or Schade guards, remembered Pet.

Unable to look at Brog a moment longer, Pet slipped out of the private room and took refuge behind the bar in the common area.

Even if someone looked over the countertop, they wouldn't see him under the overhang, but no one was looking for him.

Why would they? He was just décor. Tradius's Schade guards only grabbed him because they'd seen him with his trio.

His trio. Could he even call them that anymore, or

had they just become a duo?

They would be zero if they couldn't find a way to escape. Tradius wasn't going to just let Xavis and Desmodian go.

The senior Iknox knew about the trio's Phazer abilities. For someone like him, a Phazer would be a powerful weapon. Even worse, Tradius knew their weaknesses.

How?

Had Brog told Yaivin?

Yesterday, Pet's answer to that question would've been an automatic *no*. Now, he wasn't so sure.

While Pet hid behind the bar, the air steadily grew colder. He rubbed at his bare arms and legs to chase away the goose bumps appearing on his skin.

Sitting around wouldn't do any good. Tradius and Brog were beyond his ability to deal with, but maybe he could find Xavis and Desmodian.

Rising onto his knees, he peeked over the top of the bar.

The empty common area extended the length of the ship.

Where was everyone? Desmodian and Xavis had been removed from the private lounge under guard. If they weren't in the common area or the private lounge, they had to be somewhere in the upper half of the airship.

Scooting along on his knees, he checked around the side of the bar. No one there either. Taking a deep breath, he stepped out from his hiding place.

Staircases flanked either side of the room. Pet could only keep one in view at a time, which always put one at his back. So far, he had been overlooked, but that might not continue if he was caught wandering around.

Couches and chairs were scattered throughout the common area, each a different style to accommodate different species. He moved to the nearest cluster of furniture and ducked out of view. Based on the style, this set had been designed for species with wings. It resembled Xavis's chair in the control room of their ship.

Pet paused, listening for anyone approaching. Once certain he was still alone, he moved to the next oasis of furniture and repeated the process.

In this fashion, he made it across the room. He put his back to the wall to keep both staircases in view but startled at the touch of cold glass. A large porthole window stood behind him, and the view outside made him forget his fear of being spotted.

Pale-gray clouds surrounded the airship, allowing brief glimpses of the ground. Everything was white. A few hours ago, they had been on a beach. Now they flew over a landscape of ice and snow.

And he was wearing a piece of string masquerading as a swimsuit.

On the beach, his outfit had been perfect for the warm climate. Looking at the frozen wasteland below made him shiver.

He retreated from the window and ran up the nearest staircase.

The upper half of the airship lay under a transparent dome, with walls dividing the space into smaller areas.

At the top of the stairs, Pet stopped to watch the sky. The stars looked dull compared to the view from the *Vanguard*. Usually, he flew among them. Here he remained below.

The first few rooms he checked held only furniture positioned for sky watching. There were no doors in the upper half of the airship. Even sticking to the shadows, he would be easily spotted.

Pet almost overlooked the next room. It seemed as empty as the others, but just as he passed the doorway, he stopped and looked back. A pillar stood among the furniture, easily mistaken for an artistic centerpiece.

It was a Schade. Silent and unmoving, its pitch-black surface contrasted with the moonlit clouds beyond the dome.

Pet jumped out of the doorway.

Could Schade see? They didn't have eyes, but they navigated their environment somehow. Maybe they hadn't spotted him.

He waited, pressed against the wall, barely daring to breathe. A break in the shadows across from him caught his attention.

Another Schade stood perfectly camouflaged against the dark wall.

Pet had walked right past without noticing it.

Neither Schade moved, as if they truly were inanimate.

Either they couldn't see him, or they didn't care about him wandering around.

He moved on, looking into each room. More Schades lurked at the edges of his vision.

At least two dozen living pillars stood guard around the upper half of the airship.

He'd been helpless against one.

Two dozen would be unstoppable if the situation turned violent.

He wasn't even sure his trio would be able to fight them.

His duo?

No. Now was not the time to think about that. He had to push forward.

At the center of the upper deck, artificial lights created a glare against the glass dome, distorting the view of the sky.

He looked into the room beyond the doorway, hoping to find Xavis or Desmodian.

Brog and Tradius stood around a table, with Yaivin just off to the side. They all stared at a thin stack of something spread over the tabletop.

Was that paper?

Brog held up the top sheet from the stack to get a better look in the light, giving Pet a clear view as well.

Yes, it really was paper. Some sort of blueprint had been printed on the two-dimensional surface. Imperfection in the lines suggested it had been drawn by hand rather than computer.

Brog put the paper down and gave a low whistle. "Damn. You really have one 'a these? How'd you get it here?"

Tradius glared at the paper. "Had to bring it in pieces. The sensors around this planet forced me to hide them as parts of my ship's engine. It'll need to be assembled on site. Didn't even dare keep the blueprints on file, but paper can't be hacked. It took months of organization."

Crossing one set of arms, Brog tapped a spot on the blueprint. "Not everythin'. Still missin' a key part."

Tradius barely glanced where Brog pointed before his scowl turned into a smile. The Iknox's stoicism meant there was little difference between his expressions, but crinkling at the corners of his eyes gave him away. "Yes, the plutonium. That was tricky. Unfortunately, plutonium was swapped out in spaceships for more stable uranium a few decades ago. So I couldn't smuggle it in like the other pieces. However, I found there is a way to enrich uranium into weapons-grade plutonium." He leaned forward and placed his hands on the table, as if eager to brag about his success.

Brog barely twitched.

"If you're hintin' at somethin', you better just say it. Chemistry's not my strong suit. Didn't think it was yours either. This is a strange plan for you."

Tradius scoffed, waving his hand as if batting away an annoying insect. "A man in my position must know a little of everything. My research says uranium can be turned into plutonium through the use of heavy water. And that was easy enough to find once we arrived."

"The syzygy event? That's why you're here now?" Brog's voice revealed no emotion.

Yaivin stepped up to the table, shifting slightly sideways so the bag he carried didn't bump the edge. In contrast to his father, the younger Iknox was easy to read. Every line of his face told a story. There was hesitancy and fear but also a small sense of pride whenever his eyes drifted toward Brog.

"The syzygy brings a swarm of Aura moths. The dust from their wings reacts with the water in the ocean and creates heavy water. There's an unusually high percentage of it floating around right now. It turned out to be the easiest part to acquire." He briefly touched his father's arm, and Tradius regained his usual unbending posture.

Brog never looked at either of the Iknox, instead tracing a finger along the blueprint. "An atomic bomb seems excessive just to break into a lab."

A side-eye from Tradius sent Yaivin back into the shadows out of sight. The older Iknox then pulled another sheet of paper from the bottom of the stack to display it on top. "This lab is more heavily reinforced than most spaceships. See here, it's buried under ice. Even with a bomb of this magnitude, we'll only have a single-entry point."

Clouds above the dome parted, revealing a large swath of uninterrupted sky. Moonlight clashed with the artificial light of the room, causing Brog and Tradius to each cast two shadows in opposite directions.

One of Brog's shadows brushed Pet's feet. He retreated around the edge of the doorway, fully out of sight, but still close enough to hear the conversation.

Brog didn't sound happy. "This lab is in the middle 'a nowhere for a reason. There's some dangerous shit in there. No tellin' how it would react to an atomic bomb."

Pet imagined the spines along the Ocan's shoulders raising in irritation.

If Tradius was intimidated by Brog's posturing, his voice bore no evidence. "The technology we're looking for will be fine, and this airship will make sure we're out of the blast radius. The rest isn't our problem. But if you're concerned, maybe you can take care of it."

After what felt like an eternity, Brog spoke only two little words. "I can."

Tradius's answer sounded like victory. "That's all we need."

Movement in the doorway made Pet retreat even

farther around another corner. Keeping one eye peeking out from his new hiding spot, he watched Yaivin step from the room.

The moment the younger Iknox was out of sight from his father and Brog, he leaned against the wall with a heavy sigh. "Idiot."

Pulling open the bag on his shoulder, he looked inside.

From his distance Pet could only see the top of some sort of canister. A complicated nest of wires looped around the metal, pulsing in a rhythmic beat.

Almost as soon as Yaivin opened the bag, he closed it again. "Not much longer. Then he won't be my problem anymore."

He started moving in Pet's direction.

Pet nearly tripped over himself in his hurry to avoid being spotted. He backed away from the corner, keeping it in his sight in case Yaivin decided to turn his way.

The younger Iknox went the other direction, and Pet heaved a sigh of relief.

That sigh turned into a yelp when his back hit something solid and warm. Heavy hands spun him around and braced him against a cold wall.

Brog stood over him, half in shadow and half in moonlight. "What're you doin' here?"

Pet stuttered, pressing flat to the wall. Brog's size had never intimidated him before. Not even the first time they met and the eager Ocan grabbed him out of the blue. Now, however, Brog seemed to loom over him, blocking any rout of escape.

Brog didn't wait for an answer. "Décor shouldn't be walkin' around."

The Ocan practically lifted Pet off his feet, dragging him back the way he'd come. He struggled to keep up as Brog led him down to the enclosed lower half of the airship.

"Brog?" Pet clawed at the thick fingers encircling his biceps. "Please. What's going on? You can't really be..."

He couldn't finish the accusation. The words didn't deserve to be spoken out loud.

Instead, he ended on a pathetic plea. "Just...tell me it's okay. Please."

Damn, there came the tears. He wiped them away before they finished their journey down his cheeks.

Brog spared him a glance but gave no words as he dragged Pet along. They pushed through a door marked "employees only" into a sparse industrial area lined with rows of metal lockers. Brog finally let Pet go and opened the nearest locker. Then he grunted, slammed it closed, and opened the next one.

Swallowing his nerves, and a fair number of tears, Pet laid a hand on the Ocan's shoulders. "Brog? What're we doing?"

This finally got Brog's attention. Shadows hung below orange eyes as Brog regarded him. A hand raised toward Pet's face but stopped just before touching his cheek. Instead, it clenched into a fist and dropped back to Brog's side.

"You're overlooked right now 'cause Tradius doesn't see you as a threat. That won't last. He's smart. He'll realize you're more perceptive than typical décor." Brog turned back to the lockers and pulled out a bundle of gray fabric. "Put this on. Quickly. We don't have much time."

Holding up the fabric, Pet stared in confusion at what turned out to be a thermal suit. "But Brog…"

Brog grabbed his arm again and barely avoided shaking him. "Put it on." Then the Ocan turned away and started searching the lockers again.

Despite his shaking hands, Pet bit his lip and put on the thermal suit. He didn't bother removing his Dust Party outfit. The thermal suit was too large for a human and hung off him like a curtain billowing over an open window. He could barely move through the excess fabric. "Now what?"

Brog returned to Pet's side with more clothing but dropped it to mess with the thermal suit's collar. He pressed something that lit up lines through the gray fabric. They started out blue, but quickly cycled between a rainbow of colors.

At the same time, the fabric shrank until it fit Pet perfectly.

Brog stepped back to look him over, then pointed at the clothing he'd dumped. "Nothin' here was made for humans. That suit may not be enough. Put this on as well."

He didn't wait to see if Pet obeyed, immediately leaving to search another set of lockers. The first door he opened brought an avalanche of windboards. Brog cursed as he kicked the boards out of the way and tried a different locker.

With a sigh, Pet retrieved the clothing from the floor. It was a heavy fur coat, just a little too big for human proportions, and a pair of equally furred boots that reached past his knees. The end result made him feel like a child prancing around in adult clothes, but at least it was warm.

So distracted trying not to trip over the clomping boots, he didn't notice Brog's return.

"Good. Now come here." He dragged Pet into an even smaller room at the far end of the staff area. A single round window illuminated Brog's face like a spotlight, revealing how dull his orange eyes had become.

Like a picture of a fire, the color was right, but there was no life.

Brog didn't look at him, too busy clipping something around Pet's chest with a myriad of buckles and straps.

Pet should've been paying attention to what he was doing. It was probably important. Yet he couldn't look away from those lifeless eyes. His hand raised of its own accord and stroked the side of Brog's face.

The Ocan startled at his touch and looked up, finally meeting Pet's eyes. "Pet, I..." Brog sighed and pressed their foreheads together. "Fuck. This isn't what I meant. You shouldn't even be here. I'm sorry. For it all."

It was such a natural motion, done so many times, that when Pet felt lips press against his own, he kissed back without thought. Two of Brog's hands cupped either side of Pet's head while the other two wrapped around his waist and pulled them flush together.

Pet opened his mouth to deepen the kiss, but Brog retreated.

Their eyes stayed locked for another moment until Brog turned to face the window. "Stand back."

He pulled a lever beside the window. With a hiss of decompression, a door opened straight into empty sky.

Wind reached inside the room, threatening to yank

Pet out of the airship.

Brog steadied him. "Don't worry." He shouted to be heard over the howling wind and tapped the complex straps around Pet's chest. "It's automatic."

"What?" Pet choked on his question as Brog shoved him out the door. For a moment he hung suspended in open air, reaching for the dark safety of the airship.

Then he plummeted.

The question he'd swallowed came back up as wordless shouting. Rushing air filled his ears and tore at him as if he scraped against a wall. Yet, in the swirling chaos, he saw Brog above him with startling clarity.

The Ocan clung to the open doorframe, a pained look on his face as he watched Pet fall.

Chapter Fifteen

After

Something was wrong.

Well, many things were wrong. They were all
trapped in the arctic, with untold miles of frozen
wasteland between them and civilization, at the mercy
of a power-hungry politician. Desmodian and Xavis
were in cages, and Brog seemed to be falling apart at
the seams. Nothing happening right now could be
called *right*.

Yet that wasn't what caught Pet's attention.

Why was Tradius Vels looking at him that way?

Greedy black eyes raked over him. This wasn't the
look of someone appreciating his value. It was want.

Yaivin stepped in front of his father, breaking the
older Iknox's line of view. "You're, um…Two-Six-
Eight-Nine, right? The décor for the *Vanguard*."

Pet stood and tried to ignore the dust covering him.
"My name is Pet."

A puzzled look twisted Yaivin's expression into
something unrecognizable.

Tradius pulled the younger Iknox back to his side.
"What is it doing here?"

Yaivin dipped his head to avoid looking his father
in the eye. "The Schade brought it onboard the airship. I
don't know why it's in the lab. No one gave it any

orders. Unless…"

For the first time since its appearance, Yaivin released the bag hanging on his shoulder. It swung freely as he turned to the electrical cages. "You were trying to use your décor to escape." He stepped closer to the cages, almost within reach of the bars. Not quite close enough to grab, but almost.

Both Desmodian and Xavis tensed. Xavis stayed seated, but Desmodian struggled to his feet and *stared* Yaivin in the eye. "How could we? We've been stuck in here the whole time."

Tradius plucked his son back from the cages. "There's no way they could have given the décor any orders. But he could have."

He pointed to Brog.

Off to the side, away from both the cages and the father-son pair, Brog couldn't even stand up straight against the accusation. Most of his weight leaned against Desmodian's hammer. All he could do was raise his head enough to meet Tradius's gaze. "Why would I?"

Yaivin protested at the same time. "He wouldn't. He's on our side."

"No."

It was the first time Pet heard Tradius yell.

From the way every Iknox in the room flinched, it might have been the first time Tradius ever raised his voice.

"He's not on our side. He's manipulating us to save his little friends."

As Tradius shouted, Pet inched toward the dial on the other side of the room. Maybe, while everyone was distracted, he could reach it and shut down the generator.

Unfortunately, the Schade were dedicated to their jobs. Living pillars still surrounded the room. They would stop him the moment he tried to go for the dial, and then Tradius might figure out his real plan. The older Iknox knew he was trying to free Desmodian and Xavis, but he hadn't yet figured out how Pet planned to accomplish this.

Pet needed to keep Tradius in the dark as long as possible.

Something about the older Iknox still bothered him. That look in his eyes when he gazed at Pet was different than it had been before. During his first few interactions with Tradius, the older Iknox regarded him as something pretty but easily bought.

Pet remembered his first auction. He'd been inspected by many buyers before Mister Stiril purchased him. It was obvious from the start which were serious buyers and which were window shoppers. They looked at Pet differently. The auction staff only focused on the serious buyers. Window shoppers had been hustled along as quickly as possible.

Tradius looked at him like a window shopper.

With this revelation in mind, other details became more obvious. The intricate gold sash Tradius wore sat just a little crooked on his shoulders. He gestured more with his hands. Before he'd always stood ramrod straight but now tilted his head when he spoke.

Then Pet saw Tradius's footprints in the dust.

On the beach, Tradius's footprints had been slightly uneven due to the limp he tried to hide. The footprints in the dust were perfectly even.

Pet's growing suspicion became a certainty. He

looked back over his shoulder toward the dial, measuring the distance between himself and the wall. With some luck, he might be able to provide his own distraction and get past the Schade all at the same time.

First, he needed to seem as unthreatening as possible. He clasped his hands and softened his posture into the stance of obedient décor. It was a position he had maintained for years, and still felt distressingly familiar, but it also provided the perfect camouflage. No one paid attention to décor when they looked like they were following orders. So no one looked at him now as he gradually drew closer to the argument building between Yaivin and Tradius.

Pet kept his eyes on the floor but his attention on Tradius.

The older Iknox faced his son, pointing emphatically at Brog. "He's only pretending to help us in order to free those two."

Brog could barely hold himself up. He didn't have enough energy to argue.

Yaivin kept looking between his father and Brog. "But he was furious with the Dhen'in, and Brog's never been the type to stay in one place for long."

"Maybe not when you knew him, but he's obviously changed a lot since then."

Tradius turned, putting his back directly toward Pet.

Perfect.

Pet lunged and grabbed Tradius's sash. The Iknox was lighter than expected. He pulled too hard and nearly sent Tradius flying. At the last moment he managed to keep hold of the older Iknox and bunched his hands in the front of Tradius's toga.

Tradius tried to push him off.

Pet stumbled but kept his grip and brought the older Iknox with him. He was careful not to rip Tradius's clothes. Not yet.

Instead, he pretended to fumble with the sash. He saw the moment the Iknox realized what he was doing.

Black eyes widened, and hands shoved at Pet with new desperation. The two of them scuffled, Tradius pushing and Pet pulling.

Over Tradius's shoulder Pet saw Yaivin coming to break up the fight. He was out of time. They had nearly reached the line of Schade guards. It would have to be enough.

Taking hold of Tradius's toga in both hands, he ripped it right down the front.

The delicate fabric tore easily and parted all the way from collar to waist, leaving the Iknox's entire torso on display.

Just for good measure, Pet shoved him back toward Yaivin, making sure to turn him so everyone saw his revealed state.

A gold identifier with a curved design gleamed on his chest. It resembled a question mark and was definitely not the one belonging to Tradius Vels.

The older Iknox—whoever they were—tried to cover themself, but it was too late. They had been seen by every pair of eyes in the room.

Silence descended as the imposter clutched the remains of their clothes, no longer even trying to act like Tradius as they stared around the room in fear.

Pet laughed. Out of the corner of his eye, he noticed the shocked looks from all three of his trio. He couldn't blame them. He hated it when someone expressed one emotion while meaning another, yet here he was laughing without humor.

It felt wrong, but he forced himself to keep going. "Don't be so surprised." He caught the imposter's attention, and fearful black eyes zeroed in on him. "It's a miracle no one noticed you earlier. You're not a very good actor."

The imposter started crying, taking Pet by surprise. He had expected anger, not tears.

The Iknox dropped to his knees, weeping into his hands. "No. It's not my fault. I did everything you said."

A heavy sigh interrupted the imposter's stuttering, and Yaivin grasped the other Iknox's shoulder. "Do yourself a favor and shut up."

Yaivin's voice had lost his softness. Now it sounded like ice, a deadly combination of hard and cold. With one hand still on the weeping Iknox's shoulder, he used the other to point a small device at the imposter. Most of the device remained hidden within Yaivin's palm, with just the barrel sticking out.

It would have barely looked like a threat, except for the way the imposter scrambled to get away. "But, wait." Their limbs flailed as their hands slipped on the dusty floor. "You said if I helped you, then you'd make me Second-in-line once you became First."

Another sigh from Yaivin. "Well, that only works if you aren't discovered. Now you're useless to me."

The device flashed white, shooting out a beam of light that burned right through the imposter's chest.

He slumped dead on the floor as a pool of black blood spread around him.

Yaivin huffed, straightening his clothes and

backing away from the blood to keep it off his shoes. Furious eyes turned in Pet's direction. "Not just ordinary décor, are you?"

He slugged Pet across the face.

Pet expected a slap. The closed fist came as a surprise. Hardened patches on the Iknox's knuckles struck deep into the side of his jaw. The world spun, and he stumbled, bouncing off one of the Schade before hitting the floor.

Blood filled his mouth. He'd never tasted it before but somehow recognized it anyway. It was more metallic than he imagined.

Yaivin wasn't done. He reared a foot back and kicked Pet in the stomach. "You ruined everything."

Pet wrapped his arms around his middle to shield his ribs, and he took some of the force out of the blow by rolling with the kick. It still hurt and knocked the air out of his lungs, but at least nothing was broken.

Instead of hitting him again, Yaivin picked him off the floor and shoved him against the wall. One hand gripped Pet's throat while the other pointed something at his head.

Pet got an up-close look at the device that killed the imposter, a miniscule gun perfect for smuggling past security. He clawed at Yaivin's hand around his throat, but hard patches on the Iknox's knuckles easily fended off blunt human nails.

Pet struggled to breathe, and his vision swam. In the distance, Brog's shouting sounded like it came from underwater.

"Don't you dare hurt him." Orange sparked for a moment between Pet and Yaivin but died before taking effect. Desmodian's hammer slipped out from under

Brog's arm, and the Ocan collapsed to his knees.

Yaivin squeezed harder, completely cutting off Pet's air. "I thought you were on my side, Brog. You were so eager to hurt your friends before. What does one little décor matter?"

The muzzle of the gun dug into Pet's temple, barely an inch wide but more than enough to take Pet's life.

Spots danced in Pet's vision, and his eyes threatened to burst out of his head. No one was coming to save him this time.

Unable to remove Yaivin's hands, Pet slapped helplessly at the body in front of him. He found the strap around Yaivin's chest and followed it down to the bag hanging off the Iknox's hip. Tears dripped from his eyes, and his vision turned white, but clumsy fingers slipped into the bag and grabbed some sort of handle. It felt heavy.

That would work.

Pet swung the object at Yaivin's head with all the strength he had left.

It glanced off the side of Yaivin's temple, knocking the Iknox back.

Sliding down the wall, Pet landed on the floor with a painful jolt, coughing to breathe through his abused throat.

His ribs ached, and his stomach flipped like he was about to throw up. Through swimming vision, he looked at what he'd pulled from Yaivin's bag.

The canister had glass walls and a complicated system of electronics on each end. A living heart floated inside, surrounded by a viscus yellow liquid. Wires connected to the heart, keeping the organ beating.

Tradius's golden identifier gleamed among the wires, still attached to the heart.

Pet shouted and tossed the canister away.

It hit the floor without a scratch and rolled away. The yellow liquid clung to the canister's glass sides, and the heart flipped around, tangling in its wires.

Yaivin chased after it. Uncaring feet stomped through the blood still leaking from his dead accomplice, leaving black footprints in the dust.

"What the hell, Yaivin?" Brog wheezed through each word, staring at Yaivin and the canister with horrified eyes.

On the other side of the room, the other Iknox clustered together. They wore a variety of different colors, but all bore the same terrified expression. Some tried to flee, but Schade still guarded the door.

Pet looked up. He sat directly under the dial, just as he'd planned. Unfortunately, he would have to stand to reach it. He tried, but his head spun so badly he collapsed as soon as his weight shifted.

Directly under the whirlpool lights, Yaivin cradled the canister with the heart like a parent comforting a child. "The sensors guarding this planet are too sensitive. They would've noticed an imposter. Talking my father into coming here wasn't easy, but after that, I didn't need him anymore."

Brog trembled with the effort to even remain kneeling. More cracks opened along his skin. "He was your father."

"He was my jailer." Stepping closer to Brog, Yaivin tipped the Ocan's face up with a gentle hand to stare into his eyes. "You know what it's like, living under the control of someone like that. It's why you joined me, right?"

Pet took a deep breath. He needed to get up. He needed to hit that dial. Then his trio would be free to defend themselves.

Bracing his hands on the floor, he managed to push himself into a kneeling position.

"Liar."

Yaivin's sudden shout made Pet jump, then groan and clutch his ribs.

The Iknox still held Brog's face with one hand, digging fingers into Brog's flesh. More cracks formed under his grip, dripping orange over Yaivin's lilac skin.

"I see it in your eyes. You never wanted to help me. You were just using me to save them." With the canister holding his father's heart, Yaivin gestured wildly at Desmodian and Xavis still trapped in their cages.

Brog trembled, but his gaze remained firm as he looked up at Yaivin. "You used me as well. To help you break into this place."

Yaivin merely laughed. "It's your place to be used. Isn't that what you want? To be useful? Well, now you are."

This man was insane. They all needed to get as far away from him as possible.

Bracing his hands against the wall, Pet struggled to his feet. The dial was higher than he originally thought. Even standing with his arm stretched to its full length, he couldn't quite reach. He stood on his toes, and his fingertips brushed the edge of the panel holding the dial.

Pet's back was to Yaivin, so he couldn't see what

was happening but heard the Iknox continue to rant.

"Did you seriously think I would come all this way without knowing how to find the Relativator in this maze of a lab? Our identifiers take time to register. I needed to make sure Father's location was recorded. Once his crime was noticed, then his poor abused Second-in-line would have no choice but to stop him.

"He takes the blame. I cry over the pain of having to kill my own father and how unfortunate it is that I don't know what he did with the Relativator. Authorities won't waste resources searching for lost tech that had been abandoned anyway. Then I'd become First-in-line, and I'd be free to do whatever I want with the Relativator. It would've been perfect, and it was ruined by your overpriced trinket."

Pet had felt Yaivin's eyes on his back before. He knew the moment Yaivin looked his direction.

Out of time.

He jumped for the dial at the same time Yaivin yelled for someone to stop him. Luckily, his fingers found the knob on the first try and turned it as far as it would go.

His feet never hit the ground again. Still in midair, his arms and legs attached like magnets to a pair of Schade, one on his left side and one on his right. He hung spread-eagled between the two living pillars, stretched to the limit of his limbs.

The Schade glided over the floor, not even disturbing the dust as they brought him before Yaivin.

"You continue to be a nuisance." The Iknox's slight stature meant he had to glare up at Pet.

It would've been amusing if Pet wasn't aware of how easily his captors could rip him in half. "I thought I was just an overpriced trinket."

"What you are is stupid. I know what you're trying to do. It won't work."

Lights along the generator shone like beacons. Machinery cried out as it spun faster and faster until electrical sparks danced over the outer shell and along each branching arm. With a final shriek of metal against metal, the generator went dark.

Yet the rest of the lab remained unaffected.

Yaivin gave him a cruel smirk. "Good try. But this lab has more than one generator."

Pet matched the smirk with one of his own. "I know."

Then the whole lab went dark.

People shouted, metal clanged, and Yaivin called for someone to find a light.

Pet flinched when the Schade on either side of him began to glow.

One by one, the rest of the Schade followed suit. Pools of light allowed people to see but also made the surrounding shadows darker. Machinery twisted into ominous shapes, as if an army of giant monsters lurked just out of sight.

The abrupt changes in light gave Pet a headache. His eyelashes fluttered as he waited for his vision to adjust. Once he could focus, he immediately looked for Desmodian and Xavis.

Two cages stood empty. Their bars bent outward like hatched eggs.

"Put him down."

Purple light sparked, followed by the sound of sharp edges striking metal.

The Schade abruptly released Pet.

Taloned hands caught him before he hit the floor. "I got you."

Pet clung to Xavis, wrapping his arms around any part of the Scaacax he could find. "You're all right."

Xavis held him tight and stroked his hair. "Thanks to you. Glad you got my message. Never tried that trick with the feather before. I couldn't maintain connection with anything outside the cage. So I poured my intent and knowledge into a single feather, hoping that would allow it to function on its own as if it were me."

Pet closed his eyes and drew in deep lungfuls of Xavis's scent, basking in the comforting mix of sweetness and spice. "It worked. I'm sorry it took so long."

"Don't apologize for success. Now, can you stand?"

Pet's legs shook but held his weight. Still, Xavis kept an arm around him, and Pet had no intention of telling him to let go.

The Schade that had been holding Pet vibrated. The disks comprising their bodies reshuffled in jerky uncoordinated movements. Rust crept up the living pillars, and the disks grated against each other.

Both Schade retreated into the shadows before Pet saw the end result of Xavis's work.

A bubble of light, swirling with a mix of green and orange, led them to Desmodian and Brog. The Ocan lay flat on the ground gasping for air. Molten orange leaked from the cracks in his skin and pooled on the floor like blood.

Brog grasped blindly in Desmodian's direction. "Sorry."

"Shut up." Desmodian knelt at Brog's side and

placed a hand on the center of his chest. "Save your strength. You're burned-out."

Orange light soaked into Desmodian's hand, climbing up his arm and turning green when it reached his chest. From there it flowed down his other arm into his hammer.

Slowly the cracks along Brog's skin receded.

Desmodian shook from the strain but didn't relent until the cracks disappeared and Brog breathed normally.

Although still emaciated, the Ocan remained in one piece.

Something metal bumped against Pet. He jerked back, nearly knocking Xavis over.

"It's me." Bug rolled into sight.

The colors emanating from his trio reflected off her chair. Pet didn't let go of Xavis but reached out to her with one hand. "There you are. I was worried."

Her mechanical arms folded and unfolded several times. "You were worried? I was worried. Was that really your plan to shut off the generator? Get captured and let that Iknox beat you until you reached the dial?"

He shrugged. "Something like that. It worked for Xavis, so I figured I could try something similar."

Sharp talons pricked Pet's skin as Xavis gripped tighter. "Pet, no. Don't copy me. I'm not a role model you want to follow." He eyed Bug up and down before recognition struck. "You're the waiter from that restaurant on the beach. What're you doing here?"

Pet turned Xavis's head, forcing the Scaacax to look at him. "She's a friend. It's a long story, but I would've been lost without her."

Having a newcomer in their midst obviously made

Xavis uneasy, but he took Pet's word and nodded. "If you're Pet's friend, then you're our friend. Sounds like we owe you a lot."

A groan from Brog interrupted them. Orange light disappeared as Brog gained awareness in sudden increments like climbing stairs. First his limbs started moving, then he abruptly tried to sit up.

"Easy." Desmodian pushed Brog back down.

"Stop…" Brog flailed helplessly. "Stop him."

Xavis and Pet knelt on Brog's other side, each taking one of his hands. Pet felt every tendon shift as if Brog's skin didn't even exist.

Xavis was extra careful with his talons as he stroked Brog's head. "It's okay. The lab's got all kinds of security cameras. Yaivin's plans have been exposed. He's done."

Brog shook his head, though it looked like an involuntary spasm. "No. Yaivin's always been self-destructive. He'll take everyone down with him before he gives up."

A bright light illuminated the room as if the sun had risen indoors.

Pet shielded his eyes as he peered into the source.

Someone stood at the center of the radiance, visible only by their silhouette, and grasped the heart of the light.

It dimmed to a tolerable level, turning the room to dusk.

The container for the Relativator hung open.

Yaivin stood in front of it, holding a crystal prism in one hand and his father's heart in the other.

Xavis pushed Pet toward Bug, opening his wings to shield them.

Desmodian jumped to his feet. "Yaivin, put that back. A Relativator can't be removed from its containment."

Pet peered between feathers.

Colors and lights swirled inside the Relativator prism, as if it contained an entire galaxy.

Somewhere in the back of his brain, he noticed the Schade had disappeared, but that didn't matter as Yaivin raised the Relativator over his head.

Brog collapsed when he tried to stand. "Yaivin, don't. It'll kill you."

Shadows moved at the edge of the Relativator's light.

The other Iknox fled the room but didn't have time to get far.

Yaivin smiled with a serene mouth but pained eyes. "Sorry, Brog. You tried, but it's useless. I'm already dead."

Several things happened at once.

Yaivin smashed the Relativator at his feet.

Desmodian dove to cover Brog.

Xavis wrapped his wings around Pet and Bug.

The whole world turned black and white. Proportions stretched and distorted like an optical illusion. A shield of green and purple formed around their small group, weaker than it should be. Orange tried to join but faded. The shield stretched to protect anyone nearby but only reached a few.

Pet's senses turned inside out. He no longer felt the metal of Bug's chair or the brush of Xavis's feathers. Instead, he felt his own organs pressing against each other and the blood pumping through every inch of his veins. The sound of people shouting was replaced by the snap of synapses firing in his brain.

He could've counted every cell in his body.

It was too much. He closed his eyes and covered his ears, praying for it to pass.

His ears popped.

Had his eardrums ruptured? There'd been no pain, but everything went silent.

Pet opened his eyes. He stood alone in a black void, with small lights twinkling in the distance like stars. Bug, his trio, Yaivin, the Iknox, and even the various machines around the room were all gone.

No, not alone. The distant lights coalesced into a human shape. He'd seen the person once before, several months ago, on a recording he never should have been shown.

His own eyes looked back at him from a stranger's face.

It was himself, before he became décor. Everything looked exactly the same. Baggy clothes hid a malnourished frame. Lank hair fell in uneven lines, as if hacked away by an unsteady hand. Sickly pale skin emphasized the shadows under their eyes.

The stranger looked at him, and he looked back.

He tipped his head to the side. The stranger copied.

It was impossible to tell who moved first. Trembling hands reached toward each other.

When their fingertips touched, darkness crashed against them like a tsunami. Pet tumbled head over feet, limbs flailing in open air, and landed hard on his back.

It took a while to regain his senses. The air stung his lungs, it was so cold, and the hard surface at his back made him shiver uncontrollably. His head pounded, but he opened his eyes.

Blinding white made him immediately close them. The pain stabbing his pupils receded, and he tried again, opening his eyes slower this time.

A pale sun sat directly overhead. It reflected off the frozen landscape, making everything look much brighter despite the ominous gray clouds.

Pet lay on his back in the middle of the arctic, right at the edge of a smoldering crater. The remains of the lab stuck out of the ice in twisted structures of charred metal.

He looked around.

Bug's chair lay broken on its side. Its back faced him, and he could just see the light coming from the neural connector. Hopefully, that meant it was still working and that Bug was okay.

Just past Bug, his trio lay scattered over the ground, unconscious but breathing.

Pet sagged against the ice and closed his eyes. They were alive. That would have to be enough for now because he didn't have the strength to reach them.

Ice crunched in the rhythmic pattern of footsteps.

Pet looked toward the sound, turning his head at an awkward angle when he couldn't lift it off the ground.

A human climbed out of the crater.

What was 3155 doing here?

She stopped at the top of the crater and brushed a gray mix of soot and snow from her sensibly warm clothes. In one hand, she held something that looked like a large, geometric egg made of a dark material.

With a grunt she set the heavy device down and raised a communicator to her lips.

"Yeah. I got it. Smaller than I thought it would be. Seems like a lot of fuss for a fancy smelter." She tapped the egg-shaped device with her foot, then stopped to listen to the person on the other end of the communicator. "You were right. The electrical cages worked, but we'll need to redesign them. Solid walls instead of open bars would be better."

She stopped to listen again, surveying the landscape and the unmoving bodies scattered around. Her gaze swept toward Pet, and he closed his eyes, pretending to be unconscious.

Whatever she was doing here, instinct told him it was dangerous. With his eyes closed, he listened carefully.

"Yaivin did exactly as we thought. Even saved us the trouble of getting rid of him. Idiot blew himself up. I'm on my way back now." There was another pause as she listened again, followed by a breathy huff. "I still don't see why I can't... Fine, I won't kill him."

The communicator beeped, signaling the end of the conversation.

3155 grumbled, but her words were lost to the howling arctic wind.

Crunching footsteps came closer, uneven and one sided, probably due to the weight of the device she carried.

Pet barely kept himself from flinching when something heavy planted right next to his head. 3155 knelt at his side, close enough for him to feel the heat of her breath.

"I should just kill you now. Get it over with."

Did she know he was awake? Should he try reasoning with her?

She cursed under her breath.

Pet realized his mistake. She wasn't talking to him.

She was talking to herself.

A hand wrapped around his throat, pressing just hard enough to make breathing difficult.

Was she really going to kill him? He could try to fight her off, but in his state, she would easily overpower him.

Her hand left, and the heat of her breath disappeared. "But he would get angry if I did. You're not worth that. Enjoy your life for now. I'll take it eventually."

She picked up the heavy device and walked away.

Pet wanted to see where she went, but couldn't even muster the strength to open his eyes. His limbs may as well have been rooted to the ground for all he was able to move them.

He lay on the ice, shivering in the cold despite his thermal suit. When he'd looked around earlier, the suit's lines had been glowing bright red. Even working at full capacity, the suit still wasn't enough to keep him warm.

As unconsciousness claimed him, he worried about the others. What would happen to them if left exposed to the cold?

Even that worry disappeared when he fell unconscious and every thought went silent.

Chapter Sixteen

Before

Blood rushed in Pet's ears like crashing tides. Yet there was no water. He'd been pushed from the airship and left to the mercy of empty air.

Wind scraped over his flesh like knives.

He was falling.

Falling.

Falling.

Falling.

Gray clouds and dark sky tumbled around him. Clouds, sky, clouds, sky, clouds, sky. Somewhere out of sight lay the unforgiving ground.

No one would hear him when he died.

Pet curled in on himself, eyes closed, and braced for the final impact. Something on his back beeped. He could barely hear it but felt the vibration through his coat and thermal suit.

The beeping grew more urgent, screaming so loud it overtook the howl of the wind.

With a sudden jolt, the straps around his chest pulled him upward. For a moment it felt like he was back in the safety of his antigravity bubble on the *Vanguard*, free-floating without weight.

The illusion didn't last long.

He started falling again but slower this time. The

straps supported him like a pair of great hands gently lowering him downward.

Pet caught his breath. Was it over? Was he safe?

He looked up through tears of pain and cold. A translucent silver canopy hovered above. Thin filament threads connected the parachute to the straps around his torso, keeping him upright as he floated toward the ground.

The threads were so thin. They were probably sturdier than they looked, yet he couldn't shake the fear that they would snap at any moment.

He wrapped his arms around himself and watched the approaching ground. An endless field of ice and snow lay below. This didn't tell him much about his location. Ninety percent of planet Syzygy was frozen. He could be almost anywhere.

Which basically meant he was nowhere.

How much farther until he hit ground?

He strained to look down past his feet and gasped.

It was closer than expected and approaching fast.

In the air, his descent felt slow, but seeing the ground approach at an alarming rate, he realized how quickly he was falling.

Fear and cold shared a lot of similarities. Both penetrated deep into the body, past the bones right into the marrow.

Pet had never known fear or cold like he did as he hurtled toward the ground with no idea how to land.

Ice was a form of water, and hitting the surface of water was easier with legs tucked.

So he did the same thing.

He hit the ground at an angle. His feet touched first but found no traction on the ice. Instead of a steady landing, he slid along the ground, tumbling over himself. When he came to a stop, he sat stunned for a moment. He was fine. A little bruised, but he'd had worse from an energetic night with his trio. Whooping in relief, he threw his hands in the air and fell onto his back in the snow.

His relief was short-lived.

Wind caught the parachute still attached to his harness. It dragged Pet over the ice, scraping him against frozen edges.

He scrabbled for something to hold on to as he was reeled like a fish on a line.

He needed to get free, or he'd be dragged from one side of the arctic circle to the other. Already his fingers felt stiff with cold. Clumsy hands struggled to undo the buckles, further hindered by the gloves built into the thermal suit.

The wind shifted. It twisted the parachute and flipped Pet onto his front.

He braced a hand against the ice to protect his face, leaving him only one hand to fumble with the buckles.

Finally, he managed to free himself. The moment he undid the last buckle, the parachute was ripped away by the wind like a child taking back their favorite toy.

Pet lay panting in the snow. Ice crystals clung to his eyelashes and melted on his face. "Well, at least you're alive."

His words froze the moment they hit the air. He sighed, adding to the cloud forming around him, and sat up. A layer of ice matted down the thick fur of his coat.

Somewhere during his struggle, he'd lost one of his oversized boots. He slowly got to his feet, checking for injuries along the way. Nothing hurt beyond scrapes and bruises. Standing on one foot, he scanned the landscape for his lost boot.

There, near the spot where he first landed. A hint of silver stuck out of the snow.

The thermal suit had soles built into the feet but couldn't ward off the feeling of snow squishing between his toes. On slow, careful steps, he followed the drag mark left by his landing.

By the time he reached his boot, his foot burned from the cold, and his toes had gone numb. He sighed in relief as he slipped his foot back into the warm cavern of fur. The boots came up past his knees, and he appreciated the cover they provided. Colored lines along the thermal suit glowed bright red. It was doing its best, but this suit wasn't built for such extreme cold.

He needed to keep moving. Sitting in the middle of the arctic feeling sorry for himself would only succeed in freezing to death. The suit would eventually run out of power.

Stomping his foot to secure the boot in place, Pet turned his gaze to the sky.

A line cut through the clouds, showing the path of the airship.

Following the ship might lead him to more trouble, but it was the only hope he had. His trio weren't coming for him this time.

Pulling the hood of his coat tighter over his head, he started walking.

Hours passed in a daze. The landscape looked the same in every direction, barren and white.

There was no way to tell how far he traveled.

Moonlight reflected off the snow, turning it into an ocean of crushed diamond. Blue shadows decorated the edges of each dip and peak.

The snow acted as an insulator, absorbing every sound until it felt like he had cotton stuffed in his ears. It was a little too similar to a deprivation chamber for comfort.

He wanted to be back on the *Vanguard*, warm and safe, with his trio around him. Even being back on the beach of Starthrone Island would have been fine. At least then he would have the option to leave.

Frozen tears stuck his eyelashes together.

His trio. What was happening with them? They'd been having problems during most of their time on the island. Then, for a terrifying moment, it looked like Brog had betrayed them. Desmodian's screams played again in Pet's ears, making him wish for silence.

Yet Brog then turned around and snuck Pet off the airship to protect him.

Pet wanted to believe in Brog. He needed to believe everything Brog had done was for a reason. Surely, there had to be a plan Pet wasn't aware of.

Time passed without measure as Pet continued walking, lost in his own thoughts to distract from the cold.

The three moons weren't quite as lined up here as back on Starthrone Island.

He kept an eye on them, but they didn't seem to move. Had less time passed than he thought, or did the sky move differently in the arctic? Most of Pet's understanding of the stars came from the perspective of space. He didn't know how they were viewed from a planet.

The landscape changed so gradually that he didn't notice at first. Packed ice turned into loose snow until eventually he hiked through waist-deep powder. It made for very slow progress because he had to dig and stomp a path for himself, but the walls of snow helped block the wind.

Despite the cold, he was sweating by the time he reached the peak of a tall snowdrift. He stopped to catch his breath and survey his surroundings.

Dawn broke over the horizon, refracting off the ice and turning the white ground into a bright mosaic. Pastel pinks and oranges streaked through the lightening sky while a hint of deeper red curled its fingers over the edge of the land.

Something dark stuck out of the ground in the distance. It imitated a jagged sheaf of rock, but its angles were too perfect.

Near the structure sat a familiar airship.

Pet gave a heavy sigh.

He'd found it. Now what?

That was a question for the bottom of the snowdrift. Climbing down was harder than climbing up. Gravity threatened to send him tumbling down the slope. He tested each step before putting his full weight on any foot. Even so, he tripped several times. At one point he lost his boot again and had to spend several minutes digging it out of the snow.

At the bottom of the snowdrift, he lost sight of the structure and the airship. Thanks to the sun, he knew which way to go, but he didn't dare get too close. If he saw an opportunity to free Xavis and Desmodian, he would take it, but Brog had pushed him off the ship for a reason. He was safer away from whatever Tradius planned. Brog had taken a risk getting him out of there. Pet wouldn't disrespect that by getting caught again.

He headed in the direction of the airship. When its top peeked over the edge of another snowdrift, he hunkered down and peered over the crest.

Down below, far enough away to keep him hidden, he got his first proper view of the artificial structure beside the airship. Mostly buried, its visible portion was small, but a shadow in the ice revealed the structure's massive size.

A whole compound lay under their feet.

People gathered around the exposed part of the structure. From this distance Pet couldn't identify individuals, but basic shapes at least revealed their species.

There was no sign of Xavis or Desmodian.

Schade stood guard over the many Iknox who carried pieces of something that they assembled against the structure wall.

A new silhouette appeared among the crowd. The tall four-armed figure could only be Brog. He stood over the group like an overseer.

Knowing Brog had some level of control here gave Pet a sense of confidence.

Everything would be okay. Brog would make sure of it. Right?

This would be a great chance to search the airship for Xavis and Desmodian, but the flat white landscape didn't provide many hiding places. He couldn't get closer without being spotted.

A ripple passed through the group. Even Brog seemed agitated.

Then, all at once, the Iknox rushed back inside the airship.

The Schade followed, gliding smoothly over ice.

With little ceremony, the airship took off into the sky. It left behind nothing but a round indent in the snow.

Cold dread filled Pet's stomach. He threw himself behind the snowdrift, curling into a protective ball with his eyes shut and his hands over his face.

Even the wind died, and a heavy silence took its place. It seemed like the very planet held its breath.

A flash of light filled the air, so bright Pet could see the skeleton of his hands through his eyelids. The snowdrift collapsed. Feet upon feet of snow crashed over him like an endless ocean wave, but he didn't dare move.

Immediately following the light came a blast of sound so loud it felt like someone had punched through his ears into his brain. It shook the ground like an earthquake, bringing more snow down on top of him.

Lastly came a wave of heat worse than anything Pet had felt before. Melting snow skipped the liquid phase and turned directly to steam. It would have burned him if not for the heavy fur coat and thermal suit protecting his skin.

All at once the light and heat stopped.

Darkness returned behind Pet's eyes, and cold arctic air crystallized the steam into a cloud.

Pet pulled shaking hands away from his face. He didn't have to dig himself out of the snow drift. It was almost entirely gone.

Rolling onto his back, he looked up into a picture of pure terror.

Fire and lightning filled the sky. A burning mushroom cloud stretched so high it surpassed the natural clouds. Its upper umbrella kept expanding until it seemed to touch the horizon on every side.

This was it. This was how he died. There was no surviving this.

Pet was too shocked to even care. He just stared, scared and mesmerized, as the cloud covered everything in sight.

The edges of the cloud abruptly curled backward as if they hit a wall. Orange light formed a barrier around the mushroom cloud, slowly forcing it to retreat. The smaller it grew, the denser the light became, until the orange turned opaque. It kept condensing, bringing the mushroom cloud right back to its root.

Brog stood exposed on an open patch of ice, arms outstretched. His whole body glowed orange, even brighter than when the trio had vaporized a spaceship.

Contained within its barrier, the mushroom cloud shrank until it was small enough for Brog to hold. He squeezed the orb between all four hands, pressing tighter and tighter until his fingers blocked out the light. He shouted, and his muscles bulged as if they would break through his skin.

With a disproportionate pop, his palms met, and the remnants of the mushroom cloud winked out of existence.

The light glowing from Brog's skin remained, and smoke rose from his hands when he parted them. He collapsed to both knees, and all four arms braced against the ground.

Pet didn't move. As much as he wanted to run to Brog and comfort him, the snowdrift had melted. A few inches of snow remained, but that would only conceal him if he stayed prone. He surely wasn't the only one watching the Ocan from a distance, and Brog wouldn't thank him for getting caught again.

A tremble in the ground pulled Pet's attention away from Brog. Partially melted snow shifted as a crack formed in the ice. Before Pet could move, the ground collapsed, and he tumbled into a pit. Air rushed from his lungs when he hit the bottom. Lying on his back, he stared up through the crack in the ice at the clear sky.

He was alive. They were all alive, thanks to Brog. Any remaining doubt about the Ocan's intentions vanished.

Closing his eyes, Pet coughed as he started breathing again, imagining the mist trailing from his mouth joining the clouds far above. Brog was still on their side.

Pet would find a way to help his trio. At the end of this ordeal, all four of them would return to the stars where they belonged.

Chapter Seventeen

After

Everything was white when Pet opened his eyes, and he immediately shut them again.

Was he still in the arctic? No. It smelled wrong. The frozen wasteland had smelled sharp, cold, and a little bitter. In a way it reminded him of living on the *Vanguard* surrounded by metal but much less inviting.

Pet smelled none of that now. This place smelled clean and sterile, like air that had been filtered too many times.

Also, he was warm.

He opened his eyes again. White walls surrounded him. He lay on a white bed, dressed in white sheets, and neatly propped on a stiff white pillow.

"Where am I?" It took effort to sit up, and his head felt heavier than his neck could support.

"This is Silverbay Private Hospital."

Pet jumped and nearly fell off the narrow bed.

A pale-peach Rurarine with sky-blue highlights filled the doorway. Their chair had a minimalistic design, built into tracks along the floor, and strangely made from clear plastic.

The Rurarine came to the side of the bed. "I'm your designated nurse. You're being monitored for a concussion. Please remain still."

Pet reached up and felt a band strapped around his head. Sensors pressed against his scalp, feeding information through wires into an interface like Bug used earlier, so probably scent based.

A small screen off to the side showed a translation of the information, but it was all wavy lines and indecipherable medical jargon.

How had he gotten from the arctic to a hospital? If this Rurarine was a nurse, then they must know what happened to him.

Pet swung his legs around and perched on the edge of the bed. "What's going on? How did I get here? Where's everyone else?"

The nurse didn't respond, instead plugging their chair into the computer to review the readings. "Everything's looking good. I'll inform your Owners."

They disengaged from the computer and headed out the door without another word.

Pet jumped from the bed, throwing the sheets aside. "Wait. They're here? Where? Are they okay?" Hospitals meant injuries, possibly even death. His trio had been breathing last time he saw them, but anything could've happened while he was unconscious.

Machinery screeched as he pulled the sensor band off his head.

The nurse rushed to shut it off. "Please, remain in the bed. Everything is fine."

Pet didn't listen and stood over the nurse, staring down at them. "If everything's fine, then tell me where my trio are."

The nurse didn't answer, and Pet lost the last of his patience. He stormed out of the room, leaving the nurse shouting for him to come back.

It may have been a hospital, but the architecture reminded him of Starthrone Island.

Airy rooms with organic designs that resembled natural structures. Only the color looked different. Every wall was either solid white or clear glass.

He passed more Rurarine in simple plastic chairs on tracks.

They watched him, but no one tried to interfere.

Maybe because he was décor. People hesitated to touch something that didn't belong to them.

His limbs felt like they were made of lead, but he pressed on. The nurse said they would talk to his Owners, so his trio had to be somewhere nearby.

The first few patient rooms held unconscious Iknox. Some looked fine, but many showed obvious injuries. Lacerations, broken limbs, and even signs of frostbite.

Pet had never counted the exact number of servants that Tradius and Yaivin brought with them, but there seemed to be significantly fewer than before.

He didn't want to think about what this meant.

At the end of the hall, in a secluded wing, he hit pay dirt.

Beyond a glass divider, the grayish-blue of Brog's skin stood out starkly against white hospital sheets.

Pet searched but couldn't find a way inside.

The glass wall had no door or any seams to suggest an opening.

He could only watch from the other side as medical staff loitered around Brog's bed.

The Ocan still looked emaciated but breathed easily as if merely asleep.

One of the medical staff held a syringe against

Brog's arm. They pressed in, then held up the syringe to reveal a bent needle. The syringe was discarded into a pan holding several syringes that had evidently suffered the same fate.

The medical staff clustered together, antennae twitching in conversation.

Another member of the medical staff approached the glass wall. Red light shone down from the ceiling, scanning them, then flashed green.

A seam appeared down the center of the divider, and the glass parted.

The Rurarine moved into the room, and the glass began to seal behind them.

Just before the doorway disappeared, Pet slipped inside. No one noticed him, too intent on their discussion around Brog's bed.

One of the Rurarine seemed to be in charge. The other medical staff regularly reported information to them.

"Recent scans say this patient was at full health when they arrived on the planet a few days ago, but now they exhibit symptoms like someone who hasn't eaten in months. They desperately need a nutrient drip."

"The patient's skin is like steel. We can't get a line in."

"All three of these patients are strange. Their physiology is like nothing on record."

All three patients? That was exactly what Pet wanted to hear. Brog seemed safe for now, so Pet looked for Xavis and Desmodian. He didn't have to go far.

Xavis lay in another stark-white bed, with his wings pulled open to their full width across two tables.

The right wing was fine except for a few missing feathers. The left wing, however, bore a heavy cast.

An IV had been inserted into the Scaacax's arm, right where the tough brown skin of his forearm transitioned into soft yellow. Several bags of various liquids hung on a stand beside the bed, feeding into the needle through a tube.

At the sight of the IV, Pet shoved into the room, knocking one of the medical staff out of their chair in his hurry to get to Xavis. "What're you giving him? He can't have that."

Several months ago, when Xavis was attacked by DPS agents, the Scaacax had lain on the *Vanguard*'s medical table, screaming in pain.

Brog and Desmodian refused to give him pain medication then, due to his history of drug addiction.

Did the Rurarine doctors know about that?

Mechanical arms grabbed Pet before he reached Xavis and pulled him from the room. He fought the doctors while trying to explain at the same time. They could be hurting Xavis even more without realizing.

The doctors only cared about why Pet was out of his room.

The same nurse that greeted him when he woke up found him again. They apologized to the other medical staff for losing track of him and tried to lead him out of the secluded wing.

"I don't need to go back to bed." Pet tried to pull free from their grip. "Listen, please. He has problems with drugs. You're going to hurt him."

Unrelenting hands barely budged despite how hard he fought.

The nurse's mechanical arms had been specially

designed to restrain without causing injury. At the same time, their voice maintained a soothing tone. "Don't worry. Everything we use is safe for Scaacax."

The room spun. Pet's concussion caught up with him, and he stumbled. "Let go of me. Please. Those drugs are bad for him."

They reached the doorway leading out of the secluded wing.

Pet dug his heels into the floor and grabbed the edge of the glass with his free hand. He was ready to kick up as much of a fight as he could, but a new voice interrupted.

"What's going on?"

Pet would recognize that voice anywhere. Swallowing down the nausea climbing up his throat, he looked around and found Desmodian leaning against the entrance to another room. The Dhen'in seemed tired but otherwise uninjured.

Pet clung to the glass doorway. "Des. Help Xavis."

Desmodian reacted before Pet could even tell him what was wrong. He made a straight line for Xavis's bedside, shoving the medical staff away when they tried to intervene. One look at the drugs hanging from the rack had him growling under his breath.

Medical staff shouted as Desmodian pulled the needle from Xavis's arm.

Even the nurse holding Pet left, to help calm the situation.

The head doctor moved in front of Desmodian, grabbing for the IV. "Sir. You can't interfere with medical treatment."

Desmodian held up the tubes that had been feeding into Xavis's arm. "And you can't give him these kinds of pain meds. He's a recovered drug addict."

The head doctor pulled back. They held a conversation with another doctor, presumably using their natural language of scent because their antennae twitched in place of words.

Their conversation ended, and the head doctor turned back to Desmodian. "We have the medical information for Xavis of Xylanthia. There's no record of addiction treatment."

Desmodian ran a hand over Xavis's forehead. "Because he never received addiction treatment. He was arrested and thrown in jail."

This information set off another round of scent-based muttering between the doctors.

Pet breathed a sigh of relief.

The IV had been removed from Xavis's arm, and the medical staff were finally listening.

If Pet looked, he could probably find furniture fit for a human, but that would require effort. Instead, he took a seat on the floor. Leaning back against the wall, he closed his eyes and waited for his head to stop spinning. He'd done what he could. His trio were safe. They could take care of themselves from here.

He didn't mean to fall asleep, but he'd been worrying about his trio for so long the sudden release of that worry left him weightless and lethargic. He drifted off moments after his eyes closed and didn't wake for a long time.

****

Three days passed before they were able to leave the hospital. Out of their group, Desmodian was the least injured, so he interacted with hospital staff and answered questions when authorities came asking.

Security cameras in the lab had caught everything. That, along with the testimony of surviving Vels family members, meant Desmodian didn't have to explain much. His story matched the evidence, and the authorities left after only speaking with him for an hour.

No one asked Pet for his story.

Instead, he told his trio about 3155 during one of their rare moments alone. Medical staff constantly loitered around, so he kept his recap brief. He felt insane as he explained what he'd seen while everyone else was unconscious. She showed up in the arctic, stole something from the lab, and conversed with an unknown person who seemed to have orchestrated everything. It sounded made-up even to his own ears.

In the end, his trio advised him not to say anything.

The testimony of décor wasn't admissible in court, nor could it be counted as legal evidence. Authorities wouldn't be able to do anything with this information.

Instead, his trio promised to investigate it themselves.

Or they would once they were able to leave the hospital.

Having one of their labs broken into and subsequently destroyed did not look good for the Rurarine government.

The atomic bomb used to break into the lab set off a bunch of alarms, but it had taken authorities time to get there. They arrived shortly after Yaivin blew up the Relativator and brought survivors to a special private hospital in order to keep everything quiet. The hospital staff were used to not asking questions. It didn't take much convincing for them to ignore the trio's strange physiology.

Pet's concussion also healed after some rest.

The true difficulty came with getting Xavis and Brog back on their feet.

When Brog finally woke up, he immediately started eating everything he could get his hands on. Over the course of three days, he regained a significant percentage of his usual muscle.

Although the Ocan was still leaner than before, Pet could no longer count Brog's ribs through his clothes.

Xavis stayed unconscious until the drugs filtered out of his system. Even once he was awake, his broken wing would need to be kept in a cast for several months.

By the third day, they were finally deemed healthy enough to leave.

A private escort brought them back to Starthrone Island where the *Vanguard* waited for them. They arrived on the island just after sunset.

It was the last days of the syzygy, and the Dust Party still raged on the beach. Aura moths filled the sky in even greater numbers, completely hiding the aligned moons and most of the stars. A thick layer of dust covered the island.

If not for the orangish-pink color, it would have looked like they'd accidentally returned to the arctic.

Since waking up in the hospital, Pet had been unable to contact Bug.

Their private hospital specialized in alien medicine, while Bug had gone to a native hospital for Rurarine.

He'd been assured she was fine, but requests to talk with her had been either ignored or met with excuses until he gave up asking. It was unfortunate, but he itched to get back on their ship and return to the comfort of space. Maybe he could try contacting her again off-planet.

Their escort dropped them off at the same dock where they'd been kidnapped.

The stolen airship had already been replaced.

Seeing the *Vanguard* still sitting on the resort's landing pad caused a tight knot in Pet's chest to unwind.

He let out an audible sigh of relief. "Home at last."

Xavis boarded the ship first and disappeared into its interior.

However, when Desmodian reached the ladder, the hatch snapped shut. "Xavis? What's going on?"

The hatch didn't open. Xavis's voice filtered through the *Vanguard*'s external speakers. "You and Brog aren't getting on this ship until you settle your argument."

Brog stepped backward, looking for Xavis through the ship's windows. When he found nothing, he threw his arms up and cursed. "Come on, Xavis. We'll talk about it on the ship."

The speaker crackled, and Xavis's voice rang out stronger. "No. The two of you will just go back to ignoring it. We still have the suite for a few days. Go take some time and figure yourselves out. This can't happen again."

After that, the speaker turned off. No amount of shouting from Brog or Desmodian got another word out of Xavis. They could probably force their way onto the ship if they wanted, but they seemed loath to physically challenge Xavis in such a way.

In the end they stormed off in the direction of the island.

Pet watched their retreating backs. What should he do? He hadn't been invited onto the ship nor to the suite.

The speaker turned on, soft enough so only Pet could hear. "Pet, go with them. They're going to need some support."

"But…" Pet searched the side of the ship, wishing he could look into Xavis's eyes. "What about you?"

"I've got the ship. I'll be fine. They need you more than I do."

The speaker turned off with a final click.

With no other choice, Pet ran after Brog and Desmodian. The Dhen'in and Ocan walked side by side while Pet remained a step behind, measuring the distance between them. It was only a few inches of empty air, but it felt like a light-year.

They returned to the waterfall suite. It looked untouched. Even the extra-large nest they made from the bedding remained.

Desmodian took a seat among the pillows.

In contrast, Brog placed himself on the other side of the room. He leaned against the cave wall with his back to Desmodian, watching the falling water that hid access to the private beach.

Pet sat on a cushion in the middle of the room, directly between the two, and waited. It took longer than he thought, and he passed the time playing with the flowers floating on the stream that meandered through the stone floor.

Brog finally broke the silence, though he didn't turn around. "You don't have to say anythin'. I know I fucked up."

Desmodian sighed and braced his elbows on his

knees. "This isn't just about a single mistake, Brog."

Brog's fist hit the wall, though he refrained from cracking stone. "I know. I made every wrong decision."

"No. I mean we're both at fault. This never would've happened if we had each other's backs." He stood and moved to the edge of the stream dividing the room, just a few feet from where Pet sat. When Brog didn't respond, or even turn around, he sighed again. "Come on, Brog. Talk to me."

Brog whirled to face Desmodian. His lips pulled back in a snarl, but his eyes pinched like he was in pain. "What'd you want me to say? 'I'm sorry' ain't gonna cut it. I hurt you. It was an accident at first, but then…fuck. I pushed that button on purpose." One set of hands held onto the wall while the other clutched his head.

He was trembling.

Soft footsteps against stone marked Desmodian's passage over the bridge across the stream. He joined Brog by the waterfall and pulled the Ocan's hands away from his face. "That doesn't count. Our only hope for getting out of there was for someone to stay outside the cages. You did what you had to in order to protect us. I never held that against you."

Brog clung to Desmodian. "You don't understand. That wasn't… I was angry, but I never…" Moisture gathered in his eyes, and his face became a picture of anguish.

A sound welled up in the back of Brog's throat that Pet never expected. Was Brog crying? He leaned forward, trying to get a closer looking without moving from his spot on the floor. His hand slipped on the wet stone, and he nearly tumbled into the stream.

By the time he looked back to the pair, Desmodian had taken Brog's face in his hands, forcing the Ocan to look at him.

"What do you think I don't understand? Do you really think there's a single thought in here—" He tapped Brog's head. "—or feeling in here—" He tapped Brog's chest. "—that I don't understand as if it were my own? I know you, and you know me. That's why you pushed that button. You knew I would rather suffer than let anyone I love be hurt. Me and my damn martyr complex, right?"

Instead of providing comfort, Desmodian's words only made Brog tremble harder. He curled over until his head was level with Desmodian's shoulder. "I should'a protected you, but I was useless. All I did was hurt you."

Desmodian held him close as the Ocan wept. Brog's legs gave out, and Desmodian went with him so they both knelt on the floor.

Pet jumped to his feet but dithered on the other side of the stream. He wanted to help, but it wasn't his place to interrupt. This was between Brog and Desmodian.

Green scales brushed blue skin as Desmodian stroked a comforting hand over Brog's head. "I hurt you too. When we fought on the beach, I knew my words would hurt you. At least you hurt us to protect us. I have no such excuse. I said what I did out of petty spite, and I'm sorry about that. It was wrong, and I wish I could take it back."

Although he still cried, Brog looked up at Desmodian. "You also meant to protect me. You said gettin' involved with Yaivin would be dangerous, and you were right."

Desmodian smiled. "Being right doesn't excuse me being an asshole."

Brog's laugh turned into a wet hiccup. "An asshole and an idiot. What a pair."

Eventually, Brog's tears slowed enough for Desmodian to guide him over to the bed. They sat heavily on the mattress, right next to each other.

Pet considered leaving, but Desmodian waved him over.

"Pet, come here. Give him something to hold. It'll calm him down."

With nothing to offer but himself, Pet climbed into Brog's lap. Thick arms immediately wrapped around him and pressed him to Brog's chest. To his distress, when he hugged Brog, he reached farther than usual. It was a painful reminder that Brog wasn't back to full strength yet.

From the very first day they met, Brog had held Pet like this many times.

Pet always likened it to a child clutching a beloved toy. Only in that moment did he realize how accurate the observation had been. Knowing what he did about Brog's past, he could picture it too easily. An unloved child found comfort in his toys. Then, when he outgrew those, he sought comfort in adult ways.

Yet the inner child remained.

Pet started to hum. The wordless tune from his forgotten past brought him comfort. Maybe he could offer the same to Brog.

It seemed to work.

After a while, Brog calmed down enough to meet Pet's eyes. He looked surprised, like he hadn't realized he was holding Pet. "Ah…um…" He cleared his throat.

"Pet? Thanks, but I should be comfortin' you after what I did to you. Before, on the beach, I tried to push you into somethin' you didn't want. Then, instead 'a apologizin', I went off with Yaivin."

Although no longer openly weeping, Brog still trembled.

Pet held him tighter. "You did apologize. When you pushed me off the airship. I knew what you meant. And I'm also sorry I couldn't communicate better. You stopped when you realized I was uncomfortable. I'm the one who didn't explain properly."

Brog shook his head, almost dislodging Pet. "No, you shouldn't 'ave to explain. I was only thinkin' about myself, and I fucked up. Even after the fight with Des in the elevator, I still went back to Yaivin. That's when he let slip about Tradius's plan with the bomb. Des, I tried to warn you, but by then you'd already been taken and…I'm an idiot. Yaivin told me that on purpose to manipulate me into helpin' him. Fuck."

With a sad laugh Desmodian pressed his masked face into Brog's shoulder. "We're both idiots. I was upset about our fight, so I decided to drown my sorrows at a bar. Didn't notice them sneaking up on me until I was already in the cage."

Desmodian raised his head to face Brog directly. It was an unnecessary gesture, done only as a sign of sincerity. "I wish I could be everything you need, Brog. You need a physical relationship to be happy, and I wish I could give that to you, the same way I wished I could be what my family wanted. I couldn't change for them any more than I can change for you, and I'm sorry for that."

Brog started shaking his head before Desmodian

was even halfway through his declaration. His arms tightened around Pet. "No, Des. You shouldn't change. Not for me. Not for anyone. I want you as you are."

The smile that graced Desmodian's face was the softest expression Pet had ever seen.

The Dhen'in leaned closer and cupped a hand to the side of Brog's face. "And I want you as you are. Even if that means we're misaligned sometimes." He closed the rest of the distance between them and kissed Brog.

The Ocan froze with a surprised grunt but quickly melted into the kiss.

Pet watched, enraptured, as their mouths molded together.

Green scales and blue skin complemented each other perfectly. A flyaway strand of Desmodian's indigo hair clung to the moisture staining Brog's cheek, as if trying to wipe it away.

When they parted, Brog stared at Desmodian in wide-eyed shock. "You've never..."

Desmodian pulled back with a shrug. "I like sharing intimacy, but I knew that to you a kiss is something sexual, and I didn't want to..."

Brog finished for him. "You didn't want to lead me on."

Desmodian nodded, nervously smoothing back his hair. "As much as I love you, Brog, I'm just not attracted to you like that. It would be cruel to make promises I can't deliver."

"You don't need to." Pet only realized he'd spoken out loud when both Brog and Desmodian looked at him with confusion. A hot blush trailed all the way from his hairline to his chest. "I mean, um, Des, you shouldn't worry about that. You can make promises. I'll deliver."

His explanation apparently wasn't as good as he thought.

Brog and Desmodian shared a look, as if hoping the other had an answer.

Pet took a deep breath and tried again. "That's why you wanted a fourth in the first place, right? To act as a bridge between you. So you should be as intimate with each other as you want. I'll fill in the gaps where your sexualities don't match."

That explanation worked. Brog and Desmodian's confusion turned to understanding, but it didn't inspire delight like Pet expected. His offer only brought more concern.

"Pet." Desmodian said his name like a sigh. "That's not fair to you."

Pet scowled. "What's not fair? I'm offering."

Desmodian and Brog shook their heads, obviously about to argue further.

With a frustrated huff Pet untangled himself from Brog and stood. He crossed his arms and faced them. Their size difference meant that although Brog and Desmodian sat on the bed, he barely stood taller than them. "Look. Don't take this the wrong way, but you don't know how hard it is being on the outside watching you."

Brog and Desmodian both objected at the same time, but Pet held up a hand asking for silence.

"The three of you have this connection I'm not part of. You're seamless together, and it feels like there's no room for anyone else. I like knowing there's space for me within your relationship. More than that, I like knowing I'm necessary. That I'm not just a satellite

327

orbiting you, waiting for you to cast me off. So I'm not making this offer just for you; I'm making this offer because it's what I want."

Brog and Desmodian shared another look, and a spark of understanding passed between them like a long-distance message reaching its destination.

It was another example of the connection between his trio. This time, however, it didn't leave Pet feeling lonely. He had a place among them that only he could fill.

Brog shrugged both sets of shoulders. "He makes a good point."

Desmodian's tail twitched, knocking a few pillows from the nest. "I suppose."

Sensing they needed a moment to process what he'd said, Pet stepped away from the bed. Without anything else to wear at the hospital, he'd kept the technically stolen thermal suit. The soft body-hugging fabric may be comfortable, but he was tired of it.

While Desmodian and Brog talked, Pet peeled off the suit, revealing the Dust Party outfit he still wore underneath. The gossamer weight of the cover-up was like the first spring breeze after a long winter. His skin could finally breathe.

He folded the thermal suit and set it on a side table. The sound of running water echoed off stone walls, so he didn't notice the silence at first. When he turned back around, he found Desmodian and Brog staring at him.

Desmodian reached out to feel the hem of the cover-up, admiring the thin strands of black nebula diamonds. "Have you been wearing this the whole time?"

Pet shrugged, and the diamond netting shifted with him. "I didn't have anything else to wear, and it's comfortable."

Brog ran a hand down his side, pressing just hard enough for Pet to feel the woven pattern against his skin.

"I noticed this earlier. It's new."

Pet toyed with the draped sleeve. Maybe he should've changed into something else. "Yeah. I got it for the Dust Party. Don't worry. It's fake. It didn't cost much."

Tipping his head to the side, Desmodian gripped the netting in both hands. "Not worried about that, but..." In a strange move he brought the diamond threads to his mouth and tasted them. "I don't know who told you it's fake, but they were lying."

Remembering his trip with Bug to Ochaid's fabric shop, Pet huffed and crossed his arms. "I knew something was weird. I should return it on principle."

Two different sets of hands, one blue and one green, ushered him onto the bed.

Desmodian guided him to lay on his back and pressed against his left side. "Keep it. If they sold it to you, that means they wanted you to have it. Plus, it suits you."

Brog took the spot on Pet's right side and slipped a hand under the cover-up to toy with the string of his swimsuit. "This too. Wear it again when we can appreciate it better."

He started to untie the string, but Desmodian stopped him. "Hold on. Pet, if you're offering to be the bridge between us, then we'll accept. However, an offer can always be withdrawn. If, at any point, you become uncomfortable or no longer want this, all you need to do is say so."

Maybe it was a sign of Pet's difficulty with social interactions, but he appreciated the direct explanation. It would save him from repeating the previous misunderstanding with Brog. Giving a sincere smile, he pressed a hand to each of their faces. "I understand, but I don't think it'll be a problem. I'm very comfortable."

Brog finished removing Pet's swimsuit. "We can tell."

Pet tried to help by removing the diamond cover-up.

Brog grabbed his hands. "Leave it."

Pet meant to make a joke about them liking the wrapping more than the present but was interrupted by Desmodian kissing him. The Dhen'in's tongue slipped into his mouth like a general charging the front lines of battle. Pet forgot everything he meant to say and leaned back against the mattress, content to be conquered. He threaded his fingers through Desmodian's hair and cupped the back of the Dhen'in's head to draw him closer.

At the same time, Brog mouthed down Pet's throat, following the path of his jugular from ear to collarbone. Sharp teeth pricked his skin.

Overwhelmed by the dual attention, when Brog suddenly disappeared, Pet felt like he'd tripped over the edge of a cliff. The cool air that replaced Brog on his right side made him jump and break the kiss with Desmodian. "What?"

Desmodian stroked a hand over Pet's chest. "We don't have any lubricant, and Xavis isn't here. Brog went to find some. He'll be right back."

Gentle touches coaxed Pet to roll onto his stomach. He did, then moaned in appreciation when Desmodian knelt between his legs and pressed kisses down his spine.

When Brog returned and tossed them a small bottle, Desmodian's full body vision let him catch it one-handed without stopping the attention he lavished on Pet.

With another moan Pet buried his face in the sheets. He couldn't see what was happening, but he felt the mattress dip when Brog sat next to Desmodian. Multiple hands dragged up his legs, pushing his cover-up out of the way and raising his hips. He braced himself on his knees while his upper torso pressed into the bed.

Hands seemed to be everywhere. They stroked his thighs, his ass, his back, and even between his legs. Brog and Desmodian toyed with him, getting him worked up and leaving him to groan into the mattress.

He fisted his hands in the sheets. "Hurry up."

Out of sight behind him, Brog laughed and pinched him on the sensitive crease between thigh and ass. "Calm down. We're havin' fun here."

The sound of a bottle opening met Pet's ears, giving him hope. Scaled fingers spread the slick oil between his ass and around his hole, but never entered him.

Pet squirmed, trying and failing to push back on those fingers and get them inside him. "You're both mean. I hate you."

Brog pinched him again. "You love it."

He did. It wasn't just the sex, either. He loved everything about his trio, flaws and all. In fact, he just loved them.

The epiphany made him forget his frustration. So that was the name of his feelings for his trio.

Love.

He'd always known he cared for them but assumed love had to be more complicated. Everything he heard about love made it seem like something mysterious and incomprehensible. Surely, if regular people couldn't understand it, the emotion would be too complex for décor.

Yet in that moment it seemed simple. Love was just a deeper version of desire. It was a desire to hold someone close while at the same time propping them up, a desire to know every part of someone no matter how good or how bad, and most importantly, it was a desire to see them happy and to share that happiness with them.

At least, that's what it was for him. Maybe love felt different for others, but he liked his version. It was an intense yet comfortable feeling that he wanted to explore.

Racing thoughts halted when Desmodian finally pushed a finger inside him. Questions of love were replaced with an overwhelming need for more.

Pet begged, and he was answered. A second finger quickly joined the first, but this one felt different. It was thicker, stretching him more than he expected, and lacked the scaled texture.

Desmodian and Brog both had a finger inside him, working together to coax him open. Just thinking about it brought a hot rush of arousal, and his already-hard cock started leaking pre-cum. He wished he had a mirror so he could see them both inside him at the same time but had to settle for his imagination.

"Someone's enjoyin' this." Brog sounded too smug for his own good.

Desmodian pressed his finger in a little deeper. "He's already dripping. I don't think he's going to last long." The questing finger found Pet's prostate.

The two of them tormented Pet's deepest pleasure spot without mercy. Ecstasy spilled through his stomach and up his spine to pool in his brain, turning every nerve ending into a live wire. He panted heavily against the mattress, licking salt from his lips as sweat beaded on his skin.

Orgasm hit him so hard he didn't have time to enjoy it. He came, but he wasn't satisfied.

The fingers left.

Pet blindly reached out and grabbed onto Desmodian. "No. More."

Desmodian stayed, but Brog moved up the bed so he sat by Pet's head. "Don't worry, Pet. We're not done."

At some point, out of Pet's sight, Brog had removed his clothes. The Ocan's arousal stood proud, exposed, and in easy reach.

Pet didn't hesitate. He surged forward and wrapped his mouth around Brog's cock. The knobbed head barely fit past his lips, so his fingers danced over the ribs lining the shaft.

"Hell." Brog's hand fisted in his hair. "He's, fuck, ravenous."

Desmodian grabbed tightly onto Pet's hips. "Looks like you're not going anywhere, Brog. Enjoy it."

The Dhen'in's dual cocks pressed against Pet, teasing him before pushing inside.

Pet spread his legs wider and moaned as he was stretched open. The vibration of his voice caused Brog to thrust into his mouth. Pet gagged but pulled back just in time to avoid choking.

Above him, Brog mumbled an apology and removed his hand from Pet's head.

Pet, however, dove right back in, this time licking up and down Brog's shaft.

In contrast, Desmodian took his time and slid smoothly inside until he was sheathed all the way to the root. His dual cocks moved in opposite directions as he started thrusting.

Driving Pet right back into the jaws of ecstasy.

They fell into a rhythm as Desmodian sped up just enough to maximize their pleasure without pushing either of them to orgasm.

At the same time, Pet experimented with the best ways to pleasure Brog. He couldn't fit more than the head of the Ocan's cock in his mouth, so it took some creativity. It was bliss from both sides.

Pet could've stayed there, caught between the pair forever, but an unexpected sound caught his attention. It was similar to the wet suction as Brog slid in and out of his mouth, but it didn't fit their rhythm. Pulling his head back just enough to look up, he found Brog and Desmodian locked in a heated kiss.

They barely seemed to remember Pet was there as they clung to each other.

Pet didn't mind. The two of them needed a chance to reconnect.

He went back to sucking Brog and clenched internal muscles around Desmodian's cocks, causing the pair to share a moan. Pet also shuddered, savoring the pleasure he caused.

Desmodian slowly increased his pace until he thrust with such force that he shoved Pet forward each time. He pulled out of the kiss with Brog, panting heavily. "Fuck. I'm going to..." The warning cut off as his whole body tensed. He buried deep into Pet one last time and came with a groan.

The rush of heat filling him made Pet gasp, and he almost came again.

Brog pulled Pet's head up to get a better look at his flushed face. "Look at you, takin' it so well." He traced Pet's wet lips with a thumb, praising their skill.

Pet took it one step further, sucking Brog's thumb into his mouth while maintaining eye contact, letting the Ocan feel the dexterity of his tongue.

Desmodian abruptly pulled out and repositioned Pet to sit in his lap, back to chest. Scaled lips pressed kisses against the side of Pet's neck and spoke directly into his ear. "I think we've teased Brog enough, don't you? Time to give him some relief."

Pet eagerly agreed. He spread his legs and reached behind to wrap his arms around Desmodian's neck.

Brog jumped at the invitation. His cock still glistened with saliva as he settled between Pet's legs. Lining up, he thrust inside Pet's already-used hole.

Desmodian gripped behind Pet's knees and kept his legs open to Brog's fucking.

In typical fashion, the Ocan started at a rough, fast pace that only grew more intense.

It was ruthless and exactly what Pet wanted. He cried out each time the knobbed head and ribbed shaft of Brog's cock rubbed deep inside of him. His legs shook and went numb, but Desmodian kept him in place, pliant and open.

Pet watched Brog through lashes wet with tears, soaking up the other male's enthusiasm. However, Brog wasn't looking back at him.

The Ocan's attention locked on Desmodian.

From this angle, with Pet sitting in the Dhen'in's lap, it almost looked like Brog was fucking Desmodian as well.

Desmodian caressed down Pet's stomach until he gripped between human legs. "Such a good Pet for us." He stroked Pet's sensitive cock in time to Brog's thrusts, cool scales a torment against hot flesh.

Pet came first. Pleasure snapped tight, and his back arched with a desperate cry. He clenched around Brog, who picked up his pace and drove Pet even higher.

Desmodian kept stroking him through it, milking his orgasm to last as long as possible.

It seemed like it would never end. Fire burned through his veins. Every inch of his body felt electrified at the slightest touch.

Yet Brog only thrust harder, driving so deep he knocked the air from Pet's lungs.

The intensity of it left Pet sobbing as he rode the line between pleasure and pain.

If only he could live in that moment.

But, like all things, it had to end eventually.

Brog gave a strangled shout and shuddered as his orgasm ripped through him.

The Ocan filled Pet past his limit. Evidence of Brog's pleasure dripped down Pet's legs, onto Desmodian, and landed on the sheets below.

When it was over, all three of them were left gasping.

Brog pulled out slowly, then collapsed in a sprawled heap over the bed.

Pet could barely move, and Desmodian's hands shook as he guided them both into a more comfortable position.

They lay on either side of Brog, using his chest as a shared pillow.

Brog grunted and wrapped arms around both of them, then promptly started snoring.

Desmodian laughed under his breath. "Self-indulgent idiot." The soft smile on his lips turned the words into a compliment.

Pet placed a hand over Brog's chest, lightly tracing invisible bioluminescence.

Those lights only existed when Brog was in his element, deep under water.

Desmodian's hand covered his. Scaled fingers reached longer than human ones, but the Dhen'in curled his fingers, so their fingertips aligned. "Pet. Thank you."

Together they mapped the lines along Brog's skin. Even if they couldn't see the pattern, they knew it existed just under their touch. It only needed the right conditions to shine again.

****

The next morning, Pet couldn't stop yawning. He was exhausted, but it was the good kind of tired. It came from a short night spent getting very little sleep because he was too busy being taken by Brog and Desmodian multiple times each. He followed the two of them back to the *Vanguard*, sticking to the open path down the middle of the walkway.

Each morning, a cleaning crew shoveled the roads

clear of Aura moth dust. After a week, large dust piles lined every path, nearly turning the walkways into tunnels.

They had almost reached the end of the floating bridge to the landing pad when someone called Pet's name.

Looking back, he saw Bug quickly rolling toward him.

"Bug." He turned around and met her at the center of the bridge.

The wide ocean stretched to either side of them, with the landing pad at his back and Starthrone Island at hers.

"I wasn't sure I'd catch you before you left."

In his head Pet counted how many steps remained between him and the *Vanguard*. "You almost didn't. I tried contacting you when we were in the hospital, but I couldn't get through."

The floating bridge shifted over the waves, and the suspension on Bug's chair worked to keep her stable. "Some authorities visited me in the hospital. I overheard them talking just outside my room. Apparently, they thought we might be lying about what happened, so they didn't let me talk to anyone to keep us from *getting our stories straight*. But there wasn't much they could do when everyone's story matched the recordings on the security cameras."

Pet looked her over, searching for signs of damage or injury. "But you're all right now?" The last time he saw her she had been lying unconscious on the ice, chair in pieces. It was a relief to see both her and her chair in working order again.

Mechanical arms shrugged at the same time Bug's

antennae twitched. "As fine as I can be, although I'm probably going to have to move to a different island. I missed too many days of work. Lost my job, and there aren't many open positions right now."

"What?" Pet glared in the direction of the island. "Didn't you explain what happened?"

She rocked back and forth on her treads. "Yeah, but they already hired someone else. For the restaurant to take me back, the new person would have to lose their job, and I don't want that either. I'm just going to look elsewhere. There's nothing keeping me to this island specifically."

Steady footfalls, punctuated by the tapping of a hammer, announced Desmodian as he stepped up behind Pet. "Bug, right? Pet told us how you helped him. We want to return the favor. If you'd like, you could come with us."

Bug fidgeted so much that for a moment Pet wondered if her chair suffered an electrical shortage. "Oh, um, I don't know about living on a ship. I've never even left the planet. What would I do?"

Desmodian leaned against his hammer and draped one arm around Pet's shoulders. "If you don't want to live on a ship, we know some places where you'd fit in. Plus, if you decide you don't like it, we'll bring you right back here."

She still looked hesitant, but excitement took hold of Pet. "It'll be great. There's so much out there to see. I'm sure you'll love it. Think of it like a vacation."

As she pondered, Desmodian leaned over to whisper in Pet's ear. "Let's hope her vacation works out better than ours."

Pet elbowed him in the ribs.

After a few minutes of pacing the width of the bridge, Bug finally came to a decision. "All right. I'll give it a try. But you promise you'll bring me back if it doesn't work out?"

"Of course." Pet didn't hesitate to speak for his trio in this case. It was one answer he felt certain about.

Even without eyes, Bug turned back to face the island with wide-eyed astonishment. "I guess I'll start packing."

"I'll help you."

With her permission Pet hopped on the back of her chair.

The two of them rolled down the bridge away from the *Vanguard*. He watched the landing pad grow smaller.

Desmodian remained at the middle of the bridge, leaning against his hammer with a smile on his face.

At the far end of the bridge, Brog stood with arms crossed but spines relaxed. From that distance he looked no different than when they first arrived, as if the catastrophe in the arctic never happened.

The illusion would've been complete with Xavis there, but the Scaacax remained holed up on the *Vanguard*.

It would take more time to completely heal from their latest adventure. When they'd decided to take a vacation, this wasn't what Pet expected, but at least something good came from it in the end.

That didn't make up for all the pain they experienced since setting foot on the planet, but it did take the sting out of the wound.

Next

She sat in the chair at the rarely used desk and pulled up a display screen. A holograph floated in front of her, its pale glow the only light in the otherwise dark room. Through the door she could hear him, her true Master, moving around, but he paid no attention to her.

He was too focused on his work, staring at the same recorded images of The Void over and over again, as if they would tell him something new.

The Void had appeared at the center of their galaxy about fifty years ago, and they didn't know much more about it now than they did then. That wasn't likely to change anytime soon.

She shrugged, unconcerned. There was likely a whole team of very intelligent people dedicated to solving the mystery of The Void, but she wasn't one of them. Even if answers existed, no one would give them to her.

There were other things for her to worry about, anyway.

Certain that Master would be occupied for a while longer, she turned her attention back to the glowing display.

It had taken her months to learn how to navigate computers. Now she booted up the program she wanted easily.

Master wasn't supposed to have this. Hacking into private security systems was illegal, and he kept the program a strict secret.

He probably didn't even realize she knew it

existed, let alone knew how to use it.

The system took a minute to connect.

While she waited, she pulled out a piece of paper and a pen. The old ways of writing were barely used anymore, but tracing each letter by hand made it easier to learn how to read and write. She still struggled with literacy. The list running down the page had been painstakingly copied one letter at a time. It was lopsided and uneven but legible. Her best work yet.

Finally, the system connected, and she punched in a familiar code.

The holographic screen lit up with an image of the inside of the Gravity Well, straight from the club's security cameras. She plugged a headphone into one ear so only she would be able to hear the noise from the feed. That was an error she had made before, and it had almost gotten her in trouble.

No one could say she didn't learn from her mistakes.

Switching through the many cameras, she found the one she wanted. It showed the club's owner, Vige, talking with a pair of familiar aliens.

"So you want me to hire her?" Vige looked between the Ocan and the Dhen'in like a hunter waiting for a trap to spring. In the flashing neon of the Gravity Well, her expression was nearly impossible to read.

The Dhen'in—what was his name?—tucked his hammer into the crook of his elbow, making it as unthreatening as possible. "Come on, Vige. You're always complaining about how hard it is to keep up maintenance on this place. You could use another set of skilled hands."

Vige leaned against the bar at the front of the club,

evidently unbothered by the pounding music and the crowd. She looked over the Dhen'in's shoulder at something just out of the camera's view.

"Fine. But you owe me a favor, and I intend to collect."

Beside the Dhen'in, the Ocan's laughter could be heard even over the music. "Wouldn't expect anythin' else from you, Vige."

Sighing in frustration, she switched to another security camera, hoping for a better view of her real target. She found it, a little farther away and looking at her target's back, but there he was, standing next to a pink-and-yellow Rurarine in an elaborate chair.

What was he calling himself now? Pet. How cute and domestic. She had liked him once, back when they belonged to the same Owner. At least, she thought she had liked him. Memories from before were a bit blurred and ran together in a jumbled mess, but she couldn't recall having any negative feelings about him.

Until he'd left, and her stable life had been upended.

The camera was too far away to hear what Pet and the Rurarine were saying, so she waited and distracted herself by contemplating her list. She crossed out the word "Jewel," enjoying the feel of her pen slicing through each handwritten letter. "Jewel" was too close to "Décor."

Words like "Gem" and "Treasure" met a similar fate.

Eventually, Pet and the Rurarine wandered away from the bar and closer to the camera, allowing her to finally see their faces and hear what they were saying.

Pet smiled at the Rurarine. "See. Told you it would

work out. Let me show you around." He led the being
*and its chair through the crowd, sticking close to the
wall where there was less traffic.*

*"Are you sure? That woman didn't look happy."
The Rurarine's antennae twitched and tried to turn in
all directions at once.*

As she watched them, she shuddered. Thankfully,
her human body didn't have any appendages which
constantly moved like that. If those antennae had been
attached to her own head, she would've cut them off by
now.

On the screen, *Pet brought the Rurarine to a halt
as a particularly drunk patron stumbled into their path.
"It's fine. Vige never looks happy. It would ruin her
image. Plus, I don't know if her face is actually able to
smile. But trust me, if she didn't want to hire you, she
wouldn't. She only argued to get a favor out of my
trio."*

So the Rurarine was going to work at the club. She
heard that Pet and his alien trio had taken someone else
onto their ship. The poor Rurarine must not have been
cut out for space travel to already be looking for a new
job on land. Even if that land was an asteroid.

She couldn't blame the being for that. She hated
space travel as well and couldn't understand how Pet
lived permanently on a ship without going mad.

Maybe he was mad. That would certainly explain a
few things.

Pet and the Rurarine continued their aimless
wandering around the club, Pet pointing out people he
knew or things he thought the Rurarine should know.

She followed them from camera to camera but
grew bored. Another word was crossed off her list.

"Savage." It was the exact opposite of Pet, which she liked, but it also had plenty of negative connotations. She wanted to be feared, not mocked.

As she considered her list—was "Paragon" too presumptuous?—she idly looked up at the screen now and then. Wait, what was that strange expression on Pet's face? The male décor glared at something across the room. Following his gaze, she found an alien with large leathery wings that she surprisingly recognized.

Maddax was a dealer in anything that could be dealt. This included information. Ever since the incident on Syzygy, Pet and his little trio had been asking around about her.

How had they even known to ask? Sure, they'd seen her as the Vels' décor, but that alone shouldn't have been enough to catch their suspicion.

It was annoying, but they wouldn't find anything useful. Records would show that she had been taken from her previous Owner when Stiril was arrested, resold, and bought at auction by the Vels family. That part wasn't even a lie, so there was nothing suspicious to find.

She smiled to herself as Pet continued to glare at Maddax. It was no mystery why her fellow décor hated the man across the room. That winged alien had once supplied drugs to the Scaacax member of Pet's trio. The poor thing must be worried sick that history would repeat itself.

At least she hoped that was the case. It was a lovely thought, imagining him lying awake at night, fretting over something he couldn't control.

With an extra flourish she crossed "Paragon" off her list as well. She was no pillar of virtue.

Pet's one-sided staring contest was interrupted when the Rurarine suddenly grabbed his arm and pointed off in another direction.

"Who's that?"

At the front of the club, a robotic dancer dazzled the crowd from their stage. Neon lights reflected off a chrome finish as the dancer curled and twisted around a pole. The dancer's programming made them take the shape of whoever stood closest. At the moment they looked like a metal version of an Apha, a species half armor and half plant. Then the crowd shifted, and their body realigned into some sort of serpentine species.

Pet's glare disappeared, to be replaced with a disgustingly happy smile. "That's Oi. She works here too."

"She's so pretty."

The Rurarine fidgeted again, but it was different this time. Once-shy energy turned nervous, and mechanical arms twisted around each other like they meant to tie themselves in knots.

Pet nudged the Rurarine with his elbow. "Come on. I'll introduce you."

The pair waited at the edge of the stage for the dancer to finish. With them so close, the dancer inevitably took on a human shape, though the metal version looked more female than male.

Pet had referred to the dancer as female. Robots didn't technically have a gender, but maybe this one had chosen an identity for themselves. Watching them through the cameras, she couldn't help approving of the dancer, at least a little bit. Having an identity was important. Now, if only she could name her own.

When the dancer finished, she joined Pet and the

Rurarine at the edge of the platform. Her sensors must've shifted from Pet to the Rurarine because her body changed shape again. She almost looked like a Rurarine's chair but froze mid-transformation.

Gears ground together with a horrendous scraping sound, just before she seemed to fall apart. Her outer panels popped open, revealing the inner workings underneath. The panels floated on pistons around a central core that ticked like clockwork.

Pet flinched and drew back from the dancer, tripping over the Rurarine in the process. "What happened?"

The dancer held out one of her disassembled limbs. "This is my original form." She let the limb drop back to her side and looked up at the Rurarine. "I haven't met your species before. My sensors got confused by your chair. They couldn't tell what part is your body and what isn't, so they defaulted to my factory settings."

The Rurarine rolled out of the range of the dancer's sensors. "I'm sorry. I didn't mean to. You're not hurt, are you?"

Since Pet was now closest, the dancer automatically imitated him again. She held up an arm and flexed her fingers. Everything moved as smoothly as if it had never come apart. "No, I'm fine. It was refreshing. I haven't seen my original form since I was first brought online."

She stepped closer to the Rurarine and once again fell into her disassembled shape, this time without freezing up first.

The Rurarine rolled a little closer as well. "Oh, um. That's a relief. It would be horrible to break one of my coworkers on my first day."

The dancer looked up from studying her own body. "First day?"

A lull in the music made Pet's voice easy to hear, even through the security camera. *"Yeah. Bug's going to start working here. Vige just hired her."*

Bug? What kind of name was Bug? Looking away from the security feed, she retraced her list. Even the ones she'd crossed out would make a better name than Bug.

Yet neither Pet nor the dancer seemed unsettled by the name.

The dancer even held out a disassembled limb in greeting. "Well, good to meet you, Bug."

The mechanical arm of Bug's chair shook the offered limb in a strange facsimile of a handshake. "Actually, my name is Bugguna. Though everyone just calls me Bug."

Bugguna? It was at least better than Bug, but it still rolled off the tongue in a funny way. Shaking her head, she crossed off every remaining word from her list that included a B sound.

Oddly enough, though Pet hadn't reacted to the name Bug, he now stared at the Rurarine in shock. *"Your full name's Bugguna? How did I not know that?"*

Although she sat on the other side of the galaxy watching him on a hacked security camera, she still fought the urge to slap him upside the head. Or possibly squeeze his neck until he stopped breathing.

How did he not know his own friend's name?

Her name would not be so easily forgotten. Only a few options remained on her list. She liked the words

"Flame" and "Flare." F was a satisfying sound. The way her upper lip pulled back to reveal her teeth when she said it felt a bit like snarling.

Yet these options were too literal. They made her seem like she was trying too hard, so they were crossed out as well.

Bugguna—she refused to refer to the Rurarine as Bug—*curled her antennae toward each other as her chair's arms shrugged. "It never came up. We were a bit busy trying not to die."*

Two of the dancer's limbs planted on her center panels, mimicking the posture of someone bracing their hands on their hips. "What've you gotten up to this time, Pet?"

He raised his hands in defense. "Hey, it wasn't our fault. We were just trying to take a vacation. But it's a good story. I'm sure Bug could tell you all about it if you wanted to show her around the club. You know this place almost as well as Vige."

Bugguna fidgeted again but this time didn't back away. "That would be good. I mean, if you're not busy."

Even in her current state, the dancer's smile couldn't be mistaken for anything else. "I'm on break right now. I have time to show you the main part of the club. Later, I could show you the employee sections. That's where the real interesting stuff is."

When Bugguna turned questioning antennae his direction, Pet shooed her off. "Don't worry about me. Go have fun. You're in good hands with Oi."

He gave his eyebrows a suggestive lift.

Although Rurarine don't express emotions like a human, Bugguna still blushed a brighter shade of pink.

The dancer led the Rurarine off into the club, leaving Pet sitting alone on the edge of the stage.

This wasn't helpful. She wanted some clue into how Pet had become suspicious of her. His trio wouldn't investigate a random piece of décor just for fun, even if she and Pet had once belonged to the same Owner.

No. They suspected something, but watching them wasn't giving her any information.

On a brighter note, she'd crossed out nearly every word on her list. Only one remained, and she circled it with a big sweeping gesture.

"Feral."

Her grin stretched wide enough to show teeth, and she repeated the word to herself.

No more 3155 or 4104 or any other item number the auction house might give her. She had a name now.

The newly named Feral stowed the paper away and turned her full attention to the holographic screen where Pet continued to sit passively, watching the crowd of people move around him like a living tide.

There had to be something here she could use.

Most of Pet's attention seemed to be drawn to one side of the club.

Back at the bar, the Dhen'in and the Ocan—she still couldn't remember their names—*sat side by side. Each had a drink in their hands, and one of the Ocan's arms draped behind his companion's shoulders.*

A stranger on the Ocan's other side leaned over to speak with him.

The security camera was too far away to pick up what they said, but Feral didn't need to hear. She recognized the flirtatious body language. It was the same way Yaivin Vels had acted when he brought the Ocan back to his suite.

Feral shuddered. Why would anyone want to sleep with the four-armed giant? Not just Pet or Yaivin either. The Ocan seemed to have no end of willing bed partners.

This time, however, the Ocan only gave the stranger a polite nod before waving them away. Then the Dhen'in said something that made him laugh, and the two clinked glasses together.

What had changed? When she'd seen the pair back in Yaivin's suite, they'd practically been at each other's throats. Now, just a few weeks later, their relationship seemed better than ever.

Pet grinned like an idiot and squirmed with obvious delight at the sight of the two aliens getting along so well. Ugh, that was even worse.

She considered turning off the security feed and calling today a failure.

The grin on Pet's face suddenly dropped.

She sat up straighter in her chair, eagerly scanning the holographic screen for any clue as to what had caused the reaction.

There, on the other side of the club.

The Scaacax member of the trio sat perched on a stool all alone. His usually bright colors looked dull, and his shoulders sagged under the weight of the cast on his broken wing.

In direct contrast to the Ocan and the Dhen'in, the Scaacax looked worse than Feral had ever seen. *He threw back the contents of his drink, draining the glass in one go.*

A heavy scowl marred Pet's face as he watched the

351

Scaacax add the glass to the growing collection of already-empty ones on the table.

Feral pulled out a blank piece of paper and started a new list, slowly writing out everything she knew about the Scaacax.

For over a year now, she and Master had been looking for a way to get to the trio.

The three aliens, despite being so different, functioned as a single seamless unit.

The argument between the Dhen'in and the Ocan had been the closest they'd ever come to having an advantage over the trio, and that had happened mostly by accident.

However, the events on Syzygy had left one of the trio significantly weaker than the rest. He was in pain, and if the shaking of his hands was anything to judge by, struggling with more than just physical injuries.

Giggling under her breath, she stowed the short new list away and turned off the holographic screen. Master wouldn't be pleased to know she was messing with the computers. She would have to find another way to hint at the Scaacax's condition, but she wasn't worried. Once Master realized they finally had an opportunity to gain control of the trio, he wouldn't care about anything else.

They had their next target.

All they had to do was wait for the perfect opportunity, and soon she would bring Pet's world crashing down around him.

A word about the author...

D'Arcy Arden grew up in Akron, Ohio, where she attended creative art schools and was surrounded by beautiful country landscape. This combination cultivated an interest in literature, art, and the natural world around her. In college she earned a master's degree in Fiction Writing, which primarily taught her that there is no one way to tell a good story. So she turned around and went back for a degree in Animation as well. This love for both visual and written stories has given her a preference for stories that are memorable, easy to picture, and most importantly, fun.

Her main goal when she started writing *The Fourth State of Matter* was to provide readers with a fun story featuring the three S's—Science, Sex, and Spaceships. That was her first published novel but only the beginning of a great adventure.

https://daarden33.wixsite.com/weatheringthestorm
https://www.patreon.com/DArcyArden